NIGHT ROUNDS

The intern snapped on the light over the patient's bed. The young woman stirred and moaned softly. He tugged at the tubing attached to her central venous line. She rolled over toward him. One eye opened, blinking in the brightness.

"Doctor!" she gasped.

"It's okay," he mumbled. The woman's hair, spilling down over the pillow in the oblique lighting of the lamp, seemed spun of pure gold. The intern longed to run his fingers through it. "Soon you'll be fine."

"I am feeling better tonight, doctor." She rolled onto her back, her eyes still squinting in the light.

"It's okay," he repeated, trying not to listen. He inserted the syringe in the line, then pushed the plunger. "Soon you'll be fine."

After a few moments he slowly pulled back the bed sheet from her lifeless body . . .

D0915765

A DROP OF MURDER

BENJAMIN JOSHUA, M.D.

AVON BOOKS ◬ NEW YORK

The characters and events described in this book are entirely fictitious. Any resemblance to real people, living or dead, is purely coincidental.

The setting is intentionally real, to capture more accurately for the reader the emotional intensity of the hospital experience. The name of the hospital has been changed to protect the reputation of a fine and distinguished institution, for which the author has the greatest respect and admiration.

A DROP OF MURDER is an original publication of Avon Books. This work has never before appeared in book form.

AVON BOOKS
A division of
The Hearst Corporation
105 Madison Avenue
New York, New York 10016

Copyright © 1990 by Benjamin Joshua, M.D.
Published by arrangement with the author
Library of Congress Catalog Card Number: 89-92482
ISBN: 0-380-75794-X

First Avon Books Printing: June 1990

AVON TRADEMARK REG. U.S. PAT. OFF. AND IN OTHER COUNTRIES, MARCA REGISTRADA, HECHO EN U.S.A.

Printed in the U.S.A.

RA   10   9   8   7   6   5   4   3   2   1

To Barbara, my wife,
whose kindness and patience have seen me
through my own darkest hours

Monday Evening, September 9

The cool night air from off New York harbor had enfolded Manhattan's Upper East Side, but the streets were still baking under the hard, bright light of the street lamps. Buses, taxis, people continually hurried to their destinations without so much as a pause to mark the passage from day to night.

To Peter Lee, the aura of the busy, lively city seemed, at best, deceptive. Each traveler, he knew, was alone in his journey. Alone, and often lonely, in the crowd.

He drew in a deep, deliciously cool breath. It seemed for a moment to quench the burning feeling in his gut. But the air stank of gasoline fumes, the foul breath of civilization.

He walked down York Avenue, studying the sidewalk in the clinically impersonal streetlight. Across the street, beyond the meaningless traffic, the harsh lights reflected off the white brick face of Manhattan General Hospital. On his left was the soft, cool darkness of the shrubbery at the edge of Rockefeller University, and beyond that rose a powerful wrought iron fence. He was not sure whether the purpose of the fence was to keep the city light out or the darkness in. But beyond it, Peter knew, lay the cool, quiet solitude of the verdant, darkened campus.

A young couple approached, clinging together for warmth, for love. They tried not to stare at the wiry, dark young man, lost in his thoughts. Peter could almost feel the warmth they generated as they passed. Seeing his hospital whites, they made way for him on the sidewalk. Peter did not look at their faces. He knew what he would find there: the joy, the hope that for each of them the loneliness might, together, end. He knew it was a lie, and he could not bear to face it.

Peter continued past Sixty-sixth Street to the stone and iron gates of the sleeping campus. The watchman at the entrance noticed the hospital whites and barely lifted his head to acknowledge Peter's entry. Whites were the key to unquestioned access. Peter looked down at his own carte blanche, at the small red brown drops of dried blood, the gentian violet of countless spattered Gram stains and the yellow streaks commemorating the secretions of various splattered patients—all defacing the purity of his uniform. He looked back at the guard, hunched over his podium as if someone had hung him there. A bus flashed by the entrance. In the harsh white interior light Peter saw the sharpened features of the passengers. They remind him of the cadavers he had worked on during that first traumatic week in the medical school gross anatomy lab. Huddled together in the glaring white fluorescent light, the bus riders were being ferried off to their separate nothingnesses.

A chill ran up Peter's spine. He turned from the street and started once again up the steep drive to the administration building.

He loved to walk through the Rockefeller campus because it was dark and quiet and because he could think there. Separated from the noise, the constant distractions of the hospital, he felt that he could clear his head and straighten out his thoughts. He knew that the stress, the constant harassment of his internship, sometimes caused his thinking to ball up on him. His thoughts would lead off onto unexpected tangents and random ideas. Metaphorical figures would interrupt his concentration. For the last two months it had become increasingly more difficult to organize his workday. Sitting down to write his patient progress notes had become an unbearable exercise in frustration. Over the past few days, he had become aware that he was losing control of the situation. Which was why tonight, his on-call night, when the clamor was the most incessant, he felt the greatest need for a walk through the cool calm of the ''Rock.''

The entranceway lights of the old gray stone administration building were ablaze, but inside the halls appeared darkened, lonely. At the top of the hill, Peter turned right and followed the driveway past a series of red brick buildings connected by third story covered walkways. He knew that on that floor was the Rockefeller Hospital, a collection of patients with rare diseases, assembled for study by the research staff, like so many rare birds.

It hurt to think about the sick people inside. The thought of their dependence, their insatiable needs, pressed in on Peter as if his chest were being crushed under a huge rock. It was the part of medicine he could least tolerate: the sticky personality of the patient in desperate need, not so much for medicines, but for human caring. The demand was so intense that Peter often felt himself a dry well, unable to yield up what his patients most needed. He was keenly aware of his lack of ability to make human contact. He knew he was failing them—and he felt deeply the anguish that was all he had to share.

He turned his back on the hospital building and rounded the corner into the courtyard just beyond it. This was his favorite place in all New York City. The courtyard was a small stone-paved area between two buildings, with tall oak trees at its entrance. On the two sides it was lined with stone benches, but the far wall was the courtyard's main attraction: Beyond the waist-high stone rampart was a sweeping view of the city. Directly ahead burned the lights of the high-rise buildings on Roosevelt Island—mounds of apartments, individual lives—stacked to the sky. Beyond the island smoldered the street lamps of Queens, stretching out as far as he could see. Peter looked down from the stone wall at the dark, swirling waters of the East River, running like a moat below his rampart. The river was a black velvet ribbon, its presence marked only by the absence of light, except for the occasional scattered bits of city reflected from its inky depths.

Peter leaned over the thick stone wall and stared down its sheer outer face. The stones, blackened by the fumes of traffic, dropped eighty feet to the pavement of the East River Drive below. He watched the lanes of automobiles shooting past, each vehicle guided by an individual seeking his or her own path through the darkness. Peter's own life was more like that of the car than the driver: driven by an unseen force for reasons he could never hope to understand to a destination that was of no interest to him.

He took a series of deep breaths, closed his eyes, and hummed a single note. As he drank in the cool air he could feel the tightness in his abdomen begin to ease. His mind started to feel more clear. He could take control again.

Four shrill blasts shattered the peace of the night. Before his stomach muscles even had time to retighten, Peter Lee's left hand reflexively reached for the pocket pager attached to the waistband of his pants. His index finger depressed the button on the side of the pager; it was an act done thousands of times, often during the dead of sleep, and totally unconsciously. A cracked voice sounded above the static: "Call 3131, 3131, 3131." The Emergency Room telephone extension. That could only mean one thing: a new admission. Every third night for nearly three months he had been on call, receiving new patients as they were admitted through the Emergency Room. Interns were strictly forbidden to leave the hospital while on call. But Peter had finished his routine chores and had put his last patient to bed. Two other interns, in rotation, were scheduled to receive new admissions before his turn came up again. Peter had hoped for one or maybe two hours of peace before his next patient, enough time to wander off to the Rock to try to get his head together. The Emergency Room must be swamped to get back to him so quickly. Peter quickened his steps as he rounded the edge of the Rockefeller Hospital building. He hoped he would not be missed if it took him a few minutes to get to a telephone. He started to trot. Before him, across the dark, quiet grounds of the Rock, loomed the white monolith of Manhattan General Hospital, a gigantic tower lit with blazing white lights, against a velvety black sky. It resembled a tombstone with windows but no epitaph.

His pager went off again. "Call 3131, 3131, 3131!"

"Shit!" Peter could feel his abdominal muscles tighten, the weight press on his chest. He was letting them down. Again. He broke into a run.

"What's going on here tonight?" complained Chuck Barone. "This place is a zoo!"

"It's a full moon, I think." The receptionist snickered. "Always happens at a full moon."

A nurse—short, svelte, and bleached-blonde—sauntered into the nurses' station. "I don't know about the moon, but every one of my rooms is full." She stopped for a minute, bent over a desk, still standing, so that her already-too-short white skirt climbed up her white-stockinged legs a purposeful few inches more. She began to enter her latest patient's vital signs on a fresh Emergency Room sheet. As she recorded the pulse and blood pressure she continued, "Except for the crash room . . ."

Barone turned to her, a wry smile masking his thinly suppressed anxiety and frustration. He did not even notice her legs, which was a sure sign that the ER resident was on edge. "Goddamn it, Linda, don't mention the crash room! With all that I've got going on here, I don't even want to think what would happen if I had to handle a cardiac arrest now."

Linda Ranson knew Barone fairly well, although only on a professional basis, so far. In his few weeks working in the Emergency Room, she had come to appreciate his aggressive but affable personality and biting sense of humor. She had also come to admire his muscular, just-short-of-stocky frame and thick black hair. Only once or twice before, when the Emergency Room had been equally pressured, had she seen him lose his cool.

She finished recording the new patient's temperature and respiratory rate, slid them into a clipboard, and placed them on the counter next to Barone. He did not even move to acknowledge them, but she could sense a tenseness, a change in his breathing pattern that said what he could not: Not another one! I've still got eight others to get out of here! She silently stepped behind him, the edge of her skirt catching on his sleeve, and placed her warm, soft hands on his neck, gently massaging the tight muscles. He stopped writing, sat for a moment completely still. Slowly, like ice cream melting on a summer's day, she could feel the muscles soften and relax.

Barone settled back into his chair, his head rolled back and he tried to look up at her. He could see only the pale hair spilling over her forehead and her lively blue eyes. "Hey, you got a license for this?" he asked. He let his left hand fall down and back, stroking her stockinged calf. "You have really talented hands."

"So do you." She jumped as his fingers began to work their way over her knee and back up her thigh.

She giggled. "Well, at least we have one miraculous recovery tonight."

Barone reached over and picked up the sheaf of papers for the new patient. "Maria Figueroa, twenty-three years old, lower abdominal pain," he read off the sheet. "Good lord, not another belly pain. This must be the eighth tonight."

"She's also our eighth Maria Figueroa tonight. I think that may be some kind of record." Linda giggled again, the laugh of a girl who was not yet a mature woman but was old enough to know the difference. "At least you don't have to rush on this one. She's had the pain for three months."

"And she just happened to stroll in tonight during my shift?" asked Barone. She could sense the tension returning to his voice.

"It must be love." She shrugged.

A dark-haired nurse poked her head into the room. "Chuck, this looks like your lucky night. We've got a full house." He turned to look at her. She was not smiling.

"Do you mean—"

"Yep. The paramedics are wheeling a woman with a respiratory arrest into the crash room right now."

"Shhhhit!" He turned to Linda. "How are the other folks doing? Can they all wait?"

"All except for the old woman in room eight. She's not breathing very well."

"Goddamn it, that's all we need now: a double arrest. She's Lee's patient. Where the hell is he anyway? Page him again. Stat."

The third page came as Peter Lee was trotting down York Avenue, across Sixty-eighth Street. "Call 3131 stat. Call 3131 stat. Call 3131 stat." He had planned to come around the outside of the hospital, savoring his last few moments in the night air before coming in through the Emergency Room entrance. But the stat page meant that they not only needed him badly, but also that they had noticed his slowness as well. He turned into the Cornell Medical School entrance on Sixty-ninth Street. For a moment he thought of ducking into the medical school library and calling from the circulation desk. That would be a good cover story. He could say he had been down in the stacks.

"Call 3131 *stat!* Call 3131 *stat!* Call 3131 *stat!*" Another stat page. That could only mean big trouble in the Emergency Room, maybe even a cardiac arrest. He hurried past the library, rushed down the stairwell, and ran through the ground floor corridor toward the Emergency Room.

The hallway near the Emergency Room was more crowded. He dodged past nurses, transport people, other equally distracted interns and residents, into the ER waiting room. He threaded his way through the knots of people—families and friends of various patients—wondering which anxious group was waiting for him.

He arrived at the glassed-in front of the nurses' station, his heart pounding. "I"—he puffed—"was stat . . . paged." He was not sure whether the shortness of breath was from running or from the pressure in his chest of the anxiety and guilt.

The receptionist, a dark Hispanic woman, was talking on the telephone. She nodded, continued with her conversation on the telephone: "No, we can't wait any longer. Just have someone run the blood down here now."

She hesitated for a second, and Peter Lee broke in. "Why did you want me?"

She covered the mouthpiece. "That was Dr. Barone. He has a very sick lady for you." She shifted again to her telephone conversation. "I don't care if you have to get the head of hematology to run it down. Just do it. All of our nurses are busy, we have an arrest in the crash room, and the doctor says that the patient needs the blood now. Do you want me to tell your supervisor that a patient died because you couldn't be troubled to carry down some blood?''

There was another short pause. ''Where's Barone?'' Lee asked.

She covered the mouthpiece again. ''In the crash room. They've got a real bad one. Overdose, I think.'' She removed her hand from the mouthpiece. ''And thank you, too!'' she answered sarcastically and slammed the receiver into its cradle.

Peter ran through the ER corridor toward the crash room. A resuscitation: a wrestling match with the grim reaper with a chance of winning. Like most interns and residents, Peter always ran to an arrest and always with a tangible air of self-importance bordering on elation.

Barone was examining the patient in the crash room. She was a fortyish woman with black hair that was beginning to streak with gray. Her face was thin, almost gaunt, but not unpleasant. She was cold and ashen; both her pulse and blood pressure were low, and she breathed in shallow, infrequent gasps. Barone examined her eyes: the pupils reacted sluggishly, shrinking very slowly when he shined a flashlight into her eyes. He twisted her neck to the side. The eyes moved in their sockets, as if fixed on some point in space in front of her, like the painted eyes of a toy doll. She was completely naked, a long angry-looking red scar running down the length of her scaphoid abdomen to be lost in the mound of black pubic hair. One nurse applied cardiac monitor leads to her chest, and another inserted an intravenous needle into her arm, while Barone felt the pulses in her neck and groin, lifted her flaccid arms and legs and let them fall to the stretcher.

An ambulance attendant was speaking. ''She wasn't breathing when we arrived, but she had a pulse, so we bagged her for a while. She pinked up pretty quick, and we brought her in. We found this next to her.'' He held up a tumbler with a slurry of half-dissolved granules in its bottom and dried pasty material along its walls. It reminded Barone of a glass which had been filled with buttermilk. ''These were in the bathroom.'' The ambulance attendant produced three pill bottles, all with labels saying they had contained Seconal. One contained a few pills, but the others had only opened pill capsules.

Barone sniffed the tumbler. ''Alcohol. She mixed the contents of the capsules into the booze and drank it. Then she put the broken capsules away neatly into their containers. Jesus, what could have been going through her head?'' He looked up at the ambulance driver. ''Do we have any history? Anyone with her? Maybe a suicide note? Has she tried this before?''

The paramedic shrugged, shook his head sadly. ''Don't know very much. A hotel maid called it in. Came into the room to turn down the sheets and found her on the floor. Said the lady had just checked in an hour before. Sounds like she thought it all out beforehand and knew what she wanted to do. All we got is a name, if she used her real one when she checked in: Anne Delbert.''

Barone turned to the nurse who was assisting him. ''Has she been here before?''

Linda finished taping the intravenous needle in place, looked up. ''Don't know. They're checking for an old hospital chart now.''

''I don't like the looks of this.'' Barone circled the stretcher on which the patient lay. ''She's done much too good a job of this for an amateur: getting a hotel room, opening the capsules to get them dissolved faster, mixing them with booze. This gal has probably tried this before. And,'' he said, pointing to the abdominal scar, "I don't like that, either. God, I wish I had some history."

Linda Ranson put her hand up to motion for silence. "I can't get her blood pressure, and her pulse is very thready."

Barone looked up at the cardiac monitor. The heartbeat was still normal. "Open up the intravenous line and tilt her head back." He turned to a black nurse. "Get an ambou bag."

She reached over to the crash cart, laden with resuscitation equipment, and selected a rubber face mask with a bag attachment that looked like a clear green plastic football. She fitted the mask over the patient's nose and mouth and pumped the bag several times, forcing air into the woman's lungs.

"No good," called Linda. "Her pulse is slowing."

Barone saw Peter at the entrance to the room. "Lee, get your ass in here," he called. "Pump this lady's chest while I put in an endotracheal tube."

Peter hurried to the stretcher and leaned over the emaciated woman. He looked at her spread before him, her complexion like gray plastic in the cold, white light. She reminded him of one of the resuscitation practice dummies in the classroom. Except she looked less alive. He placed the heel of his hand over her breastbone, a few inches below her shriveled breast, and began rhythmically pumping her rib cage.

"I've got a femoral pulse," called out Linda.

"Good," said Barone. "Giver her two amps of bicarb." He turned to Peter Lee. "Can you keep pumping while I pass this endotracheal tube?" Peter nodded, not speaking, as he counted out the beat of his chest compressions.

Barone tilted the patient's head back and opened her mouth. He picked up a long, curved plastic tube, about as thick as a cigar, and deftly slipped it into her mouth, past her vocal cords, and into her trachea.

The black nurse disconnected the ambou bag from the mask and reconnected it to the endotracheal tube. Barone placed his stethoscope over the right side of the patient's chest, then over her left, as she compressed the bag.

"I've got a blood pressure," said Linda. "One twenty over seventy."

Barone smiled. "You can stop pumping now, Peter."

"Blood pressure still one ten over seventy."

"She made it."

The receptionist waved a manila folder from the door. "Just got the old hospital chart on Anne Delbert. Anyone interested?"

"Yeah," said Barone, taking the thick volume from her. He leafed through it, starting from the last few pages. He stopped, shook his head, started rifling through the earlier pages of her chart, his face reddening. "I don't believe this!"

Linda looked up from recording the blood pressure. "Hey, Barone, it was a good save, but not unbelievable."

"Not that." Barone's voice was trembling. "Her medical history. This was her third suicide attempt in the last three months."

"What could drive her to do that?" asked the black nurse.

Barone looked up from the pages of the chart. "Because she has cancer of the colon."

Peter Lee stared at the naked woman, now pink and warm. "But she only has a single scar. I thought they usually took out most of the colon for that, leaving a colostomy with a bag. . . ."

Barone turned back to the chart. "Only if they are going for a cure. In her case, the tumor was so extensive that they just closed her up. The last note on the chart, written two weeks ago, says that there was nothing that they could offer her, and that she was aware of this.

"And they gave her a prescription for Seconal. With three refills."

"The lady in the crash room is going to the medical ICU," said Barone to the receptionist as he entered the nurses' station. "Call the intern up there and tell him we've got a present for him."

"Let's see, that will be Dr. Derney," she answered.

"Right," replied Barone, plopping down into a chair. He began to scribble his notes concerning Anne Delbert's resuscitation onto her ER sheet.

Peter Lee entered the nurses' station a moment later. He leaned over Barone. "So tell me about my new admission."

Barone continued writing silently for a minute, finished a line. Without looking up he started, "Seventy-four-year-old woman from Burnham Gardens Nursing Home. Found delirious and febrile this evening. Here." He looked up, fished a sheet of green paper out of the pile on the desk, and handed it to Lee. "This is the note from the nursing home. You can read about it yourself."

Peter accepted the paper. It was a printed form, with spaces for the nursing home attendant to fill in the patient's medical history, allergies, medications, and reason for transfer to the hospital. Peter knew immediately that the information carefully recorded in the round, flowing hand would be of little use. He read it through anyway, finding out about the patient's gall bladder surgery and hysterectomy thirty years ago, and that she was given a laxative and vitamins daily.

Peter let the slip of paper sail gently down onto the desk in front of Barone. "Did you write a note yet?" he asked.

Barone looked up, squinted at the intern. "I was

busy,'' he answered. "I've got eight rooms filled with sick patients, and I couldn't get any help from the interns on the wards."

Peter let the implied rebuke slip by. "Did you find anything on your exam?"

Barone returned to filling out Anne Delbert's ER sheet. "Just some rales at the lung bases. I couldn't be sure whether she was in heart failure, so I put in a central venous line. Then the GI bleeder came in, and then the drug overdose. I didn't get back."

"Did you find out why she is in a nursing home?" asked Lee.

Barone shrugged, kept writing. "I don't know. Ambulance attendant says she's been demented for years. Talk to the family. They're in the waiting room."

Peter looked out the front of the nurses' station at the people milling about in the waiting room. He turned back to Barone. "You stat paged me twice for this?"

Barone jerked his head up; his curly black hair tossed back from his brow and his blue eyes flashed. His voice was thick with restrained anger. "If I were you I'd get my ass in there and see my patient before someone begins to wonder why it took two fucking stat pages to get you down here!"

Peter looked at Barone impassively, as if emotionally disconnected from the scene around him. Barone had the uncomfortable feeling that he had failed to register.

A moment passed before Peter asked, as if in passing, "What room is she in?"

Barone's dark eyes scanned Lee's face. The mouth seemed tense, set in a half-smiling grimace of near panic. But the nearly black, impenetrable eyes were elsewhere, their obliquity apparent. Barone shook his head. "Room twenty-five." He returned to his ER sheets, unsatisfied as if he had punched the night air.

Peter Lee picked up the new patient's papers again, scanned them for her name. He walked into the waiting room. "Is Mary Altman's family here?" he called. For a long moment no one answered. He looked around the room, searching for a silent response. Finally a heavy, middle-aged woman turned from the window, where she had been staring into the night, and caught his eye. She rose from the chair with obvious difficulty and began moving her considerable bulk, wrapped in a dirty corduroy coat, across the room toward him. Her hair was a brassy shade of yellow, heavily curled, with black roots grown out about half an inch. She looked at Peter Lee from watery blue eyes, streaked with red, under lids heavy with blue eyeshadow and black mascara. "Yes, I'm with Mrs. Altman. . . ."

"Are you her . . . ?" Peter stopped short of saying "daughter."

"Daughter-in-law." The woman emphasized the "in-law" part with an obvious sense of relief, as if this excused her from responsibility or possibly grief.

"Can you tell me why she's here?"

"Not really. The nursing home just called and said that she was sick and they were taking her here. My husband works the night shift, so I came alone."

"What is she usually like? Why is she in a nursing home?"

The woman chose to answer the second question. "Her husband died and she couldn't take care of herself no more."

"What was the matter with her?" Peter pressed.

The woman reddened, sputtered a bit. "Well, uh, she . . . uh . . . was getting a bit senile. One day she attacked her next-door neighbor. Nice woman, been living there for years. Ma said that her husband was over there, having an affair with her. O' course, he'd been dead for more than a year. So we . . ." She dropped her gaze, shrugged.

"Is she always very confused?"

The blue eyes looked up again, flashed at him from

under the mascara, revealed a sense of shame, of exposure. "How the hell would I know?"

Lee could see her discomfort but not share it. He was relentless. "Well, do you visit her often?"

The woman looked away, the beginnings of a tear in her eye. Her voice was choked. "Not really."

"When was the last time?"

There was a long pause. The woman looked back; her mascara was beginning to run down her cheek. "Last time we was there, she thought that my husband was his father. She accused me of . . . It was real nasty. That was last spring, and we haven't been back since . . . ." Her voice trailed off; then suddenly regained its strength. "Now we just pay the bills." She sobbed.

Lee was embarrassed but did not know how to console her. He hesitated for a moment, took a deep breath, and turned toward room 25.

The smell of stale urine met him at the doorway. Sickly sweet, it permeated every nursing home patient he had ever known. Mary Altman was thin and frail looking. She lay on the stretcher, breathing noisily. As he bent to look at her, the fetor of her breath was overpowering. It was an odor he knew well, the same taste as his own mouth when, on an on-call night, he worked around the clock and forgot to eat or drink. The woman's tongue was so dry it was caked with thick mucus. He guessed that no one had bothered to feed the old woman or make sure she had anything to eat for at least two days.

"Mary," he called. "Mrs. Altman! Wake up!" No response. He shook her by the shoulder, again without response. Finally, he made his hand into a fist and rubbed his knuckles along her breast bone, grinding into her chest. *"Mary!* Wake up!" The ancient eyes opened slowly, almost leisurely, their stare vacant. Her knees bent upward and her hands gradually rose toward her chest, clenched into fists. "Unnhhh," she moaned.

He sighed again and shook his head. The rest of his examination went very quickly. He looked at her eyes, noted dense cataracts; she was almost blind. The plastic catheter from the central venous line that Barone had placed, was taped to the side of her neck, like a twig grafted to a dying tree. The lungs were congested, especially the right base. Her heartbeat was surprisingly, sadly strong. He tried to bend her neck forward, meeting resistance when her chin was about halfway to her chest. She moaned again.

Stiff neck and confusion; a possible case of meningitis. She would need blood tests, a spinal tap, blood cultures, a chest X ray, and an electrocardiogram. And in the end he would probably find out that she had pneumonia from aspirating her food into her lungs at the nursing home. And she would be skewered with intravenous needles, cured with antibiotics, and sent back to her oblivion in the nursing home. All at a cost to Medicare of some $8,000.

"Jesus fucking Christ," he muttered, and shook his head.

Peter Lee sat at the desk in the back room of the 4 East nurses' station and stared out the window. During the day, while supposedly updating his patients' charts, he often sat back there and watched the scows and ships slip past on the East River. At night, the background of twinkling lights in Queens and Brooklyn spread out like a carpet to the horizon. But tonight Peter was lost in the velvety blackness of the East River itself. It seemed so deep that it swallowed him up.

He was still marveling at its inky infinity when he was suddenly aware of someone just behind his right shoulder. He turned, nearly bumping into Sylvia Blackman. Tall and slim, Sylvia's long straight chestnut brown hair contrasted with her clear gray eyes and milky complexion, which, like fine china, had a nearly translucent quality. Her aquiline nose and thin lips were set in a long, thin face that was pleasant if not beautiful in the conventional sense. But what attracted Peter most was the grace of her movement, an effortless economy of motion that allowed her to be standing behind him before he even knew someone was in the room with him.

She had been his supervising resident on 4 East for the previous month and had covered for his inexperience innumerable times, always with delicate and slightly exasperated aplomb. He was sure that the latter was her defense, to cover some deeper feelings about him. For his part, he felt a deep stirring that was far more than the usual regard of an intern for one of his first teachers. At night, in the seclusion of his own apartment, he would fantasize that she would one day confess her passion to him. But he knew it would be difficult for her to actually do it, just as it would be too hard for him, risking possible rejection. So he sat back in his chair, basking in her scent and the warmth of her nearby presence as she brushed past him and took the chair across the room.

"Well, Peter," she began. Her voice had an almost musical quality. "Mrs. Altman is certainly a sorry sight."

He stared at her, not meaning to, and became suddenly self-conscious, his eyes gliding down her lithe figure, stopping at the hem of her skirt, before he forced them to the floor and then to the write-up on the desk in front of him. "Yes," he echoed, reddening, "quite a sight." He thumbed through the carefully written history and physical exam as if looking for some forgotten fact. At least it gave him something to do with his hands . . . and his eyes.

"What do you want to do with her?"

Peter's ears began to redden again. He had not really been preparing his treatment plan. In fact, he had not been thinking about Mary Altman at all. "Well, I, uh, would like to give her, uhhmm, every chance, so . . ."

He knew immediately that was not right, but it was too late.

"Every chance? For what?" Sylvia's voice suddenly was cutting, sarcastic. "To go back and sit in that dingy nursing home, terrified by her own inability to understand the world? She's been abandoned by everyone: her son, her daughter-in-law, even her own senses. But good old Manhattan General Hospital won't give up without a fight."

The blush had spread from Peter's ears to his cheeks. "I know th—I didn't mean that we had to, uh, go to extremes. . . ."

Her soft gray eyes were cool, betraying no emotion, but there was a trace of sadness in her voice. "From her physical examination, she clearly has pneumonia in the lower lobe of her right lung. From the looks of the food remnants still inside her mouth, she probably aspirated some food. Give her penicillin and some fluids and see how she does." She stopped for a moment, looked out over the river. "If she's lucky . . ."

"Yes?"

Sylvia rose from her chair, continued to stare out the window at the swirling dark waters. "If she's lucky, her pneumonia may be resistant to penicillin and she may not wake up again in this world." Her face reddened, voice strained, at expressing acceptance of defeat. She turned swiftly and was gone, only a gentle disturbance in the air, carrying her scent, remained.

Peter marveled at her coolness. She was right, of course. Mary Altman was like an actress who had stayed on the stage a bit longer than her scene was intended to run. No longer useful to those around her, an embarrassment to herself, if only she had the wit: She had simply lived too long. The logical solution would simply be not to treat her, but at Manhattan General Hospital that was unthinkable.

Or was it? For a moment he allowed himself to consider the possibility. It might be ethically reasonable, but could it stand up to review? He could imagine the spectacle at morbidity and mortality rounds. Maurie Benson, the director of the residency training program, would tear him apart in front of thirty other interns and residents. All of the others might agree with him, but not one would stand up to Maurie and risk his own career in Peter's defense. In the end, there could be no excuse for letting a poor old lady die.

He wrote the nursing orders for Mary Altman. Carefully, he inscribed her diagnosis and condition, her diet, medicines, allergies, and required nursing care. He hesitated on the dosage of her penicillin. The standard dose for aspiration pneumonia was twelve million units per day. He thought about prescribing a low dose, to give her pneumonia a chance. He imagined again the scorn of M and M rounds. Under the glowering visage of Maurie Benson he settled on a middling figure: six million units of penicillin per day, intravenously.

He handed his orders to the ward clerk. That was the last of his new patients. At least he could try to get some sleep. He wandered out of the nurses' station toward the on-call room. As he turned the corner he walked into Shirley Kyriakos, the night nurse.

Peter stepped back, reddened as he savored her soft warmth. "I'm sorry, I was looking the other—"

"No, Dr. Lee." Her olive complexion turned crimson. "I was coming around the corner too fast. I need you to help with the central venous line on that new patient in room four-oh-eight. It just won't run right. I was going to pull it, but—"

"No," said Peter hastily. "Let me have a look at it first." He knew it could take him half an hour or more to find a good vein for a new intravenous line in a dehydrated elderly patient like Mary Altman. He was grateful that the nurse had not merely pulled the central venous catheter out. There was still a chance that he could get it to work properly. Sometimes the tip would become clogged with a small blood clot. If he could force some liquid through the catheter he might be able to blow the clot out and get the line working again. That could save him half an hour of sleep.

Peter walked across the hall into the main supply room. The walls were covered by shelves and cabinets filled with bedpans, surgical tape, tongue depressors, and other nonsterile supplies. In the center of the room was an odd collection of wheelchairs, air pumps, and stretchers that were not currently in use. Along the far wall was a table, set with half a dozen chairs, that the nurses used for coffee breaks and sometimes to eat lunch. Off to one side was a metal door with a small window in it. Peter opened it and stepped into the medication room, a long, narrow chamber, barely wider than a corridor. Along one wall was parked a metal rack, containing shelves stocked with sterile medical supplies. Each night the rack was rolled down into the basement and restocked with intravenous kits, surgical gloves, and dressings. The opposite side of the room was occupied by a long stainless steel counter. Over the counter were hung shelves containing boxes of syringes and bottles of medicines. At one end, the shelves were replaced by a stainless steel cabinet with two locks. This was the narcotics cabinet, and only one person, the senior nurse on the shift, was entrusted with a key.

Peter selected a ten-millimeter syringe from one of the boxes. He opened one of the drawers below the counter. It contained several rows of small boxes, each filled with small vials of intravenous additives. He picked up a familiar blue green ampoule, containing sodium chloride solution, and walked down the darkened hallway.

Room 408 was in the old part of the hospital, one of the last remaining rooms with four beds, one in each corner. Each bed was surrounded by a shabby orange curtain, hung from the fourteen-foot ceiling. The curtain provided the only privacy available to the occupants. Three of the curtains were drawn and dark, but the fourth was partially opened and backlit. Peter stepped through the opening. Mary Altman's wrinkled features were smoother in repose. Her dirty, yellow gray hair was spread out on a spotless white pillowcase. The sheet was pulled up to her neck. In the dim light of the single bare bulb in the bedside fixture, only the slight rise and fall of the shadows brushing the sheet as her chest rose and fell gave any indication that she was alive.

He reached over the metal bed rail and adjusted the thumbscrew on the intravenous tubing, opening it wide. Not a drop appeared in the drip chamber. He closed the thumbscrew and began to examine the clear plastic tubing, checking for a bend or kink that might have closed off the flow. He traced the tubing up to Mary Altman's neck. The clear tubing ended in a plastic hub; from there a catheter would take the fluid into the jugular vein and release it into the vena cava, near the entrance to her heart.

Peter snapped open the glass ampoule and filled his syringe from it. Removing the needle, he connected the syringe directly to the plastic hub of the central venous line and jammed down the plunger of the syringe as hard as he could. For a moment he met resistance, then he could feel a sudden give as the blood clot at the tip of the plastic tubing worked free and the fluid rushed into her heart.

Suddenly, Mary Altman's face contorted in pain. Her arms rose from the bed like white-sheathed wraiths and a horrible moan gathered in her throat. She began to reach for her neck. Peter lunged across the bed and caught her hand. She resisted with greater effort than he imagined possible, then slackened slowly as her moan trailed off.

Peter picked himself up off the bed. Mumbling, "I'm sorry Mrs. Altman," he turned his attention back to the central venous line. The syringe was still in place, plugging the line. With a sigh of relief he reconnected the intravenous tubing and opened the thumbscrew. The drip chamber immediately filled with a rapid stream of drops. Peter took a minute to slow down the stream to one drop every two seconds. He paused for a moment, grateful that he had been able to restart the line, then began to smooth the rumpled sheet.

It was not until he began to tuck the sheet across Mary Altman's chest that he realized the shadows across it were no longer moving. He placed his palm on her rib cage. Nothing. No heartbeat, no respiratory movement. He turned the light onto her face. It was ashen and dusky. He felt her neck for the carotid pulse. There was none.

A sweat broke out on his face and neck. He reached for the ampuole he had brought to the bedside and held it up to the light. Even in the yellow glare of the bedside lamp, it was clear that the label on this vial was too blue. He could feel his heart racing as he slowly turned the vial. The label was definitely blue, not blue green. It read: "Potassium chloride, 20 millequivalents per 10 milliliters." Instant death by cardiac arrest.

He looked again at Mary Altman's frail body, waxen and gray. His duty now was to call for the cardiac arrest team. Within minutes half a dozen interns and residents would be at the bedside, pounding on her chest, invading her body with tubes and needles. If they were "successful," she might live long enough to experience great agony, never understanding why it was necessary, before returning to her unloved, unkempt, unremembered nursing home existence.

And the cardiac arrest team would want to know her medical history. They would want to know what had happened immediately prior to the cardiac arrest. And he would have to tell them. Because they would need to give her special medications to counteract the potassium chloride injection. And because their blood tests, run routinely during a cardiac arrest, would pick up the potassium even if he did not tell them. And of course there would be Maurie Benson to face at the next M and M rounds. . . .

Peter was never conscious of making any decision. He just finished smoothing the sheets, then gathered his syringe and the ampoule of potassium chloride. He left the intravenous line running, turned out the light, and walked quietly down the hall to the medicine room. He pitched the syringe and ampoule into the trash can filled with dozens of other similar discards. No one would ever know what had happened. The thought brought a wave of relief, a small thrill of excitement, but no remorse.

In the hallway on the way to his on-call room, he saw Shirley emerging from another patient's room. "Mary Altman's IV is running again," he said with a trace of satisfaction in his voice. Now, even if she were found, everyone would think that she had been alive when he left the room.

"Thanks," she replied, misreading his smile.

He walked to the end of the hall and into the cramped, shabby room that doubled as a house staff office by day and sleeping quarters by night. Barely larger than the medication room, one wall of the office was occupied by a low counter that was used as a desk. It was piled high with unfinished patient reports and old X-ray films. Peter cleared a small corner of it to lay out the contents of his pockets. Then he unfolded the metal cot, and, sitting on the edge, took his shoes off. He stared at the dull gray tile of the floor. He had just killed a person, murdered another human being. That was supposed to be a cataclysmic event. Everything somehow was supposed to be different now. But he could detect no change. He could feel his socks, matted down by his having been on his feet for twenty straight hours, sticking to the soles of his feet. Nothing was different. And, he concluded, neither was he.

He turned out the light, lay on his back, and covered himself with the cool, white hospital sheets. In repose, he marveled how little different he was from Mary Altman. Both had been living, but neither knew for what. He, like her, had been dreading each day, one at a time, hoping to make it through without something awful happening. The lack of a sense of anticipation of tomorrow made them alike.

Now he had released her. He knew that neither he nor she were better or worse for it. But others might think differently. The secret must remain shared between them.

He lay on his back and stared through the darkness at the shadows cast on the ceiling of the on-call room by the lights in the courtyard. They reminded him of the images formed by the moonlight shining through the branches of the oak tree outside his bedroom window when he was a young boy. For several long moments he allowed his eyes to pick through the tenebrous forms, searching for something, he was not sure what. Finally he realized that he was not looking for a particular shadow, but rather for a feeling. What he sought was the sense of familiarity that would bring back to him the warmth and reassurance of his mother, sleeping in the next room. What he needed was the security of her telling him that, no matter how hideous they looked, the images were merely a dance of shadows.

And if he shut his eyes tightly, everything would be all right. He closed his eyes again, hoping desperately she had been right.

The lights snapped on, filling the on-call room and Peter's vision with harsh light. He could not remember having been asleep, but felt the familiar grogginess of its interruption.

"Dr. Lee?" It was Shirley's voice, coming from the half-opened door. She always stood outside when awakening the male interns, ever since she had surprised one who liked to sleep nude.

Peter rubbed his eyes and padded to the doorway. "What is it?"

Her eyes were wide, and her voice quavered. "Come quick. It's Mrs. Altman. I think she's dead!"

He shook his head and blinked his eyes. "Dead? Are you sure?" The words came without effort. He felt nothing.

She nodded her head. "I've been a nurse long enough to know," she said with a trace of irritation.

He began to put on his shoes. "Did you call the cardiac arrest team?" Now there was a slight tremor in his voice.

She shook her head. "Not yet. Should I?"

He could feel himself regaining control of his voice. "Well"—he tucked in the tails of his shirt as he stepped out of the on-call room—"if she's been dead more than five or ten minutes, they probably wouldn't do her much good. Let me take a look at her first. . . ."

Peter Lee followed the nurse dutifully down the hall to Mary Altman's bedside. As Shirley hovered at the foot of the bed, he hunched over the lifeless form, felt her neck for a carotid pulse, listened to her silent chest with his stethoscope, and shone a flashlight into her unseeing eyes. "Her skin is already cool," he noted to the anxious nurse. "She's probably been dead for at least a half hour. No use in calling the cardiac arrest team now." He checked his watch. "Time of death is two twenty-four A.M."

He walked back to the nurses' station, Shirley trailing behind this time. While she filled out the paperwork and gathered Mary Altman's personal effects in a large plastic bag, he scribbled a cursory death note: "Patient found in bed, not breathing, no pulse or heartbeat, no pupillary response to light. Skin was cool. No resuscitation attempted. Time of death 2:24 A.M." He sighed his name, then flipped to the front of the chart to find the telephone number of the next of kin. As Peter had imagined, her son received the news calmly, much as he might urinate: with some small sense of relief and little else. Peter ran through the usual patter. Did the family want an autopsy? No, the hospital would provide one without cost. No, there would be no external marks on the body. Yes, they would have her ready for the undertaker tomorrow.

Peter was halfway down the hall, back to his bed, when the accursed pager sounded shrilly. "Call 3131, 3131, 3131!"

Peter's heart sank. It was almost 3:00 A.M. There was no reason for the Emergency Room to be calling him other than to tell that there was another new admission for him, his sixth of the night. Peter knew that some interns called a new admission a "hit." Considering the feeling in his gut, this was not far from the truth. "Shit," he hissed under his breath, returning to the nurses' station to telephone the Emergency Room.

Chuck Barone answered on the first ring. "Peter?" He did not wait for a reply. "I've got a little present here for you." His voice was almost jovial.

Peter stifled a groan. "Wonderful," he answered. He could not help himself: "The last present you gave me is already in a box."

Barone's voice was suddenly serious, accusing.

"That little old lady? Mary Altman? What did you do to her?"

Peter reddened and stammered, glad that Barone could not see him. "Nothing, I, uh . . . I—"

Barone mercifully cut him short. "Well, here's a chance to redeem yourself. I've got a thirty-eight-year-old chronic alcoholic man down here vomiting buckets of blood. And Peter?" Barone did not give him time to answer. "This time I expect you down here *stat.*"

"Be right there," Peter mumbled. Barone had already hung up.

Barone's words stung like a slap across the face. As he hurried toward the elevator, Peter felt the familiar surge of adrenaline, the intern's friend. Where a few minutes before he had felt exhausted, he was now wide awake. It was a sensation he knew well, the second wind that could bring an intern through a sleepless night.

The elevator opened onto the ground floor. The corridor and waiting room were now nearly deserted. The ghostly white fluorescent lights of the nurses' station bathed the few remaining souls, curled on the couches to catch a few minutes sleep, in an eerie pale glow.

Barone was sitting at the desk in the nurses' station, writing furiously on an ER sheet. His white coat and pants were speckled with blood.

"Anybody come in with this guy?" asked Peter.

Barone stopped writing, laid down his pen. "Well, Dr. Lee. So glad you could make it." He stretched, picked up his pen. "Mr. Brown is all alone." He turned back to his writing. "Ten-year history of big-time boozing, at least a fifth a day of hard stuff, when he can get it. Cheap wine when he can't." He finished writing and put down the pen again.

"He lives alone in Harlem." Barone turned to face Peter, then stood up. "He apparently had heartburn all day and drank some muscatel to quench it. About ten o'clock this evening he became sick to his stomach and started puking blood. He shares the toilet with some neighbors down the hall, who noticed the blood and called an ambulance.''

"Have you put in a nasogastric tube?'' asked Lee.

Barone shook his head. ''Not yet. He vomited as soon as he got here''—Barone gestured toward the front of his uniform as he spoke—''and I've been trying to stabilize his blood pressure first. It was ninety over sixty lying down, but dropped to sixty palpable sitting up. So I put in a couple of big bore intravenous lines and started pumping him with saline. I sent some blood to the lab to type and cross-match. The nurse went to get a nasogastric tube and lavage set. It should just about be ready.'' He led the intern out of the nurses' station and into one of the patient rooms.

An emaciated black man lay on the stretcher. Although he was covered by a sheet up to his shoulders, his massively protuberant abdomen was immediately apparent. His dark eyes were open but dull and filmy, and he gazed nowhere in particular. Now and again he moved his arms or legs, listlessly and aimlessly. A large intravenous catheter was attached to each arm, like notes taped to a door. The man, the linens, the walls, the floor—the entire room was splattered with blood. A turquoise basin, sitting on the bedstand, was nearly filled with purple red vomitus.

"Dr. Lee.'' Barone almost smiled. ''I would like you to meet your new patient, Herbert Brown.'' Herbert Brown belched, moaned. ''He's all yours.''

A nurse, small, dark, and brisk, walked in carrying two basins, one empty and one filled with ice water. Floating on the crushed ice were two syringes and a nasogastric tube.

Barone moved out of the way. ''I'll just leave you two to get acquainted. . . .'' He gestured grandly toward the sleeping drunk and left.

Peter began to examine the patient. The face was gaunt, the eyes hollow. "Mr. Brown?" He waited a moment. "Herbie?" The man groaned in recognition.

Peter pulled back the sheet. The swollen belly, in contrast with the wasted arms and legs, looked pregnant—maybe a month overdue—with triplets. Large veins stood out darkly under the surface of the olive-colored skin, appearing to radiate from the umbilicus like fat worms, a sure sign of cirrhosis of the liver.

The veins in Herbie's stomach and esophagus would also be swollen with blood, and undoubtedly he was now bleeding because one of these distended veins, or varices, had burst. Peter took out his stethoscope and measured the blood pressure: still ninety over sixty. He cranked up the back of the stretcher, putting Herbie into a near-sitting position, and took another reading: eighty over forty. Herbert Brown had lost so much blood that he could not even maintain his blood pressure while sitting in bed.

Peter turned to the nurse, who was still standing beside him. "Can you check on the blood and get it down here, stat?"

"Right away." She turned and hurried toward the nurses' station.

Peter reached into the ice-cold water of the basin and withdrew the nasogastric tube. Chilled by the ice water, the normally soft plastic of the tube was stiffened, making it easier to pass. "Mr. Brown." Peter gripped the tube with his right hand and turned Herbie's face toward him with his left. The face was blank. "Herbie!" There was a groan of recognition. "Herbie, I want you to swallow this tube down into your stomach." There was a slight nod.

Peter smeared the end of the tube with lubricating jelly, then placed the end of it in Herbert Brown's right nostril. He began to advance the tube, meeting a slight resistance at the back of the nose. He jiggled the tube, pushed a littler harder. It slid gently into the back of the throat.

"Now Herbie, I'm going to pass the tube. I want you to try to swallow it down." No response this time, not even a groan.

Peter shrugged and began to advance the tube again. He managed about one inch before Herbie began to gag. He coughed, spat, and gagged again. His eyes opened wide and looked at Peter for the first time. The emaciated hands reached for the tube.

"No!" cried Peter, trying to defend the nasogastric tube with his free hand. "No, just try to swallow!" In desperation he withdrew the tube a half inch. Herbie's excitement began to wane. "Now, we'll try it again. Just swallow." The glazed eyes drifted off.

Peter advanced the tube another inch. Without so much as a premonitory gag, Herbie let loose a fountain, then a river of bright red blood onto the sheets, onto the floor, onto Peter's shoes, pants, and shirt. Worse, while Peter stood frozen in horror, Herbie yanked out the nasogastric tube.

"Damn it!" Peter grabbed the empty basin, too late. Herbie gagged again, spat purple clots into the basin before sinking back onto the stretcher.

The short brunette nurse poked her head in the door. "What the hell is going on here?"

"We've got a real pumper," called Peter over his shoulder, as he turned Herbie's head to the side to prevent him from choking on his own vomitus. "Where the hell is that blood transfusion?"

"The blood bank said it would take another half hour for the cross-match," she answered.

"This guy may not have another half hour. Run up to the blood bank yourself and get two units of whatever they have: typed blood if they have it, O negative if they don't."

"I'm on my way." The voice trailed off down the hall behind her.

Peter adjusted the thumbscrews on both intravenous lines to wide open. He took another blood pressure reading: seventy over thirty. He picked up the nasogastric tube, slimy with the K-Y jelly and nasal mucus and covered with blood, and held Herbie's head back. The tube slid easily through the nostril and into the back of the throat.

"Swallow, damn you, swallow," he hissed under his breath. Herbie gasped and choked.

Desperate, Peter picked up a small paper cup filled with water from the bedstand. He poured a few drops into Herbie's mouth. It began to dribble out.

"Hey, Herbie," he called. "That's my muscatel. Don't waste it!"

Reflexively, Herbie swallowed. Peter advanced the tube into his stomach.

He taped the tube to Herbie's nose to keep it in place and picked up one of the empty syringes. Working quickly, Peter pulled back the plunger on the syringe. The nasogastric tube and syringe filled with dark red liquid. He evacuated the bloody fluid, then flushed the stomach with saline. He pulled back Kool-Aid colored fluid, and repeated the lavage. By the sixth pass, the fluid was only pink tinged, and Herbert Brown was shivering visibly.

Peter lowered the head of the bed and took another blood pressure reading: seventy over thirty. Time was running out.

He was looking for a leg vein to start a third intravenous line when the brunette nurse trotted it, carrying two plastic bags of purple red blood. "Not a minute too soon." Peter reached for one of the bags, began to attach it to the intravenous line.

He had just finished hanging the second unit of blood from the intravenous pole when Barone walked by the door. "What the hell are you doing, Lee?" His voice was strained.

"What does it look like?" He turned to face Barone. "I'm trying to get some blood into this man before his tank runs dry."

Barone's face darkened as he examined the plastic sacks. "Uncross-matched whole blood?"

"Chuck, he's bleeding out." He pointed to the basin filled with red fluid.

"Uncross-matched whole blood?" Barone repeated. "You gave him this in my Emergency Room?"

"What the hell do you want me to do?"

"I want you to give him fresh frozen plasma. It has more clotting factors. And what about the cross-matched blood that I ordered for him?"

The nurse reddened. "It wasn't ready yet."

"How long would it have been?" asked Barone.

She shrugged. "The blood bank said ten or fifteen more minutes."

Barone turned on the intern. "And you couldn't wait that long?"

"Chuck." Peter was almost shouting. "He was bleeding out all over me!"

"You exposed him to uncross-matched blood because he got your shoes dirty?" Barone sneered.

Before Peter could answer, Sylvia appeared in the doorway. "What is going on?" Her voice was cool, soothing. "I could hear you all the way down by the elevators."

Barone's face reddened. "Your intern"—he nearly spat out the word like an epithet—"gave this patient uncross-matched blood."

"Sylvia," Peter blurted, "he was bleeding out. His blood pressure is only seventy over thirty."

Barone turned on him again. "I specifically ordered cross-matched packed red cells for this man. It would only have taken another fifteen minutes. In my Emergency Room—''

"Isn't he Peter's patient?" she interrupted.

"Well, of course, I called him down, but—''

"In that case, he's my patient too." Only the rise in pitch in her voice betrayed any emotion. "And, no matter what room he is in, I agree with Peter. He needs the blood. Now.'' She turned her back on Barone and began to take a blood pressure reading. Barone stood behind her for a moment, unsure, and then, still red faced, turned and left the room.

It was nearly 5:30 A.M. before Herbie Brown was stable enough to transfer up to his bed on 4 East. He bled again, not more than five minutes after Barone left the room and a full twenty minutes before the blood bank completed the cross-match. Following a second ice water lavage and two more units of cross-matched blood, Peter and Sylvia rolled Herbie's stretcher down the darkened corridor to the 4 East ward.

For almost an hour now, Herbie had not bled. Peter and Sylvia were sitting in the back room of the 4 East nurses' station, writing their respective notes for Herbie's chart.

Sylvia finished first and handed Peter two sheets of neat, round, precise lettering—always written with a fountain pen, always with violet ink. She was tired but refused to let the cumulative strain of her twenty-four-hour workday show through. Her voice even still had a hypnotic singsong. "Well, Peter, here's my write-up. Can you put it on the chart with your own?" Peter nodded, without looking up. He was writing furiously, trying to finish so that he might get back to bed for a few minutes sleep before morning rounds.

She rose, started for the door, then turned. "By the way, what do you want to do with Mr. Brown?"

Peter lifted his head, looked out the window in front

of him. The sky was becoming an ever lighter shade of gray. "You mean long term?" She could see his reflection in the window, staring out over the slate-colored cityscape. "I didn't really think . . . I mean, I guess I was just happy to get him stabilized." He stopped, squeezed his eyes shut as if trying to force the last drop of concentration out of his numbed brain. "I suppose that I'll try to get him to stop bleeding, then get him ready for discharge." He opened his eyes, turned to face her. "What are you getting at?"

Sylvia locked onto his eyes, shiny black marbles that seemed to stare right through her. "Well, you could try to do something about his varices." She tried to draw him out slowly, resisting with what force she had left the urgency of his gaze.

Peter turned from her, flushed. The bright orange disk of the sun caught his eye as the first few rays peeked over the tops of the buildings on Roosevelt Island. "You mean a shunt operation?" he asked, at length. "A bypass to reduce the pressure in his verices? I guess that is not a bad idea. I could call for a surgical consult later this . . ." He turned back to her, his voice trailed off.

She watched the young intern, hair disheveled, clothes splattered with blood, as he tried to pick up her train of thought. She knew how difficult it was to think coherently after a sleepless night filled with anxiety, responsibility, and the endless harassment of a pocket pager. She also knew the kind of toughness that he would need in the months and years ahead to make those decisions, and make them correctly, after nights even worse than this one. Her heart went out to the bedraggled young man in front of her, a kind of affection, as if for a younger brother.

"No," she said slowly, "I don't think that is a very good idea."

He knew that he was being tested again, but his mind was a blank.

"What do you think of his state of consciousness?" She led him on.

"Well." Peter rubbed his eyes, turned back to the window. Gold shards of light gleamed off the surface of the East River. "I guess he is fairly sleepy, but he is an alcoholic, and it was the middle of the night. . . ."

"No, Peter." She shook her head softly, and could not help some of her sadness coming through in her voice. "He is much more sleepy than that. The lethargy is due to the poisons that are building up in his blood-stream as a result of his liver failure. A shunt operation to divert blood away from his failing liver would only make his mental function worse."

"Of course," Peter agreed, turned again to meet her stare. "And if we can stop his bleeding and clean the toxins out of his blood, he may do all right."

Sylvia shook her head sadly, a sense of remorse creeping over her. "Not likely, Peter. First, I doubt that a thirty-eight-year-old alcoholic in this much trouble will ever do all right. And second, you, not we, are going to have to deal with him."

"What do you mean? Where will you be?" Peter gave her a quizzical look.

"In the Emergency Room." She sighed. "This was my last night on Four East. Today I rotate off service."

Peter looked at her, dazed. "I guess I knew that the rotation was nearly finished." The look in his eyes confirmed what she had already suspected: that he already had become much too attached, too dependent on her. "But I didn't know what day you were going to leave. I never even checked the schedule." He stared at the floor for a moment, as if searching for something, perhaps a way to express an inner feeling, a sensation, that was too fragile for him to frame in words. At last he gave up, finally said only, "Who will be replacing you?"

She was silent for a moment. "You mean you really don't know?"

He raised his eyes up to hers again. They were devoid of hope, the eyes of a faithful puppy that has been beaten one time too many. She shook her head slowly. "As of this morning I will be replaced by Chuck Barone."

The sunlight was already streaming in through the windows as he trudged through the semicircular solarium at the end of the 4 East corridor on the way to his on-call room. His mind had been too dulled by the endless, sleepless night for him to react to Sylvia's news. All that mattered was catching a few moments of rest.

He glanced out the picture windows of the sun room, overlooking the tall oak trees of the Rockefeller University campus. The entire midtown Manhattan skyline loomed above the dark green treetops. A shaft of bright golden light, glinting off the spire of the Chrysler Building, caught his eye. Lit from a nearly horizontal angle on a clear morning the buildings in the distance seemed almost hyperreal, so crisp and sharp, so perfect that they could only be an artist's drawing.

It was almost 6:00 A.M. Peter savored the realization that his long night on call was nearly over. He yearned for a few moments of rest, to close his eyes against the imminent beginning of another busy day.

He pulled the shades in the on-call room, returning it to semidarkness, and untied his shoes. His feet felt liberated from their hot, confining prisons. The coolness of the sheets against his clothing was soothing. Greedily, he closed his eyes and let the darkness enfold him. . . .

* * *

"Peter," she said hesitantly. The voice was soft but slightly coarsened with age, like his grandmother's. "Peter, I just wanted to thank you."

Peter Lee did not open his eyes. He knew he was still asleep and he was relishing every moment of it.

"You really shouldn't be ashamed, you know." He could feel the press of her soft but weathered hand against his own. Involuntarily he let his eyes open just a crack to see who she was.

"I knew you weren't really sleeping." It was Mary Altman. Her face was still waxen and gray, but now smiling benignly.

Peter's eyes opened wide. He started. "What are you doing here?"

"Now don't worry," she answered. "They won't miss me down in the morgue. Not at least for an hour, until the pathologists come in."

Peter's first sense of alarm was overtaken by an eerie calm. He felt uneasy in her presence, but somehow not surprised by it.

"I just wanted to thank you properly, that's all."

"For what?" asked Peter, his voice strained.

"For releasing me. You have no idea what life is like when you are old and helpless and living in a nursing home. Not only are all of your reasons for living taken away, but everyone assumes that you do not even miss them."

"Did you?" Peter's voice was little more than a croak.

"Of course I did!" Peter almost thought he saw her face color. "No intellect, no exercise, no sex—and the food is slop! The only ones who do not realize that something is missing are the fortunate ones who are already dead!"

Peter winced, recalling the events of the night. "So you are not angry with me?" he offered.

She almost laughed. "Would a slave be angry with

a man for cutting his chains? Is a baby angry when the umbilical cord is severed? By ending one stage of my existence, you have allowed me to enter another that is infinitely less unpleasant. For that you deserve a kiss.''

He looked at her cold blue lips. ''You really don't have to—''

''I insist,'' she answered. He watched, frozen in mixed fascination and horror as her ashen lips, a bit of cold spittle at the corner, approached his face.

''No!'' he started, the shout frozen in his throat. He closed his eyes and could feel the cold, smooth hardness press against his lips.

The phone rang. He opened his eyes with a start and found that he was askew on the cot, his head over the edge of the mattress, his lips pressed against the cold metal of the bed frame.

A second ring. His arm reached out reflexively and lifted the receiver. He sat up in the bed, drenched in a cold sweat, and brought the receiver to his ear. ''Yes?'' he answered thickly.

''Sorry to wake you up, doctor,'' the voice of the hospital operator was warm, alive, welcome, ''but you asked me to call you for rounds at seven A.M.''

''So I did,'' affirmed Peter, ''and thank you.'' For once he meant it.

Tuesday Morning, September 10

"Tired?" answered Barone with the forced weariness of someone who is trying to make a point. "I am practically *deceased!*"

"I know," said Sylvia, her voice almost compassionate, "it really is rough starting a new ward rotation after a night on call in the Emergency Room. . . ."

"I was up all night," agreed Barone. "Belly pains and chest pains, one after the other." He shook his head slowly and pursed his lips, it was not clear whether in disbelief or disgust.

"But," continued Sylvia, "we've all had to do it." Crisply, as if she too had not been up most of the night, she added, "We had better get on with morning rounds, so we can all get our work done and get out of here today."

Peter, more exhausted after his brief nap than before he want to bed, marveled at how fresh Sylvia looked. He was going to miss her.

Barone sighed. "I guess we had better get on with it." Sylvia accompanied them down the hall. She tried, whenever she rotated off service, to make rounds one last time to introduce the new resident to the patients she was leaving behind. Barone seemed a bit discomfited at her continued presence, but did not seem to know how to ask her to leave. Peter marched down the hall behind them, followed by the other two 4 East interns with whom he rotated the every-third-night on-call schedule. Marilyn Silver, short and chesty, had a buoyant personality that often made morning rounds just barely tolerable. Harvey Krane, by contrast, was a thin, too carefully groomed young man, with a neatly trimmed beard and effeminate manner that Peter judged was probably a homosexual affectation.

"Let's do it!" chimed Marilyn as they entered the first patient room. Harvey's lips rolled up into something approaching a sneer.

In the bed nearest the door on the left, a small man with off-color orange brown hair and a pasty yellow complexion was attacking his breakfast of eggs and toast with toothless gums. Shrunken and wizened, he gave the appearance of great age. "John Sherman," began Harvey matter-of-factly, as Barone examined the bedside chart, "is a forty-three-year-old insurance salesman with end-stage diabetic renal disease." Mr. Sherman ate without trace of recognition, let alone emotion, as his history was recited. It was not clear whether he did not understand what was being said or whether he had been stung so often by callous remarks that he chose not to listen. "He came in to begin kidney dialysis," added Harvey.

"What is his creatinine clearance?" asked Barone.

"Less than ten." Harvey flushed; he had not actually calculated it and was embarrassed to admit this on his first rounds with the new resident.

Barone knew he was bluffing. "Is that milliliters per minute or liters per hour?"

Harvey stumbled. "Well, it was, I, uh—"

"What is his creatinine running now?" Barone cut him off sharply.

Relieved that he was back on firmer ground, Harvey answered, "After the dialysis yesterday, it was six point seven."

Barone ran his eye down the chart; the last value was correct. The lesson had not been lost.

Barone set down the chart, addressed the patient himself for the first time. "Good morning, Mr. Sherman. I'm Dr. Barone. I'll be taking over from Dr. Blackman today." He waved his hand vaguely toward Sylvia. "How are you doing this morning?"

John Sherman looked up, as if he had not heard a word of the previous remarks. "I'd like some more toast," he answered. Only Marilyn smiled.

"I mean medically," Barone added with some irritation. "How are you doing medically?"

The little man shrugged. "My feet hurt."

Harvey broke in. "He has long-standing, painful diabetic nerve pains in both of his legs."

"Are you treating him for that?" Barone asked, seeming relieved that he could question one of the other doctors rather than the patient.

"No," interceded Sylvia. "What do you suggest?"

Barone turned to her. "There have been some reports in the medical journals about the use of capsaicin for that kind of pain."

She nodded, thoughtfully sucking her lower lip. "Good idea," she acceded and turned to Harvey, who was already writing the suggestion on his notepad.

John Sherman watched the byplay wordlessly. The group of young doctors moved on to the next bed without acknowledging his complaint further. He shrugged, returned to his breakfast.

A middle-aged Hispanic man sat in a chair at the side of the next bed, eating his breakfast from a hospital tray. His dark, thick hair was tinged with gray; his heavy mustache wiggled as he munched his toast. His eyes were brown and liquid, and he appeared mournful as he gazed out the bedside window at the East River. Electrode leads, attached to his chest, ran to a cardiac monitor, which announced each heartbeat with a beep.

"Alberto Hernandez is a fifty-six-year-old Hispanic male," began Marilyn. Her cheerful voice contrasted with Mr. Hernandez's expression as he pretended that he was not listening. "He was admitted"—she checked her notepad—"on September second for chest pain and had EKG and enzyme changes compatible with an acute anterior wall myocardial infarction."

Alberto Hernandez looked up. "Say, Doc? Did I have a real heart attack?" He addressed Marilyn, who flushed and looked to Sylvia, then Barone.

"This is the fourth time we have been through this," she remarked to Barone, and then to the patient: "Yes, Mr. Hernandez, you had a real heart attack."

"Not just angina"—he pronounced it so it would rhyme with "vagina"—"or something?"

"No." She shook her head, amused and exasperated at once.

"Then when can I go back to work?" he asked plaintively.

She turned to Barone. "He runs a pressing machine in a dry cleaning plant." She turned back to the patient. "Not for two months, at least. And then you will have to take a less strenuous job."

He shook his head, this time at the river, and went back to his breakfast.

"Let's see," said Barone, "he's now eight days out from his heart attack. Why does he still need a cardiac monitor?"

Marilyn's face colored and she nodded toward the doorway. The group edged out of the room, and she explained in a low voice. "The monitor is to remind Mr. Hernandez that he has had a heart attack. Technically he doesn't need it, but psychologically . . ." She shrugged. "At least the leads from the monitor tie him down to the bedside so he doesn't wander off and get into trouble."

"Whose idea was that?" Barone looked ready to pounce.

Sylvia, standing behind him, answered first, icily, "Mine."

His cheeks began to burn, but his voice was controlled, and Barone did not turn to confront her. "Well, let's get him off the monitor today. I want him up and around."

"He tries to help the nurses carry things—" Marilyn began.

"Then they should have the sense to tell him not to help." Barone cut her off. "By the way, is he getting any propranolol?"

Marilyn shrugged. "No, why?"

"Two studies," answered Barone, "have shown that it may reduce the risk of sudden cardiac death in the survivors of acute heart attacks."

Marilyn nodded and scribbled down the comment in her notebook as the group proceeded to the next bed. "Roscoe Bremmer is a fifty-six-year-old taxi driver from Queens who was admitted for high blood pressure which was out of control," said Peter. "We've stabilized him on hydrochlorothiazide and nadolol."

Barone looked at the bedside chart. "His pressure is running about one forty over ninety, still a bit on the high side." He put his stethoscope to Mr. Bremmer's chest and listened to the heart and lungs. "I'd say he has a bit of heart failure, too. What does his chest X ray look like?"

"His chest X ray . . . ?" Peter reddened, began to search through his notebook for the result.

"Showed that his heart is slightly enlarged," interrupted Sylvia.

"Probably as a result of his high blood pressure. I'd give him a drug for his hypertension that also controls his heart failure. What about prazosin?"

"We thought of that," replied Peter, "but he would

have to take that drug at least three times a day. The other two drugs he only has to take once a day.''

"Medically," Barone lectured, "the combination you chose is inferior. Why take a less effective medication, even if it is only once a day?''

"Because," broke in Sylvia, "it is better than a more effective medication that is not taken at all. Mr. Bremmer is a taxi driver. He's out driving for ten or twelve hours at a stretch.''

"That's right, Doc," agreed Bremmer. "When I'm out on the street, I don't stop for nothin'.''

"Every few months," continued Sylvia, "he comes into the hospital with his blood pressure out of control, because he forgets to take his medicine when he's out driving. This time, I wanted to put him on a regimen that his wife could make sure he would take before he left the house in the morning.''

Barone flushed. "The nadolol is probably making his heart failure worse." He addressed himself to Lee. "Start decreasing that, and begin the prazosin today." He turned and started toward the door.

Harvey followed behind, and Sylvia stalked after them, fuming. Marilyn left the room last with Peter. "One room down, fourteen to go." She sighed. "This is going to be a long morning." They followed the others out into the hallway.

Maurie Benson shielded his eyes from the strong sunlight streaming in on his left from the tall windows of the 4 East solarium. "You wanna go over that again?" he asked belligerently.

Peter Lee was sitting in the full sunlight and sweating. "Mr. Brown presented to the Emergency Room stuporous, with gastrointestinal bleeding and a significant drop in blood pressure.''

"And what did you do?" Benson almost snarled.

The sweat on Peter's brow and upper lip felt cold. "I wanted to give him some blood."

"You wanted to give him some blood?" Maurie mimicked. "You *wanted* to? What the hell were you thinking about? Why were you wasting critical time? You should have been *giving* it to him!"

The words lashed at Peter, stung him. "Well, I wanted to but—"

"But what?" Benson cut him off. "You just *do* it! You waste time with an unstable patient like that, and someday someone is going to die!" He mopped his forehead. "It's goddamn hot in here."

"No shit!" whispered the medical student seated directly behind Peter Lee. A low giggle ran through the group of students and interns. Involuntarily, a small smile began to form on Peter's lips. He bit his cheek.

Benson had not heard the remark, but the giggling made him furious. "A man comes to our Emergency Room bleeding to death and you just sit around, contemplating your navel, trying to decide whether to transfuse him? Look, I am the attending physician this month on the Four East ward. I am ultimately responsible for the medical care of every patient on this floor. And I will not stand for anything less than the very best medical practice on my service. Is that understood?"

Peter nodded mutely.

"Now, why was Mr. Brown not transfused immediately?"

Peter tried to swallow; the inside of his mouth felt like it was covered with sand. "There was no"—his voice caught, he paused, cleared his throat—"no cross-matched blood yet."

"No cross-matched blood yet?" Maurie parroted him again in ridicule. He turned to one of the third year medical students. "Under the circumstances, wouldn't you have given him uncross-matched blood?"

"I don't know," broke in Barone, "whether that is

really justified." His face reddened as Benson's gaze shifted to him. The flashing brown eyes seemed to bore into his skull. "You could always use saline or albumin to replace his lost volume if he broke loose bleeding again. And it would only take ten minutes to get the cross-matched blood, it he really needed it."

Peter felt as if a great weight had been lifted from his shoulders, as the force of Benson's tantrum now shifted to Barone. "And what if he bled to death while you were waiting for the blood bank to finish the cross-match? That kind of delay could have cost the patient his life."

"So could a transfusion reaction," shot back Barone, his voice rising.

Benson was livid. "So it was *you* who didn't transfuse him!"

"Not exactly," Peter ventured, reluctantly. "We did give him the uncross-matched blood."

"Jesus Christ!" Benson shook his head, deflated. "Let's go take a look at this patient." He picked up his battered black medical bag and led the way out of the solarium, followed by Barone and the entourage of interns and medical students in white coats, lined up like ducklings.

Marilyn Silver was just behind Peter. "Attending rounds with Benson," she whispered, "is like the Spanish Inquisition!"

Peter nodded, without turning. He dropped back a half step, whispered out the right side of his mouth: "I'm not looking forward to going through this every day for a month."

"Relax," she said. "I think he only grills the intern who was on call the night before."

"Nothing like kicking a man when he's down."

"Or a woman," added Marilyn, ruefully.

When they reached Herbert Brown's bedside, Benson was already leaning over the patient, taking his pulse.

"Heart rate is one twenty," he remarked to no one in particular, then tried to rouse the sleeping man by shaking his shoulder. Herbie only moaned.

Benson pulled the lower eyelids down, examining the pink of the eyes. "Awful pale. Lee, what is his hematocrit?"

Peter blushed. He had not yet had time to check the morning blood report. "It was thirty-two."

Benson picked up immediately on the slight hesitation. "And when was that reading done?"

Peter's color deepened. "About three A.M."

"You mean last night in the Emergency Room?"

Peter nodded. His ears burned, as if on fire.

"What time is it now, *Dr.* Lee?" He emphasized the honorific, which under normal circumstances he did not use at all.

Peter checked his watch furtively. "It's eleven-fifteen . . . sir."

Maurie's eyes were piercing. "Let me get this straight. You have an active GI bleeder in the hospital for eight hours, and you haven't even rechecked his hematocrit?" His tone was one of disbelief, as if Peter had, perhaps, forgotten to put his pants on before coming to work.

Peter's voice caught. "But I . . . I mean, we, uh . . . ." He coughed to clear his throat; it did not help. "That is, we did send a hematocrit this morning," he finally managed to rasp.

Benson stared right through Peter. He hesitated a second, then pursued. "Well, Dr. Lee. Don't keep us in suspense. What was the result?"

Peter stared blankly, mumbled, "I haven't had a chance to check it yet."

Maurie continued to stare in mock disbelief. "Well, then, why don't you go check it now?" he asked, as if addressing an idiot. Grateful for the respite, Peter hastily retreated.

Benson spent a moment examining the bedside chart, grunted as he traced out the pulse and blood pressure lines. Then he pulled back the sheet, exposing Herbert Brown's protuberant abdomen. He pressed on it, patted it with one hand. "Just like slapping a water balloon," he remarked.

He took out his stethoscope and listened over the abdomen, then the chest. When Peter rejoined them, Benson was just slipping his stethoscope back into the front pocket of his long white coat.

"The hematocrit this morning was twenty-nine," Peter announced.

Benson nodded. "But he's bleeding again. Look at this pulse line on his chart. Stable at eighty-five to ninety all morning, and now it's up to one twenty. And his blood pressure has begun to fall again." He passed the chart to Barone, who nodded. "This man's liver is shot, which is probably why he is comatose. And he needs another two units of blood, immediately." He turned to Barone. "Uncross-matched, if his blood pressure falls any further."

Barone's cheeks were burning again. "Do you really think he might have bled to death last night without the uncross-matched transfusion?"

"He should be so lucky." Benson turned and stalked out of the room.

"Pretty quiet, Marina."

The ER receptionist looked up from the romantic novel she was reading to see Sylvia Blackman standing in front of her. She was not used to the doctors in the ER paying much attention to her, particularly for the last few weeks during Dr. Barone's rotation there. She glanced down at her time sheet. "I haven't had anyone check in for over twenty minutes." At least the new ER resident looked friendly.

"Yeah, I've already seen all the patients. Now I just

have to wait for some lab test results to come back.''
Sylvia had found it easy, considerably easier than most
of the male residents, to gain the friendship of the ward
secretaries and nurses whom she worked with. The female support staff might get along with the men, and
often were more cooperative, but the added tension of
real or potential sexual relationships would always enter
in at some level. And the women would never quite
open up to the men in the same way that they would
with her. "Why don't we get a cup of coffee?"

Marina Quintanos was used to being ignored, ordered around, even yelled at by doctors that she hardly
knew. But this was the first time one had treated her as
something like an equal in her six years as an ER receptionist. "Sure," she said, lifting her hands to flip
her curly black hair up from her neck. The gesture produced a brief puff of cool air on her neck as the hair
settled back down, a sensation that she equated somehow with a feeling of freedom. "Jean?" she called to
the nurse filling out a form at the back of the nurses'
station. "Can you watch the desk for me for a few
minutes?"

The two women walked to the coffee room—a small
supply closet containing a coffee maker—in the back of
the ER. "This is going to take some getting used to,"
said Marina.

"How is that?" asked Sylvia, pouring the steaming
black liquid into two Styrofoam cups.

"Well, it usually takes a week or two before the new
ER residents even begin saying hello. I don't think the
last one ever learned my name."

Sylvia held out one of the cups, took a sip from the
other. "You mean Dr. Barone?"

Marina nodded, took the cup. "It's not as if he was
abusive or anything. He just seemed to act as if I was
some sort of servant. Like there was no need to notice
who the person was who was bringing him the charts."

She began to load the cup with spoonfuls of sugar, then coffee creamer.

Sylvia nodded, thinking of the scenes in the ER the previous night and on rounds this morning. "He certainly can be arrogant." As she sipped her coffee, a warm feeling began to rise from her stomach. "But at least he tries to be a good doc." The dark, curly-haired resident might not win a Mr. Personality contest, but he tried hard to do his best for his patients using his considerable technical skills.

"Well." Marina wrinkled her nose. "As far as I'm concerned, you can have him."

Sylvia smiled and took another sip of the coffee. "I just hope he doesn't burn out my former interns up on the ward."

"Which ward is that?" Marina stopped stirring her coffee and finally took a sip. Her face screwed up in a look of disgust, then she added another teaspoon of sugar.

"Four East," said Sylvia.

"Isn't that where that cute Dr. Lee works?"

Sylvia smiled again. "Yes," she answered, "and Dr. Krane and Dr. Silver. But the one I am really worried about is Peter Lee." She sipped her coffee, thinking about the intern who felt too keenly the problems of all his patients. Unlike Barone, he had never learned to insulate himself from their pain. "He is already having a tough time adjusting to his internship. And an overbearing resident is not what he needs right now."

Marina took another sip of her coffee, looked like she could barely swallow it, but forced a big smile. "Well, any time you think he needs some TLC, just send him down to me."

Sylvia looked at the attractive young woman across from her. She was struck by the contrast between the pleasant, fashionably dressed receptionist, whose major concern in life seemed to be her social relationships, and the troubled young intern she had left behind on the ward. "Sure." She drained her cup of coffee. "You may be exactly what he needs."

Marina walked into the empty patient room across the hall. "Yeah," she said, pouring the rest of her coffee down the sink, "maybe I could take him to a disco or something."

Peter Lee found Marilyn hunched over John Sherman, trying to find a fresh vein for an intravenous line. Beads of sweat stood out on her forehead as she gently tapped each scarred-over, tired vein with her forefinger, trying to find one that might still accept an intravenous needle. Six hastily applied Band-Aids on John Sherman's other forearm commemorated as many prior unsuccessful attempts. Six used needles dripped blood onto the sheet, and John Sherman sat among them dripping sweat.

Finally she found a likely candidate. She did not look up as she said, "I'll be with you in just a minute," to Peter. She scrubbed the skin with an alcohol wipe, then carefully unwrapped a fresh intravenous needle. Holding it by its plastic attachment, she slid the needle along the skin until its sharp point bit into John Sherman's flesh. He winced, and there was a brief whistling sound of air rushing through his front teeth as he sucked in an involuntary gasp.

"I'm sorry, Mr. Sherman. I know this hurts . . ." She began the nearly automatic refrain, supposed somehow to comfort the patient. "I'll be as quick as I can." But the needle in her hand leisurely explored the flesh of his forearm, pushing against the wall of the recalcitrant vein, sliding under it and then along its side. Finally the tip of the needle bit into the wall of the vein. She advanced it a bit further. There was no blood return through the needle, so she pulled back again slightly.

A bit of blood leaked out of the vein, surrounded the needle. The vein collapsed.

"Goddamn it!" She pulled the needle out. John Sherman winced again, as much from the pain of the needle pulling back through the flesh of his forearm as because he knew there would now have to be another attempt.

Placing a Band-Aid over the seventh wound, Marilyn's voice was solicitous. "I'm sorry, sir, but I have to leave for a minute. I'll be right back." Mr. Sherman showed no sign of regret.

"That goddamn fag Krane!" she spat out, as soon as they had reached the hallway. "He signed out to me early so he could go downtown and meet one of his boyfriends." She looked slightly suspiciously at Peter, decided to back off a bit. "I mean, that's all right, to leave early. Let the on-call intern handle your patients. But at least he should have put in his fucking IVs before he took off!"

Peter felt vaguely guilty without knowing quite why. He returned her gaze for a moment, then his eyes dropped to her breasts, taut against the oxford cloth of her shirtfront, and then to his own sign-out sheet. He handed her the half sheet of paper as they walked toward the nurses' station.

"I have twelve patients." He began to run down the list. "Berman is six days out from his heart attack. He's doing fine. Brown is the alcoholic with cirrhosis we saw this morning during Benson's rounds."

"Benson was pretty rough on you," she broke in.

Peter shrugged, began to blush. "The patient has been stable all day. You need to check a blood count this evening."

"Benson's?" she tried to joke.

Peter looked up, baffled. There was a brief pause before he smiled. "Sorry. I was up all night with Brown."

She nodded sympathetically. "I hope he's a little kinder tonight."

He forced a smile, returned to his checkout list. "Loftus is a woman with pancreatic pseudocyst . . ." He continued his litany. Marilyn studied the sign-out sheet as he spoke. He watched her small, fine hands as she placed check marks in red ink next to each lab test that she was asked to perform, circled each blood pressure she was to check.

"Anything else, Peter?" she asked as he finished. Her voice seemed, to him, to caress the syllables of his name. Involuntarily his eyes drifted down to the white cloth of her hospital skirt, stretched across her full thighs.

"Dr. Lee!" His reverie was broken by the call of one of the evening nurses. She was hurrying down the hall, her eyes fixed on him.

"Mr. Brown in four-oh-two has begun to throw up blood again."

Peter looked toward Marilyn, groping for a sign that she would handle this emergency for him, let him go home after thirty-six hours on duty, set him free. If there had been any hint of softness a few seconds before, it was gone now. Her face was a closed door.

"I'll get it," said Peter wearily to the nurse. "Be there in a minute. Just get some iced saline and a couple of emesis basins, and meet me at the bedside." Peter turned back to Marilyn. Her face was a mixture of embarrassment, guilt, and relief. "I'll handle this before I leave," he promised. "Hope you have a good night." He hurried away to Herbert Brown's bedside, exhausted but not too tired for his stomach to knot up in fear of what he might find there.

Herbert Brown was flat-out comatose. The sheets, the pillowcase, even a bedside towel were all soaked with blood. His pulse was rapid and thready, and Peter could barely obtain a blood pressure reading.

"He's shocky," Peter said to the ward nurse, as she brought the lavage equipment into the room. "He needs more blood. Get two units of blood up here, stat." She hurried out.

He set to work, first opening both of the intravenous lines to maximum rate. Then he began to lavage the stomach again, flushing with clear iced saline, drawing back syringe after syringe of Hawaiian Punch–colored fluid. By the sixth pass, when the nurse returned, the stomach fluid was the color of pink lemonade.

"The blood will take about half an hour," she said timidly.

Peter flared. "Half an hour? I said *stat*. That means now!"

She shrugged, her cheeks flushed. "They say that the dispatch service is running late."

Peter stared at her in disbelief. "And what about you?"

She shook her head. "I can't leave the floor. I'm the only RN on duty."

"And the nurse's aides?" Peter's voice was rising both in pitch and volume.

She looked down at her shoes, the floor. "They're both at dinner. Union rules. They get a thirty-minute break for every four hours on duty. . . ."

Peter did not wait to hear the rest of the excuse. He stalked off toward the blood bank, the frustration catching in his throat. He had been on call for thirty-six hours straight. He had not even eaten since breakfast. But he could not interrupt the dinner of the nurse's aides. Not to save a man's life. After all, they had already put in their four hours. . . .

The anger choked him, and a hot tear welled in his eyes. As he passed through the door to 4 East he slammed it with his fist. Despite the doorstop, the knob hit the wall with enough force to leave its impression there.

He retrieved the blood from the blood bank, started the transfusion, and left the hospital quietly, without saying good-bye to Marilyn. Before they could hurt him again.

The elevator door slid shut with a dull thud, and the dingy, fluorescent-lit car began its slow ascent to the eighth floor. Peter let go of the Door Close button, which he had been pushing to ensure that he would ride alone. He did not like the forced conversations, or even more awkward silence, when he shared the ride. He studied the safety certificate above the control panel. It had expired two months earlier. Not unlike myself. Peter allowed himself a smile.

Beep, beep, beep. The silence was shattered by his pocket pager. "Call 3187, 3187, 3187." Even through the tinny tones of the pager's minute speaker, the urgency in Marilyn's voice was apparent.

He could feel the heat of anger rising in his throat. "Can't leave me alone for a fucking minute!" He swore under his breath, even though he was alone. He wanted to slam the elevator door with his fist, but his hand was still too sore from pounding the door in the hospital corridor.

He trudged down the cold blank fluorescent-lit hall to the blue-painted metal door of his apartment and undid both locks. He opened the door, hesitated for a second, then slammed it shut. It did not make him feel any better. He shrugged off his white jacket and dialed the 4 East phone number.

"Dr. Silver, please," he told the ward clerk who answered.

There was an electronic pause, as he waited on hold for Marilyn to come to the telephone. She finally picked up. "Peter?"

Again he thought he heard a softness, an eagerness in her voice. "Yes. Did you call me?"

"I did. One of the nurses just told me about Herbie Brown. Why didn't you let me know yourself?"

He did not want to admit that he had been afraid that if he stayed another minute, he would have been saddled with some other scut work. "I guess I was just so tired from being up all night last night that I wasn't thinking." Any intern would understand that.

"Well, is there anything special you would like me to do tonight?"

Peter resisted the temptation. "Have the nurses lavage him every few hours." He sighed. "And you will need to get a 'crit six hours after the end of his transfusion."

"That will be about three A.M." He could feel the pain in her voice. "Looks like this is going to be another wonderful night."

He refused to let himself feel guilty. "Yeah," he answered numbly, "another one."

After hanging up the telephone, Peter went into his tiny kitchen alcove and opened the refrigerator. It was almost empty. He removed a small dish of leftover lasagna and a beer.

Maryann had cooked the lasagna for him last Sunday, but even after two days it was rich and spicy. He nibbled the lasagna as he opened his second beer. His eyes rested on Maryann's photo on his shelf and lingered over her warm brown eyes. Her full, dark brown hair framed her face with its smooth, milky, translucent complexion. Despite the cold lasagna, Peter could almost taste her full warm lips.

He put the empty plate in the sink and dialed her number. She answered on the fourth ring. "Hello?" Her voice was breathy.

"Hi, Maryann. It's Peter." He could still hear her breathing. "Did you just come in?"

She hesitated for a minute. "No, no . . ." There was a pause. "I was just, uh . . . indisposed."

Peter smiled. "Oh, sorry. Perfect timing, as usual." He snuggled down into his chair. "I just got out of the hospital and was thinking about you. Do you think that we could get together tonight?"

She drew in a breath sharply; the sound of it was like a cold blast of wind. "Tonight?" She hesitated, cleared her throat. "You want to get together tonight?" Her voice was distant, as if she were talking loudly but not directly into the telephone. There was another pause. "Gee . . . I don't think so, Peter. Not tonight."

Peter flushed. "Why not?" He was not going to give up so easily.

"I . . . I just don't think tonight is such a good idea." She paused again. He said nothing. "I mean, you're always so *tired* after being on call . . ."

Peter's throat tightened; his voice was harsh. "Anyone would be tired after staying up all night on call. And so maybe I don't"—he tried to swallow, was unable—"perform so well those nights. But I still need you. I need to be with you."

"Well, I have needs too, Peter." Her voice had lost its hesitancy. "You are on call every third night, so that's out, and the next night you're too tired. And then on the third night . . ." She did not need to finish the sentence.

"Sunday was a fluke. So I fell asleep after dinner."

"It wasn't that you fell asleep! It was when!" she blurted out. He could hear a creaking in the background. Bedsprings?

"You know I can't perform after a heavy meal," he retorted.

"And what was the excuse last Thursday? And the Monday before that?"

Then he heard it in the background. The sound of someone . . . no . . . unmistakably, the sound of a *man* clearing his throat. "Maryann, is there someone there with you?"

The hesitation told the entire story. Finally she answered coolly, "It's really none of your business."

Peter could feel his stomach rise up in his throat. The taste of the lasagna, again. Bitter. "There is, isn't there? You've got another guy there with you right now!"

"Peter, that is none of your business," she repeated. "Even if I did, what difference would it make to you? You don't own me." She hesitated, then spat it out, "And you certainly don't need me!"

He was choking on his rage, trying desperately to keep it out of his voice. "Need you? I need you *now!* I can't believe that you are doing this to me!"

"Peter," she hissed, her voice now a hoarse whisper, "if you had shown this much emotion with me last Sunday, I wouldn't be!"

The line went dead.

Peter slammed the telephone receiver down into the cradle. He lifted it, began dialing again, then slammed it down once more. "Bitch!" he yelled. "Bitch, bitch, bitch!" He stifled a sob, could not hold back the next. His eyes welled up, and he lay facedown on the couch, the hot tears running down his cheeks.

It was already past sunset, and the room was rapidly darkening. The night enfolded him.

Barone blinked in the flat fluorescent brightness as he entered the Emergency Room. Through the glass doors he could see the darkness outside. He turned to the ER receptionist. "I can't believe that it's dark already."

"Day's getting shorter, you know." She did not look up from her crossword puzzle. Behind her, Sylvia Blackman was gathering up her medical bag and her purse.

"It's already after eight o'clock," she said. "Summer can't last forever."

"Finished with your shift?" he asked Sylvia as she left the nurses' station.

"You don't think they would let me out of here if I wasn't," she responded wryly.

"No." He shrugged. "Not really. I guess I'll walk back to the apartment house with you."

She did not answer. The glass doors to the ER slid open as they approached. The cool night air felt soft, balmy.

"You're here awfully late," she said.

Barone looked at his watch out of habit. He knew it was 8:15. "I guess so. I just had to catch up on some old charts. I'm always behind on dictating my discharge summaries."

She smiled. "Aren't we all."

He nodded, too vigorously. "I wanted to get through some of the backlog before the charts start rolling in from Four East."

"I know," she agreed, "after two months on the ward, I'm three months behind."

"At least the ER rotation ought to give you a chance to catch up."

"Sure." She grimaced. "Dictate charts. Just exactly what I want to do after a twelve-hour shift in the Emergency Room."

He smiled briefly, turned toward her. "You know Benson really lit into me on ward rounds this morning."

She looked at him for the first time. "You mean about Herbie Brown?"

He nodded.

She stopped for a second, looked directly into his eyes. "Well, you deserved it." She turned and continued walking.

Barone had to hurry to draw even with her. "I may

have been wrong in the ER last night,'' he insisted, ''but you didn't have to make a point of it in front of the intern.'' He refused to mention Peter by name. ''It is going to be much more difficult working with him now.''

''It wasn't Peter's fault that he was right,'' she said.

''No.'' Barone reddened. ''But after you came in on his side, it was very hard for me to back off gracefully.''

They stopped under the pink orange glow of the sodium streetlights in front of the house staff apartment building. Sylvia turned to him, her gray eyes glowering. ''Chuck, you always come on so strong, acting as if you know everything. It's no wonder people have the compulsion to prove that you don't. I don't hammer at everyone I meet, but you just''—she shrugged—''invite it.''

Barone stared at the sidewalk. ''Are you going inside?''

''No,'' she answered. ''I was going to the grocery store down the block to buy something for dinner.''

''Well,'' he said, ''I was on my way to Sparky's pub for some dinner. Can I buy you a burger?''

She reddened, took a moment too long to answer. ''Sure,'' she said softly. ''Why not.''

They began walking again. ''You know,'' she said, ''you really shouldn't worry about Benson. He does that kind of thing to everybody.''

''I know.'' Barone nodded. ''I hear he's a real schmuck.''

Sylvia laughed. ''More than you know. He's made a career of it.''

''How do you mean?'' asked Barone.

''Have you heard of Bensonhurst?''

Barone thought a minute. They stopped at the door to the pub. ''Do you mean that big, expensive condominium development out on Long Island?'' He opened the door.

"That's just part of it," she called back as the music blasted from the door. They slipped by the bar area and found a table in the back corner, farthest from the music. "Bensonhurst is an entire village"—she was nearly shouting to be heard—"with homes, shopping centers, schools. Practically all of it was built—"

"By the Benson family," Barone finished.

Sylvia glared for a moment, then continued. "They've built homes in Brooklyn, operate rental apartments in Queens."

"And Maurie's from *that* Benson family?" asked Barone in disbelief. "What the hell is he doing here?"

"Maurie's always been a schmuck." She scanned the menu chalked on a blackboard on the back wall.

A waitress approached. "Can I get you folks anything from the bar?"

Barone shook his head. Sylvia said, "I'd like a bacon cheeseburger. Rare."

"Make that two," said Barone, "with fries." He looked at Sylvia. She nodded. "And a Michelob dark for me."

"Two Michelobs." Sylvia smiled for the first time, turned back to Barone. She began again. "When Benson was eighteen he inherited twenty million dollars. That took all the fun out of life for him. He could have, or be, almost anything he wanted." The beers arrived; she took a swallow. "No challenge.

"So Maurie went into medicine precisely because he knew that he would have to make it on his own as a doctor. He turned his back on his family—they'd given him too much and spoiled everything for him. When he saw how much fun it was to kick his family, he decided to combine careers. Now he's a doctor who kicks around doctors."

"A sadist?" asked Barone.

"Not exactly," she answered. "He's really good to his patients. Maybe too good." She sipped her beer, huddled conspiratorially with Barone. "He's always willing to drop everything for one of his patients. Stays at the hospital day and night, hardly ever leaves. It may be his way of kicking himself."

The hamburgers arrived. "I heard he's particularly tough on women." He held her eye as he bit into the sandwich.

Sylvia chewed for a moment. "He usually beats up on someone for a good reason. But I think he takes particular delight in beating on female residents."

Barone chuckled.

Her cheeks colored. "I don't think that's so—"

He shook his head. "No, I'm not laughing at what you said," he interjected hastily. "It's just that you reminded me of an incident with Benson."

She waited, not smiling.

"It was really pretty crude," he began.

She nodded, eyes wide.

"One day I was eating lunch in the cafeteria, sitting at one of the tables reserved for the hospital staff, when Benson comes in, shouting at his resident Janice Wolcott. 'Goddamn women,' he was yelling. 'Can't make a goddamn decision.'

"They sat down at the next table, and one of the other residents, Steve Turner, began to defend her. He said that women were no more indecisive than men.

"Benson just blew up. 'Men and women are built differently,' he shouted. 'They think differently. And women cannot make a decision.'

"Turner, who never knows when to stop, began again. 'You have no reason to say that. Women can think just as well as men and make decisions just as well too,' he said. Benson was already turning red, and Janice, who had been on service with Benson all month, was pulling at Turner's sleeve to get him to stop. He continued anyway. 'There's absolutely no evidence for a sex difference. . . .'

"Well, Benson just blew up. He began screaming, and the entire cafeteria stopped to listen. 'You think there's no sex difference?' he shouted. 'You think there's no difference between men and women? Well, let me tell you one thing, buddy, that is never going to change—' " Barone stopped, looked to Sylvia. "This is a direct quote, you understand."

She nodded.

Barone continued. "Well, Benson's voice is the only sound in the cafeteria. With two hundred sets of eyes on him he says, 'One thing is never going to change: We will always be the fuckers, and they will always be the fuckees.' "

Sylvia's cheeks reddened. "A direct quote?"

"Direct."

"As I said." She shook her head, took the last bite of her sandwich. "He's made a career of being a schmuck."

It was after 2 A.M. when Peter Lee awoke. He was sure that he had been dreaming and that it had been unpleasant—he felt the tenseness in the pit of his stomach—but the content of his dream dissolved into his waking consciousness, eluding his grasp and leaving only a residue of anxiety. He pulled himself to a sitting position on the sofa and looked out the window. The face of the high-rise building across the street was awash in the pink orange glow of the street lamps. Only the fact that all but a few of the windows were dark betrayed the lateness of the hour.

Peter walked to his own window and looked down at the street. Several people were standing in front of the entranceway to the apartment house across the street, talking and laughing. A woman was walking her dog near the street corner. The entire city was insomniac. Peter pulled on his shoes and went out for a walk.

Even the cool evening air did nothing to extinguish Peter's smoldering thoughts. The knot of people across the street was still there, still laughing. Peter turned from them and walked up Seventieth Street towards Central Park.

The traffic on First Avenue was light but continuous. Peter waited on the corner for the light and crossed the broad boulevard.

When he reached Second Avenue, he reflexively turned uptown toward Maryann's apartment. He had not planned to go to her, but he suddenly seemed drawn as if by an unseen force. He needed to feel her warmth, though he knew it would no longer be there for him. The thought tore at him as he walked toward Seventy-third Street, pulled by a magnetism he could not resist.

He reached the glass-enclosed entrance to her building and froze, his feet suddenly rooted to the pavement. If he went inside he would commit himself to the confrontation, to the pain. Rejection was all but certain.

Peter stood for a minute, five minutes, perhaps an hour. He finally become aware of a figure staring at him from the entranceway. The doorman recognized Peter, held open the glass door for him to enter. He was committed.

"It sure is late, doctor."

Peter smiled weakly and mumbled something about on-call schedules. The doorman smiled and nodded.

"Shall I call up Miss Polino for you?" Peter knew it was the doorman's job to announce visitors, but he could not approach Maryann through a third person, could not bear the agony of yet another person sharing his rejection. He blushed. "Actually, it is rather late. Can I call her myself?"

The doorman looked puzzled. "Well, it's the management policy . . ."

Peter fished in his pocket and handed the man a ten dollar bill.

"But under the circumstances, you might need some privacy." He winked. "So while you're watching the desk here, I'll just be out front getting a breath of fresh air."

Peter stepped behind the desk and began to dial the telephone. On the third digit he hung up.

He picked up the phone again, but did not dial. His hand hovered over the telephone, frozen, trembling. He felt cold. Cold and alone. What if she were waiting for him, sitting by the telephone? What if he woke her up, and she refused to talk? What if the man with her answered the phone? He would be putting everything on the turn of a phone dial. He could not move.

A loud buzz blared in his ear, the telephone's off-the-hook signal. He reached to hang up the phone, but found himself dialing again instead. She might be waiting for him!

This time he dialed the entire phone number before hanging up. His hand was on the telephone, still shaking, when the doorman pulled the front door open. "All done?" He smiled lecherously.

"No!" Peter panicked. He could see Maryann, standing in her doorway, inviting him inside, pressing him to her warm, soft breast. "No, it's just that, uh, the, uh, line is busy.

"At three A.M.?" asked the doorman. "That's one busy lady you got there." He leered, closed the door again and turned into the night, whistling.

Frantically, Peter dialed again. He had to talk to her before the doorman intruded again. He felt like he had as a small child, standing at the end of the high diving board, afraid to jump into the pool. He was afraid of the fall, but feared more the scorn of his friends who were watching from the poolside. The telephone handset, slick with the sweat from his palm, almost slid from his grasp as the telephone rang.

"Hello?" Maryann's voice had the soft, dreamy quality that he knew so well from when they lay in bed together after making love. "Who is this?" Her voice was almost slurred. Maybe she had taken a sleeping pill. It would not be fair to approach her when she was drugged, half asleep. Summoning his last shred of courage, Peter laid the telephone back in its cradle, gently.

He pulled open the front door and nodded to the doorman, who was leaning against the tiled facade of the building, whistling tunelessly and watching the taxis cruise by. "Thank you," said Peter, without emotion.

The doorman shook his head. "Sure," he said. "Anytime."

Peter walked down Second Avenue, staring into the tail lights of receding traffic. It was so unfair. The hospital, the internship, were eating him alive. They swallowed his life, in thirty-six-hour gulps, digesting his emotions and humanity. His bones had been picked clean of any positive sentiments. He was empty, used up.

Maryann had been his only real human contact. She had kept him alive, fleshed out his skeletal existence. But now he had been stripped of Maryann as well. By monopolizing his time and his energy, the hospital had ensured he would have none left for her.

He passed under the cable car to Roosevelt Island, at Fifty-ninth Street. A car, lighted from within, was sliding along the cable, past the front of the Queensborough bridge, toward Peter.

That was what he needed: a home on an island, surrounded by the busy world, yet apart from it. Able to reach the rest of the world, to melt into its flow of activity when he wanted and able to escape its clamor and incessant demands when they reached too high a pitch for him to bear. Peter watched the car as it passed over Second Avenue. It, too, was empty.

He turned onto Fifty-seventh Street and started toward Fifth Avenue. The store windows were filled with the luxuries of existence. Sleek leather goods competed with Oriental vases and leopard coats for attention. In one storefront, a crystal table was on display. He stared at its ornate curves. The sign read: "$30,000." Could such extravagance exist in the same world as Herbie Brown? Was life just one big long bad joke, designed to make you salivate for things you could never have, then leave you bleeding your guts out?

He turned, began walking back toward the East River. The most unfair part, he thought, was that he could not even mourn for himself. No matter how intolerable his own life became, it never approached the misery of his patients. Compared to Herbie Brown, he was eating at a $30,000 crystal table.

It was infuriating. As unhappy and desperate as he was, there was always someone even less fortunate to lay claim to his time. He could gain no comfort from the fact that his position was more favorable than those he served. Rather, it tore at him that their wants and needs might even justify the destruction of his own happiness.

Endless nights on call, punctuated by dysphonic blasts from his pocket pager, slogging through rivers of urine, fountains of blood. In the process of serving other human beings, he had lost his own humanity. The world had lost its charm, its sense of humor.

He reached Sutton Place and turned uptown again, walking through the cool canyon formed by the luxurious apartments and town houses of the rich. Humor, he thought, is fundamentally the juxtaposition of incongruities, things that did not really belong together. For him there were no incongruities left. No high times to accentuate the lows. His world was being inexorably crushed until the gray juices of his life ran out of him.

Peter stopped in one of the small plazas amid the town houses facing the river. He stepped to the edge of the stone fence overlooking the water, watched its surface eddies roil darkly beneath him. He could no more stop the flow of his degradation than he could halt those currents. He was trapped, being swept downstream, condemned to spend and exhaust his energies among dark currents, unable to affect his ultimate direction.

He turned back to the street and continued uptown. The dark stone supports of the Queensborough Bridge loomed ahead. As he passed beneath them he wondered if the rock was naturally black or if it had only become darkened, after millennia of purity, through its brief contact with humankind.

Just past the bridge, the lights of the riverside helicopter landing pad were shining up into the empty night. He turned into the deserted parking lot, then past the landing pad, onto the paved jogging path that ran along the East River. The track, too, was deserted, except for a few derelicts, sleeping on the park benches along its length.

He began to drift along the track. On his left a fence separated him from the traffic on the East River Drive. Beyond that, in the pink orange glow of the streetlights, loomed the dark, rough-stoned face of Rockefeller University. Built on land which had once sloped gently to the edge of the East River, the Rock had been built level with York Avenue and New York Hospital by filling in the slope and erecting a huge stone retaining wall. Running the entire length of the campus, the wall, topped by parapets, looked like it belonged to an ancient castle. In the darkness of the night, it was not difficult to imagine peasants atop the wall, fending off an invading army by heaving boulders down the sheer, eighty-foot drop. Peter stared through the glare of the street lamps, trying to find the outlines of the buildings behind the parapets, looking for the location, on the other side of the wall, of his on-call oasis. The wall resisted even the intrusion of his gaze.

Peter came to the most deserted spot along the track, and stopped along the rail, overlooking the East River. He stared once more into its depths. He had not even been aware of the decision which had begun to form in his mind, but instantly it seemed both right and unavoidable. Almost, thought Peter, as if the decision had been made without him.

The most important decision of my life, thought Peter, lifting one leg over the rail, and he was merely swept along, by an invisible force, like so much flotsam upon the river. Still, there was no question that the only hope of release from the unending pain was to withdraw from the contest. He lifted over his other leg and sat on the railing, the heels of his shoes balanced against a shallow shelf of pavement that protruded beyond the rail.

There was no hope of fighting the East River currents. He would not even try. His body would be swept out into the New York harbor, where, with any luck, it might never be found.

He looked up at the apartment houses on Roosevelt Island, a hundred yards across the river. Most of the lights were out, but here and there a window glowed into the night without lighting up the darkness appreciably.

He would be adding a small amount of grief to the lives of those he left behind. His father would probably grieve for as short time as he felt was seemly. Secretly, he might be relieved. His mother, were she alive, would have understood. And Maryann . . . she might feel responsible. He savored that.

Not many people at the hospital would really care. Maurie would probably be annoyed that he would have

to rearrange the on-call schedule. Barone would probably celebrate.

And Sylvia. She would be the only one who would
really mourn, the only one who might really be hurt.
He stiffened as he prepared to spring out into the night.
He sniffed the air, the smell of the sewage at his feet. A
wave of nausea began to rise in his gut.

Maybe Sylvia would just think he was being cow-
ardly. She had gone through an internship. She had
shared the workload, the frustration with him for the
last month. But she was going on. Would she look down
on him for taking the easy way out?

Surely Herbie Brown had no such choice. He could
not slip off the stage quietly while no one was looking.
And even Anne Delbert, by taking a drug overdose,
had chosen to deal with the unfairness of the world by
a deliberate act, rather than merely allowing herself to
be swept, by whatever currents prevailed, into oblivion.

Peter was aware suddenly that his breath was coming
hard. A sense of doom closed over him, choked him,
grabbed his heart like a huge, frigid hand within his
chest. His hands and feet began to feel numb. His legs
felt rubbery, could no longer support his weight. He
collapsed back against the rail, his knees shaking.

Slowly Peter worked one leg up over the rail. He
nearly slipped, grasped the railing desperately with his
free hand, steadied himself. He worked the other leg
over, stumbled through the darkness on rubbery knees
until he found a park bench. He collapsed onto the
bench, bent over limply with his chest against his knees,
his face in his hands. The hot tears ran over his fingers,
onto the asphalt pavement, burning their way into the
earth.

To leave an impression. If there was a goal on earth
worth having, that must be it. To leave life at his nadir
was to admit his own impotence, the futility of his existence.

In the depths of his depression he found solace in the thought that by continuing he could do no worse. Because he already considered himself dead, he was free to use his life to defy those who had stolen it from him. He could not abandon Herbie Brown, Anne Delbert . . . Mary Altman. Losers, like him, they had even been deprived of the choice to make their own end. If there was a purpose for continuing, that must be it.

The ground at his feet was beginning to glow orange red. He raised his head to see the rosy halo of dawn's first light outlining the buildings on Roosevelt Island. As he watched, one of the apartment lights snapped on.

In life he had found only death; now in death he would find life. He rose and started toward the footbridge at Seventy-first Street, over the East River Drive. He felt a weight lift from him as he ascended the ramp. The vertical face of Manhatten General Hospital, just ahead, was suffused with the morning's red glow. There was work to be done.

Wednesday Morning, September 11

"Herbie had a rough night." Marilyn's voice was a bit higher than usual, straining not to crack. Her hair was oily and matted. She wore glasses instead of her usual contact lenses, and had on no makeup. The front of her blouse was speckled with red blotches.

"I don't know," said Harvey Krane. "He looks pretty good compared to you."

Marilyn gave him a sick smile and a kick in the ankle. Turning to address Peter and Chuck Barone, she continued, "He started gushing again about ten o'clock. Lost about three units before we could get him to stop."

"How much blood did you replace?" asked Barone.

"All three units," she answered proudly. She had done it all. Both she and her patient had survived the night. Not even Barone could find fault with that.

Barone frowned anyway. "That's a lot of blood. You could have put him into congestive heart failure."

Marilyn's cheeks colored. "His lungs were clear," she replied defensively, "and we gave him the blood very slowly."

Barone pursed his lips, nodded. He lifted the sheet from Herbie Brown, exposing the abdomen, protruding like a small brown hill in the morning light. "Help me roll him over, so we can listen to his lungs."

Peter and Harvey obediently pushed Herbie's shoulder and hip, rolling him onto his side. Barone put his stethoscope to his ears and listened. It sounded like crinkling cellophane.

"His lungs are loaded with fluid." He motioned to Marilyn to listen for herself. "He needed a central venous line last night to monitor his right heart pressure during the fluid load."

Marilyn listened, nodded sheepishly. "Well, I didn't think—"

"Apparently not," Barone cut her off sharply. Suddenly he turned. "Peter, have you put in a central line before?"

Peter swallowed. "I, uh, once, well, I've watched a couple of times and tried to—"

"Good," Barone interrupted again. "I'll help you. Meet me back here after rounds."

They let Herbie Brown roll onto his back. Harvey perfunctorily pulled the sheet halfway up his abdomen; it slid back to his groin.

"In the next bed," began Marilyn, her voice quavering, "we have Mr. Jonathan Tripp, a carpenter from Queens, who was admitted last night for . . ."

"Have you got the central line tray?" asked Barone. Peter nodded.

"Two sets of gloves? And an extra syringe?"

Peter nodded again.

"Then we're ready to begin," said Barone. "Tilt the foot of the bed up, so the blood will drain toward his head."

Peter obediently pressed the buttons on the bedside controls. The automatic bed lurched into action, tilted back until the veins on Herbie Brown's neck stood out like fat, brown worms.

"You have to prep him first. Scrub the right side of his neck all the way up to the angle of his jaw and all the way down to his shoulder." Barone grasped Herbie Brown's jaw and pulled it to the left side, exposing the right side of the neck. He rested the palm of his other hand on Herbie's forehead, pressing the head into the pillow and preventing the man from turning his neck accidentally during the procedure.

Peter poured the syrupy brown iodine disinfectant onto a cotton gauze pad and began to paint Herbie's neck with it. Then he unwrapped a sterile sheet and donned a pair of sterile surgical gloves. He spread the sheet over Herbie's head, so that the entire head of the bed was covered by the cool blue green cloth, except for Herbie's neck, which was exposed by a four-inch fenestration in the center of the drape.

The sheet, mused Peter, was as much for the doctor as for the patient. It is so much easier to cut the skin of an isolated neck or arm or abdomen, when it appears disconnected from its human owner. The drapes allow the doctor to avoid identifying with the patient, to separate himself from the pain. They prevent the doctor from becoming too emotionally involved, which would increase the chance of error. Hence the necessity for the blue green shield.

Peter smoothed the drape over the neck and began to attach a fourteen-gauge needle to a plastic syringe. "You want to come in two finger's breadths above the clavicle," instructed Barone, demonstrating with two fingers held up to his own collarbone, "at the back edge of the sternocleidomastoid muscle." He indicated the thick band of muscle running up toward the angle of the jaw from his own collarbone.

Peter found the muscle, a thin fibrous strip on the neck, and measured two finger's breadths up along it. Taking a deep breath, Peter jabbed the thick needle into the neck, piercing the skin.

"Now, slowly advance the needle, pulling back gently on the plunger, until you get free flow of blood into the syringe. That will be the internal jugular vein."

Peter Lee pushed the needle slowly into the fibrous

tissue of the neck, until it was buried, all three inches worth, right to the hilt. No blood in the syringe. He looked up. Barone was scowling. "Try again."

Peter pulled the needle out. Blood welled up through the hole which the needle, as long as a tenpenny nail, had left in the neck. He pressed a cotton gauze pad against the hole for a moment. The bleeding slowed, and he tried another penetration through the same hole.

"Aim a little higher this time," Barone urged, using his finger to point out the direction in which he wanted Peter to push the needle. Peter could feel the resistance as the needle tip cut through the muscles and tendons of the neck.

Suddenly, Herbie Brown lurched forward, head rising off the pillow as if he were trying to sit up. Barone fought to keep the delirious man from impaling his neck on the needle. The syringe jerked, separated from the needle, and fell from Peter's hand onto the sterile sheet. Blood oozed around the needle, still protruding from the neck.

"Ummmhhh!" moaned Herbie as he tried to roll over onto his right side.

"Stop him!" yelled Barone, losing his grip on the slippery skin of Herbie's chin. Trying desperately to avoid contaminating the sterile field, Peter leaned over, resting his elbow on Herbie's right shoulder. Bearing down with all of his weight, he was just able to keep Herbie pinned to the bed.

The man with the pregnant abdomen, who until that moment had been comatose, struggled with unexpected strength to free himself.

"Nurse, nurse!" screamed Barone.

Three aides answered, one of them a burly orderly. In a melee of flailing arms and legs, the five of them managed to subdue Herbie Brown. When he was at last under control, Peter began to search for the needle. He straightened the drape, adjusting the hole to expose, once again, the neck. He plucked the bloody needle from the oozing skin and applied another gauze pad to stop the bleeding.

"Try again," Barone demanded fiercely, pinning Herbie's head to the pillow under the blood-soaked drape.

Peter's legs felt rubbery. His fingers, slippery with blood, struggled to control the syringe as he guided the needle in as carefully as he could. He felt a bead of sweat run down his brow and along his nose as he advanced the needle again to its hilt. No blood. "Again," said Barone, his voice a harsh whisper.

Drops of sweat began to fall from Peter's face and brow, wetting the drape, one even landing on the exposed neck. He plunged in the needle, time and again, trying to ignore the feeling of resistance as its tip tore through the tissues of the neck. Blood was now oozing from four different punctures, and the neck was becoming swollen. Peter swallowed hard. "Again," demanded Barone.

On the seventh attempt, the plunger of the syringe, which Peter had been pulling back on gently, suddenly gave way as the syringe filled effortlessly with dark red blood.

"That's the jugular vein," said Barone. "Now hold that needle in place and gently detach the syringe."

A wave of light-headedness passed over Peter, as he struggled to control the shaking of his right hand while he carefully removed the syringe. In his left hand he held the needle, buried two inches into the oozing neck. As soon as Peter disconnected the syringe, a stream of warm, sticky blood began trickling out of the hilt of the needle. It rolled down Peter's gloved hand, covered the neck, and soaked the drape.

"Put in the catheter!" barked Barone.

Peter looked around for the thin plastic tube, the size of a strand of spaghetti. "It must have slipped away when Herbie moved,'' said Peter as he lifted the drape, ignoring the rapidly expanding dark stain.

"Then cover the opening of the needle with your finger!'' screeched Barone. "Quick, before he bleeds out!''

Peter capped the end of the needle with his left thumb. One of the nurses opened another sterile package, and Peter slipped a fresh catheter out.

"Now thread the catheter through the needle, into the internal jugular vein.'' Barone's voice was barely controlled.

Peter removed his thumb from the end of the needle. Blood gushed out again, forming a crimson stream, until he stanched it by passing the catheter into the needle. The blood ran back through the catheter, until a nurse attached the other end to an intravenous line.

"Open up the IV,'' ordered Barone. The column of clear fluid pushed the blood in the catheter back into the neck, as the line ran clear.

Barone sighed, audibly relieved. "Okay. It looks like the catheter is in place. Now slip the needle out.''

Peter held the catheter in place as he gently worked the needle back along it, until it was free of the neck. Blood oozed around the catheter, a single clear plastic tube which now protruded directly from the neck. Peter wiped it clean with another gauze pad. He placed a plastic clip around the needle to prevent it from causing any damage.

"Now suture the line in place,'' directed Barone.

Peter opened a sterile packet of surgical silk, attached to a small curved needle. He placed a single small stitch and began to tie it in place.

"Careful now,'' cautioned Barone. "I know one intern who spent half the afternoon sweating over a central line. Then he accidentally ran the suture needle through the catheter and had to start all over.''

Peter smiled weakly as he tried to steady his hand

while tying the suture to the plastic catheter. "That intern," he asked, "that wouldn't by any chance have been you?"

One of the nurses suppressed a giggle. Barone glared at her, then at Peter. He released his hold on Herbie's head, stepped back from the bedside. "Just bandage the patient, doctor." He turned and left.

"Herbie Brown?"

Peter Lee's consciousness jerked back to the cramped 4 East nurses' office. He was dimly aware that he had been staring out the window, his mind floating on the silver gray currents of the East River.

"Peter," asked Harvey Krane, exasperated, "are you going to finish your sign-out or not?"

Peter focused on the dapper young man in front of him. His eyes drifted from the close-cropped hair to the too-neat beard. Harvey's lips were pink, wet, and . . . precise. He could not think of a more apt description for the sharp vermilion borders.

"Jesus Christ!" Harvey slammed down his clipboard; his school tie flapped in the sudden gust, then fluttered to rest against his white oxford cloth shirt. "Peter, this is the third time you've just drifted off. And you weren't even on call last night! Where is your head today?"

Peter stared blankly at the gunmetal gray eyes. Harvey's auburn-fringed eyelids drifted down, then fluttered up again, birdlike. "Do you really think Herbie is going to make it?" asked Peter.

Krane took a short, deep breath, then expelled slowly. He shook his head. "Not a snowball's chance in hell. How is his renal function holding out?"

Peter's mind snapped back once more to his check-out list. He ran down the page, found Herbie's latest laboratory reports. "His creatinine is up to three point one today."

"Is he going into hepatorenal shutdown?"

Peter shrugged. "I don't know. His blood volume is so poor that his kidneys haven't had much of a chance."

"How many units of blood have you replaced so far?"

"I'm not really sure," answered Peter, "maybe ten or twelve, all together."

"You might as well be pouring it down a sewer." Harvey shook his head. "Last guy that I took care of like this ended up dying of black box disease."

Peter's brow furrowed. "What is that?"

"That's something the technicians down in the biochemistry laboratory first noticed. They don't have that much to do, now that all of the tests are automated. But they have to keep an eye on the printout from the computerized blood chemistry analyzer, to make sure it doesn't go on the blink in the middle of a batch of blood samples. So they sit there, watching the printout, which is like a column of numbers, and the machine prints a black box next to each one that is out of the normal range. One day they had a contest to see which patient in the hospital had the most black boxes on his lab report."

Harvey leaned back into his chair, his fingers interlaced behind his neck, elbows out to the side. His gray eyes scanned the ceiling. "The winner had fifteen black boxes out of a total of twenty tests. When they called up the ward to tell the intern that his patient had won, the ward clerk told them that the woman had died just a few minutes earlier.

"The winner the next day had fourteen black boxes. He died that night. Pretty soon the technicians began to notice that anyone with fourteen or more black boxes on their lab report invariably left the hospital in a black box themselves. Hence, black box disease." Harvey snickered, the thin, precise lips curling briefly.

Peter was silent, staring ahead. "Is that true?"

Harvey leaned forward. "Of course it is!"

"But why do they die?" Peter's eyes stared past Krane into the indeterminate distance. "What is the cause of death?"

Harvey shrugged. "How should I know? What is the usual cause of death? Too much life? Herbie has at least ten good reasons to die. Any one of those black boxes could kill him. I guess they all will. It's always the same: multiple systems failure. You work like a dog to correct one problem, and two others show up to take its place. First the liver goes, then the kidneys, then the heart, then the lungs, and pretty soon the patient just stops breathing, and you can't resuscitate him. As if his poor body just quits."

Peter nodded, pulled Herbie's chart from the rack, turned to the laboratory reports, and counted. "Herbie already has fifteen black boxes."

"Then he's a dead man." Krane shrugged. "What if he goes tonight?"

Peter shrugged in turn. "I don't think we need to take any heroic measures in supporting him. I would not call the cardiac arrest team. Just let him go peacefully."

"Does the family agree with that?" asked Krane.

"I've never seen any family with him." Peter turned to the window again and focused on a bit of flotsam, bobbing up and down as it floated along the river.

"What does Barone think?"

Peter shrugged without turning. The floating speck seemed to be a brown paper bag, empty, riding the currents.

"Well, I want his opinion," said Harvey, picking up the telephone receiver. He dialed Barone's pager, then spoke mechanically. "Chuck, please call Harvey at 5346, 5346, 5346." He put down the telephone.

The brown paper bag was twisting in the currents, bobbing up and down, finally disappeared beneath the dull gray surface. Peter did not hear the telephone ring. He was jerked back, once again to the tiny office by a tugging at his sleeve.

Harvey's face was florid. "He wants a full court press." He handed the receiver to Peter. "Full arrest procedure. Here, you talk to him."

Peter took the telephone reluctantly. He turned back again to the window, tried to find the paper bag again. "Yes?"

"Peter?" Barone's voice was harsh. "What the hell are you doing up there, making a do-not-resuscitate decision without consulting your resident or the attending physician?"

Peter could feel the heat rise from his cheeks. "Didn't Harvey tell you what we discussed? About the black boxes."

"Peter." Barone was furious. "That is pure, un-adulterated, one hundred percent, grade A bullshit! Herbie has widespread disease but no specific reason to die. Do you really think that I would have wasted half of my morning with you, putting in the central venous line, if we were just going to give up on him?

"Every life-threatening event since his admission is potentially reversible. Every problem he has is treatable. Your job, *doctor*"—he emphasized the title sarcastically—"is to see that he is *treated*. Not abandoned. Let the morticians bury him."

"Reversible?" Peter asked, incredulous. "Can we reverse his life-style? The man was living in a gutter, drinking himself to death. Is it really in his best interest to drag him, at great cost and pain, back to where he started?"

"I can't evaluate his life for him," answered Barone coldly. "But I will not have a patient on my service dying of neglect. You will resuscitate him and provide full care to the last."

"To the last?" Peter was shouting, out of control.

"To the last what? To the last drop of *his* blood? To the last scream of *his* agony? Do you really want the cardiac arrest team to smash his ribs trying to compress his heart? Do you think he would make it through an arrest procedure, let alone live to leave the hospital?"

"I'm a doctor, not a clairvoyant," answered Barone, his voice edged with ice. "I don't claim to know what will happen to him. I just know that life is too precious to let it slip away, ever, without doing everything I can to save it. He's my patient, and you will resuscitate him if necessary. Is that clear?" The line went dead before Peter could answer.

"I guess that's settled," mumbled Krane, shaking his head. He crossed out the do-not-resuscitate order written next to Herbie's name on the sign-out sheet. "Now what about Mary Clemmons? What if she has more chest pain?"

"Can I help you?" asked Sandy, the evening nurse, hunched over her dinner. Peter glanced at the salad in a Tupperware container, drenched with Russian dressing. The obese woman was shoveling forkfuls of greens into her mouth, dripping pink dressing on the fabric of her tunic, tightly stretched over her burgeoning bosom.

"No," said Peter, walked through the main supply room, past the nurses' lunch table, toward the adjacent medicine room. "I just need to draw up some saline to clear an IV line. You on a diet?"

Sandy smiled at her salad, gobbled another forkful. "Always."

Peter closed the door to the medicine room and searched the drawers for the familiar blue-capped vials. Mary Altman, he now realized, had not been an accident. He had not intended to kill her, of course. But in the grand scheme of things, his role in her death had been a part of his education, more important than learning how to put in a central venous line or interpret a serum sodium level. She had taught him about the dignity of death. His hand closed on a vial, turned it over. The label read:

Potassium chloride.
20 milliequivalents per 10 milliliters

He paused to listen for sounds in the hall to be sure no one was coming toward the medicine room. He could hear Mary, the nurses' aide on the evening shift, chatting next door with Sandy.

He plunged the needle into the vial, began to fill the syringe. He listened again. The conversation had stopped. Footsteps were approaching.

Quickly, he pulled out the needle, tossed the vial into the garbage can. He was capping the syringe as Mary opened the door to the medicine room.

She jumped back. "Oh, Dr. Lee." She blushed. "I was just going to get a Tylenol. I have an awful headache."

Peter nodded, smiled. "Sure, go ahead." He forced an outer calm, held open the door for her, then exited.

At Herbie Brown's bedside Peter paused to check the central venous line, making sure that it was running freely. The drops of intravenous fluid ran unimpeded, one after another, through the drip chamber. This liquid was not just a way to feed Herbie Brown. It was Barone's way of controlling them both—patient and intern—forcing them through the motions of their tragic ballet, alternately bleeding and stoking the crimson fire. He wanted to perpetuate the agony for both of them until he left the ward. And then, for all Barone cared, they could both go to hell in whatever way they found most expedient.

Peter uncapped the syringe and drove the needle into a rubber-stopped side inlet in the plastic intravenous line. He began to push down the plunger of the syringe.

The potassium solution caused a faint pattern of turbulence in the intravenous fluid as it rushed by the needle tip. Swirls ran down the line, like puffs of smoke wafted on a fresh breeze. Herbie soon would be free, Peter thought. Free at last from the ultimate burden: to live in agony because someone else thinks that you should.

The rubber tip of the syringe plunger reached the hub of the syringe. Gently, Peter removed it, capped the needle. He lifted Herbie Brown's wrist and felt his life's pulse. For a moment, as the postassium ran down the plastic tubing, the pulse was thready but persistent. Then the potassium entered the right atrium of Herbie's heart, which relaxed almost immediately. The blood flowed lazily into his right ventricle, which was too thick to be paralyzed immediately. Instead, it continued pumping blood, through his lungs and back into the left side of the heart. As it flowed from here into his aorta, a portion was diverted into his coronary arteries. As the potassium filtered through the heart tissue, the muscle slackened. Within seconds the pulse was feeble. A minute later Herbie Brown stopped breathing and was pulseless.

Peter Lee placed the limp arm back down on the bed, gathered his syringe, and walked away. At least one of them would find peace tonight.

"Lasagna!" Barone snorted indignantly. He speared a flaccid white noodle with his fork, sauce dripping from it in splats onto his plate. "My mother makes lasagna"—his eyes rolled toward heaven—"but this, this . . . stuff, this isn't lasagna. They have no right to use the name." He allowed the noodle to drop limply back on the plate.

Sylvia Blackman was stifling a giggle. "So your mother makes good lasagna?"

" 'Good?' " replied Barone, a look of incredulity

on his face. "Did the Romans build 'good' roads? Was Michelangelo a 'good' artist? Her lasagna is exquisite! The hospital cafeteria cooks couldn't hold a candle to her lasagna. If they did, they would probably burn it!"

Sylvia burst out laughing.

"You really have to taste her lasagna," continued Barone. "I'll have her invite you out to Queens one Friday night."

"I'd like that." She nodded, blushing slightly. "Of course"—she looked down at her plate—"I would probably never be able to eat here again. . . ."

Barone took another bite, his face screwed up in disgust. "No harm in that." He took a gulp of water, looked relieved. "How are things in the Emergency Room tonight?"

Sylvia turned her attention to a piece of cherry pie at the corner of her tray. "It was pretty quiet when I left for dinner. Only a lady with belly pain, waiting for her amylase to come back from the lab, and a couple of people with backaches."

"Just try to keep things quiet," said Barone. "I'm on call tonight with Harvey Krane, and I don't like to leave him alone with new patients."

"Why not?" asked Sylvia, cutting the tip off her wedge of pie with the edge of her fork. "Are you worried that he'll make a pass at one of the men?"

Barone's cheeks colored. "Of course not. I mean, I don't even know for sure that he is gay."

"No?" asked Sylvia. "Have you ever tried to reach him at home when he's not on call?"

Barone shook his head.

"Well, I did once. One of his patients went sour in the middle of the night, and I had to ask him some questions. A young man's voice answered the phone, not Harvey, and when I asked for Dr. Krane he mumbled 'Okay,' like he was still asleep. Then I could hear them rolling around in the bed as he transferred the phone to Harvey.''

Barone squirmed in his seat. "Well, I never had that pleasure. But that's not why I don't trust him. Harvey is just too . . . too prissy. Superficially, he's neat as can be, but underneath it all he's a mess. Take his nursing orders. His are the most legible, most compulsively all-inclusive I've ever seen. He practically tells the nurses when and how to blow the patient's nose. But he prescribes the medicines mechanically, as if he just wrote down all of the recommendations directly from a text-book without considering all of the patient's other medications or medical problems. For example, last week he prescribed propranolol for a patient's chest pain. The man then had a massive asthmatic attack caused by the propranolol and almost died."

Sylvia nodded. "I once had an intern like that." She leaned across the table conspiratorially. "Had to check all of his orders"—she pointed with the pie on the end of her fork for emphasis—"on every patient."

"In any case," Barone continued, "I would still rather trust Harvey's judgment than Peter Lee's."

Sylvia set down her fork. Her eyes flashed. "Let's not get into that again. He may not be the sharpest intern in his class, but I think he's competent. Just because he had the nerve to argue with you . . . and be right . . .''

Barone shook his head. "I know I was wrong about Herbie Brown needing the blood. Everyone from you to Maurie Benson has told me about it. I also know that sometimes I tend to be too bullheaded. It's part of my personality." His voice softened. "But the odd thing about that argument with Peter is how completely he relied upon you for support. Since you've left the service, the nurses tell me he's been like a different person. And I've been watching his work carefully. He's been overlooking laboratory tests, forgetting to write orders. I think he has a crush on you.''

It was Sylvia's turn to blush. She turned her attention back to her cherry pie. "I don't think so, Chuck. We had a very . . . professional relationship.'' She chewed her pie thoughtfully.

"Amazing!" She shook her head suddenly.

"What?" asked Barone.

"How they can make a piece of cardboard look just like a cherry pie.'' She swallowed with disgust.

Barone chuckled. As he leaned back in his chair, his pager sounded: three short shrill blasts, then a repeat. The pager code for a cardiac arrest.

Barone was bolt upright in an instant. As a medical resident on call, he was part of the resuscitation team. Sylvia leaned across the table to listen to his pager. "Cardiac arrest, Four East. Cardiac arrest, Four East."

Without a word, Barone was gone.

Herbie Brown's room was crowded with nurses, technicians, medical students, and interns. One nurse was holding an oxygen mask across Herbie's face and squeezing a rubber ambou bag to force air into his lungs. Another nurse, a pretty short blonde, was sitting on her knees astride Herbie's protuberant abdomen. Her skirt had ridden up and the hem was tight across her mid thighs, as she pumped courageously on Herbie's chest.

What a shame, thought Barone incongruously, that Herbie Brown did not live to see this.

"All right," he shouted above the din. "Everyone but the arrest team out of the room." Twelve onlookers immediately fell silent, then stepped back to let Barone by. No one left.

"Has he had any bicarb?" asked Barone.

The short nurse, pumping on Herbie's chest, shook her head. "Not yet.''

"Okay," barked Barone to a third nurse standing by the medication cart. "Give him one amp." He turned to the nurse holding the oxygen mask. "How long has he been out?"

"We don't know." She pumped the ambou bag. "Sandy"—she inclined her head toward the 4 East staff nurse—"found him cold and pulseless. We have no idea when it happened."

"Better make it two amps of bicarb, then," said Barone to the nurse by the medication cart. "Any pulse at all now?"

"I don't know," answered the blonde, still pumping. "We haven't stopped to check yet."

"Then stop for a second," ordered Barone, placing his index finger over the femoral artery in Herbie's groin. "No pulse. Continue pumping." She began again immediately. "How long have you been working?"

"We've been here nearly four minutes," answered the nurse injecting the bicarb.

"Okay," said Barone to one of the medical students. "Moore, you set up the electrocardiogram." A tall, wiry student in a short white coat stepped forward and began attaching electrocardiogram electrodes to Herbie's emaciated limbs.

Barone turned again to the medication nurse. "I need a syringe to draw some electrolytes and one to draw a blood gas. And when you're done with that give him a third amp of bicarb."

She handed him the first syringe. Barone palpated Herbie's groin again. He could faintly feel the pulse of blood in the femoral artery as each chest compression forced blood from the heart into the arteries. He swabbed the area with alcohol, then plunged the two-inch needle into the groin until it filled with a rapid flow of dark, purple blood. He withdrew the syringe, exchanged it for the second, and drew another sample.

"Send these off stat." He handed the second syringe to the nurse.

He turned to the electrocardiogram machine. "Stop pumping for a minute." He held up one hand as if directing traffic. The electrical trace, which had been rising and falling with each chest compression, went flat. "Okay, resume pumping. Give him an amp of epi, and prepare to shock him."

A nurse rolled the defibrillator to the bedside. Barone squirted electrode gel on the metal paddles and rubbed them together to spread the clear paste around for better electrical contact.

The blonde nurse stopped pumping and climbed down from the bed. Barone turned to the medical student who was watching the electrocardiogram. "Anything?" he asked.

"Flat line."

"All right, everybody off!" Barone leaned over Herbie's body, applied the paddles to his chest. "Ready?" There was no dissent. He pushed the red button on the paddle.

Herbie's body arched as if someone had kicked him, throwing Barone back. "Any cardiac rhythm yet?" he asked.

"Still flat."

"Damn," whispered Barone as he began compressing Herbie's chest himself. "It's going to be a long night."

The Emergency Room was empty, and the night clerk had turned off most of the fluorescent lights, so that the usual flat white glare was reduced to a shadowy ghost land. Barone did not disturb the night clerk, who had nodded off. He walked straight back through the ER to the on-call room at the end of the hall.

He opened the door slowly. The light was on. Sylvia was seated at a small desk, poring over a medical journal. "What is it this time?" she asked without looking up. "Another belly pain?"

"Would you believe a pain in the ass?" answered Barone.

Sylvia spun around in surprise, smiled at Barone.

"I was just in the neighborhood," he explained lamely, holding out a Styrofoam cup. "I came down to get a Coke from the cafeteria. Would you like some?"

Sylvia nodded and held out an empty coffee cup. "Sure. How are things on the wards?"

"Can't complain," he answered, pouring some soda into her cup. "We only got three new admissions. I'd have been done a lot earlier if it hadn't been for that cardiac arrest."

"The one on Four East?" Sylvia took a swallow. "Who was it?"

"Herbie Brown. The nurses found him cold and pulseless. He must have been dead a hell of a long time before we arrived. His electrocardiogram was flat line, and we never got any kind of heart response."

"Sounds awful. How long did you work on him?"

"Over an hour," said Barone.

Sylvia drained her Coke, stood up and started across the room. "That's a long time for a man who had a flat line EKG when you started." She sat down on the on-call bed, her hand stroking the smooth, cool surface of the pillowcase.

"I know," said Barone. "I just couldn't give up though. Not while there was even the faintest hope. . . ."

"I guess we all feel like that." She nodded. "But Herbie was a pretty sick man when he came in."

"I know that, too," Barone replied. He sat down on the foot of the bed, his back to her. "But the longer I see patients, the more I become convinced that doctors, even good doctors, can't always be sure who is going to die and who is going to make it. I don't ever want to make the mistake of giving up too soon.''

''Me either,'' said Sylvia, ''but you also have to consider the cost. Sometimes, even if you can pull the patient through, the cost, in agony for the patient, is not worth it. Especially if the patient faces a life of continued pain and misery with his disease.''

Barone's shoulders slumped. He allowed himself to fall backward onto the bed. His head landed in Sylvia's lap. He stared into her soft, gray eyes. ''I know that too.''

He closed his eyes, and Sylvia brushed a strand of hair from his forehead. In a moment, he was asleep.

Thursday Afternoon, September 12

Peter Lee sat in the 4 East nurses' station, his eyes fixed on the burning orange glow of the setting sun reflected in the windows of the apartment buildings across the East River on Roosevelt Island. It was almost as if the building were aflame.

He was tired. He had been up most of the previous night, struggling with his conscience. As a physician, it was his duty to relieve suffering and to prolong life. Usually the two ideas were congruent.

But not always. He had clearly relieved Herbie Brown's suffering, just as he had Mary Altman's. But in fulfilling the first half of his commitment, he had violated the second.

He had become more agitated as he sought exoneration from a part of himself that he no longer controlled. Finally, the volume of his frustration had exceeded the capacity of his small, barren room. He had taken to the streets and walked until dawn in the open, where the constant pulse of the city life at least could reassure him that he was not alone.

The rest of the day had been a disaster. Nothing he could say on morning rounds had met with Barone's approval. Only by being quiet and inconspicuous as possible had he survived the savage attacks by Maurie Benson's rounds. All afternoon he had tried to carry out his chores, but never seemed able to scratch the surface. And now the other interns had all checked out, and he was on his own again, on call for the rest of the night.

"Peter?" He turned around. It was Lauren, one of the evening shift nurses. The orange glow from the window reflected faintly from her white uniform. Peter stared at the luminescence of the cloth, pulled tight across her full bosom and waist. "Peter, are you listening?" She blinked, waiting for a sign of recognition.

"Sure." He shook his head, continued to stare at her hips.

"Well, there's a transfer patient for you in bed fourteen B." He did not answer. "Peter, did you hear me?"

He blinked, looked up at her face. Her blue gray eyes showed concern. Pale yellow, straight hair, falling limply to her shoulders, framed her face.

"Room fourteen B," he repeated, eyes fixed on hers, but somehow glassy, not making contact. "Who is the patient?"

Lauren Nyquist squirmed uncomfortably under his gaze and was relieved to look away to check her clipboard. "A transfer from the medical intensive care unit. A woman named Anne Delbert."

"Okay," he said, reaching for his medical bag. "Is she sick?"

Lauren shrugged. "Looks okay to me." She turned and headed down the hall.

"Mrs. Delbert? I'm Dr. Lee." He introduced himself as he came into the room. A thin, angular appearing woman was lying quietly on the bed, in the deepening shadows of the evening, her face toward the wall. She made no move to acknowledge him.

Peter walked around the bed. In the gathering darkness, her eyes seemed hooded, almost hollow. It was not until he touched her shoulder and she looked up at him that he recognized her: the woman from the Emergency Room, with colon cancer, who had taken a drug overdose. He had helped Barone to save her.

Her eyes were red and watery, but had long since exhausted their supply of tears. She faced Peter silently.

Peter felt a wave of nausea as he surveyed the bony arms and sunken abdomen, outlined against her nightgown by the bony protuberances of her chest wall and her hips. "My name is Dr. Lee," he repeated, his voice suddenly hoarse. "I'm going to be taking care of you on this ward."

She blinked, but did not answer.

"I'd like to take your history and examine you."

She blinked again. Peter felt her dark eyes boring into him. His cheeks colored.

"Leave me alone." She turned back to the wall.

"Mrs. Delbert," he pleaded, "I just have to ask a few questions."

He heard a dry, muffled sobbing sound. "Why won't you let me be? I've had colon cancer for two years. They did an operation, removed part of my colon, but couldn't get it all out. I vomited my guts out on chemotherapy for nine months, but six months later the cancer was back, eating into my sacral bone. For four months the pain has been so bad that I can't even sit down."

She turned back toward him, glaring angrily. Inexplicably, he felt guilty. "They irradiated me, they gave me pain medicines until I was so snowed that I couldn't recognize my own children. And the pain is still there, boring into me. . . ." She broke into sobs again.

Peter wanted to comfort her. He wanted to let her know that he shared in her anguish, even if his own pain was not physical. He hovered at the bedside for a moment, wanted to put his arm around her. The best he could find to say was: "May I see your abdomen?"

She breathed a sigh of acquiescence, lay back in the bed, raised her nightgown. He began a perfunctory examination of her emaciated body. Her liver was hard and knobby, swollen. He felt a hard, enlarged lymph node in her groin; only scant wisps of pubic hair remained. Her breasts were flattened and sagging like deflated balloons. They did little to cover the bony rib cage. Taped to the side of her neck was a central venous line that the resident in the intensive care unit had inserted to monitor her cardiac and fluid status while she was recovering from the overdose. A brown curly wig covered her nearly bald skull.

The physical examination passed wordlessly, each participant ignoring the other as best as possible, given the unavoidable intimacy of the encounter. At the finish, Peter helped rearrange her nightgown.

He looked into the watery, brown eyes once more. He could not help himself. "Did you really want to die?" he heard himself ask.

For the first time she seemed possessed by a spark of life. "Damn right I did!"

"Then why did you take the overdose in a place where they could find you?"

A sob wracked the frail body. "The first time, I took the overdose at home in my own bedroom. My husband had agreed to let me go. But when I started gasping for air, he panicked and called for an ambulance. The second time, I overdosed while the rest of the family was out of the house. My husband came back early and called for help again. This time, I thought I did everything right. I checked into a hotel, even opened the capsules up so they would dissolve faster. But then the hotel maid . . ." She looked up into his face, her features contorted with a mixture of contempt and pleading. "I tried, goddamn it, I really tried. . . ." The tears finally came.

Peter felt empty inside. "Yes, you did," was all he could think to say. He swallowed hard. His throat was dry. "Yes, you did."

* * *

Barone set down the dictating machine handset, rubbed his eyes, and looked at his watch. Five minutes to eight o'clock. He picked up the handset again and hurriedly dictated the remainder of the hospital discharge summary for Sadie Collins. "On the tenth hospital day the patient was discharged in good condition, taking hydrochlorothiazide, fifty milligrams, BID. She will return to the Valleyview Nursing Home where she will be seen by Dr. Willard Thomas in one week. This concludes the dictation. Please send copies of the discharge summary to Dr. Thomas, Dr. Marilyn Silver, and to me. Thank you."

He looked at his watch again. Three minutes to eight. He popped the cassette out of the dictating machine and left it, with the hospital chart, in the medical records In box. He hurriedly exited into the hallway, which not coincidentally happened to be directly across from the Emergency Room. The proximity made medical records more rapidly available to the Emergency Room. In some cases, noted Barone with a smile, it could also work the other way.

He hesitated for a moment as he entered the ER, deliberately slowed his pace. Sauntering across the Emergency Room, he took a single furtive glance at the glassed-in nurses' station. Sylvia was not there.

He stopped at the receptionist's desk to ask: "Is Dr. Blackman in back seeing one of the patients?"

The receptionist did not look up from the insurance form she was filling out. "Sylvia? She got off a few minutes ago. Her evening coverage relieved her a little early."

Barone could not disguise his disappointment. "You mean she left already?"

The receptionist finally looked up and shrugged in answer. Barone bolted for the Emergency Room entrance. Maybe she had just left. Maybe he could find her on the street.

Moving at full speed, he reached the electric sliding door and had to pull himself up short to avoid hitting it. He waited for the door to open. It took nearly a second before the motor kicked in. It seemed like forever.

The door began to open lethargically. He slipped through, stopped at the sidewalk, looked both up the street and down. She was nowhere in sight.

Perhaps she had just gone home. It was more brazen to call her than just to meet by "accident," but . . . And what if she had someone with her . . .

"Chuck!"

The voice was melodic, so soft that he was not even sure he heard it. He looked up the street again. She was nowhere in sight. Maybe it had just been his imagination.

"Chuck!" Louder. He was sure about it this time. And the voice was coming from *behind* him. He spun around. Sylvia was emerging from the on-call room at the back of the Emergency Room, her overnight bag slung over her thin shoulder.

The door began to close again. Swearing softly, he stepped back onto the mat, waited another eternity for it to open again.

Sylvia was wearing faded blue jeans that hung from her hips, and a red knit top. The clingy red fabric outlined her small pointed breasts, then dived dramatically across her flat abdomen to the beltless waistband of her jeans. With deliberate effort, he focused on her clear, bright eyes. "You're looking pretty casual for an ER doc," he began.

Sylvia smiled and tossed her straight chestnut hair back over her shoulder. "I change clothes in the on-call room as soon as I come off duty. After drunks have been vomiting all over my hospital whites for twelve hours''—she patted her overnight bag—''the last thing I want to do is to wear them home.''

Barone smiled. ''I know what you mean.'' They began to walk together toward the house staff apartment building. ''On my last night on call as an intern, I admitted one of the sickest guys I ever saw. He was an alcoholic''—Barone's voice fell quieter for a moment—''a lot like Herbie Brown, actually. While I was bent over him, listening to his heart, I heard this loud gurgling sound. Suddenly he threw up a bellyfull of blood all over me.''

''Yuck! Did he bleed out?'' Sylvia asked.

Barone nodded. ''He tried to. But I kept the sucker going. All night long, I kept running to the blood bank. It took twenty units. But when morning came, and my internship was finally done, I knew I could keep anyone alive. Both of us had made it: He had gotten through the night, and I had survived my internship. That night, after dinner, I burned that set of whites.''

Sylvia's muffled giggle seemed to float through the soft evening air. ''Was your internship that rough on you?''

Barone nodded. ''It was the toughest thing I have ever done. I came to it from the laboratory, you know.'' He caught her pale, gray eyes for a moment. She nodded. ''I did my PhD degree during medical school, and so I spent every moment of my elective time working on my research. During the first few months of my internship, I was so green that I was scared to death that I would make a mistake that would hurt someone.''

''Did you?'' asked Sylvia.

''Not really,'' answered Barone, shaking his head. ''It took a while for me to realize that the intern is not supposed to know how to practice medicine. You just have to make sure that you call for help when you need it and that you follow the advice of more experienced doctors. But I was always afraid that the next moment

I would be called to the Emergency Room to take care of a horrendously sick patient, and that I would not know what to do. I would get this sinking feeling in the pit of my stomach every time I got called to the ER for a new admission. I even had nightmares about it.''

''I know.'' Sylvia looked into the distance. ''My nightmare was that I would get a call from the nurses, the day after I had been on call, that my new patient, Mr. Jones, was dying. And I would try to think who Mr. Jones was, and then I would remember that he had been sent up from the Emergency Room the night before and I had forgotten all about him.'' They arrived in front of the lobby of the apartment building. She turned to Barone. ''What made your nightmare stop coming?''

Barone looked down, his eye catching briefly on the gap between her shirt and jeans, then resting on his shoes. ''It never happened.'' He looked back into her eyes. ''By Christmas, I realized that in six months, my nightmare patient had never shown up. And I already knew a lot more medicine than when I had started. And finally, I began to believe that maybe that patient never would come. It made things easier. Not easy, but easier. What about your nightmare?''

She cocked her head and shrugged. ''It did happen. At two A.M. one night, I had just finished seeing all of my new patients and I was finally done writing up all of their histories and physical exam results. I was looking over the charts one last time before going to bed, to make sure that the nurses would not have to wake me up a half hour later for something trivial.

''Anyway, there in the rack was a hospital chart for a new patient, one I had never heard of. And my name was listed on the chart as the staff doctor. No one had told me about him.

''Well, I hit the ceiling. The night nurse said that the patient had been there since three in the afternoon, and she thought the evening nurse had told me about him. I called the evening nurse at home, woke her out of a sound sleep, but she said that she thought the day nurse had told me about the patient. The day nurse said that the patient had been transferred to the ward from the cardiac care unit while the shifts were changing, and she thought the evening nurse would inform me. And meanwhile, here is this cardiac patient, fresh from the CCU, sitting in a major teaching hospital, with no doctor at all.''

''So what happened?'' asked Barone.

Sylvia smiled. ''I went in to see the patient. He was mostly upset because he was hungry. I had never written any orders for the nurses to feed him, so no one had brought him a dinner. I ordered him up a sandwich, wrote my note, and half an hour later I was in bed. I never had the nightmare again.''

Barone looked up at the front of the building, cleared his throat. ''Say, I was just going to go get something for dinner. Would you like to join me?'' To Barone it sounded rehearsed. It was.

Sylvia ignored his awkwardness. ''Sure, but not with you looking like that.'' She pointed to Barone's blood-splattered white pants.

He colored. ''I guess I can go upstairs and change. I'll be back in a minute. . . .'' He started toward the doorway.

''No,'' she said, starting after him. ''Let's both go upstairs. I can cook something up for us.'' She followed him inside.

The one room apartment was airless and spartan to the point of being drab. Sylvia followed Barone into the dim room, setting down her bag in the corner by the door. He switched on a floor lamp. A warm yellowish light suffused the room.

Sylvia stepped into the living room. There was a small kitchen table with two chairs on her left, next to a tiny kitchen area. On the right were bookshelves of cinder blocks and unfinished boards, and the entrance to a small bathroom. The shelves were loaded down with medical texts, research tomes on cardiology, and a small library of philosophy books. She recognized *Les Jeux Sont Fait* by Sartre and *Mensch und Ubermensch* by Nietzsche. On the top shelf was a small component stereo. There were no novels on the shelves, no pictures on the walls.

The far wall consisted of three windows, the only ones in the apartment. Under them was a bed, a nightstand, and a dresser. An easy chair was set in the corner, next to the floor lamp. Barone opened one of the windows, and the dull, off-white curtain flapped in the cool night breeze. The street sounds drifted in—traffic, buses, chatter and laughter, the life signs of the city.

"Now let's see what there is to eat." Barone opened the small, boxy refrigerator, under the counter in the kitchenette. Sylvia squatted to examine its contents. It was nearly as bare as the room that contained it. There was some orange juice, milk, a half-dozen eggs, a few bagels, and half a stick of butter.

Barone stood behind her, could not take his eyes off the gap between the jeans and her blouse, which had opened much wider. "Would you like the strip steaks or should we splurge and broil the lobster tonight?" he joked.

Sylvia pulled open the tiny freezer compartment. Three more bagels gathered frost inside. "I suppose we could ask the butler to go out and pick up some pâté de foie gras."

Barone chuckled. "Sure you wouldn't like to go back to plan A and find a nice restaurant?"

She closed the door and straighted up. "I'm convinced."

"I'll change, then," he said. "Would you like a drink while you're waiting?"

She nodded. "Sure."

"How about some scotch?" He opened a cabinet.

"With some ice and water," she answered.

"Terrible thing to do to a good whiskey." He shuddered, poured the amber liquid into two kitchen tumblers.

Sylvia took her drink and crossed over to the windows. She took a sip of the cold, smoky liquid, then looked down at the street. Pedestrians were walking their dogs, hurrying to appointments, delivering pizzas: a mural in motion.

She took a long pull at her drink. "Chuck." She turned, settled back into the easy chair. "Do you ever find it unnerving living in a city with so many people around you that you never get to know?"

Barone shook his head. "I was brought up here. It seems natural to me."

She took another sip, glanced out the window. "I grew up in a small town where I knew most of the people. And I always felt that I had some measure of control over my surroundings. In the city, there are so many people, so many strangers, all crowded in together. A man walks his dog at three A.M., it barks and wakes a woman, who can't fall back to sleep, so in the morning she is irate and yells at her kid, who disrupts the classroom. You cram ten million people together in one area, and they start bouncing off each other at crazy angles like some gigantic, insane game of billiards. Even a man walking his dog can affect the lives of thousands of other people. In a city like New York, the static of everyday life can be deafening." She took a swallow of her drink. "Sometimes I think that is why there are so many crazy people in this city. The continual commotion drives them to extremes." She slouched back into the chair, the drink balanced on her abdomen, rising and falling with each breath.

Barone shrugged. "Or maybe the people who are

already crazy are drawn here, because the lack of order reflects the way they feel inside. Or maybe the constant activity, all around them, makes them feel that they are still a part of the world. Anyway, only Manhattan is like that, not the whole city. The area I come from in Queens is much quieter. Probably not much different from the area where you grew up.''

Sylvia smiled wryly. "Do you really think Queens is like Iowa City?''

"Is that where you're from?''

Sylvia straightened up, took another swallow of the smoky liquid from her glass. "Not really. I was born in New Jersey, but when I was four years old Daddy was offered a job at the University of Iowa.''

"Is he a professor?''

Sylvia shook her head slowly, her voice quavering slightly. "He was a professor, in biochemistry. He died when I was fifteen.'' She took another pull of her drink, and stared out the window, her eyes becoming glassy. Awkwardly, she continued. "He was a depressive. When I was a little girl he would sit at home, unshaven in his pajamas, sometimes for a month at a time. He would stay in bed all day and pace the floors at night. I remember getting up to go to the bathroom one night. I heard him in the living room and started down the stairs. When I got halfway down I saw him sitting in his easy chair, eyes red, actually sobbing. On the coffee table was the handgun that he kept for target practice. I was scared, but I continued down the stairs to ask him if he was all right. He just sniffed and hugged me close, and I went to sleep in his arms.

"The next morning, Mom called the doctor, and Dad was admitted to the university psychiatric hospital for electric shock therapy. He came home three weeks later. He wasn't depressed anymore, but he never had the same fiery intellectual curiosity. It was as if it had been burnt out of him.

"By the time I was in high school, he had been through shock therapy twice more. In between, he took antidepressant medications. He complained that he couldn't concentrate on his research, and students and associates stopped coming to work in his laboratory. As he watched his research career shrivel, my father seemed to shrink into himself as well.

"One day my mother got a call from the hospital Emergency Room. My father's technician had found him lying facedown on the floor in the lab. Next to him was an empty bottle of bungarotoxin, a snake venom he had been experimenting with, and an empty syringe. He had taken a dose that was large enough to kill an elephant." She drained her glass, held it out to Barone to refill.

He took the glass from her, thankful for the chance to get up and move. He poured some more scotch and sat down on the edge of the bed across from her, offering her the glass.

She accepted it gratefully, took another swallow. "That is why I decided to become a doctor. I was going to be a psychiatrist. I had to understand what had happened to my father. Then, when I was a third year medical student, I realized that the psychiatrists did not understand it either. Depression is just a disease, and in my father it had merely run its course. What happened to my father happens to countless other people, through no fault of their own. Most important, I realized that I was not responsible for it either."

"That's the hardest thing to learn," said Barone. "It took me a long time to understand that my patients come to me with their illnesses. I can make them better or worse, but I am not responsible for their being sick in the first place."

Sylvia nodded. "It's like an emotional safety valve. Whenever I get too involved with a patient's problems, I have to take a step back and remind myself that I didn't cause their problems, I'm just there to try to help.''

Barone sipped his drink. ''It may sound callous, but I don't think it is good for the patient if the doctor gets too emotionally involved. It fogs his . . . or her professional judgment.''

Sylvia straightened in the chair. ''That's what made me give up on psychiatry. I felt that the closer I got to the patient, the more it hurt me to share their problems, and the less good I could do. It was that feeling of professional impotence that made me leave psychiatry for internal medicine.''

Barone drained his glass and set it down on the nightstand. ''I never really made the conscious decision to go into medicine.'' He sighed. ''It just seemed that it was expected of me. When I was a child, I was good at math and science, and I liked biology. Everyone said that I should be a doctor, and when I went away to college, my family and friends expected that I would sign up for a premed curriculum, and I guess I did too. The only departure was when I decided during medical school to take off a few years to do a PhD. My mother was incredulous. 'You want to leave medical school to do research? Do you know how many kids are dying just to get into medical school, and here you are walking out of it? And what for? So you can become some sort of professor? How much money can you make as a teacher?' She kept telling me that I should set up a private practice when I finished. She couldn't believe anyone who could earn big money as a private practitioner would prefer to work as a teacher and researcher.''

Sylvia finished her drink and set it down on the nightstand next to his. She pushed forward in the chair and stood up and rose unsteadily to her feet. Barone stood up and took her arm to steady her. The skin on the inside of her forearm was warm and soft. ''That's

what happens after two drinks on an empty stomach."
She gave an embarrassed smile.

"That's right." He continued to hold her arm. "I almost forgot about dinner."

She looked down at his blood-speckled pants, tugged playfully at his belt buckle. "I thought you were going to change those first."

He looked down at her fingers, still resting on his belt buckle. She was close enough for him to smell the faintly floral scent of her cologne. Gently, he pulled her closer until their foreheads, then noses touched. He kissed her lightly, then more deeply, her tongue gliding over his own. She pressed against him until he could feel the hardness of her nipples straining against the thin material of her blouse. His arms caressed her shoulders, the small of her back, then drifted down beneath the waistline of her jeans. He lifted the material of her skirt up gently, until he could feel the softness of her buttock. He pulled her hips tightly against him.

Her fingers caressed the back of his neck, ran under his collar. Slowly, he worked his hands up her back, massaging her, pressing her against him. He pulled the red skirt up over her head, began kissing the soft, smooth skin of her neck, her chest, her breasts.

Barone sat down on the edge of the bed and unfastened her jeans, pulling them down, along with her panties, to the floor. His fingers kneaded the soft skin of her buttocks, drawing her closer until he buried his face in the softness of her lower belly, kissing and licking the velvety skin.

She ran her fingers through his hair, pressing his head against her hips. As he found his way into her mound of pubic hair, she giggled, then pushed him backward onto the bed. Bending over, she unfastened his belt, drew his pants down. Kneeling between his legs, she gently massaged the skin of his thighs, working her fingers slowly up his groin to the velvety skin of his erection.

Finally she crept back up onto the bed and, sitting astride him, unbuttoned his shirt. He pulled her down against him, feeling the warm press of her nipples against his bare chest as they kissed deeply. Teasing, she glided the wet softness of her crotch along the shaft of his penis. When at last he could stand it no longer, he dropped his hands to her hips, pushed them down over his throbbing erection. Holding her buttocks, he drove deeper and deeper into her, until he heard her breath catch and felt an involuntary shudder. A moment later he felt the convulsive spasm in his own groin, as he climaxed, exploding inside of her.

For a minute they lay still, savoring the closeness of the moment. Then, silently, she lifted herself off him, and they lay together in the softness of the bed, enfolded in each other's arms, and the deepening night.

Peter sank back into the cool sheets of the on-call room cot, not even bothering to remove his shoes. He still had a few chores to do on the ward, but they seemed to take so long. Perhaps a few minutes' rest would refresh him. He allowed his eyes to close. Just for a moment.

The sensation of relief, at shutting out the world, was like stepping out into a cool, misty night. He longed for the grounds of the Rockefeller campus, for the tranquility, for the solitude.

And at the same time, as he felt the knot of tension in his belly begin to unwind, he was aware of another need. Just as he found himself slipping farther and farther from the people around him, he was most keenly aware of the need for someone, one special person whom he could be close to.

It was at the height of his pain and frustration with human relationships that, paradoxically, he was most strongly driven by his sexual needs. Perhaps as a sub-stitute for real emotional contact, perhaps as a way back, something to cling to while weathering out the storm. But it was there, adding to the fires in his gut, fanning the flames.

Sometimes simply thinking about a woman would calm him, caress some deep crevice of his soul. Sylvia could have that effect on him. Her cool gentleness had provided a lifeline to him over the previous month.

He already missed the opportunities, supposedly while discussing a new patient, that he took to stare into the gray mists of her eyes. The set of her head, the way she would toss her hair when he managed to say something clever: she was a part of his consciousness that seemed, now, to burn itself more deeply than ever into his thoughts.

He could see her as he drifted off to sleep, talking to him with that wistful patience, the words perfectly formed by her soft, vermilion lips. He wanted to kiss her, had to hold himself back. He was not sure what to do, how to do it.

He could smell the floral scent that always permeated her hair. As if in a dream, his hand reached out, stroked the silky tresses, applied gentle pressure to her back, pulled her into his embrace.

He saw her eyes flutter closed, sensed the anticipa-tion as her lips drew together, then slightly parted. Then suddenly, from between them, came a shrill bleating sound, *Beep, beep, beep!*

He looked into her eyes, now open wide, terrified as the involuntary, scratchy voice emitted from between her parted lips, "Dr. Lee, call 3131, 3131, 3131 . . ."

Peter Lee shook his head. The room was black, he was alone. His hand reached out automatically and felt for the button to turn off his pager. The voice stopped. When he switched on the light he was in his on-call room.

He reached for the telephone, grudgingly dialed it. "This is Dr. Lee. Someone paged."

"Just a minute." He almost fell back asleep during the wait.

"Peter." It was Burt Rhinehart, the Emergency Room resident. "I've got an admission for you. Twenty-eight-year-old woman with acute myelocytic leukemia, being treated with chemotherapy for her first relapse. Her white blood count bottomed out Monday at two hundred, and she's here tonight with fever, shortness of breath, and pneumonia of the left lower lobe of her lung on the chest X ray. I put in a central venous line and started her on a saline drip, She just left here on a stretcher, so she should be up to Four East in a few minutes."

Peter was silent.

"Any questions?" Rhinehart waited a few seconds. "Peter? Did you hear me?"

Another hesitation. "Yeah," Peter finally responded, still trying to sort the shattered fragments of his dream from Rhinehart's rapid-fire recitation. "How old did you say she was?"

"It's all in my note," Rhinehart cut him off, annoyed. "Have a good night." The line clicked dead before Peter could respond.

By the time he had pulled on his shoes, the night nurse was knocking softly on the door. "Dr. Lee?"

"Yes?" he answered.

"There's a new patient on the floor for you. A young girl, and she looks pretty sick."

"Be right there," said Peter, checking his watch— 3:30 A.M.

Peter smoothed his hair into place with his fingers and yawned as he padded down the darkened 4 East corridor toward the nurses' station. The night nurse was sitting at the desk. "What room is she in?" he asked.

"Four-oh-eight B." She did not look up from her work. "Her name is Suzanne Grayson."

Room 408 was dark except for a single reading light, illuminating the head of bed B. The rest of the room was bathed in shadows, lit only by the glow reflected off the stark white sheets and pillow, and from the pale skin of the girl lying upon them. The classic beauty of her high cheekbones accentuated the fullness of her rounded lips. Her eyes were closed, and the soft brown lashes brushed the nearly translucent skin beneath them. Her face was framed by light gold ringlets of hair. Stray backlit curls created the effect of a halo. She lay so still that Peter could not help but feel that she might have been carved from marble.

Suddenly, a shaking chill racked her body, and her eyelids fluttered open. Peter gasped, surprised to see her move. "I'm sorry." He recovered. "I didn't know that you were awake."

Her wide gray eyes fixed on Peter. "Are you my doctor?" she asked. The voice was slightly hoarse, but still soft and warm. Her cheeks began to flush.

For a long moment, Peter could find no words. Then, swallowing hard, he replied, "Yes. I'm Dr. Lee."

She reached out a hand from beneath the sheets. Peter shook it, clumsily. It was dry and very warm. He was disappointed to realize that the color in her cheeks was probably a fever, rather than a girlish blush.

"I'm Suzi Grayson," she said.

Peter cleared his throat and swallowed again. His mouth had suddenly become very dry. "Well, Miss Grayson," he began, "what is your problem tonight?" He pulled closed the drapes around the bed.

She sat up a bit. "You know," she said, as if it were a stubbed toe, "that I have leukemia?"

Peter nodded. "When did it start?"

"About two years ago, I started to get very tired and my skin began to bruise very easily. Then I got a nosebleed, and when I went to the doctor, he did a blood count. He said I had to come into the hospital.''

Peter nodded. ''And what happened the first time in the hospital?''

''They did a lot of tests,'' she said. ''A bone marrow, a spinal tap. Then they gave me chemotherapy. It made me really sick, and all my hair fell out.'' Peter could not imagine her in that condition. He did not even try. ''But finally I went into remission, and I felt pretty good. It lasted for over a year. Then two weeks ago I started to get bruises again.

''I went back to the clinic, and they found my white blood count was back up. So they gave me some more chemotherapy. I went back to the doctor three days ago, on Monday, and he said that my white blood count was very low, and that I should call him if I felt sick in any way.

''This morning I had a slight cough when I woke up, but I thought it would just go away. By dinner time, I was short of breath and it hurt to breathe.'' She held the left side of her chest. ''By the time I got to the Emergency Room I was burning up with fever, and my teeth were chattering from the chills.''

Peter nodded. ''Have you been coughing?''

''Since this afternoon.'' She nodded back. ''A little yellow mucus.''

''Okay,'' said Peter. ''I'll have the nurse bring in a specimen cup so we can collect some sputum for lab tests.''

He opened his medical bag and started his exam. Her pulse was racing (probably, he realized disappointedly, from the fever). Systematically he looked into her nose, ears, and mouth, and poked over her neck and spine for sore spots. The central venous line that Rhinehart had inserted in the ER was taped to the side of her neck. He unfastened the back of her hospital gown and let it slide forward over her hunched shoulders. When he tapped his fingers against her ribs, the lower part of the left side of the chest gave off a dull note. Through his stethoscope, the breath sounds over her left lung sounded like crumpling cellophane. "Say 'Eeeeee,' " he asked. She did as she was told, but the sound that Peter heard was more like the bleating of a goat: "Ay-ay-ay-ay . . ." There was fluid between her lung and chest wall, distorting the sound.

"Please sit back on the bed," he asked, and as she lay back, Peter pushed the hospital gown further forward on her arms, exposing her chest. Her small, rounded breasts heaved with the exertion of breathing. Peter listened to her heart, his stethoscope pressed against the small mound of her left breast. He placed his hand over her heart, cupping the breast, to feel the pulsing of the heart beneath it. The skin was warm and soft against his palm.

Peter realized, almost with a start, that he was enjoying this examination. This intimate contact with strangers usually embarrassed him, and he rushed through it. Tonight, he thought, despite the fact that it was almost 4 A.M., he had taken his time. As he turned his attention to the right breast, he realized that he was blushing. He looked at Suzi Grayson to see if she had noticed. She was lying completely still, with her eyes tightly closed.

Reluctantly, he finished and pulled the gown back up to her shoulders. Then he pushed the sheet down to her lower abdomen and lifted the lower edge of the hospital gown, exposing her midriff. He listened to, poked, and prodded the soft skin of her abdomen. He could feel the taut abdominal muscles beneath her skin. Under the umbilicus, a thin line of downy hairs extended downward beneath the sheet. He lifted one edge of the sheet, until he could see where the hair blossomed into a triangular thicket between her legs. He followed the curve of her thigh and ran his finger over the warm moist skin of the groin, feeling for swollen lymph nodes. He did the same on the other side.

He pulled the gown back down over her, tucking it around her hips. She opened her eyes, flushed again but this time not from her fever.

Peter, who could feel the heat from his own cheeks, put on his best professional manner. "It looks like you've caught a bad case of pneumonia." His voice sounded more grave than he had intended. She looked up toward him, the gray eyes wide. "I think you have some fluid built up over the left lung," he continued. "While you were down in the Emergency Room, did they send you for any X-ray tests where you had to lie on your side?"

She shook her head.

"Well, we're going to have to send you back down for some more films. Meanwhile, try to cough up some sputum for me to examine."

"Okay, Dr. Lee." She hesitated for a second, the gray eyes appealing to him. She waited for him to say something, then finally asked, "Will I get better from this?"

Peter stepped back from the bedside, hoping the dim light would hide the color in his own cheeks. "Of course," he said. "We'll give you some antibiotics, and in a few days you'll be fine." He wished he felt as confident as he tried to sound.

Peter sat at the desk in the back of the 4 East nurses' station, paging through Suzi Grayson's hospital chart. She had been in the hospital so many times during the last years that the chart had been bound into two thick volumes. Soon, thought Peter, there will be three.

The story, as he put it together from the hurriedly written notes of a dozen other interns and medical students who had cared for her, was essentially as she had related it, embellished by the details of endless lists of chemotherapeutic drugs that she had been given. Most of the drugs Peter recognized; a few were experimental. He was shaken to realize that, if this had happened a dozen years earlier, she would have been dead by this point in her disease. So fresh, he thought, so full of life, and already living on borrowed time.

He wrote down his history and physical examination. As he was writing the nursing orders, Shirley, the night nurse, set a small paper cup down on the desk in front of him.

"Sputum sample from Grayson?" he asked, timidly.

She nodded, pursed her lips. "Must be. Even our kitchen can't prepare anything this disgusting."

He finished the nursing orders, set them down on the front desk, and carried the sputum sample into the small laboratory in the corner of the examining room, across from the nurses' station. There was a mucinous yellow globule streaked with blood in the corner of the cup. He picked up a bit of the sputum on the end of a cotton swab and smeared it over the surface of a glass microscope slide. Peter let the thin film dry a minute, then placed the slide on a rack over a small, blue-stained pan. One at a time, he flooded the surface of the slide with a series of dyes, to stain it for bacteria. Then he placed the freshly stained specimen onto the stage of the small lab microscope and examined it. Against a pinkish background, he could see clusters of red-stained cells, Suzi Grayson's precious few white cells, which had been mobilized to fight the infection. Scattered among these were clumps of tiny violet-blue dots, looking like miniature clusters of grapes: a staph or strep infection.

He turned off the microscope light. Ordinarily, that sort of pneumonia would be easily cured by antibiotics. But Suzi Grayson had leukemia, and her resistance to infection was at a low ebb. And then there was the possibility that the fluid that had built up around her left lung might be infected too.

Peter took the elevator down to the ground level, where X rays were done at night, next door to the Emergency Room. He entered a small room, permanently dark except for the ghostly white shadows given off by the bank of white fluorescent X-ray view boxes on one wall. Seated in front of them was a short, mousy-looking young woman—the night radiology resident. She was speaking into the microphone of a cassette recorder: ". . . The carpal and metacarpal bones appear normal. There is no evidence of fracture—" She broke off as Peter approached. Her small, thick lips formed a little smile as she regarded Peter owlishly through her thick glasses. "Hi, Peter. The technician just brought in the lateral decubitus films on your patient"—her eyes flicked briefly down to scan the list in front of her—"Grayson."

She reached into a bin set into a cabinet next to her chair and fished out a large manila folder. The resident pulled out three large sheets of X-ray film and set the first two, oriented vertically, in front of the fluorescent view boxes. The third she turned horizontally and placed next to the first two.

She pointed to the film on the left. "There is pneumonia of the left lower lobe." Her finger traced out a white area near Suzi Grayson's heart.

Peter nodded.

"On the lateral film"—she turned to the second upright X ray—"there is blunting of the costophrenic angle," pointing to the lower corner of the chest wall.

"However"—she pointed to the third film, in which Suzi Grayson's chest was pictured while she was lying on her left side, rather than standing up—"we do not see much fluid, which we would expect to layer out over the dependent chest wall, if it were there." She pointed to the clearly distinguishable margin of the ribs.

"I don't think there's enough fluid in there for you to tap with a needle."

She watched intently while Peter studied the X rays. He could not bring himself to imagine driving a needle into Suzi Grayson's thin, frail chest, to try to draw off some fluid. He was revolted even by the thought of it. The disgust showed on his face, despite his silent relief at the radiologist's assessment. "Thank you," he offered.

"Sure," the resident answered resignedly, misreading the expression on his face. "Any time." She returned to her dictation.

Peter sat at the desk in the back office of the 4 East nurses' station, writing the antibiotic orders for Suzi Grayson. As he signed his name, he noticed that the page seemed to glow a faintly orange yellow color. It took a moment for him to realize that it was lit by the first rays of dawn, streaming through the window, mingling with the cold, white fluorescent lights above.

He looked over the towers and smokestacks of Roosevelt Island, framed in orange-gold light. The first rays of morning sun, poking through the low-lying cloud cover, were burning the mist off the East River. Here and there, small gold glints of light reflected from the currents, before being swallowed up by the random, inky swells. The night was again yielding, reluctantly and, inevitably, temporarily to another day.

Friday Morning, September 13

Sunlight filtered through the venetian blinds in Chuck Barone's apartment, casting a zebralike pattern across the bed beneath them. For a while Barone played a game of hide and seek with the sun, intermittently re-settling himself so that this eyes were between the stripes of light. Eventually he could no longer adjust the angle of his head to avoid the sunlight. As he began to roll over he was conscious of the soft warmth of an arm sprawled across his chest. He opened his eyes, and a moment later Sylvia opened one eye too. Wordlessly, they slid into each other's arms, enjoying the warmth of each other's body. She pressed her hand against the small of his back to draw him closer.

"Have you been awake long?" she whispered.

"Just for a minute. How about you?"

She pressed her cheek to his, whispered into his ear. "I've been awake, on and off, since dawn. I was afraid . . ."

Barone pulled back to look into her soft, gray eyes. A tear was forming in the corner of her left eye. "Afraid of what?"

She rolled onto her back, looked away. "Afraid that you wouldn't hold me like this in the morning." She sniffled. "Afraid it wouldn't be like last night."

Barone reached across her for a tissue, dabbed her eye. "You mean you were afraid I wouldn't respect you in the morning?'' He could not avoid a hint of amusement in his voice.

She snatched the tissue from his hand, blew her nose. Her face reddened, and he could feel her body beneath him become taut. "You don't have to be sarcastic about it, Chuck. It's just that, well, this sounds corny, but nothing like last night has ever happened to me. I mean, sure, I've had boyfriends"—her cheeks blushed a deeper shade of crimson—"and we've gone to . . . I mean, we've been . . ."

"You don't have to confess to me, Syl—"

"No." She began to pull away, frustrated. "You don't understand. I'm not afraid of . . . intimacy. It's just that this has been so damned fast. I don't know what to make of it. I don't know if I can . . . if I want to keep up at this pace. A relationship should have some time to develop. . . ."

He pulled her back to him, kissed her softly on the cheek. "I don't do this every night either, Sylvia," he whispered into her ear. He could feel the tautness begin to melt, folded her head in against his shoulder. "In fact"—he stroked the back of her head—"I couldn't even imagine it, until last night." He kissed her on the cheek, then the neck. "Until you."

She kissed him on the lips lightly, then deeply. They made love tenderly, leisurely in the morning light.

Sylvia came out of the bathroom, wrapped in a fluffy blue towel and drying her hair with another. "I'm famished!" She plopped herself down on the end of the bed. "You know, Barone, you still owe me a dinner from last night."

Barone, already dressed, bent down to examine the contents of the refrigerator. "Let's see, what would you like—"

"I'll have the croissants and quail eggs, I think," she broke in. "Jesus, Chuck, with a refrigerator that empty I would think that you could remember what's in it.''

Barone laughed. ''Okay, then it's bagels and eggs.'' He began taking the ingredients out of the refrigerator. ''Eggs, butter, bagels, milk . . . You know we could still go out for something to eat.''

She came up behind him, wrapped her arms about his middle. ''No,'' she said. ''I don't want to go out this morning.'' She released him. ''But don't think this gets you off the hook for dinner.''

Barone watched her dress from the corner of his eye as he busied himself frying the eggs and toasting the bagels. She let the towel drop unself-consciously. Her body was thin, her hipbones standing out against the soft pale skin, like a young girl's. But the rounded buttocks and small, firm breasts gave her body a look of fullness and maturity that was more consistent with her intense lovemaking.

As she pulled on her clothes, Barone flipped the eggs expertly onto the two plates and set them down on the small kitchen table.

They ate greedily. ''I can't remember eggs tasting this good,'' said Barone between bites.

Sylvia nodded, tore off a piece of bagel, and used it to wipe egg yolk from her plate. ''It might have something to do with not eating dinner last night.''

Barone nodded, smiled lecherously. ''Really? I was too busy to notice.''

She threw a bit of bagel at him. It bounced off his chest and landed in his plate. He popped it into his mouth.

They both laughed. Then, thoughtfully staring at the eggs in his plate, he said, ''You know I always go to my mother's house for dinner on Friday nights.'' He looked up from his plate, caught her eye expectantly. ''Would you like to go with me tonight?''

She stopped chewing for a moment, swallowed. ''I

would really like that,'' she said. ''Does she live near here?''

Barone nodded. ''Not far. Just across the bridge in Queens. You'll love her; she's a sweet old busybody. And her pasta is out of this world.'' He kissed his fingertips and rolled his eyes upward.

Sylvia chuckled. ''I guess we can go when I get off from the Emergency Room. Maybe I can get someone to cover for me so I can leave an hour early. Burt Rhinehart owes me a favor.''

Barone nodded again. ''Good idea.''

The blinds in Marilyn Silver's apartment were drawn, as were the curtains over them, so that only the electronic rasp from her alarm clock admitted that another day had begun. She rolled across to the empty side of her double bed to turn it off. She deliberately placed the clock across from the side she slept on, because the movement across the cool sheets to turn it off helped awaken her. The clock's placement also made the nightstand look more balanced. She did not like the look of emptiness.

She arose from the bed, allowing her flannel nightgown, which always rode up around her hips, to fall back as she stood. She padded across the room and turned on the television to catch the morning news. The bright colors instantly filled the screen, reflecting an eerie glow off the bare walls of the room. Marilyn put up a pot of coffee to brew, expertly maneuvering in the dim light, almost without opening her eyes.

The morning news announcer was a young, blonde woman. Her face, usually reflecting the fullness of youth, had been unusually rounded recently. As the camera backed up from her, it was apparent that her abdomen was beginning to swell. The gossip columnists said it would be twins.

Marilyn yawned, stretched. She shrugged off her

nightgown, letting it fall to the floor. She looked down at her own body, her large rounded breasts and hips reflecting the glow of the television screen. She could feel her body approaching overripeness. Her days as a young girl were over, her time as a nubile young woman nearly so. All while she spent her life looking after elderly patients who did not know who or where they were, let alone who was taking care of them, and at what sacrifice.

She went into the bathroom, urinated, and turned on the shower. While she waited for the water to warm up, she surveyed her body again in the harsh fluorescent light. Her breasts were definitely more saggy, and the extra weight on her hips was beginning to look more like a roll. She pulled back the shower curtain, stepped into the tub, and soaped up, rubbing her fingers over the slick softness of her skin as if to erase the extra poundage.

She dressed quickly, hiding her breasts in an oversized blouse and her hips in white hospital pants. She applied her makeup sparingly; she did not spend long at the mirror. As she drank her morning coffee, she thumbed through the latest *New England Journal of Medicine,* looking for articles on renal failure. She had to present a case to Maurie Benson and wanted to one-up him. She only hoped that Barone's copy of the magazine had not arrived in the mail yet; he could always be counted on to try to show up everyone by quoting the latest articles. Harvey, of course, would not have read the journal yet; he spent every night off with his gay friends on the Lower East Side. Peter Lee she could never be sure about. He was very intense and sometimes seemed to be right on top of things. But lately he had been very distant, almost as if he were distracted by something. She guessed that it had something to do with their last resident, Sylvia, leaving the ward. He really seemed to have a crush on her, and Barone was not making it any easier.

Marilyn finished her coffee and rinsed the cup, then picked up her overnight bag. Tonight she would be on call, she noted with a mental grimace. She stepped out of her apartment into the windowless, dimly lit hallway. As she locked her door, she thought she heard whispering and maybe even a giggle from the other end of the hall. Two shadowy figures were clinging together in front of one of the doorways. Chuck Barone lived at that end of the hallway, but she was not sure which apartment was his, and besides, he lived alone.

Not until she reached the elevators, halfway down the hall, was she sure about Barone's short, muscular form. And only when they almost met, in front of the elevator doors, did she recognize Sylvia, carrying her overnight bag. Marilyn tried not to stare.

"Good morning," said Sylvia, a bit awkwardly, to her former intern.

"Good morning," replied Marilyn, forcing a cheerful note. Barone acknowledged her with a nod. She looked away again, her cheeks burning.

They rode the elevator down together in silence. Sylvia got off on the tenth floor, to return to her own apartment. She kissed Barone good-bye chastely, lingering only a second too long for Marilyn to believe that it was casual.

Marilyn and Barone walked together to the hospital, exchanging comments on the weather, traffic, and hospital staff, skillfully avoiding the topic that interested each of them the most. With more than a little relief, she excused herself at the 4 East entrance, and walked to the on-call room to deposit her overnight bag.

Peter Lee was lying on his back in the on-call bed, fully clothed, on top of the sheets, trying to catch a few minutes sleep before morning rounds. She tiptoed quietly to the closet, stowing her bag on the floor as silently as possible.

Peter stirred anyway. "Is that you, Marilyn?" he asked groggily. "It's okay. I'm not really asleep anyway. I just finished with my last admission twenty minutes ago."

"You poor dear," she answered, a note of genuine pity in her voice. "Is this the first time you've gotten to bed all night?"

"No." Peter sat up on the side of the bed, rubbed his eyes. "I caught a couple of hours of sleep between one-thirty and three-thirty."

"I hope I do that well tonight," she replied. "After all, somebody has to stay awake around here. And after what I saw as I was coming out of my apartment this morning, I don't think our resident is going to be paying a lot of attention. . . ."

Peter Lee stared out from the 4 East solarium windows down along the East River towards the Queensborough Bridge. It was lit so brightly by the midmorning sun that it appeared etched in place, too sharply drawn to be real. He followed the progress of a cable car from Roosevelt Island, bound for midtown Manhattan. The small gondola seemed like a toy, suspended over the East River. It moved so slowly past the bridge that it seemed to be suspended in time as well as space: It constituted its own frame of reference. The river could slip past below, the traffic could flow over the bridge, but the gondola was above it all, insulated.

"Dr. Lee, are you with us?" rasped Maurie Benson. Peter felt his attention jerked back to the balding, mustachioed man dominating the center of the room. Peter's first impulse was to answer honestly "no," but instead he found himself nodding dumbly.

"Well then, what are your alternatives in the patient

presenting with acute renal failure?'' Maurie pounded away.

Peter had deliberately chosen a chair in the shadows away from the glaring sunlight streaming in through the windows, but he could feel the beads of sweat begin to break out on his brow, as he tried to think of a cogent answer. ''Well, uh,'' he stumbled, fighting to organize his thoughts. ''I guess I would, uh, first do either peritoneal dialysis . . . or hemodialysis.''

''Why?'' Maurie's glare was even hotter than the sunlight.

''To buy some time, to see if the patient's own kidneys might recover.''

Maurie snorted, nodded his head in grudging approval. ''And what would your criteria be for initiating therapy?''

Peter considered for a few seconds. ''I would dialyze the patient when the creatinine reached about six point zero.''

''And how would you determine when to stop dialysis?'' asked Maurie relentlessly.

''When the creatinine reached above three point zero to four point zero?''

It was more of a question than an answer, but Maurie seemed satisfied. He turned his attention to Marilyn Silver. ''And what kind of side effects would you have to watch out for?''

Marilyn struggled to answer. ''I would be concerned about bleeding, uhmmm . . . infection . . . uhh . . .''

Peter could feel himself sliding back into his own world. The cable car . . . if only Maurie weren't such a hard ass . . . if only he could escape . . .

''And now, Dr. Lee, do you have any other cases to present?''

Peter was yanked back to the solarium again, found himself nodding again dumbly. He would have to describe his middle of the night admission. ''About three A.M.," he began, "I admitted a twenty-eight-year-old woman with acute myelocytic leukemia for . . ." He detailed Suzi Grayson's history and physical exam for Benson, in the time-honored format of a formal presentation. Nowhere in his presentation, Peter noted as he mechanically gave the details of the chest sounds and serum chemistries, was there a place to describe the golden halo of hair or the softness of her skin.

"There was evidence of pneumonia and fluid build up over the left lower lung, but the remainder of the exam was normal," he concluded.

"And what did her X rays show?" Maurie's face was impassive, an expression that could mean that he liked the answers he was given or that he was bored or, more often, that he was about to pounce.

Peter thought he knew what Maurie was getting at, decided to play out the game of cat and mouse. "There was consolidation of the left lower lobe." He gave the obvious results, then hesitated. "And the left costophrenic angle was blunted." Maurie was going to have to stop being coy and come after him if he wanted the full answer.

"And the lateral decubitus films?" Maurie's impatience was beginning to show.

"A small amount of fluid layered out."

Maurie could hold back no longer. "Did you tap it?" His tongue flicked out over his lip, his eyes boring into Peter.

Peter could feel himself reflexively recoil, pressing against the back of the chair, as if it were a trapdoor he could retreat through. "There wasn't enough fluid to tap."

Benson's face darkened. "And how did you determine that?"

Peter felt his face flush, his voice strain. His mouth was suddenly dry. "The, uh, the radiologist on call said that—"

"The *radiologist?*" Maurie interrupted. "And who was that? A first year resident? Did he examine the patient?"

"Actually it was a woman, and she—"

"I don't care if it was a goddamn eunuch down there," Benson exploded. The snickering from the medical students only fueled his fury. "Since when does a *physician* rely on the word of a technical consultant, who has never seen the patient, to direct his care?"

Peter's voice trembled, out of control. "The radiologist is an MD. She is trained in examining X-ray films. I just didn't think—"

Benson cut him off again. "That's obvious. Let's go examine this patient." He grabbed his medical bag and stalked out of the solarium.

The entire group—Barone, the interns, the medical students—crowded around Suzi Grayson's bed. Benson examined her carefully, beginning with her eyes and skin. "She looks febrile. What is her temperature?"

Peter picked up the bedside chart. "Still one hundred and one."

Benson, without acknowledging the reply, asked the young woman to bend forward in the bed, and began to repeat the exam Peter had done the previous night. He tapped his fingers against her chest wall and made a pen mark on her back where the sound changed from a healthy resonant note to a dull thud. Then he had her breathe deeply while he listened to her chest with his stethoscope. He made a second set of marks. Benson was quick, efficient, with no wasted motion. A perfect machine, thought Peter, watching Suzi Grayson wriggle slightly under Benson's touch: No wonder the patients always complained that his fingers were as cold as steel.

Finally Benson straightened himself, stepped back from the bed. "Thank you, miss," he said perfunctorily to Suzi Grayson. "The doctors will be working to help you get over this." Then he turned to the medical students. "I would like each of you to examine this chest." Not a young woman, thought Peter, or even a patient, just a chest. "And be ready to discuss your findings at rounds Monday." He turned to Barone, ignoring Peter. "I would like to speak with you and Dr. Lee for a moment outside." He brushed past them out into the hallway.

Peter and Barone followed. Benson led the way to the 4 East on-call room, held the door open for the two young doctors. No one was inside; it was like walking into an ambush. As soon as he had closed the door behind them, Benson turned so quickly that Peter had to catch himself against the desk to keep from falling backward.

"Dr. Barone." He glowered, ignoring Peter entirely. "You will have that woman's chest tapped. This morning!"

Before Barone could answer, Benson had turned again and was out the door.

"Have you got everything together?" Barone asked Peter, who was assembling his equipment at Suzi Grayson's bedside.

"I think so. Betadine, four-by-four's, lidocaine, syringe—"

"Don't forget a sterile vial and a jar."

Peter blushed. "I don't think that there will be enough fluid for us to need a jar. . . ."

Barone, scanning the equipment on the bedside table, answered without looking at his intern. "If you can see any fluid on a chest X ray, there is at least two hundred fifty milliliters in there. I'll get a jar—you get started."

Peter, grateful for Barone's absence, turned to his patient. "Miss Grayson, do you remember last night that I said some fluid had built up on your lungs?"

She nodded, eyes questioning, afraid.

"Well," said Peter, trying to be reassuring, knowing he was not, "we are going to need to draw some of that fluid off to check it and make sure it is not infected."

She lay back in the bed, her head encircled by golden brown ringlets. She nodded again, her eyes reflecting fear, but her voice bespoke trust. "Of course, doctor."

"Do you feel strong enough to sit up?"

She nodded a third time and began pulling herself weakly forward. Peter placed an arm under her shoulder to help. The skin exposed by the open back of her hospital gown was warm and soft, and Peter could feel the movements of her ribs as her chest heaved. He helped her gently to swing her feet over the side of the bed. The skin of her legs was pale and translucent, like fine china.

He brought the bedside table closer, placed a pillow on it. "Now I would like you to lean forward and rest your head on this table." She folded her arms on the pillow, then laid her head down. She looked up at Peter, eyes wet with repressed tears.

Peter did not know how to respond to her fear. He wanted to tell her that it would be all right, that she had nothing to fear. But he knew that Maurie's clinical judgment was as good as his interpersonal relationships were bad. If Maurie were right, if she indeed had infected fluid around her lung, then she was in for a very rough time. He could not tell her that. Finally he looked away and walked around the other side of the bed.

Without speaking, he began to push her hospital gown forward on her arms, exposing her back entirely. The shafts of sunlight, brushing over her skin, exposed the heaving of her ribs under the soft, pale skin.

"I am going to put some iodine soap on your back now," he cautioned. "It will feel cold, but it won't hurt."

He watched her back move as she nodded silently.

He began painting her skin with the sticky brown soap, once, twice, three times. Then he covered her back with a sterile drape. Only a small patch of yellow brown–stained skin, raised by her seventh and eighth ribs, was visible though the small fenestration in the drape.

Barone returned as Peter put on his sterile gloves and began to lay out his instruments on another sterile towel. "How high is the fluid in the chest?" asked Barone.

"Up to the seventh rib," answered Peter, filling a small syringe with lidocaine. "I'm going to numb up the skin now." He spoke over Suzi's shoulder. He could see the drape shift slightly as she nodded.

He pushed the needle tip just beneath the skin covering her eighth rib. She jumped slightly as the needle penetrated, then inhaled sharply and held her breath as he began to inject the anesthetic into the skin. As he pulled the needle out, the chest began to move rhythmically again.

Peter picked up another larger syringe, with a needle as large as a tenpenny nail. He touched the tip to the anesthetized area on her back. "Does that hurt?"

"Just feel pressure," came the muffled reply.

Peter looked up to Barone, who nodded. With a small shove, he pushed the massive needle into the skin over the eighth rib. Abruptly the needle came to a stop as its tip bit into the bone beneath. He could feel the syringe pull from his hand as Suzi Grayson jumped slightly.

"Sorry," he mumbled, and aimed the needle slightly higher, to clear the top edge of the rib. This time it continued to plunge in, unimpeded. Millimeter by millimeter, he advanced the needle, pulling back on the plunger of the syringe. He began to sweat as the needle sank in deeper. He pulled on the plunger again. Still no fluid.

How much farther could he go? If he had overestimated the fluid level in ·her chest, the needle would pierce her lung. It might even cause it to collapse, which in her weakened state might kill her. He stopped and looked up at Barone, who only nodded again.

Of course, Maurie Benson had confirmed the physical exam, and he had demanded that the tap be done. And with Barone approving every step, no one could criticize him if the worst happened. But Barone was not holding the needle, and it was not his hand that might collapse her lung. His hand trembling, sweating inside the tight rubber glove, Peter began again to advance the needle, steeling himself for a sudden gush of air as he drove it into her lung.

Nothing. He pushed a millimeter further. Still nothing. The huge needle seemed interminable. Another millimeter.

The plunger suddenly pulled back freely, as the syringe filled with murky, straw-colored fluid. Peter released a breath he had not known he was holding. "Okay now, Miss Grayson, we've got the needle in place. I'm going to draw off as much fluid as possible."

Suzi Grayson sighed audibly, as Peter began to suction fluid from her chest. He handed syringe after syringe to Barone, who filled a variety of test tubes and small bottles for laboratory tests. Finally, they began to fill Barone's jar. By the time they were done, it contained 300 milliliters of fluid that looked like chicken soup.

"I can breathe a lot easier now, doctor." She smiled, relieved, as Peter helped settle her back into the bed.

He smiled back, wishing he could say the same for himself. "I'm sure that fluid pressing on your lung made it harder to breathe. We have to do some tests on it, so we can get you over this infection."

She closed her eyes. "I hope so, doctor."

Peter watched her for a moment, said to himself, "So do I."

By the time Peter had cleaned up at the bedside and filled out the requisitions for the special tests on the fluid, Barone was already in the 4 East laboratory, examining the fluid under the microscope. "Looks like it is infected," he said as Peter walked in.

"Any organisms?" asked Peter, collapsing onto a lab stool.

"Not yet," answered Barone, without looking up from the microscope. "But even if we don't see them, the fluid could still be due to an infection."

"Or her leukemia," added Peter.

"Or to her leukemia," Barone agreed. "If you hadn't started her on antibiotics last night, we could rely on the bacterial culture of the fluid to tell us whether it was infected. But by now, even if the fluid were infected, the antibiotics could prevent the organism from growing out in culture—"

"I had to start antibiotics last night," Peter protested. "She would have died without them."

Barone continued looking through the microscope, hunting for the telltale bacteria that would confirm Peter's ineptitude. "As it is now, she might die because of the antibiotics. They won't be able to cure her if the fluid around her lungs is infected. That will require placing a chest tube to drain the fluid from around her lung.

"But a chest tube is dangerous, and we can't put one in without a diagnosis. And because you started her on antibiotics before doing the chest tap, we can't make the diagnosis."

Peter grasped the edge of the lab table, digging his fingernails into the unyielding surface until the nail beds turned white. "It can't happen. It can't."

Barone looked up from the microscope for the first time. Peter Lee was staring at his own reflection in the glass door of the laboratory cabinet. "It can," Barone said. "You just better hope like hell it doesn't."

The late evening sun washed the face of the hospital in glowing red and orange. As Barone walked the last block, he felt a sense of anticipation mixed with a slight anxiety that was very different from his usual clinical detachment as he walked to work. The previous night had been so utterly without precedent in his experience that he did not know what to expect tonight.

Occasionally he had slept with some of his girl-friends, one even on the first date. But there had always been a sort of emotional fencing involved, each parrying the emotional if not the physical thrusts of the other. Always the big question, Where is this relationship going? intruded itself on the pure physical pleasure. Always the result had been, for that reason, less than totally satisfying.

But it had been so natural with Sylvia that he had not even thought about the "relationship." She had opened up to him like a rare orchid, letting him into the center of her being to savor her soft sweetness. He was at once enthralled by her bloom and apprehensive that he might find it perishable.

He had not even used a condom! He, a young physician in New York, the AIDS capital of the universe! But the thought had not even occurred to him, not for personal protection, not even for birth control. He could be rational about sex, but with Sylvia it was something different. Not a physical relationship but something more personal, even . . . spiritual. He had to be as close to her as he could get. In the final moments, he could not even tolerate that fraction of a millimeter of separation.

He looked up, surprised to find that he was standing in front of the Emergency Room doors. As he walked in, the desk clerk looked up briefly, without comment, then returned to her work, smiling. Barone ignored her, and not seeing Sylvia in the glassed-in nurses' station, walked past it back to the on-call room. He stopped at the door, not sure if he should just enter, as he usually did. He knocked first.

"Come on in," answered Sylvia from within.

He opened the door to find her adjusting a lavender sweater that clung tightly. The color of the sweater accentuated the slightly violet makeup on her eyelids. Barone hesitated for a moment, then crossed the room and kissed her softly, then deeply. He knew instinctively that it was right; she yielded into his arms.

"That's one hell of a hello," Sylvia breathed, not moving.

Barone smiled. They kissed again. "It just seemed like the right thing to do," he answered simply.

"Can't argue with that." She smiled back, straightened her sweater again, then opened the door. "Come on. We better get going or I think we'll never make it to your mother's house."

Barone held the door for her, then followed her out of the on-call room. "Who is covering for you?"

"Burt Rhinehart. He came in an hour early. He owes me a few hours."

"I better not ask why," gibed Barone.

Her cheeks flushed slightly, but she smiled. "No, you better not."

Walking toward the subway, with the sun slipping behind the tall buildings, the streets were lit with a pale orange luminance. Once out of sight of the hospital, Sylvia walked closer to Barone, and he put his arm around her shoulder. Unconsciously, they walked in step.

As they waited for the train, clinging together on the platform, Barone began, "Maurie Benson really laid into Peter Lee on rounds today."

Sylvia stepped back, looked up at him. "What did he do, this time?"

"Last night he admitted a young woman with leukemia who had pneumonia and a fluid around her lung. He didn't tap the fluid, just started antibiotics. When he presented the case this morning, I thought Maurie was going to explode."

"Did Maurie yell at him?"

"Not really. He was just quietly furious, criticizing Peter in front of the entire group . . . and the patient."

Sylvia pressed against Barone, shuddering slightly. "That man should be muzzled. Why didn't the resident on call with Peter catch the mistake last night?"

Barone shrugged. "The woman came in at three A.M. I guess that by the time Peter was finished with her it was nearly morning, and he figured it was pointless to get the on-call resident out of bed to check his work. He told me on ward rounds that he had admitted the woman, but he said it was just a case of pneumonia. So I told him to save her presentation for attending rounds."

Sylvia shuddered again. "I'm worried about Peter."

"So am I," said Barone.

She looked up at his face. There was a hint of triumph in his look of concern. "Peter would never have made a mistake like that when he was on service with me," she said.

Barone could not let it drop. "In other words, you would have covered for him better?" He knew before he finished that it was a mistake.

Sylvia turned to face him, flushed. "No, he was careful." She reddened further. "And if he had a question, he always called his resident."

Barone's cheeks colored too. "What are you saying? That he had to call you all the time for help?" He could not avoid a hint of jealousy in his voice.

She nodded, eyes flashing defiance. "When I was his

resident, he called me. Sometimes his judgment was a bit off, but he knew when to call for help. I think that he's scared of you, afraid to ask for help.''

Of course he called, thought Barone. I would call for help myself if I knew that you would be answering. But he said; ''Well, lately he's been very distant. He doesn't say very much and keeps drifting off during rounds, as if he were preoccupied by something.''

A rumbling sound began to build as the train neared the station. ''Internship can be very rough,'' she said. ''You're his resident. I think you should sit down with him and see if you can—''

The rest of her words were lost in the roar of the approaching train. They entered the car and sat huddled together on the plastic seat, each of them silently grateful that the noise of the train and the press of the crowd made further conversation impossible.

Peter Lee was struggling to finish his progress notes. After spending a long day on call, and a seemingly longer one, after a sleepless night, at the hospital, he had finished his chores and signed out to Marilyn. Peter then took his patient charts back with him to the on-call room, hoping in the quiet of the dingy little room to quickly pen the few required lines to mark the daily course of his patients' hospital stay.

But he found it difficult to concentrate, draw his attention to the blank pages in front of him. Every little distraction of the day came back to haunt him, tear at him as he tried to make sense of what had happened to him and his patients during the previous twenty-four hours.

He had been staring fixedly at an open chart for what could have been a few minutes—or perhaps an hour—when he heard the door open. Lauren Nyquist craned her head around the door frame, gave a little shake so that the straight blonde hair cascaded down away from her face. "Dr. Lee. I'm so glad I found you." She slipped into the room, let the door close behind her. She was standing in front of Peter, her arms behind her back in the stance of a little girl about to ask a favor, close enough that the scent of her not-too-subtle perfume seemed to wash over him.

Peter watched with a growing sense of anticipation, as she produced a syringe from behind her back. "I need you to give this medicine to Mrs. Delbert."

He could feel the deflation, struggled not to show it.

"I'm sorry to ask you, doctor," she continued quickly, taking his lack of response for annoyance, "but the new hospital policy requires the charge nurse to give intravenous narcotics, and she's . . ."

"At dinner," Peter said flatly.

She looked at him quizzically. "How did you . . ."

Peter shook his head. "It doesn't matter."

He walked down the corridor to Anne Delbert's room. She was lying on her back this time, her face set in a tight grimace, her arms drawn up over her lower abdomen.

"Mrs. Delbert?" The woman opened her eyes, winced. "I brought you some pain medication."

There was a hint of gratitude, perhaps even something more in her eyes, as she nodded her head. Peter began to administer the medication into the injection port in her intravenous line. Within seconds the tension and pain etched into her face began to soften, as an audible gasp escaped from her lips.

In a spontaneous gesture of relief that transcended mere words, she raised a bony hand, grasped Peter's free hand. He froze, did not know how to respond. He had dreamed of human contact, longed for it, but in his dreams he had imagined Sylvia's soft, sensuous touch, the lingering caress of her hand. This rough, skeletal hand, grasping his own, begging for a squeeze in return, was not, could not substitute for what he had longed for. It served only as a stark reminder of his own inability to make contact, his failure at having let Sylvia slip away.

Clumsily, he withdrew his own hand, mumbled a few words, and hastily departed from the room.

Maria Barone's neighborhood in Queens might as well have been in a different country from the busy streets of Manhattan. She lived on a tidy, well-kept street of duplex homes, all identical, every one of them spotless. Each presented a tiny patch of closely cropped green lawn in front; the monotony was broken only by an occasional statue of the Virgin Mary, planted squarely in front of the house. It was the sort of neighborhood where, if you forget your street number, you might never find your home.

Chuck and Sylvia were greeted at the front door, simultaneously, by Maria Barone and by the fragrance of her tomato sauce, which Chuck noted, "was world famous . . . or at least it should be." Sylvia did not argue.

Maria was a short, plump woman with black hair pulled straight back from a soft, round face. She guided them into the living room. Even before the introductions were completed, she was wagging her head from side to side. "So thin, so thin," she clucked, running a practiced eye over Sylvia's frame, the same way she might inspect a chicken at the butcher shop.

"Now don't start, Ma." Barone was embarrassed.

She took no note of her son, continued shaking her head. "I'll just get supper ready," she said with what sounded to be a note of sympathy in her voice.

When she left the room, Barone stood facing Sylvia, put his hands on her shoulders. "She really doesn't mean anything by it. It's just that, in the old country . . ."

Sylvia smiled. "I think she's . . . concerned. And very cute."

Barone smiled back, relieved. "Not everyone appreciates the way she shows her . . . concern."

"Well I do," answered Sylvia. 'I think she's a dear."

The dinner was a symphony of prosciutto and melon, fettuccine al pesto, and veal marsala, punctuated by insalata mista and conducted by Maria Barone using a carafe of chianti as a baton. "Does anybody care for dessert?" she challenged.

Chuck pushed himself back from the table. He placed one hand over his distended belly. "I don't know, Ma. What have you got?"

"Cassata." She smiled.

Barone winced playfully, then broke out in a grin. "You got me where it hurts. I . . ." He looked at Sylvia. "We will both have some."

Sylvia waited until she left the room. "I'm not really hungry, Chuck. . . ."

"I know," he answered. "Neither am I. But she only makes cassata for special occasions. Anyone can cook pasta or veal, but only real Italians can made cassata. You can't turn her down."

Sylvia smiled and took Chuck's beefy hand in both of her own. Looking around the room she pointed to a framed photograph of short, stout, dark, bearded man. "Is . . . was that your father?"

Barone nodded. "He died three years ago of a heart attack."

"If he ate your mother's cooking all the time, he probably had the world's record for blood cholesterol levels."

Barone nodded. "He never ate anywhere else. She's been really lonely the last few years. That was one of the reasons I returned to New York for my residency."

"Don't you have any brothers or sisters?" Sylvia

scanned the photographs around the room for a telltale likeness.

"My sister lives in Baltimore." He pointed to a gold-framed photograph on the opposite wall. "She has two children, whom my mother adores. But she can't bring herself to sell the house. She has lived here all her life. All her friends are here. And this is where she lived for twenty-eight years with Dad . . ."

Maria Barone carried in three plates of cassata. It was rich with ricotta cheese, moist with rum, and just sweet enough to deserve its special place on Maria's menu.

"This is delicious," said Sylvia appreciatively.

Maria smiled. "Such a pleasure to cook for you, my child." She looked around the room. "This house is too empty."

Barone blushed. "I come visit almost every Friday night."

Maria got up, stood behind her son, and placed her hands on his shoulders. "Of course you do." She kissed him on the cheek. "And your sister, Lisa, comes to visit with the children every summer and at Christmas." She sat down again. "But that's not the same thing."

Sylvia nodded. "My mother is"—she hesitated, looked to Chuck—"a widow too. My sister still lives at home with her, but I know that my father . . . and I . . . have left a big, empty space in her life."

Maria sniffed. "Eat up, child. You are too skinny."

Peter walked back to the medicine room to dispose of the syringe. Lauren Nyquist was standing in the corner of the room, by the window, examining two oval shaped pills in the dull fluorescent light. "Can you help me?" she said as he entered.

Peter pitched the empty syringe. The scent of her

perfume filled the tiny room. "Sure." He started toward her.

She held up the little pills. They were virtually identical. "I dropped one of Mr. Denton's pills into Mrs. Segovia's medication cup. Can you read the lettering on them?"

She held the pills up for him to examine. The writing was nearly microscopic, forcing him to lean over her.

"I think it says . . ." He squinted, felt the warmth and softness of her hip pressing against his thigh, her shoulder against his chest. The rise and fall of her chest, pushing against him as she breathed, was mesmerizing.

Long suppressed feelings of warmth began to melt the knot of tension in his stomach. He leaned further forward, as if to see the pills better, pressing against her, his hand now resting on her back, caressing her golden tresses as they brushed her shoulder.

As if he were watching himself in a movie, in slow motion, Peter saw his arm enfold her, pulling her gently toward him, the same movements that he had imagined, envisioned with Sylvia. He leaned his face forward, expecting to see her eyes flutter closed, the lips part.

Only Lauren's face was red. She started to pull away. Peter was confused, leaned against her more forcefully, closed his eyes to kiss her . . .

The red-hot sting of her hand against his cheek was like an explosion in his subconscious, letting loose a torrent of emotions that had been dammed within him. He grasped her wrist, twisted it back, pushed her against the stainless steel counter. He was flooded with hate, anger, even as his body became sexually aroused by the contact and the struggle.

Then, a sudden, sharp, white-hot pain shot through his groin. His desire was suddenly swamped by a wave of nausea as she smashed the knee of her free leg again, then a third time into his crotch.

Racked by a spasm of pain, he released her and

crumpled onto the floor. "You pig!" She kicked him, retreated to the corner of the tiny room, by the window, as if she would use it to escape if he advanced toward her. "Get out of here! Get out now!"

Gradually, the searing pain subsided and Peter found he could roll to his knees, then stand. Wordlessly, he stumbled through the doorway, then out of the hospital, into the cool of the night.

The ride home in the subway, after a heavy meal, was soporific. Sylvia curled up against Chuck's shoulder and would have fallen asleep but for the lurching. As they walked from the subway to their apartment building, they huddled together against the night chill. "Would you like to come up to my place?" she whispered in his ear, as they approached the elevator.

"I thought you would never ask." He pushed the button for her floor.

Although the floor plan of her apartment was nominally identical to that of Barone's, it was difficult to find the similarity once in the door. The walls and carpets were a soft gray. Under the windows were oak bookcases, and in one corner was a brown suede reading chair and floor lamp. On the near side of the floor lamp was a small oak desk. Across the room, her carefully made bed was covered by a gray and beige quilt. A graceful Japanese print was hung above the bed.

"Would you like something to drink?" she asked.

"Sure," said Barone. "Do you have any brandy?"

She nodded, reached into the cupboard for the glasses.

"That was very thoughtful, the way you made my mother feel comfortable when she was feeling sorry for herself. I think she likes you."

Sylvia smiled, carried over two snifters. "And I like her too. She's a lot like my own mother. Even though she does make better cassata."

Barone took a swallow of the brandy and settled down into the suede chair. "I'm really glad that you like her."

Sylvia took a sip from her glass, sat down on the wide arm of the chair. She swung her legs over Barone's and put her arm behind his head, whispered into his ear. "Not only do I like her, but I think I'm beginning to fall in love with her son."

The words came without surprise or even thought. "That's a good thing"—he stared into her eyes— "because I think I'm in love with you too."

She slid her free arm around his neck and nestled against his shoulder. After a moment he kissed her forehead, her cheek, her lips. They kissed softly at first, unhurriedly, nibbling at each other. Barone set down his glass, softly put his arm about her waist and pulled her down onto his lap. The softness of her breasts, straining against the sweater, pressed against his chest.

He kissed her more deeply, responding to an increasing sense of urgency in her lips. Sylvia unbuttoned the top of his shirt and began to run her fingers across his chest, caressing him.

He pulled her even closer, pushed her sweater up, and unfastened her brassiere, running his nails down her bare back, massaging her shoulder blades. Slowly, he lifted the sweater over her head, nuzzling her soft, small breasts and taking her hardened nipples into his mouth. After a long moment, she stood up, unfastened her skirt, and let it fall to the floor. He placed one hand on each hip and drew her closer, nibbling at the soft skin of her belly. As he reached the downy pubic hair, he drew her panties lower, working his way down until she ground her hips against his face uncontrollably, shuddering as his lips caressed her softness.

Finally, she pulled him up, hungrily kissed his lips, pressing her warmth against him. His hands fell to her buttocks, kneading the soft skin, pulling her against him until she could feel the heat from his loins.

Gently, she unfastened his pants and sat down on the edge of the bed. She slowly caressed him, nibbled at the soft skin of the inner side of his thighs, working her way upward until she was running her tongue and lips over his erection. Then suddenly she stopped and lay back on the bed, pulling him down on top of her. Her legs clasped around him, drawing him into her. She whispered hoarsely as she kissed his ear, then neck, "I need you Chuck. Now."

Peter Lee walked south along York Avenue, mechanically retracing his steps from the previous nights, letting the cool evening breeze take some of the heat from his stinging, red cheeks. It was Lauren's fault, he knew that. She had been leading him on. He turned off York Avenue, walked through the heliport parking lot toward the East River.

The walk along the river was nearly deserted. Peter passed the sheer, black, craggy face of Rockefeller University. It was a sickness, he reflected, that made women act that way. The need to swell a man's desire, then watch him beg or crawl away frustrated. He could feel the heat rise again in his cheeks as he remembered his humiliation. Sylvia had done the same thing to him. And so had Anne Delbert. Or had she? It didn't matter. If she had not done it to him, it was only because he had not given her the chance.

The white, illuminated face of Manhattan General Hospital rose in the distance. It was beautiful, alluring, like the alabaster face of a sophisticated woman. From the unlit side, facing the East River, Peter could see that behind the glittering facade the building was bathed in darkness. My mistress, thought Peter, riddled inside with disease and decay. Waiting for me, he realized, like Anne Delbert, just lying there, waiting for the opportunity to humiliate me again. He crossed the East

River Drive on the footbridge at Seventy-first Street and headed for the hospital's back entrance.

Barone had been wrong to save her in the Emergency Room. It was her right to die. Certainly, thought Peter, the woman had the right to take her life to end her own suffering. And helping a person to achieve that goal could only be considered an act of kindness. How much greater an act of charity, then, if in so doing the suffering of others was prevented as well?

Peter passed through the hospital's rear entrance, took the elevator to the fourth floor. Too much decay, he thought, too much sickness: a cancer. He could cut it out. He was the doctor. A surgeon of the emotions. Peter found himself walking down the darkened corridor toward 4 East.

"Dr. Lee, what are you doing here?"

Peter suddenly found himself face-to-face with Maureen Donnatelli, the night nurse, emerging from one of the darkened doorways. "Isn't this your night off?"

Peter blushed, thankful for the cover of darkness. "Yes, uh, of course it is, but I wanted to check on a patient . . . Suzi Grayson."

The night nurse nodded her head. "Sleeping like a baby. Now why don't you go on home and do the same?"

Peter stared down the darkened hallway. "I will, in a few minutes, but I'd just like to check on her first."

The nurse shrugged and continued down the hall on her rounds. Peter went to Suzi Grayson's room, stood inside the doorway. It was dark, and he could hear the sounds of her rhythmic breathing. He waited a moment, then stepped back into the hallway. Maureen was in another room, checking a pulse or taking someone's temperature.

He continued down the corridor to the clean supply room, peeked inside. It was empty. He slipped in and entered the medicine room. It too was deserted. He quickly located a ten-milliliter syringe. Then he opened a vial of potassium chloride and plunged in the needle.

Silently he slipped across the hall to Anne Delbert's room. She stirred at the sound of Peter's approach. He switched on the light at her bedside, watched her drawn face and wasted arms as she rolled over. Her eyes fluttered open. "Dr. Lee?" she asked, shielding her eyes to penetrate the gloom beyond the circle of light cast by her lamp. "What are you doing here so late?"

"I came to see how you were feeling." He reached out impulsively, took her hand in his own.

She rolled onto her back and smiled wanly. "I feel a bit better, doctor. The pain medicine is holding me longer." She squeezed his hand again as if to pull him downward to sit with her at the side of the bed.

Even in the hospital, thought Peter, lying in bed, dying of cancer, she could not resist playing her feminine games. He set her hand down on the bed. Reluctantly, she loosed her grip. "I know how hard it is for you," he said, reaching into his pocket for the syringe.

"Is that more pain medicine?" she asked.

"Even better," answered Peter, searching for the injection port on her central venous line. "This will let you sleep."

She nodded gratefully. "That's what I need."

"Of course," cooed Peter, plunging the needle into the injection port. "This is exactly what you need." Peter pushed the plunger of the syringe, forcing the potassium chloride into her heart.

She nodded and closed her eyes. A few seconds later her face contorted, she began to raise her head and her arms. Then, just as suddenly, she collapsed back onto the pillow, her skin clammy and gray. Her breaths came slower and more labored, then ceased.

Peter turned off the light.

* * *

Barone awoke under the soft quilt, in the pitch-black darkness of the apartment. He reached out an arm, instinctively, for Sylvia's warmth, but found her pillow empty.

The bed creaked. He could feel it shift as she sat down on the opposite side. "Sylvia?" he asked, feeling foolish.

She took a sharp breath. "Yes," was all she could manage in response.

He sat up, moved across the bed to enfold her in his arms. She seemed like a small child in his embrace, huddled against him, shivering. "Are you all right?" he asked.

"No," she gasped again, wrenched forward, jack-knifing her body. "I've got stomach cramps." He heard the sound of her breath whistle against her teeth as she suddenly gasped. "And I'm nauseous."

He placed his hand on her shoulder, slowly began to message her back. Gradually she relaxed, her breathing becoming more regular, until she straightened up, let her head fall back against her chest.

He held her for a moment, then laid her back against the pillow. Slowly he stroked her cheek, then her hair, until the even sound of her breathing told him that she had fallen back asleep.

The first orange rays of dawn caught Peter by surprise as they peeked up over Queens, illuminating the steps of the East River walkway on which he was sitting. He had no idea how long he had been sitting there. After spending most of the night walking aimlessly about the Upper East Side, he had been unable to return to his apartment, afraid of the darkness he would find there. Afraid of being truly alone. He stood up stiffly, started south down the walkway.

In the distance he could see the hospital, glowing orange as if colored with luminescent warpaint by the early morning sun. He had known his internship would be difficult, but he had never expected a war: his skill pitted against decay, his courage against sickness. And the first rule of war, thought Peter, was that someone has to die.

Saturday Morning, September 14

Barone dressed quietly in the soft early morning light that was filtering in through Sylvia's drawn drapes. She lay huddled under an extra blanket, only the top of her head showing. Barone yawned and padded over to her side of the bed. As he bent down to kiss her forehead, she raised her head slightly, nearly bumping into him.

"I'm sorry, sweetheart," he began. "I didn't mean to wake you."

Sylvia smiled weakly, pulled her legs back from the edge of the bed so that he could sit beside her. "You didn't wake me," she whispered. "I haven't really been to sleep yet."

Barone reached under the covers for her hand. "I know." He remembered awakening several times as Sylvia slipped out of bed to go to the bathroom. "It wasn't the greatest sleeping night for either of us." He found her hand, caressed it.

Sylvia snuggled up to him, held his hand to her breast and kissed it. "I'm just glad that you're still feeling well."

Barone looked down at her, feeling vaguely guilty. "I guess I should apologize for taking you to my mother's last night. But no one else has ever had this kind of reaction to her cooking. . . ."

Sylvia sat up suddenly, cheeks turning red. "Chuck, that is the nastiest thing I have ever heard you say! Your mother is a dear, and this has nothing to do with the wonderful dinner she served us."

"I suppose you're right." He shrugged. "Most food poisoning takes at least six hours to—"

"Chuck, that's enough!" The sharpness and force of her voice belied her frail, wan appearance. "Some things don't require scientific proof." She fell back into bed.

Barone reached over and hugged her to him. She kissed his ear. "Now you better get off to your morning rounds," she whispered. "I have the day off in ER. I'll be okay here." She kissed him on the cheek. "But I'll feel better if I know that you are coming back to see me later." She reached over to a drawer in her nightstand, took out a key, pressed it into his palm.

He squeezed her again and wordlessly, silently left her to try to sleep in the soft, gray light.

Morning rounds were smoother, more mechanical than usual. Harvey Krane, his beard meticulously trimmed, clothes carefully matched and pressed, was going on call. He was therefore paying more attention than usual and compulsively wrote notes on the status of each patient: which temperatures, blood pressures, and hematocrits he would have to check on later that day. Marilyn, coming off call, was rumpled and tired looking. She wore no makeup, and her chirpy voice seemed strained and taut as she described the previous evening's events. Peter was the most unkempt of all, which struck Barone as odd since he had been off the previous night. Peter's clothes looked slept in. His hair was uncombed and his beard stubbly. Peter was too distracted to offer even token resistance to Baron's criticisms, and mostly just nodded agreement.

As they walked down the hall between patient rooms, Harvey caught Marilyn's arm and pulled her back a half step. "What happened to Peter?" he whispered.

She shrugged. "I guess he must have had a big night," she responded wearily.

Harvey smiled, almost leered, "Maybe he spent it with Sylvia."

Marilyn shook her head. "I don't think so."

Harvey stopped in his place. "What do you mean?"

Marilyn turned to face him, her voice becoming a whisper, but considerably more animated. "Barone lives at the other end of my hall in my apartment building. Yesterday morning I saw him come out of his apartment . . . with Sylvia."

Harvey stroked his beard. "Do you suppose that is why Barone is such a pussycat this morning?"

"I don't really care"—she turned and started walking again—"as long as he lets me get my work done and get out of here."

Suddenly Barone, leading the procession, stopped short, turned to Marilyn. "Aren't we missing someone?"

She looked at him quizzically. "Who?"

"Anne Delbert. Wasn't she in that last room?"

Marilyn flushed. "She . . . she died last night."

Barone's face darkened. "What the hell happened?"

Marilyn stared resignedly at the floor. "I don't really know. The night nurse called me early this morning. She found her dead in her bed during her four A.M. rounds."

"Did you try to resuscitate her?"

Marilyn shook her head. "She was cold and blue. It must have happened at least an hour earlier. Besides, she has orders on her chart not to resuscitate—"

"I don't care what her orders said!" Barone sputtered. "I resuscitated her myself in the Emergency Room. She was very depressed when she took her tranquilizer overdose. She has remained depressed in the hospital. Now she dies mysteriously in the hospital three days later. Did it ever occur to you that she might have tried it again?''

"Come on, Chuck." Harvey tried to intercede. "She had terminal cancer.''

"What is that supposed to mean?'' asked Barone menacingly.

"Don't you think she has the right to decide for herself whether she is going to live or die?''

Barone turned on him, choking back his rage. "No! Never! The physician's responsibility is always to maintain life. Even against the patient's immediate wishes. Anyone who deliberately wants to die has, by definition, a sickness of the mind—depression. My job is to heal that sickness, not promote it. I would consider it a disaster if Anne Delbert had managed to overdose in the hospital under my care.''

There was an uncomfortable silence in the hallway when Barone paused, as the nurses and the orderlies who had stopped to listen self-consciously went back to their chores. Finally he began again, more calmly. "Now I want to know precisely why she died.''

"I wrote on her death certificate that she died of colon cancer,'' responded Marilyn, still looking at the floor.

"That's naive, Marilyn. She had colon cancer, but it was not going to kill her in the immediate future. Did you draw a blood sample from her for drug screening?''

Marilyn shook her head. "She was already dead, Chuck.''

"Did you at least get an autopsy?''

"The family agreed to a full postmortem.'' Marilyn nodded wearily.

Barone took a deep breath, expelled it slowly. "They should be able to get some blood at the autopsy.'' He looked at his watch. "They should be doing it soon. Why don't you finish rounds without me. I'm going to the morgue to see if I can get them to do a drug screen.''

The collective sigh of relief, as Barone strode off toward the elevators, was audible the entire length of the corridor.

Barone could feel his temper cool as he walked the obscure and purposely unmarked corridor that led to the autopsy suite. At the end of the hall was a pair of heavy doors, bearing only the words ENTRY RESTRICTED TO AUTHORIZED PERSONNEL. He rang the buzzer by the side of the door.

While he waited, he reconsidered his outburst during rounds. He knew that much of his testiness was due to his concern about Sylvia. Marilyn was a competent enough intern, and she was probably right that Anne Delbert was not salvageable by the time she got there. But Anne Delbert had been a save, damn it. His save. And he was not going to let her slip away without an explanation.

"Who is it?" asked a scratchy voice from a small speaker above the buzzer.

"Dr. Barone. I want to talk with the pathologist doing the Delbert autopsy."

Another buzzer sounded, and he pushed open the door to the morgue. Immediately in front of him was a blank wall. As he walked down a short hallway to his right, a man looked up at him briefly from his desk. Barone knew that the hallway was formed by a false wall to prevent outsiders from seeing into the autopsy room and to give the autopsy assistant time to scrutinize new arrivals before they could see the rest of the suite.

The autopsy room itself was large, with a high ceiling crisscrossed by forced-air ventilation ducts that provided a complete change of room air every twelve minutes. The floors and walls, up to chest height, were tiled in pale green porcelain. The floor sloped down to a drain at one end. The room was bathed in flat, clinical fluorescent light. Lined up parallel to each other, but perpendicular to the length of the room at ten-foot intervals, were three gleaming stainless steel autopsy tables. On the one farthest from the door lay Anne Delbert's body.

The abdomen and chest had been laid open by a single longitudal incision. The internal organs had been removed, en bloc, and were laid out on the table at her feet for inspection. In a large weighing pan lay her liver, purple and glistening, and studded with yellow balls of cancer.

Her face was covered by the skin of her scalp, which had been pulled forward to expose the skull. The pathologist and his assistant were removing the brain. Barone, waiting for them to finish, examined the stomach, which had been sliced open lengthwise. Its surface was velvety, resembling a small, wrinkled rug.

The assistant, a young black man, was the first to look up. "One of yours?" he asked rhetorically. No one came down to the morgue to watch autopsies for fun.

"Yes," he answered, studying the cut surface of the lungs.

The pathologist, a tall, wiry man with a bad complexion, lay the brain into a stainless steel pan, then looked up at Barone, curious to see who was invading his turf. A smile began to form on his craggy face. "Why, Chuck! I read in the chart about your heroic effort in the Emergency Room."

Barone smiled ruefully. "Didn't do much good, I guess." He gestured at the hollow body on the table. Burt Jacobi, the second year pathology resident, had been in Barone's medical school class. "What have you found?" Barone asked.

Jacobi walked around to the foot of the table, pointing at the colon. "Stage D carcinoma of the colon, involving the mesentery and paraortic lymph nodes. The liver"—he pointed to the weighing pan—"contains multiple metastases. So far the lungs and brain look clean, though.''

Barone frowned. ''Any immediate cause of death?''

''None yet.''

''No pulmonary or cardiac emboli? We see a lot of problems with blood clots in colon cancer patients.''

''So do we.'' Jacobi nodded, a trace of annoyance in his voice. ''We opened the pulmonary and coronary arteries looking for clots. Nothing anywhere.'' He pointed down at the pink, veined softball-sized organ lying in the stainless steel pan. ''Not even in the brain.''

Jacobi picked up a fine forceps and gently began to tease the arteries free from the surface of the brain. Barone watched over his shoulder as Jacobi traced the slender vessels which the evening before had carried nourishment and oxygen to Anne Delbert's brain.

''No evidence of emboli here.'' Jacobi looked up.

''Then what killed her?'' asked Barone.

Jacobi shrugged. ''I don't know. Sometimes we never find out.''

''How often does that happen?''

Jacobi shrugged again. ''Maybe one in ten cases.''

Barone sighed resignedly. ''So the failure to find a cause of death doesn't really mean much.''

''No,'' answered Jacobi, lifting the brain onto the weighing pan. ''One thousand four hundred thirty grams,'' he called out to the assistant, who penciled the number down. He turned back to Barone. ''It really doesn't mean very much, Chuck, except that you are running way ahead of the averages.''

''What is that supposed to mean?'' Now it was Barone's turn to be annoyed.

''It means''—Jacobi took the brain from the weighing pan and placed it gently into a jar of formaldehyde—''that this is the third negative autopsy on one of your patients in the last week.''

''Three?''

"Sure." Jacobi pulled off his rubber gloves and reached beneath his plastic apron to pull out a pocket appointment book. "I remember because I did all three autopsies myself. Here we go—Mary Altman, Herbie Brown, and now Anne Delbert."

"No cause of death on the other two?" Barone, looking slightly dazed, plopped himself down heavily onto one of the high stools at the foot of the autopsy table.

"Nope," said Jacobi, shaking his head.

"The odds against that happening by coincidence," mumbled Barone, "must be . . . what? thirty to one?"

"Actually, they are much worse. Each negative autopsy is an independent event. That makes the odds against three in a row—"

"A thousand-to-one shot," answered Barone, staring blankly at the wall across the room.

"Well, not quite that bad," averted Jacobi. "We do a lot of autopsies down here. In a series of a hundred autopsies, the chances of finding three negatives ones in a row is about one in ten. How many of your patients have we done this year?"

Barone looked back at Jacobi. "Five."

"Only five?" answered Jacobi. "Are you sure?"

Barone nodded. "At the end of each year, Maurie Benson holds an awards banquet, and hands out a Black Cloud Award to the resident who lost the most patients during the preceding year. It makes all of the medical residents more aware of the mortality rates. Until last week, I had only two deaths on my service all year. Both of them were autopsied. I wasn't even in the running for the Black Cloud Award . . . until now."

"Tough luck," said Jacobi, somewhat less than sympathetically.

"And all three within the last week," continued Barone. "Do you think it is possible—"

"That some one is killing your patients to make you look bad?" Jacobi taunted him.

"Be serious, Burt," Barone fumed. "This may not all be coincidental."

Jacobi looked at him curiously. "You really mean it, don't you."

Barone nodded.

"Well." Jacobi furrowed his brow. "Has there been any change in your service in the last week?"

Barone nodded. "I started back on the Four East ward."

"Did all of your patients die in the same part of the ward or during the same nursing shift?"

Barone nodded. "They all died during the night."

Jacobi's eyes widened. "It could be someone on that shift. Did all three patients have the same nurse?"

"I don't know," answered Barone. "I'll have to check the records."

"What about the doctors?"

Barone thought for a moment. "Yes, all three were patients of Peter Lee." He stopped for a moment. "But Herbie Brown and Anne Delbert died during the night while Harvey Krane and Marilyn Silver were on call."

"Sounds to me like you better check the nursing log."

Barone nodded and rose to leave. "By the way." He turned back to Jacobi from the doorway. "Could you take some blood from Anne Delbert for a drug and toxicology screen?"

Jacobi smiled. "I'll send a full set of blood tests to the lab."

Sylvia rolled over slowly onto her side, fighting another wave of nausea. She closed her eyes, breathed deeply, once, twice, then again, until the visceral surge began to subside. Tentatively, she pushed herself to a sitting position, let her feet slide over the side of the bed. She sat a minute with her feet dangling before she tried to stand.

As soon as her weight shifted forward, she felt herself being overcome by a sense of instability, then she was suddenly rushing toward the bathroom, retching.

She made it in time but only because her stomach was already empty and there was nothing left inside her but a small amount of thin mucus, which she spat into the toilet bowl. Sinking to her knees, Sylvia sat on the bathroom mat in front of the bowl with her legs folded back and outward, as she used to sit when playing jacks as a young girl.

Helpless, she thought. A competent, professional woman brought to a state of complete helplessness by a viral organism so small that you cannot see it even with a microscope.

And that was not the only reason that she was feeling out of control. She had always thought that she would be able to choose the time and place, and certainly the man, when she finally fell in love. There had been more than a few eager boyfriends over the years, and she had had no trouble controlling the relationships. She decided what they would do and when they would do it. And when she had made up her mind, as a sophomore in college, that it was time that she lost her virginity, she had chosen the guy and planned everything herself, right down to having a package of condoms in her purse. Even if sex was not everything she had hoped it would be, even if it had not swept her away in the kind of emotional torrent she had read about in romance novels as a young girl, she had always had the sense that it was something that she could handle.

And here she was, completely out of control over Chuck Barone! He was not even the sort of man that she really liked, or at least not the sort that she had realized before that she liked. Because now, without her permission, he represented exactly what she could not live without. As soon as she was in his arms, her self-control just seemed to melt. All of the things she had anticipated about her eventual lover, all of the scenes of slow, languorous love that she had fantasized, gave way in a matter of seconds to the urgent, burning need to be as close to him, as physically close, as possible.

Sylvia suddenly wrenched forward as another wave of nausea rolled over her, then ebbed, leaving her panting over the edge of the bowl. It took another minute of slow, even, forced breathing, before she felt able to sit back down again on her haunches, kneeling in front of the toilet as if it were some sort of idol and she were paying obeisance.

Damn Barone, she thought. Damn him for taking away my sense of control! Damn him for having to leave me here like this. And, God, I hope he gets back soon!

A garbage scow was making its way slowly down the East River, its progress nearly imperceptible. The surface of the river was flat and gray with small white eddies matching the sky above. Barone watched from the window of the 4 East nurses' station office as the scow drifted toward the Queensborough Bridge. He looked back to the sheaf of papers spread out on the desk in front of him and once more scanned the nursing assignments for the past week. Monday night, when Mary Altman had died, Shirley Kyriakos had been the night nurse. Herbie Brown had died during the evening shift, when Sandy Herman was the charge nurse. On Friday, when Anne Delbert had died, the nursing schedule switched, and Lauren Nyquist had been scheduled as the night nurse, but her name was crossed out and Maureen Donnatelli had been penciled in. Three nights, three different nurses. The three unexplained deaths on his service—on Peter Lee's service—

had been a statistical freak. Other than the distinct possibility of his winning the Black Cloud Award, there was no cause for alarm.

Barone stretched and placed the nursing assignment sheets back into a manilla folder. His biggest problem would be to explain to Shelly Cohen, the head nurse, what he had been looking for in her records.

Barone stepped out of the office and handed the folder to the ward clerk. "Please page Shelly for me," he requested.

The clerk looked up at Barone. "She's at lunch. Maureen Donnatelli is the charge nurse."

"Didn't she work last night?"

The clerk shrugged. "She's in room four-oh-two. You can ask for yourself."

An uneasy feeling welled up from his stomach. If Maureen was working today, then who was on service last night? Had the nursing records been faked?

He found Maureen changing the linens of a bed-bound patient. She had rolled him against the opposite railing while she worked on the near side of the bed. She looked up as Barone approached.

"Maureen, can I ask you a question?"

"Sure," she answered, smoothing the sheet, "if you help me roll Mr. Burton here back toward me so I can finish the other side of the bed. My back is killing me."

"Is that a chronic problem?" asked Barone, walking around the bed.

"Only when I work double shifts," she answered.

"Oh, were you on last night?" Barone asked nonchalantly.

She paused and placed her hands against the small of her back, pushing forward against her spine. "They needed me to fill in when Lauren Nyquist, who was supposed to work a double, got sick and had to go home. I decided to work last night and today, so I could get the rest of the weekend off."

"That's rough," Barone sympathized.

"Oh, I'm not complaining." She helped Barone roll the patient to the other side of the bed. "Not compared to the hours that you doctors keep. Why just last night Dr. Lee was here at midnight to check up on one of his patients."

Peter Lee sat in the 4 East on-call room. The small table in front of him was littered with six patient charts. After Barone had walked off halfway during rounds to attend the Delbert autopsy, the remainder of the morning ritual had been brief. The interns then went about their chores—drawing blood, restarting intravenous lines, writing nursing orders. But for Peter it seemed to take an especially long time to get things done.

He needed three trips to the supply room before he had all of the items he needed to start Mr. Bergen's IV. Then he missed the vein, an easy forearm vein, three times and had to try the other arm. Writing his orders seemed to take forever. He could not concentrate. Mostly, he kept coming back to the thought of Barone examining Anne Delbert's body. The image stuck in his mind like a fish bone caught in the throat. It hurt him that Barone could not leave her in peace. After all she had been through, it was only right.

Once or twice it even crossed his mind that Barone might find something to link him with her death. But it had been quick and clean. There was no way to trace him—nothing, in fact, to trace. Unless, of course, they checked the fingerprints on the intravenous tubing. (No, the nurses would have thrown that out before sending the body to the morgue.) Or on the syringe. (No way to associate that with Anne Delbert.) Or what about . . .

He could not keep the thoughts away. They kept intruding into his work routine like alien beings not part of his own mind but rather thrust in from outside by a force beyond his control.

And it wasn't as if he had anything to feel guilty about. He had helped Anne Delbert. He had released her from pain and misery. He knew he was right. But the thoughts, the images kept coming.

Peter stared at the blank page in the chart in front of him. He had to write a progress note on Roscoe Bremmer. He held the pen, poised to write, but could not collect his thoughts. Barone was ruining his life. He looked down at the paper, saw Barone examining Anne Delbert's naked body. No, the woman was not Anne Delbert. It was Sylvia. *His* Sylvia, lying naked in front of Barone. *His* Sylvia, lying in Barone's bed. The image of Sylvia on the bed fused with that of Anne Delbert on the autopsy table. Peter felt a scream welling in the back of his throat. He stifled the voice within, let out only a muffled groan. Rubbing his eyes, he put his head down on the chart, sobbed silently. No tears would come.

Barone stood at the desk in the medical records room, waiting for the receptionist to finish taking a telephone request from the Emergency Room. He stared at the row upon row of floor-to-ceiling shelving, piled high with patient records, filed by birth dates. Several clerks in blue coats scurried through the morbid library locating charts.

The receptionist finally looked up at Barone. "Can I help you, doctor?" she asked in a tired voice that did not seem as if she meant it.

"Yes," answered Barone. "I would like to see the medical records on two patients: Mary Altman and Herbert Brown."

"Do you have their chart numbers?" asked the clerk, who suddenly seemed enlivened by the possibility that she might be able to turn down his request and send him to another office.

She seemed crestfallen when Barone pulled two index cards from his pocket, stamped with the hospital plates of the two patients. For each new patient, he routinely made up an index card, on which he jotted down the details of the case for his own files. The receptionist entered the numbers into her computer terminal as she read them off the cards. "I'm sorry, sir," she said, not sounding a bit sorry. "They're both deceased."

Barone snapped his fingers in feigned amazement. "Goddamn. I thought something was wrong with them on rounds this morning."

"Sir?" The girl looked up, puzzled.

Barone snorted. "I know they're both dead. I want the charts anyway."

The receptionist frowned, tapped the keys of her terminal once more. "Both charts are signed out to pathology." She sounded satisfied at last that she could not help him with his request.

"Thank you," said Barone, not feeling very thankful.

She looked up from her computer terminal, shaking her head gently as she watched him leave.

"Are you all right, Peter?" Harvey Krane placed a hand on his shoulder. It felt warm, soft. Comforting.

Peter sniffed, lifted his head from the desk. "I'm okay," he mumbled, turning to look at Harvey. His eyes were red, but dry.

"Is it Barone?" asked Harvey, simply.

Peter nodded wordlessly, blinked, tried to swallow. He stared out the window across the room at the dull, gray day.

"He's been riding you pretty hard. Everything that goes wrong on the ward, Maury blames on Barone, and Barone blames it on you." Harvey lifted his hand from Peter's shoulder, sat down across from him in a beat-up wooden desk chair.

Peter looked past him, out the window. He had had no idea Harvey was so sympathetic. And his touch was so soft. Almost involuntarily Peter nodded. "I think it has something to do with Sylvia," he said, not looking at Harvey.

"Probably." Harvey settled into the chair, eyeing Peter carefully. "I understand Barone has been getting pretty friendly with her. He might resent your . . . friendship with Sylvia."

Peter focused on Harvey for the first time. The warm gray eyes seemed as soft as his hands. "I can't believe that Sylvia would do this . . . That she would find . . . do . . . with Barone . . ." His voice was choked off by a rising spasm of his throat muscles.

Harvey leaned forward in his chair, his eyes locked on Peter's. "Women can be like that. They feel differently about relationships than"— his voice hitched slightly—"than a man does. Women want permanence and constant attention."

Peter stared into Harvey's eyes, lost in a trance. "I could have given her that."

"Of course you could." Harvey nodded solicitously. "But you are a man. You need something different, something more than that."

Peter searched the face across from him for a clue. "And what does a man need?"

Harvey's tongue flicked briefly out of the corner of his mouth, focusing Peter's attention on the perfect pink lips surrounded by the carefully cropped beard. As Harvey opened his mouth to answer, the lips seemed to envelop Peter. "Release," they answered.

Burt Jacobi was taking specimens for microscopic examination when Barone returned. Carefully slitting open the adrenal gland, he barely looked up when Barone entered. "Back again already? Have another death on your service?" he needled.

"No thanks," said Barone. "Three in one week seems to be enough."

Jacobi snorted, almost cutting his finger. Reluctantly, he looked up. "What can I do for you?"

Barone stared at the bits and pieces of organs on the autopsy table. At the next table, the assistant was sewing Anne Delbert's body closed with heavy twine. "I need to see the charts of the three patients from my service who died."

"Over there." Jacobi gestured over his shoulder to a small corner room. "They should still be in the morgue office." He returned to his slicing.

The office was a dimly lit cubicle that had been partitioned from the remainder of the autopsy room. Every surface was piled high with patient charts. It took Barone nearly fifteen minutes to locate the charts of the three patients from 4 East. He removed a pile of medical records from the only chair in the room, set them on the floor, then settled into the chair to review each chart, day by day.

He cleared off a space on the small desk and laid out the three charts, each of them open to the Emergency Room note he had written when the patient had first come to the hospital for his or her final admission. He scanned his notes, the nurses' notes, the intern and resident admission notes: nothing unusual. Next he paged through the doctor's progress notes. Most of these were written by Peter Lee or by himself, although occasionally he found a note scrawled by a consultant or one of the other interns covering the patient on night call. The style was dry medicalese, and Peter Lee's notes were even less informative than those of most interns. Each of the patients was thought to be improving, and then each of the records terminated abruptly in a death note: "Patient discovered cyanotic and pulseless and without respirations. Pupils fixed. No breath sounds. Declared dead at . . ." For Herbie Brown, there had been an attempt at resuscitation. Mary Altman and Anne Delbert had been cold when they were found, and no attempt had been made to revive them.

Next Barone reviewed the nurses' notes for each patient. Despite being filled with cryptic abbreviations such as "OOB x 2" (patient out of bed twice) and "BM x 1", it was clear that each of the three patients was stable or improving up until the time that he or she was suddenly found dead. Each nurse's record also terminated in a stereotyped death note, noting the time of death, disposition of the body, and who claimed the personal items of the patient. There was no mention, by any of the hospital personnel, that it was in any way unusual for these patients, in the midst of improving, suddenly to be found dead. Barone marveled: Only in a hospital could three medically stable individuals turn up dead in one week, and no one even think it was unusual.

He turned to the laboratory reports. Each chart contained a computer printout of the results of the laboratory tests from that admission. Vertically arranged in rows were the dates and times at which each laboratory specimen had been received in the laboratory office. The names of the different tests were set up in columns, across the page. Under the title of each test a normal range of values was printed:

Date/Time	Serum Sodium (normal: 135 to 145 meq/l)	Serum Potassium (normal 3.5 to 5.0 meq/l)	Serum Chloride (normal 105 to 115 meq/l)	Serum Bicarbonate (normal 18 to 26 meq/l)
9/3, 9:36 P.M.	137	3.3	109	23
9/5, 10:27 A.M.	142	3.9	110	23

Every result that fell outside of the normal range was marked by the lab computer with a black box. Barone's eyes scanned the columns of numbers. Mary Altman had come in dehydrated, and her serum sodium had been too high. But her last blood sample showed this was improving. In fact, the only abnormality in her last blood sample was a moderate elevation of her serum potassium to 6.8. Barone cross-checked the time of this last sample with her time of death. It had been drawn about six hours after her death, presumably as a routine pathological sample during her autopsy.

Barone flipped through the pages of laboratory reports on Herbie Brown. Whole columns of results were followed by black boxes, but it was clear that all of the abnormalities were improving, up to the very last lab report. The timing for this blood sample revealed that it was drawn during the resuscitation attempt. Herbie Brown's final potassium value had jumped from 3.7 earlier that evening all the way to 6.9.

Finally Barone checked Anne Delbert's chart. Only her liver tests had been abnormal, which was not surprising, considering what he had seen of that organ on the autopsy table. All of the serum sodium and potassium reports were normal, up to the last one drawn the previous morning before she was found dead.

Barone closed the chart and leaned back in the chair, sighed. No help, really. It had seemed as if a pattern might emerge with the serum potassium values, but Barone knew these were often high postmortem. And Anne Delbert's values were flat-out normal. He stared at the cold fluorescent ceiling lights for a moment. No inspiration was forthcoming.

Barone lifted himself from the chair and walked back into the autopsy room. Jacobi was recording the numbers of his tissue samples and his assistant was rinsing Anne Delbert's blood off the dissecting instruments.

Barone grunted his thanks as he passed Jacobi, who nodded his affirmation silently. Then, as he reached the hallway leading out of the autopsy room, Barone turned as an afterthought. "Burt?" he asked tentatively.

Jacobi looked up, slightly annoyed. "What is it now?"

Barone flushed. "I'm sorry to disturb you, but I've noticed that the postmortem serum potassium values on the two other patients were pretty high. How much does that normally go up after death?"

"How high were they?" Jacobi shot back, showing a glimmer of interest.

"Six point eight and six point nine."

"How long after death were the samples taken?"

Barone frowned. "The first one was taken at autopsy, six hours after death. The second one was drawn during the resuscitation attempt."

Jacobi frowned. "Well, in that case, both of those values are really on the borderline. After death, potassium leaks out of the blood cells, the muscles, and the brain. Normally, this increases serum potassium by roughly zero point one millequivalents per liter each hour. But during a resuscitation attempt, there can be a lot of muscle damage. If the resuscitation is going well, and the blood circulates adequately, it can pick up a lot of potassium."

"How high can it go?"

Jacobi thought for a minute. "Usually to between six point zero and six point five. But occasionally I've seen it near seven point zero. Never more than that, though." The telephone rang. Jacobi nodded to the diener. "Can you answer that?"

Barone watched the diener walk over to the wall telephone. The man started to write down a message. "So the values of six point eight and six point nine for my patients are suspicious—"

"But inconclusive." Jacobi completed the sentence for him.

"You know," continued Barone, "I can't help but feel that there is something going on here. Something wrong. Only I can't put my finger on it."

The diener interrupted, slipped the telephone message into Jacobi's hand. He scanned it and handed it to Barone. "Maybe you're right."

On the paper was neatly printed:

LABORATORY TELEPHONE REPORT
Postmortem blood: Anne Delbert
Sodium 3.8
Potassium 7.3
Chloride 106
Bicarbonate 26

Peter Lee stared again at the blank sheet of paper in front of him. It was stamped at the top with the name "James McLaughlin" followed by his hospital number, address, and birth date. In half an hour, Peter had not been able to write anything at all. Disconnected facts—a chest X ray, blood counts, the patient's fluid intake—paraded through his mind without forming a recognizable pattern. He simply could not organize his thoughts into a coherent clinical impression.

It was like everything else in his life, thought Peter: broken and fragmented. He loved Sylvia, but his affection was not returned, at least not openly. Deep inside, he knew, she still loved him. The way his mother had loved him, even after his father had driven her away.

He leaned back in the chair, eyes closed. The images crowded in: X rays, lab reports, patients. Sylvia's face, so much like that of his mother. She had wanted him to take good care of his patients, and with her help, he had. Every afternoon at checkout rounds, she had reviewed his work, picked up the small errors. More importantly, she had put things into perspective, provided a touchstone for him.

Without her help, he was adrift in a sea of pain, his own and others'. Bits of flotsam—the patient charts, prescriptions, lab reports—floated by him. But when Peter reached out for them, they floated and bobbed just beyond his grasp. He could no more rebuild his life than a castaway could rebuild his yacht from the bits of debris floating on the ocean the morning after a storm.

Peter squeezed his eyes shut, shook his head. When he opened his eyes there was only the chart of James McLaughlin. He thumbed through the laboratory reports. "Serum sodium . . . chest X rays . . . sputum cultures . . ." He could not organize the facts in his head.

The medication pages, filled with drugs, dosages, and times of administration, provided no help. He flipped through the nurses' notes. The day nurse for the last shift had written, "Patient complains of continuing cough." Peter mechanically transferred the information to his own note.

His hand poised over the page, Peter tried to finish the note. "Think, damn you," he muttered, but his mind was numb, the same feeling in his brain as he sometimes felt in his hand after sleeping on it all night. Finally, he finished the note, as he had each of the others that day, "Progress continues." He signed the note and closed the chart.

Peter dropped the charts off at the nurses' station as he left the ward. He knew his work was futile. Even when he did it well (and even he could tell that he was no longer doing that), he only ministered to those who would improve anyway without his help and prolonged the agony of those who were sure to die despite it.

Barone walked home from the hospital in the fading evening light, staring at the gray sidewalk of Seventieth

Street. Three high serum potassiums. That was too much of a coincidence. And at least one of them was well out of the range that could be accounted for by natural circumstances.

If he were right, and if these three patients' high serum potassium levels had something to do with their deaths, then it was likely the patient had been deliberately overdosed. This was more than just a morbid intellectual exercise with Burt Jacobi. It was triple murder.

Barone opened the door to his apartment building and crossed the lobby. Of course, none of the serum potassium values were in the clearly lethal range. It would be difficult to prove that an injection of potassium had been the cause of death. But why would anyone go to the trouble of injecting three patients with potassium, and then kill them some other way? And if they had not died of the high serum potassium, what had killed them?

The elevator door opened. Barone stepped inside and, almost without thinking, pressed the button for Sylvia's floor. He gravitated toward her; he needed her help.

He fumbled in his pocket, found the key that Sylvia had given him, opened the door. The room was dim with the failing twilight.

"Chuck?" she called out to him. Her voice seemed thinner, more weak than even that morning.

He sat on the edge of the bed and gently caressed her hand. "Are you all right?"

"Not really." She smiled weakly and reached over to turn on the lamp. "I've been nauseous all day. I threw up twice."

Barone stared into her eyes. Usually clear and gray they now seemed glazed. He ran his fingers over her cheek. "I'm sorry, sweetheart." He leaned over and embraced her. His lips brushed against her forehead. The skin was hot and dry. "You'll be okay now. I'll stay with you.'' He laid her gently back against the pillows.

"Why are you so late?'' she asked. "I thought this was going to be a simple Saturday rounds. Out by noon.'' She looked at the clock. "It's almost seven o'clock.''

Barone stared at the purplish gray light filtering in through the blinds. He hesitated to bring her into this. But he needed her insight, her judgment.

At last he answered: "I've been looking into some deaths on my service.''

Sylvia propped herself up on one elbow. "You mean Mary Altman and Herbie Brown?''

Barone nodded. "And there was a third one last night: Anne Delbert.''

"The lady with the colon cancer? The one you saved in the ER?''

Barone smiled wryly. "Resuscitated, but not saved. It turned out her colon cancer was inoperable, and she had constant pain.''

"What happened to her?'' Sylvia asked.

"No one is sure.'' He shrugged. "The night nurse found her dead. Marilyn Silver didn't even call for the cardiac arrest team. The body was already cold, so she just pronounced her dead.''

"You sound as if the death was a surprise.''

"It was. I know she had terminal cancer, but there was no reason for her to die suddenly last night.''

Sylvia sat herself up against the pillows. "People with cancer can die suddenly for lots of reasons. She could have had a pulmonary embolus. Or a hemorrhage in her brain.''

Barone nodded. "That's why I went down to the morgue to watch the autopsy. I went over the entire case with Burt Jacobi.''

Sylvia shivered involuntarily. "That man is a real ghoul.''

"Yes," Barone agreed, "but a very smart one. He really knows his stuff. And he found no cause of death. Not for Anne Delbert, and not for either of the other patients."

"That can happen," mused Sylvia.

"Yes," he agreed again, "but not to me."

"Chuck, what makes you better than anyone else? No doctor likes to see his patients die. But we generally don't take it as a personal affront."

Barone stood up, began pacing in front of the windows as he talked. "I know that I tend to take things too personally, Sylvia. I've been worried that I might be blowing this up out of proportion. But these are three *lives* we are talking about. That's why I need your perspective on this. Do you really think I am making too much of it?"

Sylvia sat up gingerly on the edge of the bed, chose her words carefully. "Is there any reason, other than the timing that makes you suspicious?"

Barone sat down in the chair across from her. "Two things. First, all three patients had high serum potassium levels."

"How high?"

"Six point eight and six point nine in the first two. I was about to write the whole thing off when the potassium level on Anne Delbert came back: seven point three. Jacobi thinks the first two are high, but within the limits of what they can see at autopsy. But the last one is out of the ballpark for postmortem changes."

"It could be a lab error. Maybe the blood specimens were hemolyzed."

Barone shook his head. "Not very likely for all three specimens."

"No," she answered. "I suppose not. But that's still pretty thin evidence. What else have you got?"

Barone took a deep breath, looked down at the floor.

"All three patients belonged to Peter Lee, and he was present on the floor when each of them died."

Sylvia's cheeks turned cherry red. "Of course he was there! He's an intern on the goddamned floor. He's there at least one hundred hours a week."

Barone looked up, caught Sylvia's eyes. The gray in them was smoldering. "I knew you would react this way. It was one of the reasons that I wanted to talk to you before doing anything else." He stood up and began pacing again.

"You know that I have had a"—his voice caught in his throat—"a personality conflict with Peter since that night in the ER. You also know that I feel strongly about"—he hesitated again—"about our relationship. . . ."

He sat down suddenly across from Sylvia. The gray of her eyes was softer now. "Oh hell, Sylvia, I love you. I know that I feel jealous that you had a relationship with Peter. . . ."

Sylvia raised herself from the bed unsteadily, stood with her back to him, looking out the slats in the window blinds. "He was my intern," she said slowly. "We had no . . ." She shook her head in frustration, sat down heavily on the arm of Barone's chair. "We shared our patients, nothing else." Her face was flushed, but not with fever. "It was nothing like . . ." She leaned back against his shoulder.

"I know, Sylvia, I know." He tucked her head in against his shoulder. "But Peter doesn't. He practically worships you. And I know that his feelings about you have a very strong effect on the way I think about him. Mary Altman died while Peter was on call. Herbie Brown died just after he checked out for the evening. Peter was probably the last person to see each of them alive, but that could just be coincidence."

He stroked her hair, continued carefully. "But Anne Delbert died late last night, when Marilyn Silver was on call. One of the night nurses happened to see Peter on the floor about an hour before her body was found."

Sylvia pulled away from him. "That's still not good enough." Her voice was soft, flat. "It could still be a coincidence."

"I know that," Barone answered. "But it could be something . . . more than that. Sylvia, for the first time in my life I just don't trust my own instincts. If it were anyone other than Peter I would probably have reported this already."

"Or decided to overlook it," she interjected.

He nodded vigorously. "Exactly. I just am not sure that I am being completely rational."

Sylvia slipped her arm behind his muscular neck. They sat for a long moment in the soft yellow glow of the bedside lamp, listening to each other's breathing. Finally she murmured, "I think I have the same problem."

He drew her toward him, kissed her on the forehead, then lightly on the lips. She nuzzled her head against his shoulder. "I love you too, Chuck. Peter is just a friend. But I would hate to see you pursue this. Everyone knows that we are seeing each other. If nothing turned up, they would assume it was jealousy . . ." Her voice trailed off.

"I also think I know Peter pretty well," she continued. "I can't believe that he has anything to do with this string of deaths. In all the time that I worked with him, I never saw anything that made me think he was capable of . . . murder.

"Every instinct I have is crying out for me to tell you that you should drop this. And that is exactly why I don't trust myself to decide, either." She looked up into his eyes. "I don't think there is any choice. You have to take this to Maurie Benson."

Peter Lee picked his way along the East River track, trying to avoid the joggers and the piles of dog crap.

Even on a cold gray late afternoon, there were both runners and dogs about, each engaged in their customary activity. The surface of the river reflected the flat gray of the sky, only here and there broken by a white crested eddy, as evidence of the roiling undertow.

Harvey's comments stuck in his mind like a dagger stabbed between his ribs. No, he corrected himself, Harvey had not placed the dagger, he had just twisted it a bit. Sylvia had been the one who had betrayed him.

Sweet Sylvia! He knew that she had cared for him. They had worked so well together, through the night, side by side. She had always been gentle and supportive. Her quiet strength, her calm had made the pain of watching his patients' suffering almost bearable for him. She had never said anything to him about her feelings, but he knew that she was in love with him.

It could not be Sylvia's fault. A love like theirs could not just die. It had to have been killed. By an interloper. By Barone.

Peter could not really blame her. After all, he had been reticent to show his affection. The timing had been all wrong, the opportunity never quite right.

But she had to know how he felt! Everyone did! Harvey had said so! Marilyn knew, too. Only a demon like Barone could come into the midst of such a sweet, pure relationship and subvert it with sex.

He knew that was the answer. Barone had seduced Sylvia. His Sylvia. He could have to win her back. And then he could deal with Barone. . . .

In the failing twilight, a few remaining joggers and a pair of lovers walking hand-in-hand avoided the intense young man standing along the railing, looking distractedly out over the river. As they approached him and heard him talking heatedly to himself, they gave him wide berth. A dog, unleashed by its owner to take an evening run, sniffed at Peter Lee's pants leg. Without looking, without even thinking, Peter kicked his leg back, viciously catching the animal's chest with his heel. There was a crunching sound as the shoe broke several ribs, then the animal, before it could complain, was sailing back through the air. The dog hit the ground, stunned, then began to bleat piteously. Peter Lee walked the other direction, into the night.

Barone sat in the chair, cradling Sylvia with his arm, staring at the ceiling in the dim lamplight. She had fallen asleep against his shoulder, long before they might have gotten around to making love. The rise and fall of her chest against his arm was hypnotizing.

He knew that she was right, as usual. He had to take his suspicions to Maurie. Benson had to know eventually. He would have to make the decision to dismiss Peter Lee from the residency training program. But Barone was the fourth resident to supervise Peter and the only one to have had a significant problem with him. And Benson was sure to bring up his personal relationship with Sylvia.

As Peter walked west toward Central Park a light rain began to fall. He huddled under his windbreaker, blinking as the small droplets hit his eyelashes. The wetness felt good against the burning of his cheeks. He knew he had to pull himself together, but it was so hard to think clearly. Whenever he seemed to be following a train of thought, he would suddenly find himself derailed, thinking about Sylvia. Even when he could follow an idea for a few moments, the thoughts would seem to twist and turn, suddenly changing into something else. The only consistent thread seemed to be the pain of rejection and futility—in everything he did.

He shivered, his hair matted by the rain, no longer even noticing the raindrops. A couple passed, sharing an umbrella. They shied away from the strange young man, mumbling to himself as he walked blindly into the night. Peter did not even noticed them. And neither they, nor he, realized that some of the drops running down his cheeks were tears.

Sunday Morning, September 15

Marilyn Silver looked down at the front of her oxford cloth shirt and pulled nervously at the lowest button. The shirtfront always tended to gap open between the buttons holding the strong fabric tautly across her ample breasts. It was an effect that she often found useful: She had noticed that she could almost at will attract a man's eyes to her bosom, a technique that was both disarming and distracting. Other times she wished that she was flat chested, such as when she talked before a group of colleagues and found herself checking her shirtfront every thirty seconds. This morning she was sitting in the 4 East nurses' station across from Harvey Krane, who, she knew, probably would not care to look even if her shirt opened entirely. It was his indifference to that personal feature about which she was least insecure that made her so uncomfortable with him.

"Where do you think they could be?" Harvey examined his watch. As usual, every hair was in place, his beard perfectly trimmed. She marveled that, after a night on call, even his clothes looked freshly pressed. "I would really like to get out of here early today." The perfect pink lips spoke each word a little too precisely.

Marilyn purposefully looked out the window, as if she expected to see Peter Lee or Chuck Barone floating by on a barge on the East River. "It's not like Barone to be late.'' She looked back at Harvey. "Did he ever check back with you about Anne Delbert?''

Krane shook his head. "He never even came back for checkout rounds. That was really spooky. Barone is always so compulsive about rounds.''

Marilyn nodded, pursed her lips. "He was really broken up about her death. I guess, after saving her in the ER, he kind of felt responsible for her.''

"Like the old Chinese custom?''

She nodded again. "Something like that. You don't think he holds me responsible for her death, do you?''

Harvey shrugged. "Who can tell with Barone? Since he's been seeing Sylvia he's really come unglued. One minute he bawls you out for not resuscitating a dead patient, then the next minute he disappears, leaving me with forty live ones. Anyway, I wouldn't worry too much if I were you. No one can criticize your handling of the case. Even if Anne Delbert had not been terminally ill with cancer, she was certainly way beyond resuscitation when you found her.''

Marilyn looked down at her shirtfront again, blushing. "Thanks, Harvey, but you really don't have to—''

"No,'' he insisted, "the one who was really at fault there was Peter Lee.''

Marilyn looked up quizzically. "Peter?''

"Yes.'' Harvey nodded forcefully. "Have you read any of his notes lately?''

"I have noticed that they have been getting pretty sketchy—''

"Sketchy? How about nonexistent. And when he does write a note it says nothing. Like last night, one of Peter's patients, Mr. McLaughlin could hardly breathe. His pneumonia was so bad that his right lung was almost entirely consolidated. I had to transfer him to the respiratory intensive care unit. When I went to check his chest X ray from yesterday afternoon, it was much worse. And what did Peter write in his progress note yesterday? 'Progress continues.' He had never even looked at the X ray!"

" 'Progress continues,' " mused Marilyn. "That was also Peter's last note on Anne Delbert. He has been really distant lately. I wonder how much of this is because Barone is dating Sylvia?"

Harvey was impatient. "What if it is? He hasn't got the right to sacrifice patient care on the basis of some"— he caught himself—"some emotional involvement."

"Especially if it is with a woman?" Marilyn asked softly, almost involuntarily.

Harvey reddened. "With anyone!" He hesitated, then continued in a tensely controlled harsh whisper. "I've been on call for twenty-six hours, and this is my only Sunday off this month. I just want to get the hell out of here."

"I see," said Marilyn archly. "As long as you get out on time, you would be willing to leave your patients with Peter on call tonight."

"Are you volunteering?" Harvey nearly hissed.

Marilyn blushed, did not answer. She too wanted to start rounds so she could get her work done and get on with her day. She stared out the window again, searching for the lost intern and resident on the gray face of the East River.

A nurses' aide interrupted. "Dr. Barone just called from the Emergency Room. He wants you to meet him there."

Barone stood outside the examining room, poised to enter. Then he rocked back on his heels and folded his arms, bringing one hand up to cradle his chin. He stared intently at the tiled floor, rocking from his heels to his toes and back again. Finally he turned, nearly running over Marilyn Silver, who had been standing wordlessly behind him, waiting for a proper moment to speak.

"What the—" He barely stopped short of knocking her down.

Marilyn blushed. "I'm sorry. We just got your message and—"

"I know," Barone interrupted. "I completely forgot about rounds. It's just that Sylvia is so . . ." His voice trailed off, his eyes fixed on the examining room door.

"Is she hurt?" asked Harvey.

Barone shook his head, not turning to acknowledge Harvey. "No, she was up all night, vomiting. I thought she just had the flu. But this morning she was so weak, she couldn't even stand. I had to call an ambulance."

Burt Rhinehart, the ER resident, emerged from the examining room. "She's pretty dehydrated, probably from all the vomiting. But I think she has more than just the flu. The right upper quadrant of her abdomen is tender, and she's a bit jaundiced. I think she has hepatitis."

"Hepatitis!" Barone's eyes were wide. "And jaundice! I didn't even notice—"

"The jaundice is pretty mild. If it developed gradually over a few days, it would be fairly easy to overlook."

"A few days! Overlooked! I can't believe . . ." Barone sank back against a stretcher cart parked in the hallway.

"Listen, Chuck." Rhinehart's voice lost its professional edge. "You weren't exactly examining her under bright fluorescent lights. You know that incandescent lighting casts a yellowish tint. And when the lights are low . . ." He shrugged, his right eyebrow arching suggestively.

Barone suddenly pushed him away, slamming the young doctor with such force that he hit the opposite wall of the hallway with a thud. He stood, back pressed against the wall, while Marilyn nervously edged her way between the two.

"He didn't make Sylvia sick, Chuck."

Barone flared again. "Are you insinuating that I did?"

Marilyn backed away a half step. "That's not fair, Chuck. I didn't say that. You know as well as I do that lots of medical personnel get hepatitis, mostly from patient contact."

Barone slumped against the stretcher again. He rubbed his eyes; the lashes glistened with suppressed tears. "I know, Marilyn, I know. But I can't help thinking that if I had recognized it, I could have done something. . . ."

"You know there's nothing you could have done."

Barone shook his head silently, his right hand cupped over his eyes.

Rhinehart silently walked into the nurses' station and conferred with the clerk. He returned a moment later. "She's going to Four East."

Barone looked up, his face drained of color. "You can't do that. Four East is my ward."

Rhinehart shrugged, seeming to enjoy his intransigence. "Sorry, but she has to go into an isolation room. The only one open in the entire hospital is on Four East. I'll have the ward team from Four West cover her."

Barone nodded mutely.

Barone, Marilyn, and Harvey rode the elevator to 4 East with Sylvia. She lay quietly on the stretcher, her eyes closed, an intravenous solution dripping into her thin arm. In the fluorescent light of the elevator, her skin was only slightly yellow, about the color of a light suntan. Barone squeezed her hand, and she blinked at him, smiled. He could see now that the whites of her eyes were also off-color. He cursed himself silently.

Barone helped the Emergency Room nurse push the stretcher to the 4 East nurses' station. It was a trip he had made more than a hundred times with patients, but now part of himself lay on the stretcher. Everything, the high ceilings, the faded hallway tiles, the wooden rails along the hallway, seemed new and vaguely unreal, the way a familiar name, repeated multiple times, begins to lose its original meaning and sound strange.

Peter Lee met them at the nurses' station. He was still wearing the rumpled shirt and pants from the previous night, his hair uncombed, face unshaven, and eyes bloodshot. He asked, of no one in particular, "Is Sylvia okay?"

Barone nodded silently. His first impulse was to shield her from Peter, but he knew Sylvia would never allow it.

Sylvia stirred, rolled onto her side. "I'm all right," she mumbled.

"What happened?" Peter eyed Sylvia like a child whose pet had been struck by a passing car.

"Hepatitis," answered Barone curtly. "She was vomiting all night. She's going to be on our floor, but the Four West team will take care of her."

"She seems so weak." Peter reached for her hand.

Barone bristled, despite (or perhaps because) he recognized in Peter's voice a concern that mirrored his own. All he said was: "The nurses will put her to bed. Come on, let's make rounds."

Barone examined his watch as he walked down the hall to Maurie Benson's office. Rounds had been considerably shorter than usual. There had been none of the typical battles; each participant had been, in his or her own way, too distracted to fight.

Barone hoped that Maurie would still be in his office. He knew that when Benson was on service he would come in early, every day of the week to examine the patients. Maurie once had explained that he wanted to check the patients before the phone started ringing and the day's appointments began. The residents not so secretly suspected that Maurie came in early to check up on the patients who had come in the night before, so he could read up on their diseases, to show up the residents if they missed anything at attending rounds later in the morning.

The wooden door to Maurie's office was old and beaten up, with a translucent glass panel on which was stenciled the room number 327 and Maurie's name and title in gothic black letters. The light from a desk lamp showed through the glass. Barone knocked and entered without waiting for an answer.

Maurie was seated at his desk, poring over a computer printout. "Come in," he said belatedly, without lifting his head. The room was small and dingy, furnished in hand-me-down furniture, from the department of medicine office, which had recently been refurbished. The furnishings of the office bespoke both the lack of concern its occupant had for the trappings of power and the level of esteem that the hospital administration showed for a man who devoted his life to training residents, rather than producing research. It was no accident, thought Barone, that Benson's name was applied to the door in a manner so impermanent that a janitor working with a razor blade could, in three minutes time, end his tenure.

Barone sat in a faded green chair, its vinyl cushion held together by tape, while Maurie finished examining the printout. "If our hospital census does not pick up," he muttered, "we will have to cut back on residency positions." Finally he looked up, and seeing Barone, stiffened slightly. "What can I do for you, Chuck?"

Barone swallowed hard. His throat was suddenly dry. "I want to discuss a problem on my service."

Maurie nodded.

"As you know, we have had three deaths on my ward in the last week."

Maurie nodded again. "That's right: Altman, Brown, and Delbert."

Barone tried to swallow again. "All three patients were autopsied. I talked to the pathology resident who was responsible for the postmortems. He could find no cause of death. In any of the three."

Maurie considered for a minute. "Well, there's nothing unusual in that. The pathologists end up shrugging after lots of autopsies. But at least we know that none of your three patients had very long to live in any case."

Barone nodded. "But there was no particular reason for any of the three to die at the times that they did."

Maurie shrugged. "It happens. What's the matter, Barone, are you afraid that you'll get the Black Cloud Award? I can't declare them not dead, you know, just so you won't look bad."

Barone flushed. "That's not what concerns me." He tried to swallow, again unsuccessfully, then finally blurted out: "I think they may have been killed."

Maurie sat still in his chair as the taunting half smile slowly dissolved from his face. "What are you saying, Barone?" The tone was tough, even for Maurie.

"I mean that I think all three may have been murdered."

"For what reason?" Maurie shot back.

Barone shrugged. "I don't know."

"How do you propose that they were killed? The pathologist found no cause of death—"

"Yes, but there was one abnormality in all three cases. The serum potassium was too high."

"That could be lethal." Maurie nodded. "How high was it?"

"Six point eight, six point nine, and seven point three."

Benson snorted. "Were those postmortem levels?"

Barone nodded.

"Those numbers are not all that high for postmortem

potassium levels. Even more important, they are not high enough to stop a healthy heart.''

"But all three are unexplainedly elevated," insisted Barone. "That is too much of a coincidence, unless they were deliberately injected with potassium—"

"But not enough to kill them," finished Maurie, his eyes narrowing into slits. "And just who do you think this nonpotassium nonmurderer might be?"

Barone held his breath for a second, then exhaled slowly. "Peter Lee."

"Peter Lee," Benson repeated, tonelessly.

"Yes." Barone nodded. "He was present on the ward during the nights of all three deaths. And he was not even on call two of those nights."

Benson leaned back in his chair, as if examining the ceiling. "I see, and now you want to make it a capital offense for an intern to show concern for a patient by visiting him on a night off."

"I know it's just an inference," added Barone lamely, "but what if I am right?"

"An inference?" Maurie leaned across the desk. "How about a slander? You want me to believe that one of our own interns is inexplicably going around at night murdering the patients whose lives he has worked all day to save? And what would you have me do?"

Again Barone found it impossible to swallow. "I think that Peter should be suspended until we work this out."

Maurie sat on the edge of his chair, as if about to pounce. "Do you realize what you are saying, Barone? You want me to suspend one of our interns on suspicion of murder. And do you think that I should call the New York police to investigate? If not, I could be held as an accessory after the fact."

Barone lowered his eyes. "I guess you would have to call them in."

Maurie nodded, licked his lower lip. "And if I told

the police, how long do you think that it would take for the press to find out? I can see the banner headline in the *New York Times:* 'Intern Suspended for Killing Three at Manhattan General Hospital.' And what do you think that would do to our fucking census?'' He slapped the sheaf of computer printout down on the desk.

Maurie stopped for a moment to compose himself. "Chuck, you are a good resident, but you are letting this thing between you and Peter Lee get out of hand. Everyone in the hospital knows that he had a crush on Sylvia. And your relationship with her is no secret. If I could split up you and Peter, I would. But it's too late now to change the schedule. So you are just going to have to live with each other for the rest of the month.''

Barone kept his eyes fixed on the computer printout on Maurie's desk. He struggled to control his quavering voice. "Peter's work has been getting progressively worse lately.''

"Don't you think I know that?'' retorted Maurie. "I read the patient charts every morning. His notes are miserable, when he bothers to write them at all. His performance at rounds has been even worse. But I hold *you* responsible for that, Barone. You are the resident. You're supposed to watch those interns like a hawk. When one of them stumbles, you're supposed to pick him up and help him out—not stick in the knife and give it a twist.''

Barone glared at Benson across the desk. "I can't do his goddamned job for him.''

"No?'' asked Maurie. "Well maybe you should. In view of Peter's background, I think that you are going to have to make a special effort to give him the support that he needs.''

Barone held his breath again, then exhaled slowly. "In view of Peter's background . . . ?''

Maurie reddened, dismissed the comment with a wave of his hand. "I think we've beaten this thing into the ground. I'll expect you to watch Peter's work very closely."

He returned to his printout as Barone slipped out through the beat-up door.

Peter Lee stared out of the window in the 4 East nurses' station. Below him the East River flowed by, gray and lifeless, carrying along small bits of debris in its mindless currents. His thoughts kept returning to Sylvia, lying on the stretcher like a wounded animal. His Sylvia! And Barone had missed the jaundice. Bullshit. Barone never missed anything clinically. He had to have done it on purpose. He was hiding something. Maybe Barone was a hepatitis carrier. That must be it! The selfish bastard had stolen his Sylvia, then infected her.

"Can I check out now?" It was more a demand than a question. Harvey sat down and unfolded a sheet of paper listing the names of his patients and the clinical status of each one.

Peter did not answer. Harvey began anyway: "Langhorn has ulcerative colitis. He's stable, with minimal rectal bleeding, but you need to check his 'crit about ten P.M. Wiesky is six days postmyocardial infarction, with no complications. Sheehan is . . ." He droned on, recounting the status of each patient and what tests or examinations they would need that evening. "And Gorman is recovering from pneumonia, should go home tomorrow." Harvey looked up from his sheet. Peter was still staring out the window. "Did you hear what I said?"

Peter looked back suddenly, the intensity of his pain focused upon Harvey's soft gray eyes. "Gorman, pneumonia," he parroted. "Sure, I heard." They both knew he was lying.

"Look." Harvey dropped his eyes to the sign-out sheet to avoid Peter's gaze. "It's written down here. If there are any problems, you can call me at home. We . . . I mean, I should be there after nine o'clock." He looked back up; Peter's black, unseeing eyes were boring into him. Finally he managed, "Is it Sylvia's hepatitis?"

Peter blinked, and his eyes became dewy. He sniffed. "That bastard Barone. First he seduces her, then he . . ." The words trailed off.

Harvey nodded agreement. "Barone is an asshole. But it's not all his fault. I mean, with all due respect to Sylvia—she's a great resident and all—but women are just inherently . . . unreliable."

Peter's eyes flashed anger, and Harvey instinctively backed off. "I mean, Peter, she's a great lady. But all women are unpredictable."

Peter sniffed again. "I can't understand what made Sylvia go out with Barone."

Harvey's voice was soothing. "Of course not. No real man can. Women will do that to you. But you can always understand another man." He stood up, placed a soft hand on Peter's shoulder.

It was warm, comforting. "I just wish she weren't so sick."

Harvey placed his arm around Peter's shoulder. There was no resistance. Rather Peter huddled under the wing of the first sympathetic human contact he had had in days. "Me too," said Harvey hollowly. "Me too."

Barone sat at Sylvia's bedside, watching her sleep. He had never before been aware how uncomfortable the bedside chairs in the hospital rooms really were. As he shifted in his seat, watching the afternoon sun glint off the drops in the intravenous chamber, Sylvia began to stir.

"Chuck?" she murmured, blinking in the shaft of sunlight falling across her face.

Barone reached out and brushed a strand of hair from her face. "I'm here, Sylvia."

She held his palm against her face, kissed it. "How long have I been asleep?"

"All day, almost." Barone hitched the chair up closer to the bed. "You were pretty tired after last night."

Sylvia nodded, studied the intravenous line. "I guess that I must have gotten pretty dehydrated from all the vomiting." She stared across the room, out the window, trying to get her bearings. "What ward am I in?"

"Four East. It was the only ward in the hospital with an open isolation room."

"Four East?" She was incredulous. "But that means—"

"The Four West house staff will be taking care of you," he interjected. "Too many conflicts in the Four East group."

"You mean Peter?" she asked, a sharp edge to her voice.

"I mean that I wouldn't trust myself to take care of your medical problems."

"Well, I would trust you. And Peter too."

Barone stroked her hand. "Take it easy, Syl. We all agreed that it would be better if the Four West team took over. Barry Grant is the resident, and he's very good."

Sylvia propped herself up on one elbow. "Did you talk to Maurie?"

Barone looked down at the floor. "I saw him for a few minutes this morning. He was mostly concerned about the hospital census and what would happen if the story got out about a crazed intern killing his patients. I don't think he took my theory seriously at all."

"Or at least he doesn't want to take your theory seriously."

"No one would want to believe that kind of story.

Anyway, he has a point. If I am wrong, it would be very damaging. Both to the hospital and to Peter.''

Sylvia's cheeks colored slightly. ''And what if you're right?''

Barone shrugged. ''What can I do? Maurie's only response was to make me responsible for watching over Peter more closely. But he said one thing that kind of disturbed me. Something about, how 'given Peter's background,' I should be especially careful to provide the support that he needs.''

''What did he mean about Peter's background?''

''I don't know. That's what is bothering me. When I asked him what he meant, Maurie just cut me off. Like he had said something that he was not supposed to have let out.'' Barone stopped for a moment. ''I wonder if Peter had some sort of trouble in medical school.''

''Academic trouble?'' Sylvia asked.

Barone nodded.

''I don't think so. Peter once told me that when he graduated medical school he was elected to Alpha Omega Alpha, the medical honor society.''

''What medical school did he go to?'' Barone queried.

''Johns Hopkins. He grew up in Baltimore.''

Barone shrugged. ''Well, he certainly didn't have any problem with his academic background. I wonder what Maurie could have meant?''

Sylvia shrugged. ''Perhaps he meant something emotional. Peter has been pretty withdrawn lately.''

''I know,'' Barone agreed. ''By the way''—he cleared his throat—''I switched my call night around so that I would always be here when Peter is on call.''

''You mean that you don't trust him with me on the ward.''

Barone smiled, squeezed her hand. ''Maurie's orders.''

* * *

Sylvia only picked at her dinner; each forkful was a major effort. Urged on by Barone, she took small bites of mashed potatoes. No amount of exhortation could persuade her to attack the shriveled piece of baked chicken on her plate.

After dinner he held her hand in silence. She fell back asleep as the sunlight faded, and he continued to cradle her hand for nearly an hour. Watching the intravenous line drip its nourishment into her veins, he kept turning the problem of Peter Lee's "background" over and over in his mind. If Maurie had not been referring to Peter's education, then what had he meant? Was he referring to Peter's family? Even Sylvia did not know much about that. And how could he check into Peter's family background? He certainly could not ask Peter.

It was like trying to get the medical history on a comatose patient. Invariably, the part of the history that the people who brought the patient into the hospital did not know (or would not tell you) turned out to be the most crucial in diagnosing the cause of the coma. And the patient was no help. So the only way to get any useful information was to check the patient's old medical records.

Gently, Barone released Sylvia's limp hand and straightened up in the dim light of her bedside lamp. He kissed her cheek softly and walked into the hall toward the telephone in the nurses' station. Then, thinking better of it, he reversed himself and walked back down the hall into an empty patient room. In the faint light from the doorway, he dialed the number of the hospital security office.

"Sergeant Etrick speaking."

"Hello, sargeant." Barone spoke softly, his back turned to the doorway. "This is Dr. Barone. I forgot my stethoscope in one of the department of medicine offices this morning. Can you let me in to retrieve it? I'm on call tonight and I need it."

There was a short silence as the security guard logged in the call. "Okay, Doc. What room should I meet you at?"

Barone recalled the beat-up old wooden door. "Room 327."

The security guard showed up, red faced and puffing. Like so many security personnel, he was a retired policeman in his fifties, who had finally been unable to pass the service physical exam. Barone guessed that, despite his emphysema from thirty years of smoking and his fifty extra pounds, the guard would be quite agile mentally. He had carefully left his own stethoscope behind in the on-call room.

The older man picked through a large ring of keys. "What does this stethoscope of yours look like?" The tone sounded as if he just wanted to help search for it, but the eyes studied Barone's face for any flicker of doubt.

Barone was prepared. Coolly, he described Maurie's distinctive stethoscope. "It has gray ear plugs, clear tubing and a silver chestpiece with a black rubber ring."

The guard nodded gravely, fitting the key into the lock and opening the door. He flipped on the light, and Barone looked across the room. As usual, Maurie had left his stethoscope on his bookshelf.

Stalling, he looked around for a minute, hoping the guard would tire of the search and leave. Barone looked behind the desk, on chairs, on filing cabinets. "I hope Dr. Benson didn't lock it in his desk."

The guard did not move from his post at the door, where he could watch the entire room. Barone tugged at the desk drawer. It was locked. "Look under the desk blotter," the guard offered.

Barone looked up quizzically. "The stethoscope is much too large to hide under a desk blotter."

The guard chuckled and finally walked across the

room. "Not the stethoscope, doc." He lifted the corner of the blotter and fished out a small silver key. "The desk key. It's like people who leave their extra house key under the welcome mat or in the mailbox. They think they're being smart, but every thief in the business knows where to look. And every cop too. They may as well not bother to lock the door in the first place. And business men always leave their desk keys in the office."

"Doctors too," added Barone, opening the top desk drawer, then each of the lower drawers. He studied each one intently, shifted a few papers. It was no use. The ex-cop would not go off and leave him alone.

Closing the last drawer, Barone lifted his eyes up to the bookshelf and "discovered" the stethoscope. "There's the little devil." He quickly pocketed the instrument to prevent the guard from seeing Maurie's name engraved on the neckpiece.

The guard did not care. The stethoscope matched the description. He was relieved that he could leave now and write up his report. If Dr. Benson called in on Monday morning about a missing stethoscope, they would not have to look very far. He watched as Barone locked the desk and replaced the key, then stepped out into the hall.

Barone turned off the light and pulled the door of the darkened office closed behind him. He tried the lock and pushed against the door to be sure it was closed. "Goodnight, doc." The guard started toward the elevators.

"G'night. And thanks," Barone called after him, then started off down the hall in the other direction. He rounded the corner and continued down the hall toward 3 East. About fifty feet down the corridor, he stopped and waited. He heard the sound of the elevator doors near Maurie's office open and close. Then he waited another minute, until he heard only the sound of his own heart pounding in his ears.

Slowly, noiselessly, he tiptoed back to the corner. Pressed against the wall, he looked down the empty hall. He walked back, past Benson's office as casually as he could. No one by the elevators. Back he went to the dark, beaten-up old door of room 327. He tried the knob. The door opened. Barone slipped inside, reset the latch, which he had pushed open while turning off the office light. The door closed noiselessly behind him.

Barone replaced the stethoscope on the bookcase, then took his penlight, the one that he used to examine patients' eyes and throats, from his shirt pocket. He shone it on the file cabinets in the corner. Say ahhh, he thought, opening the top drawer, marked *A-H*, of the leftmost file cabinet. It contained a forest of patient record folders, alphabetized by last name. The lower drawers in that cabinet contained patients *I-M*, *N-R*, and *S-Z*.

The top drawer of the middle file cabinet was also marked *A-H*, but the file folders inside, filled with notes and copies of papers from medical journals, were labeled with various clinical topics from ABDOMINAL PAIN to HSV-ENCEPHALITIS. Each of the other drawers in that cabinet were similar.

The drawers of the rightmost file cabinet were labeled CORRESPONDENCE, PAPERS, REPRINTS, and ADMINISTRATION. Barone tried the first drawer. The cabinet was locked.

He turned his penlight to the desk and lifted the corner of the blotter. The desk key glinted back at him. He opened the desk and pulled out the middle drawer. In the back, he had noticed earlier, was an ashtray filled with keys. A stubby brass one fit the locked file cabinet.

The top drawer contained file folders labeled with the names of various correspondents, last name first. There was no ''Lee, Peter'' folder among them. The second drawer was filled with a dusty collection of manuscripts that Maurie was ostensibly "preparing for publication." Most had been through multiple revisions and were yellowed at the edges. In the third drawer were reprints of published papers that Maurie had authored. The drawer was nearly filled by hundreds of copies of the few papers that Maurie had published, but which no one had written to request.

The files in the fourth drawer were separated by dividers labeled by years. Barone ran his eyes over the folders, stopping at his own name, filed under the year he had begun his internship. He resisted the temptation to look into his own record or that of Sylvia. The final section was labeled with the current year. As he removed Peter Lee's file, he heard footsteps in the hall. Extinguishing his light, he froze as he heard someone, huffing and puffing, approach the door. The lock rattled once, then again. Satisfied that the office was indeed locked, the footsteps receded down the hall. The old bastard had not even trusted Barone to lock the door.

Clutching Peter Lee's file to his chest, Barone sat back in the corner, around the side of the file cabinet, where his light could not be seen by anyone walking by the door. The medical school transcript was as good as Sylvia had been led to expect. Peter had graduated from Hopkins with honors, the eighteenth in a class of one hundred-twenty. The faculty letters of recommendation contained the usual laudatory, impersonal comments: "An excellent student," "Did careful patient examinations and workups." Barone skimmed through the compilation of medical school faculty evaluations, looking for any hint of irregularity. He finally arrived at the last paragraph.

Throughout his four years at Johns Hopkins, Peter Lee has been an exemplary student. His outstanding performance fully vindicated the judgment of this

this faculty in accepting a student with his background . . .

Background! There was that word again!

Despite his history of personal problems (see enclosed letter) Peter has continued to be a stable, conscientious, and academically outstanding student. We are pleased to recommend him to you without reservations.

Barone flipped to the last page of the file. It was a letter, on University of Maryland letterhead, from a Dr. Martin Davies in the department of psychiatry. It began:

I am writing this letter in support of Mr. Peter Lee's application for medical residency, not as a faculty advisor, but as his physician and friend. Peter was under my care as a patient at the University of Maryland Psychiatric Hospital during the summer between his junior and senior years in college. He insisted upon disclosing this information in his medical school applications and was rewarded for his honesty with rejection at eight of nine schools, including, to our shame, our own institution. Only the Johns Hopkins University had the courage to accept this remarkable young man on the basis of his performance in their research laboratories during his final year as an undergraduate. As a faculty member, I understand the reluctance of schools, overwhelmed by qualified applicants, to accept a young man with a "psychiatric history." But as a psychiatrist, I must condemn the attitude that the seeking of psychiatric care should carry such a social stigma that it could deprive a patient of employment for which he was otherwise qualified. It should be considered a mark of courage and strength, not weakness, for a young man such as Peter, who was even then planning a medical education, to seek psychiatric care when necessary.

Barone skipped through the letter's recounting of unkind comments that had been made by members of various medical school admission committees that had refused Peter Lee admission.

I laud the courage of the Johns Hopkins Medical School, whose decision has been vindicated by the exemplary performance of this young man. My professional opinion is that, after five healthy years, Peter Lee is no more likely to suffer a recurrence of his former difficulties than is any other randomly chosen student to contract the same problem. If you have any questions regarding his fitness for further medical training, please call me at the number listed on the letterhead. Peter Lee has given me full permission to discuss any aspect of his case with residency program directors, in detail.

At the bottom of the page was a note, dated the previous October and signed by Maurie himself, stating that Dr. Davies had indeed been contacted, and that Peter Lee was not to be considered an ''impaired candidate.''

Peter Lee stared into the light bulb of the desk lamp in the on-call room. Its brightness kept the night at bay, and Peter was very glad of that. But it hurt to stare at the bare filament—it created blind spots in his vision, green hazy blotches that brought back to him those images, hidden in the green haze of his subconscious, that he found it hurt too much to look back on.

He glared at the blank sheet of paper on the chart in

front of him, the green spots dancing and flashing upon it. Behind the spots he could see the image of his mother visiting him at the psychiatric hospital. She would come to see him each day on the locked ward, and the barred doors and windows would glide open, releasing him into the sunlight. Only under her protection had he been able to find any peace.

Then his father had tried to prevent her visits. She came less frequently, then not at all. Through the days and weeks of gloom and solitude he had yearned for the warmth of her love. He could feel the emptiness in the pit of his stomach even now.

He laid down his unused pen and rubbed his eyes. The image of the locked ward would not go away. He walked out into the hallway, hoping to escape the unbidden visions, aching for a sympathetic human voice, for the warmth of another person's touch.

The long, darkened corridor was lit by a beam of light emanating from the nurses' station and by the light coming from the doorway of a nearby patient room. Almost involuntarily, he found himself drawn toward the open doorway.

Inside, Suzi Grayson was propped in her bed, reading in the light of her bedside lamp. She looked up suddenly as Peter approached. "Oh, it's you, Dr. Lee." She drew her legs up under the sheet, then swung them over the side of the bed to face her visitor. "I didn't know you were still here."

Peter stared at the smooth, white skin of her knees and thighs, revealed by the short hospital gown. He rocked from one foot to another in front of her. "Yes, it's, uh, my, uh, on-call night." He tried to bring his eyes up to her face, but they seemed irresistibly drawn to the dark triangle formed by the hospital gown, stretched across the dark *V* formed by her exposed thighs.

"I'm doing a lot better this evening." She shifted

uncomfortably on the bed. He continued to stare at her legs. Uneasily, she sat back a bit further on the bed. "Dr. Lee, are you all right?"

Peter did not answer, but with a suddenness that took both of them by surprise, deliberately and woodenly placed one hand on her knee. Gently, he began to stroke her soft, warm skin.

She began to blush. "Dr. Lee!" He did not answer her; the hand began gradually to work its way up her thigh. "You stop that!" she cried in a hoarse whisper, trying to brush his hand away.

He grabbed her wrist and pulled her toward him. She stretched out her other arm, pushing against his chest. "Don't . . . stop . . ." she gasped as he leaned forward, wedging one knee between her thighs. As he pulled her against him, crushing her soft breasts against his solid chest, she managed to free one hand and brought her palm down sharply against one cheek.

Peter froze. He loosed his grip, and she wriggled free of his embrace, scooting back across the bed, cowering against the headboard like a cornered animal. Her eyes were wide with fear, the corners of her mouth pulled back in a grimace. "I'll scream," she threatened. Her voice was a hoarse whisper.

Peter stood, hunched over the bed for what seemed an eternity. His eyes seemed to reflect not lust or even anger, but rather confusion. She watched, fascinated despite her fear, as the face above her expressed a panoply of frustrations and anxieties in rapid sequence. Finally, wordlessly, he straightened up and, eyes glazed, backed away from the bed.

The skin of his cheek still stung where she had slapped him. He could feel the burning heat rising from his cheek, as it had when, as an adolescent, his father had humiliated him by slapping his face in public.

He stepped back from the bed, both cheeks now

burning. Suddenly he turned and dashed from the room, back toward the dark solitude of the on-call room, leaving the stunned young woman, nearly as confused as himself, huddled against the pillow.

Monday Morning, September 16

The red morning sun, reflected off the white face of the hospital pavilion across the courtyard, suffused Sylvia's room with an orange glow. Barone awoke to find himself curled up in a bedside chair, covered with a thin hospital blanket; one of the nurses must have covered him during the night. He arose stiffly and stretched.

Sylvia was already awake, watching him as he painfully straightened his limbs. "I hear they used to have chairs like that in medieval torture chambers."

He bent over, kissed her cheek. "Good morning, sweetheart."

"You really need a shave, Chuck." She smiled weakly.

He rubbed the fingers of one hand across the stubble on his chin. "Very observant. Have you been awake long?"

She nodded, stared across the room. "I've been thinking about what you told me last night about Peter."

Barone leaned backward and rotated his head on his shoulders. "You mean his psychiatric problems?"

"You know, it doesn't necessarily mean that he is having the same trouble now."

Barone shrugged, as much a sign of resignation as an exercise. "I agree. This could all be unrelated. But it has to be explored."

"How?" she asked. "You certainly can't ask Benson about it."

"Sure." Barone chuckled. "I can just see that. 'Pardon me, Maurie, but I was rummaging through your confidential files last night, and I happened to notice a letter from Peter Lee's shrink. What did he tell you about Peter's psychiatric diagnosis . . . ?' "

Sylvia smiled again. "I suppose you could call up Dr. Davies yourself."

Barone shook his head. "Peter's psychiatric history is privileged information. He won't discuss it, even with another doctor, unless I can convince him that it is a medical emergency. And if I tell him that, Davies will probably call Maurie to ask him how Peter is doing."

Sylvia propped herself up in the bed. "Maybe you could imply that you are a hospital administrator, and you just needed some information to approve Peter for continuing his residency next year."

Barone shook his head again. "He would probably try to sugarcoat Peter's history. Remember, this is the same psychiatrist who put his name on the letter recommending Peter in the first place. If I pressed him for information, he might get suspicious and tell me to talk to Maurie. Or he might call Maurie himself."

Sylvia let herself fall back against the pillows, studied the ceiling for a minute. "Didn't you say that he was an inpatient at the University of Maryland psychiatric hospital?"

Barone's face lit up. "Of course! Sylvia, you're a genius! There have to be hospital records from his admission. I'll check into them right after morning rounds."

Morning rounds again were quiet. Peter Lee seemed more disheveled and distracted than could be accounted for even by a long night on call. Barone, for his part, nearly ignored Peter, and concentrated his flagging attention on the patients and the other two interns. Marilyn and Harvey both sensed the tension and wisely chose to remain as silent as possible.

Even attending rounds were exceptionally benign, as Maurie went out of his way to avoid upsetting Peter. When the case presentations were awkward and incomplete, Maurie just nodded and asked Barone for clarification. At the end of rounds, Maurie examined the new patients' charts and found that Peter had not completed any of his admission notes. Maurie grunted and read through Barone's more complete notes, countersigning them to signify his approval.

After rounds, when the interns and students drifted off to lunch, Barone went back to the residents' on-call room. He telephoned the University of Maryland Health Science Center and asked to speak with the medical records department.

"May I help you?"

"Yes, this is Dr. Gray at Manhatten General Hospital. We have admitted a Mr. Peter Lee to our psychiatric wing, and he is pretty violent. All he will tell us is that Dr. Davies treated him in your hospital six years ago. Can you give me some information on him?"

"I'm very sorry, doctor," the clerk demurred, "but our hospital policy does not allow us to read medical records over the telephone."

Barone had expected that. "Well," he purred, "I can understand that. Our hospital has the same policy. But in matters of life or death we sometimes bend the rules. . . ."

"Life or death?" The clerk sounded uncertain.

"Yes," answered Barone. "The patient's EKG shows a possible heart attack, but we need to know what his old EKG reading was. Of course, if you can't help me, I'll have to talk to your supervisor. But if he is really having a heart attack—"

"That's okay, doctor. I'll go get his chart."

The line was silent for a few minutes, then she returned. "His EKG was normal."

"Was that before or after his shock treatments?" Barone pushed on.

Another silence as she paged through the chart. "After."

"Hmmm." Barone tried again. "Can you tell me what medicines he was on at the time?"

"Now, doctor, I really can't go into—"

"It could affect his EKG," offered Barone, quickly.

He could hear the sound of the pages of the chart turning. "The only medicines were haloperidol and desipramine," she came back.

Barone tried once more. "Well, that's very helpful. Thank you very much. One more last thing. What was his discharge diagnosis?"

Another short silence. "Psychotic depression." Her voice was chilly.

Barone knew he was finished. "Thank you," he said. "We'll be writing formally for the full record."

Barone laid the phone down gently. "Psychotic depression." That explained why Davies and Maurie had been willing to give Peter a chance. Depression was so unpredictable an illness that it was quite possible for a patient to suffer a complete breakdown, and then recover and live normally for the rest of his life. True, many patients had recurrences. But, these were so erratic that it would not be fair to brand a patient as "emotionally impaired" for the rest of his life on the basis of one hospitalization.

But recurrences did happen. And Peter Lee had become increasingly disorganized and distant. Could it be that he was beginning another breakdown? And did that have anything to do with the three deaths? It was all too great a coincidence not to be related.

But how could he convince Maurie? He could not bring up Peter's psychiatric history; that was supposed to be confidential. And Maurie had originally approved Peter's application for internship. It would be an admission of error for him to back down now. And Maurie would never admit that he had been wrong.

Barone started back to Sylvia's room. If there was a diplomatic way to get through to Maurie, she would find it.

When he peeked in the door, Sylvia was asleep again, her lunch untouched on the bedside tray. Barone shook his head. He knew the food service workers would soon take back the full tray if she did not get up to eat. And Sylvia needed to eat to keep up her strength. He uncovered the plate of greenish meatloaf and overdone string beans, unwrapped the slice of bread and buttered it, then set the tray in front of Sylvia on the bed.

Gently, he leaned over her and shook her shoulder. "Syl, it's time to eat your lunch."

No response.

He shook her shoulder again. In a louder voice, he called: "Sylvia, it's time to get up."

Still no movement.

His pulse beating in his ears, Barone rolled Sylvia onto her back. She was limp, like a rag doll. He leaned over, put an ear by her face. No sounds of breathing.

The sweat began to break out on his forehead. He pushed two fingers into the side of Sylvia's neck, feeling for the carotid pulse. Nothing. He moved his fingers up to just below the angle of the jaw.

A faint pulse. Then Sylvia gasped, a shallow breath. And a deeper one. And another, until she was breathing rapidly and deeply. Then the breathing slowed down again and stopped.

Grimly, Barone marked the time on his watch. It seemed like an eternity as the seconds ticked by. Cold sweat dripped from his forehead. Twenty seconds—still not breathing. He reached his two fingers again to feel her carotid pulse. They were slippery against her skin.

The pulse was still present, still faint. A full half minute passed before she gasped again and went through another cycle of breaths.

Cheyne-Stokes respiration, thought Barone. A sign of coma. His fingers trembled as he lifted back Sylvia's eyelids. Her soft gray eyes seemed glazed, staring off without comprehension into space. He hugged her limp body to him, sobbing noiselessly against her shoulder. "My God, Sylvia, my God. I should never have left you alone. What has he done to you?"

The neurologist finished his examination and emerged from Sylvia's room, medical bag tucked under his arm. A small, dark man, with heavy-rimmed glasses, Angelo diCharo was one of the best neurologists ever to have trained at Manhattan General Hospital.

He stood next to Barone in the hallway, watching the disheveled resident stare blankly down the corridor, for nearly a full minute before interrupting his trance. "Chuck?" he said quietly.

Barone nodded, turned to diCharo.

"Chuck, I think that Sylvia has slipped into an hepatic coma caused by her liver failure."

Barone nodded, swallowed. "Are you sure, Angelo?"

The neurologist stiffened, despite himself. "We will need some confirmatory tests, but this is a classic case—"

"I mean," interrupted Barone, "that it's nothing . . . I mean, can you be sure that there is no other problem?"

diCharo shrugged. "Such as what?"

"Well"—Barone looked at the floor—"we've had a rash of unexplained deaths on this ward."

The neurologist blinked furiously behind the heavy black frames. "Are you suggesting that someone could have deliberately . . . ?"

"I'm not suggesting anything. But if you don't look for something, you don't find it." That was one of the neurologist's favorite aphorisms, told innumerable times to disbelieving medical residents when he suggested an arcane diagnosis.

diCharo bristled at hearing his own words thrown back at him. "Yes, Chuck, but this is a serious charge. I'll have the lab check her blood and urine for drugs and poisons. But before you talk idly of an in-house Lucrezia Borgia, you had better have some facts. Hospital administrators are like Roman emperors"—he unconsciously drew on his own ethnic history—"they only want to hear good news. And if the news is bad, they will most likely want to behead the messenger."

Barone was grim. "And if no one ever tells them the bad news?"

The neurologist shrugged again. "Then the empire comes crashing down around their heads."

Peter Lee left the hospital as soon as morning rounds were finished. He no longer could tolerate even the pretense of performing his patient care work. It had become obvious to him that Barone was stepping in, pretending to cover for him, but really forcing Peter out of the way, in the same way he had done with Sylvia. Until there was no room for him anymore at the hospital, and he could no longer stand even to be there.

He walked across town, toward the openness of Central Park. He had hoped that he might find refuge in the cool green spaces, but soon felt that they only accentuated his personal sense of emptiness. Seeking activity in which to submerge his own loneliness, he left the park, turned down Broadway.

The streets were crowded with tourists, shoppers, business people. Millions of people in the city, all of them strangers, to each other as much as to Peter. There seemed to be some cold comfort in that.

He was jostled back and forth by the flow of the midday traffic, passed a booth advertising a striptease show with a video. He was mesmerized by the image of the girl on the screen nearly bursting out of a diaphanous negligee, seeming to be looking directly at him. Her wet tongue darted over her lips as she motioned him closer. He stepped up to the screen, looked into her eyes with growing fascination.

He wanted her, could feel the yearning deep in the pit of his belly, the way he had with Sylvia, with Lauren Nyquist, with Suzi Grayson.

The girl on the screen seemed to be staring into his soul, pulling him toward her with a magnetic attraction. It was a feeling that was all too familiar, as if his heart were hooked like a fish, being reeled in. She would play with him for a while, dangle him on a string, like Sylvia had done, like Suzi Grayson had done. Let him feel her attraction, and then reject him.

Harvey had been right. It was a trick, a ploy that women used to control a man, to belittle him. Even he could see that now, staring at the voluptuous woman on the screen, her manipulations as transparent as her lingerie.

Peter lifted one hand. He had a right to control his own destiny. No one could take it from him.

His fist smashed down into the screen. There was a blinding flash of light, then a small explosion and smoke poured out of the shattered picture tube. A knot of people gathered, asked one another what had happened.

Peter's knuckles were bruised, bleeding. He sucked at the blood. It tasted salty. The tears of the damned.

The disheveled young man melted back into the crowd and was gone.

Barone sat by Sylvia's bedside, watching the shadows dissolve into the darkness as the light faded from the room. Her breathing pattern was still cyclical. Except when the nurses periodically repositioned her in the bed, she did not move.

The laboratory tests ordered by diCharo had confirmed the diagnosis of coma caused by liver failure. More important, all the other laboratory tests had been normal. There was no trace of any sedative drugs in her system—and her potassium level was normal. But even though he realized that Peter Lee had had nothing to do with Sylvia's condition, Barone still could not forgive Peter for having distracted him from Sylvia's bedside while she had been slipping away.

Late in the afternoon, Barone had conferred with both Harvey and Marilyn, checking out the status of each of their patients. No one had seen Peter Lee since morning rounds; the nurses said that he had not even answered his pager. Barone reflected that if any other intern had disappeared during the working day, he would have been furious. In this case, though, he merely felt relieved. He had examined Peter's patients himself and written progress notes for them, too—the first that had been recorded in most of their charts for three or four days. Normally he would also have resented having to do this "intern's work." But the chores had given him an excuse not to be at Sylvia's bedside when Barry Grant, the 4 West resident, put in a central venous line to follow Sylvia's fluid balance better while she was in coma. Barone could not imagine watching the procedure, which he had performed himself so many times, knowing that the neck beneath the blue-green sheet was the same one he had rested his head against the night before. In any case, it gave him a sense of satisfaction to expunge the decaying influence of Peter Lee's care from the patient charts.

Now, in the last rays of evening light, Barone sat once again at Sylvia's bedside, watching her chest rise and fall rhythmically and then, once again, slow down and stop. For another thirty seconds he lived through the agony of waiting for her breathing to resume, reliving the convulsive moment when he had thought that she was dead.

He waited for what seemed an eternity, and then waited some more, and just when he was sure that she would not start breathing again, she saw her chest begin to heave, almost at full inspiration. In the failing light, he had failed to see her first few shallow breaths.

Damn Peter Lee, thought Barone. Damn him for making this unbearable illness even worse. Damn him for making me think that Sylvia had been murdered. He buried his face in his hands and leaned forward against the bed, sobbing silently.

Then Barone, gasping for air, rocked back in his seat. He was not going to leave Sylvia alone again. Not in a hospital with a deranged intern who might be murdering patients.

Barone flipped on the switch on Sylvia's bedside lamp and took up the vigil.

The entranceway guard at Manhattan General Hospital almost stopped the disheveled young man at the door. His hair was uncombed and his clothes in disarray. But the guard recognized the face of one of the interns and, shaking his head, let him pass.

The elevator up to 4 East was unoccupied, and no one saw him enter the darkened hallway. He waited in the shadows of the doorway of an empty room until the night nurse left the nurses' station to check on one of her patients. Then he slipped into the medicine room and quickly located a vial of potassium chloride. He found a ten-milliliter syringe and filled it from the vial.

He looked outside the medicine room door. There was no sign of the night nurse. Slowly, he crept down the hall, moving from doorway to doorway until he disappeared into one of the darkened rooms and closed the door behind him.

The long walk had accentuated the sensation of emptiness and frustration he felt inside. He needed more than mere warmth or the pleasure of a physical relationship with a woman. He needed a sense of reassurance, of control.

He snapped on the light over the bed. The young woman stirred, turned away from the light, moaned softly. Then, as the intern tugged at the tubing attached to her central venous line, searching for an injection port, she rolled over toward him. One eye opened, blinked in the brightness of the bedside lamp.

"Dr. Lee!" she gasped.

"It's okay, Suzi," he mumbled, fumbling with a plastic syringe. Her hair, spilling down over the pillow, reflected the golden color of the oblique lighting. Peter longed to run his fingers through it, to touch, to hold her: another of life's pleasures that had been dangled in front of him, then withheld, jerked back suddenly and forever beyond his reach. To Peter her beauty and her unapproachability were the essence of femininity. "Soon you'll be fine."

"I am feeling better tonight, doctor." She rolled onto her back, eyes still squinting in the unaccustomed light. "You know, I decided not to tell anyone about last night," she offered, watching him uncertainly.

"It's okay, Suzi," he repeated, trying not to listen to her. He knew better than to believe her. Too often he had listened to women, responded to them; too often he had suffered the punishment of their rejection. He could not have her, and he could not live without her. Therefore, she could not be allowed to live without him. He pushed the plunger of the syringe. "Soon you'll be fine."

She felt a slight burning in her chest, then a dull coldness began to sweep over her. "What was that medicine?" she asked groggily.

"It's okay," were the last words she heard. "It's

okay, Suzi,'' he said softly as her body became limp. ''Soon you'll be fine.''

A tear began to creep down his dirty cheek as Peter Lee gently ran his fingers through her hair, stroked her cheek. Mary Altman's death had been an accident, Herbie Brown and Anne Delbert he had killed out of compassion, as much for himself as for them. But now, he knew, he had perfected his tool, his instrument of control. Suzi Grayson would have died soon anyway from her leukemia if not her pneumonia. He had saved her that pain, while taking control of their relationship, of his own life.

Slowly he lifted back the sheet. ''It's okay, Suzi,'' he mumbled, as he pulled back her hospital gown, began to explore the lifeless body. ''Soon you'll be mine.'' He ran his hands over the warm soft skin of her breasts, stroked the smooth areola. Sliding into bed next to her, he could feel the warmth of his erection, pressing against the front of his pants. Kissing her still-warm cheek, he used his free hand to unfasten his pants, releasing his erection against the smooth skin of her thigh. He probed her soft, brown pubic hair, pushed her legs apart and mounted her. The warmth of her vagina finally penetrated the frigid emptiness of his loins. At last he felt what he had been searching for: the sense of being enveloped by the warmth and security that he, and at long last, only he could control.

''Soon, Sylvia,'' he murmured into the unhearing ear. ''Soon you'll be mine.''

''Code blue, Four East! Code blue, Four East!''

Barone began to surface from the inky blackness of his sleep as the shrill bleating from his pager repeated: ''Code blue, Four East! Code blue, Four East!''

In the hazy consciousness of half wakefulness, he thought that he had forgotten to turn off his pager before going to sleep.

"Code blue, Four East! Code blue, Four East!" Barone began to reach for his pager, then realized that the alert was coming from the loudspeakers in the hall outside Sylvia's room. He was still in the hospital! And there was a cardiac arrest on *his* ward!

Barone leaped from his chair, scrambled for the door. The night nurse was pushing the crash cart toward Suzi Grayson's room.

He helped her swing the cart into the room. Marilyn Silver was already on the bed, kneeling over the lifeless, blue body, rhythmically compressing the chest.

She looked up, almost in tears, not missing a single compression. "Chuck!" She pumped. "Am I glad to see you." Pump. "I got called to Suzi's bedside"—pump—"and when I got here"—pump—"she was blue and cold." Pump. "I knew you would want me"—pump—"to resuscitate her." Pump. "But I really didn't expect you"—pump—"to show up to help!" Pump again.

Barone picked up the woman's arm. It was cool and fell limply back to the bed. "What happened?"

Marilyn continued pumping on the chest while Barone placed an oxygen mask over the face and pumped air into her lungs. "I don't know." Pump. "She was all right on rounds this morning."

"What did Peter say when he signed her out to you?"

Marilyn turned a deeper shade of red. "He never showed up for sign-out rounds." Pump. "I haven't seen him since Maurie's rounds"—pump—"this morning."

An anesthesia resident poked his head in the door. "Does she need to be intubated?"

Barone nodded, moved around the side of the bed. He helped hold Suzi Grayson's head in position so that the anesthesiologist could pass an endotracheal tube. Standing next to Marilyn, his voice was a harsh whisper. "Why the hell didn't you tell me when Peter failed to show up for sign-out rounds?"

Marilyn continued pumping, red-faced and puffing. "Because I didn't think"—pump—"that I should get involved in your . . ." pump, pump, pump ". . . your personal affairs with Peter." Pump.

"Personal affairs?" Barone spat out the words, startling the nurse who was applying electrocardiogram leads to the arms and legs. "I am the resident on this ward. This isn't some goddamned game we're playing here. People's lives are at stake. It's my responsibility to know when things go wrong."

"Well in that case"—Marilyn pumped, puffed—"there's an awful lot for you to catch up on!"

Barone's blue eyes flashed at her. "We have more important things here than your personal opinion of me. Like why this girl, who was improving when I saw her on rounds this afternoon, has suddenly had a cardiac arrest."

Barone bent over to read the EKG strip. "Stop for a minute," he ordered.

Marilyn straightened up. Her face was beet red. A resident from another floor slipped in beside her to take over the chest compression.

"Flat line," pronounced Barone. "Give her an amp of calcium and one of epi, and then two amps of bicarb." The resident began pumping the chest.

"Chuck." Marilyn was still panting. "Suzi Grayson had leukemia. She had severe pneumonia and a pleural effusion—"

"Her leukemia had been in remission," interrupted Barone, "and she was recovering from the pneumonia. This morning she looked great. And now she's cold and dead."

"Sometimes that happens, Chuck."

"No, it doesn't!" Barone snapped at his intern. "Not on my service! Here." He handed her an empty syringe. "Draw some blood for electrolytes."

* * *

Barone trudged down the darkened corridor toward the nurses' station. He sat down at the desk in the nurses' station and stared blindly at the wall in front of him. No amount of chest compression or artificial respiration or medication had been able to revive Suzi Grayson. Four patients dead on 4 East, on his ward, with no explanation.

Marilyn helped the night nurse push the crash cart down the hall from Suzi Grayson's room. She stopped at the nurses' station, flopped down into a chair beside Barone. "Sorry, Chuck," she offered lamely.

He continued to stare straight ahead. "That's four in one week. Two on your call nights."

Marilyn's cheeks began to color again. "Just what the hell is that supposed to imply?"

Barone finally turned to her, his voice a hoarse whisper. "If four people suddenly were found dead, in one week, in a single apartment building, what would you think?"

"This isn't an apartment building, Chuck," Marilyn protested. "This is a hospital."

"I see." Barone interpreted facetiously. "It's all right for people to die, as long as they do it in a hospital."

Marilyn started to respond, then thought better of it. "I'll phone the family," she said at last.

"Try to get autopsy permission." He pushed the telephone toward her.

Marilyn flipped through Suzi Grayson's chart to the face page, dialed the telephone number listed under next of kin. Barone picked up the extension phone to listen.

A man's voice answered on the third ring. "Hello," he said thickly. Then, "My God, what time is it . . . ?"

Marilyn interrupted. "Mr. Grayson?"

"Uh-huh," the voice mumbled.

"This is Dr. Silver at New York Hospital. I am calling about your daughter, Suzi."

There was a gasp of comprehension at the other end.

This was the long-dreaded call that he had stayed awake, so many nights, thinking about, when Suzi had first been diagnosed with leukemia. Instantly the voice was attentive, polite, falsely hopeful. "Yes, doctor, what is it?"

Marilyn could hear stirring sounds in the background and a woman's voice. "Henry, what is it?" She swallowed hard and continued. "I'm afraid, Mr. Grayson, that Suzi has taken a turn for the worse."

"She's not dying or anything, is she?" he asked. She could hear the woman's voice in the background: "Oh my God!"

"Well." Marilyn swallowed, tried again to break the news as softly as possible. "She has become very sick and—"

"We'll be there in ten minutes."

The line went dead.

The elevator opened on 4 East, disgorging Henry and Elizabeth Grayson into the half light of the sleeping ward. Barone hurried down the corridor to meet them, Marilyn a half step behind.

Mr. Grayson was a bearish man in his fifties, round faced and balding, with a neatly trimmed mustache. His eyes were red and watery. His wife was a dumpy woman with graying hair. She wore a rumpled house-dress and no stockings. He wore a wrinkled white shirt and suit pants, probably from the previous evening.

"How is she doing, doctor?" The man rushed over to grasp Barone's outstretched hand.

"Is she going to be all right?" asked the woman, waddling behind her husband.

Barone's face was solemn. As Marilyn caught up with him, he began: "I'm sorry, folks." He shook his head slowly. "But she didn't make it—"

He was cut short by a wail of grief from the middle-aged woman. "My baby . . ." She buried her face in her husband's shoulder, alternating muffled shrieks and gasps. The man faced Barone, his eyelids puffy, tears welling. "Is she dead, doctor?" he said simply.

Barone nodded.

He closed his eyes and hugged his wife close to him. "Our only child," he said softly to no one and to everyone. "She was all we had." He began to sob, tucking his face into the tangled nest of his wife's uncombed hair.

Barone was silent for a minute. Marilyn could not remember seeing him more human than as he waited, motionless, for the couple to compose themselves. Finally, he patted Mrs. Grayson on the wrist and asked, "Would you like to see her?"

The woman nodded, still sobbing, and Barone led them down the hall to the room, which the nurses had cleared of life support equipment. Suzi Grayson's body lay, cold and blue, under a single white sheet, eyes staring blankly at the light fixture on the ceiling. Her face was drawn in a half grimace. Barone left the sobbing couple alone for their last moments with their daughter.

Several minutes later, the Grayson's emerged into the half-lit hallway. Barone met them at the door and led them back to the lights of the nurses' station.

"Mr. and Mrs. Grayson," he began in a soft voice, "I know it is always difficult to make a decision at"—he searched for the right words, proceeded lamely—"at a time like this. But before you leave we have to discuss one more problem." He turned to Marilyn, who was busying herself filling out some forms, then back to the Graysons. "When a person dies in a hospital, particularly a young person, and we really don't know what happened to her, we need to perform an autopsy to determine the cause of death."

He waited for a reaction, but the couple stared at him

blankly. Finally, the woman mumbled, without comprehension, "An autopsy . . . ?"

"Yes." Barone was relieved to pick up on her cue, grateful to end the silence. "We need to examine the body. It's really like an operation. But it doesn't hurt her, of course. Just to find out why she died." Barone mopped the sweat from his brow. "You see, she was doing so—"

"No." Mr. Grayson's response was soft but firm. "No," he repeated. "It's against our religion to have an autopsy."

Barone swallowed. "Your religion?"

Mr. Grayson nodded. "We're Jewish. It's against Orthodox Jewish law to do an autopsy."

Mrs. Grayson stared at him blankly. "But Henry, we're not Orthodox. . . ."

He glared at her. "We are on this one," he declared defiantly.

"But look," Barone broke in, "I'm sure that your religious laws are humane. If the lives of other people could be saved, wouldn't an autopsy be permitted?"

Grayson shook his head violently. His face began to flush. "No, there is no exception. No autopsy."

"But, Mr. Grayson," Barone continued, "perhaps if we could talk to your rabbi, we might get an expert opinion on this—"

"*No!*" Grayson shouted so loudly that the night nurse turned to glare at him. "No," he repeated in a stage whisper. "No rabbi. And no autopsy. I said no autopsy, and that's final. You doctors had our little girl for over a year. Chemotherapy, radiation, intravenous, spinal taps—you used her for a guinea pig long enough. We brought her for help, and for a year you stuck needles into her, made her even sicker. You practiced on her, you made her life miserable. And now she is dead. Let her rest in peace."

His wife tugged at his sleeve, tried to quiet him. "Henry, please—"

He turned on her, "Don't you hush me! They killed our daughter. They have no right to ask for an autopsy. No right!" He choked back a sob of grief.

"Henry," she soothed, "come with me." She tried to lead him down the hall toward the elevators.

"Mrs. Grayson." Barone tried one last time, ignoring the sobbing older man as he followed her down the hall. "I know how you feel. We all loved Suzi. But she's gone now. We won't hurt her. But we can save lives, perhaps someone else's daughter, if we can learn from her death."

The woman shook her head, sniffled, continued down the hall. Without looking at Barone she answered: "It's all over now. She was all we had. There's nothing left." She led her broken husband into the waiting elevator and they were gone.

Tuesday Morning, September 17

The sun, peeking over the edge of the apartment complex on Roosevelt Island, lit the east face of Manhattan General Hospital a brilliant orange red. The light reflected back on the East River, casting an amber glow over the first stirrings of life along the waterway: a garbage scow slowly making its way downriver, a flock of seagulls winging lazily overhead, a few joggers out to beat the early morning crush. A pile of old newspapers on a park bench swayed gently, almost rhythmically, in the soft morning breeze. Suddenly the mound began to shift. Frightened by the sudden movement and the crinkling sound of the brittle pages, a small terrier, sniffing about the legs of the bench, ran yelping back to one of the joggers. The pile of papers rose from the bench, revealing an equally rumpled and discarded human being who had been sleeping on the bench beneath them. He stretched, yawned, sat up. Stiffly, he walked to the rail by the walkway, leaned over it and peered down into the still dark waters of the East River. Peter Lee was relieved that he could not see his own reflection.

He bent backward to stretch his neck muscles. Pawing his beard, Peter briefly considered returning home to shave. But he knew he could not go back there. The memories—of Maryann, of Sylvia, of the hated Barone—would flood his mind with pain before he could even open the door. Twice he had tried to go home, and twice he had been driven away by the demons who dwelt there. He had not changed clothes, nor washed, in three days. His eyes felt gritty, and he was even more tired than when he had fallen asleep. But sleep was another refuge to which he was less than willing to return. The darkness would close in on him, the nightmares would begin again. His mother would die, Sylvia would die, he would kill them both. He had already seen the visions, three times in the last night alone. He could not suffer it again.

The thin, dirty young man stumbled up the stairs of the Seventy-first Street overpass, to cross the East River Drive. He paused halfway across the concrete footbridge and looked out over the oncoming traffic, already pouring into midtown Manhattan. He gritted his teeth and twisted his fingers into the chain-link fence, built to protect the motorists from the habits of Manhattan children who liked to drop bricks on passing autos. The cars keep coming, thought Peter, they keep passing me by without even knowing I am here. Nobody knows I am here. Nobody knows who I really am. There's no way to reach them. He imagined that behind him, on the far side of the bridge, all the cars would find that the road had been replaced by a bottomless chasm. They could drive past him, only to fall off the edge of the earth. He found his fingers shaking the chain-link fence; over the rattling of the metal he realized he was shouting at the passing cars: "It serves you right, you bastards! It serves you all right!" The cars continued to swish by. No one noticed him railing his defiance into oblivion.

Exhausted by his futile effort, he crossed the bridge and trudged slowly up Seventieth Street to the small Italian delicatessen near the hospital. By that time of the morning there was usually a crush of customers, standing in the New York version of a line, elbowing their way to the counter to order a quick breakfast. Today, although the shop was as crowded as usual, no one pressed against or pushed Peter. He imagined a cloud of impenetrable distance around himself, a personal aura of isolation. The nearby patrons appreciated the aura as being primarily olfactory.

As he approached the front of the line, the counter man recognized him. "The usual, doc?" he asked, eyeing the young man suspiciously.

Peter nodded, watching the man prepare his meager breakfast.

"Coffee light and a buttered bagel." The man put down the small white paper bag on the countertop and rung up the sale. Peter handed him a bill.

"Rough night, doc?" the counter man asked as he made change. When he looked up, Peter was already wandering out the door. The man shrugged and dropped the coins back into the cash register.

Peter sat on the steps of the medical school entrance on York Avenue, munching his bagel and sipping coffee. He stared at the shoes and legs of those who hurried up the steps around him, into the medical center. His bagel was gone and the coffee cup long emptied by the time he noticed that one pair of scuffed black shoes had stopped next to him. He followed the polyester pant legs up to the hawklike gaze of Maurie Benson.

"You okay, Lee," he more ordered than asked.

Peter, without thinking, nodded the expected answer, allowed Maurie to help him to his feet. They entered through the revolving door, walked through the vestibule of the medical school. The tall, marble clad walls of the foyer reminded Peter of a tomb; the huge wooden plaque at the far end, inscribed with the names of the hospital and medical school's largest donors, seemed to Peter a fitting headstone. Maurie led him up to his small dark office on the third floor. The young man sat woodenly, said nothing.

"Peter." Maurie began uncharacteristically slowly,

taking special care in choosing his words. "Has there been anything, either at the hospital or at home that has upset you lately?"

Peter could not describe, for the little man sitting across from him, the awe and terror of his life. He could not even begin to try. All he could manage was to nod mutely.

"Is there anything that I, uh, that is, myself or any other doctors at the medical center, can help you with?"

Peter began to nod, then shook his head.

Maurie leaned across the desk blotter, extending his open palms. "Peter, you know that Dr. Davies told me all about your . . . that is, the trouble you had while you were in college. Anyone can become depressed. Almost everybody does, sometimes."

Peter nodded. The words slipped by him like the autos on the expressway.

"And internship is one of the most stressful times in a young doctor's life. Did you know that more than half our interns, every year become depressed enough to request to see a staff psychiatrist?"

Peter started to nod again, then stopped short. So that was it. They wanted him to see a psychiatrist. The thought of being hospitalized, incarcerated, sent a cold shiver up his spine.

"At any time during the year," Benson pushed on, "up to one fourth of our interns are taking antidepressant medications. Peter"—he reached his hand out across the desk blotter to the bewildered young man—"there is no shame in being human, in having human emotions when you watch your patients die. But we are professionals. We have to take care of ourselves. We cannot let our emotions interfere with our work."

Maurie leaned back and stared into the middle distance, avoiding direct eye contact with the immobile intern. "Peter, I've been reviewing your work lately. Frankly, your notes have not been up to your usual high standards, and your workups . . ." Maurie allowed his voice to trail off dramatically, then hunched forward, looking directly into Peter's bloodshot, burning black eyes. "Well, Peter, I think that they reflect the fact that you have not been your usual self lately. We have all noticed it."

Peter, uncomfortable under Maurie's scrutiny, looked self-consciously down at the floor. Grateful for the release from Peter's gaze, Maurie continued to deliver his lecture to Peter's smudged forehead. "I think that you have become depressed again, Peter. I'm going to relieve you, temporarily, of your ward responsibilities, and," he continued, hurriedly, "I would like to have you see Dr. van Arsdale, our house staff psychiatric liaison."

Peter continued to stare at the floor.

"Will you see him?"

Peter found himself nodding mutely.

"Well, it's settled then." Benson sighed audibly. "Have the house staff secretary make you an appointment for today with Dr. van Arsdale." He ushered Peter to the door, his arm hovering above Peter's shoulders, as if repelled from actually touching him by an unseen magnetic force. "I know you are going to do just fine, Peter. We'll keep your place in the program open until Dr. van Arsdale says it is all right for you to come back." He opened the door. "Good luck, Peter." He shook the soiled hand briefly, then dropped it, closed the door.

Peter Lee stood in the hallway, blinking in the morning light suffusing the ground glass panel in Maurie's door. He watched the shadowy form of the residency director recede into the room, then he turned to walk down the comfortable gloom of the hospital corridor.

Benson sank back into his chair with the inner satisfaction of one who has performed a difficult task, and, by his own estimation, acquitted himself well. As he slowly sipped his first cup of coffee of the day, he reflected that, at one stroke, he had solved all of his problems on 4 East. By relieving Peter Lee of his patient care responsibilities, he had taken the force out of Barone's argument that the three deaths had to be investigated. And, it had become increasingly clear, Peter really did need the psychiatric help.

He leaned back, looking at the ceiling, his hands folded over his upper abdomen. He could pull an intern from an elective rotation to cover Peter Lee's patients. Barone would probably be satisfied just to have Lee off his service. And more important, he had spared the hospital the enormous embarrassment and expense that would have been involved if word of a suspected murderer had reached the press.

A sharp knock on the door startled Benson from his reverie.

"Come in," he called, leaning his chair back into the upright position.

The door opened and Chuck Barone peered in around the edge. "Can I see you for a few minutes?"

Benson gestured expansively to the chair across from him. "Come on in."

Barone sat down, shifting uneasily in the hard wooden seat. "I want to talk to you about the situation on Four East."

Benson smiled easily and rocked forward, resting his elbows on the desk top. "Yes," he said. "I needed to speak with you this morning about that."

Barone slumped visibly in his chair. "You did?"

Benson nodded gravely. "I've been reading through Peter Lee's charts. His workups have been superficial, when he has even bothered to write them up for the record, and he has written no progress notes for several days."

"I know," Barone interjected. "I've been filling in, writing progress notes on his patients."

"And that's commendable," Benson continued, "but it's not fair to ask you to continue to cover for him indefinitely. In my opinion, he is clinically depressed and cannot continue to provide the excellent patient care that this hospital demands. I have already seen Peter Lee this morning and relieved him of his patient care responsibilities, effective immediately." He took a sip of coffee, sank back into his chair. "I will recall an intern from an elective to replace him later today."

Barone was silent for a moment. "I don't know what to say," he finally began. "I came down here to tell you that there was another unexpected death on the ward last night."

Benson began to pale. "What happened? Who was it?"

"Suzi Grayson. She was found around two A.M., cold and blue, just like the others, with no reason for her death. We could not resuscitate her."

Benson's fingers gripped the arms of his chair. His knuckles were white. "What do you mean no cause for her death. She had pneumonia—"

"Which was responding to antibiotics," interrupted Barone. "And her leukemia was under control."

"Could it have been a pulmonary embolus?" asked Maurie, almost hopefully.

"I don't know." Barone shrugged. "Her parents refused an autopsy."

Benson sighed with apparent relief. "Well, then, I suppose we will never know."

Barone shifted uncomfortably in his chair. "That's why I came to you, sir. I would like you to approach the Grayson family to try one more time to get them to agree to an autopsy."

"You want me to do what?" asked Maurie in disbelief.

Barone's voice quavered. "You always tell the house staff that, if a family is reluctant to approve an autopsy, we should notify the attending physician on the service so that he can try. Well, you are the attending doctor on Four East this month. I would like your help."

Benson's cheeks began to color. "And if they refuse?"

"Then"—Barone swallowed hard—"then I would like to call the New York medical examiner, to force an autopsy."

Benson struggled to control himself. "Barone, this 'mystery murderer' theory of yours has gotten way out of control. I am as concerned as you that we have four unexplained deaths on Four East. But there is no reason to think that the first three deaths were anything more than a bad series of coincidences. And there is certainly no reason to link Suzi Grayson's death with the other three."

Barone shook his head. "That's not true, sir." He took a deep breath before playing his trump card. "I sent off Suzi Grayson's blood to the lab for electrolytes. Her potassium was seven-point-two"

Benson stared at the young resident for a moment, then suddenly exploded. "Is that it, Sherlock? Do you want me to drag the name of the hospital through the mud so you can get another inconclusive autopsy? Don't you realize what will happen if I call the medical examiner? They will want to know why we need to have an autopsy. And the minute we mention suspicion of murder, they will have to call in the police. Every newspaper and television station in town gets a copy of the daily ME's report and the police blotter.

"Do you know what they would do to us if the word got out that the hospital was investigating four possible murders of patients? Within a few days, the hospital would be empty. It costs nearly one million dollars a day to run this medical center, empty or full, and we require a ninety percent occupancy rate just to break even. A fall of just thirty percent in our daily census would cause us to lose over a quarter of a million dollars a day. The hospital would be ruined. We would have to close wards, cut our services, cut our nursing staff''—he eyed Barone—''cut our residency training programs. And all so you could avenge yourself on Peter Lee for having a crush on your girlfriend.''

Benson got up from his chair, circled the desk, looking down on Barone's bent head. ''I have suspended Peter Lee. Not because he might be a murderer, not even because you had a quarrel with him, but because he was not performing up to our standards. He is a sick young man. He is depressed and unable to function. He needs support, not suspicion.''

Benson sat down on the edge of the desk, clasped his hands in his lap. ''Now, I am not implying that your theory has any validity, but suppose, for a moment, that your suspicion is correct. It seems to me that the best thing we could do would be to get Peter off the ward and to let the rest of the matter lie in peace.''

Barone sat, crumpled in his chair, staring at the floor. ''I don't think you understand, Maurie,'' he began, afraid to raise his eyes to meet Benson's searing gaze. ''Suzi Grayson died last night''—he finally looked up, his cool blue eyes latching onto Benson's—''when Peter Lee was not on call. Merely relieving him of his responsibilities is not enough. The hospital guards have to be alerted to deny him admission to the hospital grounds at any time of day or night.''

Benson's jaw dropped. ''I don't believe I am hearing this. Are you implying that Peter Lee sneaked back into the hospital last night to kill Suzi Grayson?''

Barone nodded mutely.

Benson stood up, began pacing. ''Did anybody see him here? A nurse, a guard . . . anyone?''

Barone shrugged. "We could try calling the night guards at home—"

"You will do nothing of the sort!" Benson exploded. "I have had it with your smug theories, Barone. I cannot bar Peter Lee from the hospital grounds. He has legitimate reasons for coming here." Maurie swallowed, began again in a lower tone. "And if I did prohibit him from entering the hospital, how could I explain it? Rumors would be flying all over the medical center. I might just as well call up the *New York Times* and give them the story."

"But the patients—" began Barone.

"The patients will do just fine," interrupted Benson. "Which is more than I can say for you if I hear of you bringing this up again. Now get out of here!"

Barone rose slowly from the chair and shuffled to the door. He looked back over his shoulder as he let himself out. Maurie was scribbling furiously on a report, studiously ignoring him. He closed the door gently behind him.

"What about Lyme disease?" asked Maurie Benson.

The beads of sweat on the new intern's forehead glistened in the bright sunlight streaming in through the windows of the 4 East solarium. He mopped his brow and shrugged. "I really didn't consider that diagnosis."

Stuart Korman had replaced Peter Lee on 4 East only hours before. He had barely had time to meet his new patients. And Maurie was already beating on him.

Maurie turned to one of the third-year medical students rotating through the medical ward. "Perhaps one of our junior medical students can tell us how Lyme disease presents. Mr. Turner?"

The student did not miss a second in showing off. "Arthritis, fever, and sometimes meningitis."

"And what is the causative organism?"

"A spirochete, carried by the tick *Ixodes dammini,*" came the prompt reply.

Of course the junior medical students know this, thought Barone. We covered it in rounds last week. Before Korman was here.

"Now, Dr. Korman"—Maurie stressed the title "Doctor" sarcastically—"what can you tell us about leptospirosis?"

The intern sucked at his upper lip, was about to answer, when a nurse, entering the room, mercifully stopped the proceedings. "Dr. Benson?"

Maurie rolled his eyes. "Yes. What is it that you think is so important that you must disturb our rounds?"

She stopped in the doorway, frozen by the blast of contempt. "Dr. Benson." Her voice was taut, controlled. "I just wanted to let you know that there are two men here to see you—"

"Well, they will have to wait until after rounds," Maurie cut her off. "Send them to my office on the third floor."

She shrugged, started to close the door, when two men pushed past her into the solarium. The taller of the two, a dark young man in khaki pants, a white shirt, and a tie, spoke first. "Dr. Benson?" He addressed himself to Maurie.

Maurie nodded, irritated. "What is it?"

"We're from the New York City medical examiner's office," interrupted the shorter, balding man, taking out a handkerchief to wipe his forehead. "We'd like to talk to you about doing an autopsy on your patient, Suzanne Grayson."

The color drained from Maurie's face. Quietly, he dismissed the interns and medical students. Beckoning Barone to follow, he led the two men into the residents' on-call room. "What can I do to help?" he asked suspiciously.

The shorter man extended his hand. "My name is Dr. Bernard Glass, assistant medical examiner." They shook hands briefly. "My associate"—he gestured over his shoulder—"is Dr. Michael Mancia."

The younger man flipped open a small notebook. "We got a call this morning from a Dr. Baron"—he squinted at the scrawl in his book—"uh, Dr. B-A-R-O-N-E, who claimed to be a resident at this hospital."

"Used to be a resident at this hospital." Maurie scowled at the cringing resident."

"What's that?"

"He's standing right here." Maurie pointed. "Get on with it."

The short man opened a notebook of his own, continued. "He said that a Suzanne Grayson, a patient on this ward, had died during the night of unknown causes. He tried to get autopsy permission, but the family was not cooperative."

"That's right." Benson nodded.

"If she was a patient in the hospital, I would guess that she must have been ill."

Maurie pursed his lips. "That's the usual reason we keep them here."

The taller man broke in. "We don't need this facetiousness, doctor. We're just here to do our job. Now why did she enter the hospital?"

"She had leukemia and a supervening pneumonia with an empyema."

"Is there any reason, in this case, to suspect that her death may not have been due to the condition that caused her to enter the hospital?"

Benson answered a fraction of a second too quickly. "Not really."

"Then what was the cause of death?" persisted Mancia.

For the first time, beads of sweat broke out on Maurie's forehead. "We don't really know for sure. It may have been her pneumonia."

"We have been told," Glass broke in, "that she was improving."

The younger man frowned. "Look, Dr. Benson, we know that people in the hospital sometimes die of unknown causes. But this lady had a very high potassium level." The older man glared at him, slapped his notebook shut. "And we know that three other patients have died on this ward in the last eight days, all of unknown causes, all with unexplained high potassium levels."

"None of the potassium levels were in the lethal range," replied Maurie.

"No," answered the younger man. "Maybe not. But I think the whole story is suspicious. I want to do an autopsy on the Grayson woman—"

Maurie bristled, started to answer.

"Unless," said Mancia coolly, slowly, "you would rather that we exhume the other three bodies first."

"Look, doctor," the older man interceded. "No one is accusing you or the hospital of anything. But the ME's office has a job to do: *investigation.* If we passed by a tip like this, and there was anything to it, we'd end up looking awfully bad. We can't afford not to look into this."

"Of course," agreed Maurie, swallowing his anger. "My only concern is that this be done as discreetly as possible. I don't think for one minute that there is anything to this . . . this series of coincidences. But if the news of an investigation got out, it would irreparably damage the reputation of this hospital."

"Of course," said the older man. "We'll do what we can to keep this quiet."

The younger man winced. "Now, which way is the morgue?"

Maurie led them to the elevator, Barone following. The older man shook Benson's hand. "Thanks for your cooperation, Dr. Benson. I would like you to send us an attending physician's statement about Suzanne Grayson at your earliest convenience.''

The elevator door opened and the two medical examiners entered. Barone could barely overhear the younger man, speaking heatedly: *''You* can hush it up, Bernie. *I* don't want to be an assistant ME for the rest of my life.''

Peter Lee sat in the dazzling noonday sun, alone on a bench in the square concrete park adjacent to the Sixty-eighth Street schoolyard. The bench was poured concrete, as was every other surface in the park, except for the giant sandbox. Every other bench was packed with four and even five people; Peter sat alone.

A few young doctors from the hospital drifted through the park, on their way back from the ice cream shop on Sixty-sixth Street. They licked carefully at their rapidly melting ice cream cones. None of them noticed the vagabond sitting alone on the bench, just another displaced, homeless person in a city in which they were so numerous that most people considered them a part of the scenery.

Most of the others sitting on the park benches were young mothers, watching their young children play. Several were already pregnant again. Peter marveled at this display of fecundity in the midst of the sterile cityscape.

He stood up and began walking aimlessly up one street, turning onto the next, whichever way the traffic lights and honking taxis let him pass. Walking *nowhere,* he decided, had a lot of advantages over walking *somewhere:* You never went the wrong way, you never arrived too early or too late, and you were never disappointed when you arrived. He felt the warm sun beating on his head, peeled off his windbreaker, letting it trail over his shoulder. Indian summer. The last interval of warmth before the world again grows cold and barren.

He started across Park Avenue and had reached the center island when the light changed. He walked down the narrow parkway, hemmed in by onrushing autos on either side. The view down the avenue was unobstructed all the way to the gilt dome of the Helmsley Building, glistening in the midday sun. Behind that relatively modest structure, with its Victorian display of architectural individuality, rose the monolithic Pan Am Building, dark and foreboding. The avenue was like a canyon with steel and glass walls. And Peter Lee, unable to turn to either side, continued down the center of the parkway, drawn toward the golden dome.

He had been unable to tell Maurie how great his relief had been when he had been suspended from his patient care responsibilities. He had known that he had not been able to take proper care of his patients for some time. Each examination, every prescription had been a struggle. Each time he punctured a patient to start an intravenous line or draw blood, it was like penetrating his own flesh. No, it actually hurt him much more than it seemed to hurt his patients. He could not tell anyone how he felt, and that only intensified his pain.

Not since Sylvia had there been anyone that he could talk to. She would always listen, smile. Her gentleness always salved his inner pain.

Until Barone had taken her away from him.

He reached the foot of the Helmsley building and stood helplessly facing its stone wall, staring at the unbroken gray expanse. People rushed up Forty-seventh Street on either side, shoved past one another, ignoring him. He stood frozen, for how long he did not know. He could not decide which way to turn. Neither way seemed to hold any promise. Finally, as the sun began to fall behind the tall buildings to his right and the late afternoon shadows began to lengthen, he noticed a small dark space under a balustrade to his left. Curling up into the shadow, he pressed his burning cheek against the cold stone and drifted off into a fitful sleep.

Maurie Benson carefully closed the door to his office before saying a word. "I have been sitting in here, thinking all afternoon," he began soberly. Barone squirmed in the hard wooden chair. Maurie, deliberate and controlled, was even more intimidating than he was during an outburst.

"I didn't want to overreact," he continued. "Considering our conversation this morning, I think that you owe me an explanation for unilaterally calling the ME's office."

Barone shrugged involuntarily. He knew that Maurie had already considered and rehearsed an answer to any possible response. The show of coolheadedness and reason could only be Maurie's way of leading up to a vicious attack. At length, Barone responded: "Would you have called?"

This was apparently not one of the answers Maurie had rehearsed. Puzzled, he snapped back, "Of course not."

Barone stared into Maurie's smoldering brown eyes. "Well, then, somebody had to do it."

Maurie started pacing back and forth, the fury inside showing through the thin coating of civility. "Somebody had to carry on your sick little war against Peter Lee? Is that what you mean? Wasn't it enough for you to take Sylvia from him? To grind his self-respect under your heel during rounds every morning? To drive him into a deep depression that may have ruined his career? I suspended him from his internship, Barone. What more could you want?" He turned to face Barone. "Why did you also have to drag the hospital into this by accusing him of murder?"

Barone stood his ground. "I never accused him or anybody else. I never even mentioned his name to the ME."

"No." Maurie shook his head in mock reasonableness. "Of course not. All you did was to tell the ME that you thought someone had murdered four patients on Four East. You never expected that their investigation might implicate Peter Lee—"

"I never mentioned murder, Maurie," Barone interrupted. "I told them that we had four unexplained deaths and that we needed to get an autopsy."

"And you never for a minute thought the ME's office would consider the possibility of murder," agreed Maurie sarcastically.

"I can't help what they think. I just knew that we needed to get an autopsy on Suzi Grayson."

"So you could prove that Peter Lee was murdering his patients."

"So that I could find out why so many of *my* patients were dying with no explanation. Look, if the autopsy is normal, we will all be able to rest easier."

Maurie shook his head, sat down on the edge of his desk. "The autopsy is already abnormal."

Barone looked puzzled. "How could you—"

"The serum potassium is elevated. That is bound to lead to inquiries about the other patients."

"You were never concerned about the potassium levels before."

"I never thought they were elevated enough to account for any of the deaths. But that won't stop them from being fatal for the hospital. You may not be aware of this, Barone, but financially this hospital runs very close to the edge. Like every teaching hospital, we lose money on patient care but make it up on charitable contributions. This hospital is kept afloat by our big donors. This is very much a 'society' hospital, and appearances are very important to our overall viability.

"Once word gets out that we had a string of mysterious deaths, there will be no way to stuff the genie back into the bottle. For a hospital of this size, our cash reserves are dangerously low. We could go under in a matter of weeks."

Maurie stood up, stared out his office window, his back turned to Barone. "I have spent the entire afternoon talking to deputy mayors and assistant police commissioneers, and the ME himself. We all agree that there is no reason to air this bit of dirty linen in public. At least not until the autopsy is complete. At considerable risk to their own political careers, they have imposed a news blackout. If the autopsy turns up anything, it could be very difficult for them to explain why they participated in what will, in retrospect, look suspiciously like a cover-up. And so we had to promise them certain concessions."

Maurie turned back to face Barone slowly, giving the impact of his words time to sink in. "I had to promise them to do everything in my power to prevent a fifth death while they are keeping quiet about the other four. The Four East medical and nursing personnel are being reassigned to other parts of the hospital, no more than two to any one ward. If there are any more deaths, the suspects will be pinpointed.

"Furthermore, by mutual agreement, all of the doctors who were directly responsible for the care of the four patients will be temporarily relieved of their patient care assignments. Peter Lee, of course, has already been suspended. I guess that just leaves you, Dr. Barone."

Barone blanched, gripped the edge of his chair for support. But Maurie was not finished. He circled the desk, coming to a stop directly in front of the trembling resident. "In addition, the deputy police commissioner, at my suggestion, has personally requested that all of the former Four East personnel be barred from entering that ward. In your case, Dr. Barone, as you now have no other business here, I have asked the hospital security force to prevent you from even entering the hospital building.''

Barone's cheeks began to color. "But Sylvia—"

Benson cut him off, a smile of satisfaction creeping across his face. "She will remain on Four East. If you telephone the hospital information desk, they will keep you informed about her condition.''

Maurie walked around the desk, turned again, looked out the window. "There should be a guard outside the door, waiting to escort you off the premises.''

The security guard was polite but firm. No, Barone could not go up to 4 East to see Sylvia one last time. Yes, they were under orders to proceed to the nearest exit. No, he would not be permitted to reenter the hospital or its grounds. Yes, the hospital administration had authorized the use of any degree of force that was necessary to prevent him from returning, including the use of firearms.

The guard kept an iron grip on Barone's left elbow all the way to the front door of the hospital. He released him, shoved Barone into the revolving door, and pushed it halfway around. Then he stood in front of the door, on the inside, staring past Barone at the semicircular driveway, not moving. Barone began to leave, then stopped in the courtyard in front of the hospital and turned back toward the monolithic white building. From either side of the main tower, the two patient pavilions reached out to enclose the courtyard, like stone arms reaching out for him in a cold embrace.

He had never thought, after spending thousands of selfless hours in the care of patients on these wards, that his career at New York Hospital would end with his being forcibly ejected. His eyes began to well with tears, and he turned again and began to walk quickly away, hoping that no one would see.

Although it was already late afternoon, Barone realized that he had never before left the hospital so early in the day. The rush hour crowds surprised him, and he let himself be carried along by the stream of people, too discouraged to choose his own direction. Like a small craft cast adrift in a sea of people, Barone was washed by the waves of commuters, back and forth across the Upper East Side.

For the first time in his memory, he suddenly had no place to go. No school to attend, no job to go back to. The uncertainty of his future loomed in front of him like an open sea.

And he had lost his compass. Sylvia, the only one he could turn to, was being held captive, beyond his reach. He could not even tell his mother what had happened. He could not bear to tell her that her son, the doctor, had been unceremoniously suspended. Kicked out.

As the evening light began to fade, Barone found himself standing in front of his own apartment building. He looked at the uniformed doorman at the front entrance, wondering whether he would also be denied access to his own apartment. The building was, in fact, owned by the hospital, and therefore technically part of the hospital premises. Barone walked past the doorman with as casual an air as he could muster. The man did not even look up.

He took the elevator up to his apartment. A rush of stale air greeted him as he opened the door. He had not been back for three days. It was almost as if he had never lived there at all. The bed, the lamp, even the food in the refrigerator seemed foreign to him. The room was as lifeless as a mausoleum, a monument to a person who had been, but was no more. Barone showered, shaved, changed clothes. Then he closed the door of his airless cell behind him and took the elevator down to Sylvia's apartment.

He opened the door slowly, using the key she had given him. Sylvia's scent was still in the air, the indescribable soft sweetness of the air that surrounded her. He inhaled deeply, switched on the light, and closed the door softly behind him. Sitting on the edge of her bed, his hand stroked the coverlet. Overcome by a choking heat from deep in his breast, he allowed himself to fall back on the bed, wracked by convulsive spasms of sobbing. But no tears would come.

Somehow, he knew, he could bear up to the disgrace of being suspended from his residency. He could even learn to live with being a chief suspect in the deaths of four of his own patients. He might not be allowed to finish his residency. He certainly would never be accepted for a prestigious fellowship after his residency. But somehow, somewhere, he would have gotten back into medical practice. He would have survived.

But not without Sylvia. Over little more than a week's time, he had drawn closer to her than he ever had to another person. He was comfortable with her; he could tell her anything. He was in love with her, and he knew that she loved him too.

He could not, would not be separated from her. Not on account of Peter Lee. Not by Maurie Benson. Not under any circumstance. He struggled to his feet, switched off the light, locked up the apartment. Whatever the cost, he had to see Sylvia.

Barone took the elevator to the building's subbasement, a maze of intersecting corridors leading to the maintenance office, various power generators and, at the far side of the building, the tunnel. When the hospital had been constructed in the 1920s, the planners had laid out a network of tunnels to connect all of the main buildings underground. For the most part, the tunnel system was used only by building maintenance crews. The tunnels housed large steam pipes, bringing heat from the main power plant across the street from the hospital. In the summer, when the temperature in the tunnels sometimes approached 120 degrees, very few people used them. In the winter, especially during a snowstorm, residents taking a call from their apartments could be found scurrying back and forth through the tunnel at all times of the night.

Barone started into the tunnel, was met by a blast of hot air. He unbuttoned his collar as he walked down the slope into the first leg of the tunnel. The floor quickly dropped off, then leveled out. The corridor took a sharp turn as it crossed under York Avenue. He stopped at the corner; the next leg was clear. Quickly, he made his way along the corridor, staying near the wall. He turned the next corner and the next without seeing anyone. Finally, he turned into the last segment of the tunnel, leading into the hospital subbasement. Cooks and orderlies scurried along the corridor at the end of the tunnel, but there were no guards to be seen. Reaching the end of the tunnel, Barone slowly craned his neck, glanced briefly around the corner. No guards in either direction. He walked hurriedly from one hallway to the next toward the elevators running up to 4 East.

He pushed the call button for the elevator, then retired into a corner, studying a bulletin board while he waited. There was an opening for a cook's assistant in the hospital cafeteria. Someone was selling a used air conditioner. A new blood donation drive was beginning.

The elevator finally arrived. Barone watched, out of the corner of his vision, as two maintenance men emerged. He waited for them to walk down the hall, for the elevator door to begin to close, before he swiftly ducked inside. He pushed the button for the fourth floor, then stood at the back, staring at the floor. When two women got on at the ground floor, he slouched behind the taller one.

On the fourth floor, he pushed past the other passengers into the corridor and immediately turned the corner. Stopping in front of the board showing the roster of patients on the ward, he waited for the elevator doors to close. Cautiously he glanced to either side. No security guards in either direction. Slowly, he began to make his way to Sylvia's room.

Trying not to be conspicuous while avoiding the appearance of furtiveness was exhausting work. He drifted down the hall, eyes downcast, stopping to examine bulletin boards, posters, even fire extinguishers, to allow himself a sidelong glance. He was studying the nurses' night duty schedule, before attempting to drift unnoticed past the nurses' station, when Sandy, the plump, blonde nurse on the evening shift, turned the corner too sharply, while looking back over her shoulder at an orderly she was fond of. Her large, soft breasts plowed into Barone's chest before she caught herself.

"Chuck!" Her face reddened as she reflexively stepped back.

He quickly grasped her wrist and pulled her around the corner into an empty patient room. "Are you all right, Sandy?"

She nodded dumbly, staring at his face as if he were a ghost. "Chuck, I don't know . . ." She gasped. "It's just that . . . they told us . . . that you had been suspended . . . that you were not permitted to come up here."

"Maurie sure didn't waste any time." He shook his head bitterly.

She smoothed her dress, began to catch her breath. "Chuck, it's just awful. The head of nursing administration stopped here and said that if we see you we have to call security."

He grimaced, nodded. "Sure, you know me: vicious, hardened criminal." He stopped, took her hand. "Look, Sandy, I don't want you to get into any trouble over this. I just want to see Sylvia."

Her cheeks began to flush as she studied his face for a minute, probed his blue eyes. "Chuck, you have to promise never to let anyone know that I told you this. It could cost me my job."

Barone nodded gravely. "I promise."

She hesitated for a moment, then whispered. "They've moved Sylvia. Benson said you would try to see her. The woman in her old bed is a security guard. So is the old man sitting in a chair down the hall, near the door to her room. She's lying with her back to the door, so that when you come into the room to see her, the old man can block the doorway behind you. They plan to arrest you for trespassing."

Barone nodded again. "And where are they keeping Sylvia now?"

"Two rooms back down the hall. There is a security guard in with her, but she went to dinner. I'm supposed to keep an eye on the room."

Barone considered for a minute. "Can I . . . ?"

She stopped him, raised a forefinger to his lips. "Don't ask, Chuck. I didn't even see you. If I do see you, I'll have to call a security guard. But I won't be going into Sylvia's room for the next ten minutes."

He kissed her finger. "Thank you."

She blushed, then made a show of looking around the room blithely as if it were entirely empty, before stepping out into the hall. "Karen," he heard her calling to the nurses' aide on duty, "there's something I want to show you back in the medicine room. . . ."

Barone waited until he could no longer hear their steps, then peeked around the corner. The old man was buried in his newspaper. Barone edged out into the hall and made his way to the fire extinguisher outside Sylvia's new room. After checking the old man once more, he slipped into the room.

Sylvia was propped on her right side by pillows. He bent over her and brushed a comma of dark hair from her face, kissed her forehead. She did not stir.

Barone sat in the chair beside the bed and took her hand in his own. The fingers were limp and the skin was clearly yellow tinged. If only he had noticed that earlier! He was so proud of his medical knowledge. And the one time in his life when he had had the opportunity to use it to help someone he loved, he had blown it. He might just as well be a truck mechanic, for all the good his training had done.

He lowered the bed rail and buried his face in her shoulder. Despite the fetor hepatis, the sweet odor that penetrated her breath as a result of the liver failure, he could still detect Sylvia's own scent. He closed his eyes, let it fill his nostrils, overwhelming his other senses. Hot tears rolled off his cheeks and began to wet the neck of Sylvia's hospital gown.

He choked back a sob, wondered how much time he had left. Or whether he ought to leave at all. If the guards caught him at Sylvia's bedside, Maurie would finally have his pretext to dismiss him permanently. But at least it would show he could stand up to Maurie; it would show the world his love for Sylvia.

Or would it? Thanks to Maurie, he was now one of the chief suspects for the deaths on 4 East. How would it look now, his sneaking back onto the ward. Would they think that he was trying to kill Sylvia too?

Barone shuddered. No one but he, and Maurie, would know the truth. The publicity would wreck his career. And, of course, there would be no public recognition at all when he was finally cleared. Meanwhile, his mother would have to live with the accusation that her son was a murderer.

He raised himself slowly from the chair, wiping his

eyes with the heel of his hand. Sylvia would never have let him give up. She would have told him to fight, to get to the bottom of the problem, whatever way he could. He lifted her hand and kissed the fingers. For you, he thought. At least there would be a guard in with you tonight, to protect you.

He slipped out into the hall, found his way back through the tunnels, without being recognized.

A soft rain was pattering against the balustrade overhead, fat drops rolling off the edge of the railing onto the sidewalk, washing it free of the accumulated dirt of the day. Peter Lee hugged his body against the warm, solid stone of the face of the building, his bulwark against a world too cold and too harsh to face. Now and then a warm drop splashed against his exposed cheek, causing him to huddle still closer to the wall.

He watched the pairs of feet, clad in leather, walking past him. If only he could be protected like that, his entire self, separated from the world by a pliable shield, a leather cocoon that could keep out the vicissitudes of the world.

A pair of highly polished black leather men's oxfords stopped directly in front of him. "Come on, get up from there." Peter followed the blue gabardine pant legs up from the shoes, to the blue tunic and the outstretched billy club of the uniformed patrolman. "Come on, no loitering. This is private property." He poked at Peter's shoulder with the free end of the club. "Up and out now."

Peter began to stir. The patrolman poked him again in the shoulder. Impulsively, as much to help pull himself to his feet as to protect himself, Peter grasped the end of the club. Thinking that the vagrant was trying to steal his weapon, the patrolman tried to shake the club loose. Failing that, he delivered an openhanded slap to Peter's cheek.

The skin of his cheek stung, unleashing a flood of memories of his humiliation at the hands of Lauren Nyquist, Suzi Grayson. He grabbed the club more tightly, pulling the patrolman forward until he stumbled over Peter, kicking his leg. The sudden, sharp pain ignited a flash of rage. Peter reached up, punched the patrolman in the mouth. The man lost his grip on the club for a second, long enough for Peter to pull it completely away. The patrolman lashed out at Peter, who struck at him with the club once again. A small crowd began to gather as the patrolman tried to defend himself. Peter smashed the free end of the club against the man's arms. By now the patrolman was cowering on the sidewalk, Peter standing over him, beating him again and again. No one in the crowd moved to help.

Peter swung the club with as much force as he could, felt a sharp snap, as if a branch had been broken. The patrolman's arm fell away from his head, the hand bent back at an awkward angle. The next blow fell against the newly exposed left side of the patrolman's skull. Blood trickled from the ear. Peter swung again, felt a crunch, as the left side of the man's head caved in. The patrolman crumpled in a heap.

Peter dropped the club and stared at the growing knot of onlookers. He no longer felt angry. He no longer felt the sting of the slap, the pain of the patrolman's kick. He no longer felt anything at all. That was the best he remembered feeling in a long time, the best he could hope for. The crowd of awestruck passersby parted as he walked toward the street. No one tried to stop him.

He walked up Park Avenue, then over to Madison, before turning toward Central Park. The police vans, with flashing red lights, sped past him in the opposite direction. By the time the police had questioned the few bystanders who remained, all they could learn was that a young man, a street vagrant, had beaten a police officer to death.

Half of the onlookers thought the policeman had started the brawl, half thought it was the young man. No one could give a good description of the assailant, other than that he was dirty and disheveled. By the time the all-points bulletin was issued, Peter Lee was huddled beneath an outcropping of rock in Central Park, near the Sixty-seventh Street zoo. He watched the police cruisers drift by with bemused detachment. The darkness of the night was deepening.

Barone sat in the gloom of his apartment, bathed in the flickering light of the television screen. He had unconsciously turned on the news, which came on at 10:00 P.M. on the local station. He tried to watch the news before going to bed on nights when he was not on call. Tonight he sat numbly, staring as the images of local fires, bridge dedications, and political speeches flashed on the screen.

Suddenly, there was a female reporter, bathed in bright light, standing before the familiar white-lit facade. He got up from his chair and crossed to the television, turning up the volume.

". . . Rumors tonight that there have been a string of unexplained deaths at Manhattan General. An anonymous but highly reliable source has informed this reporter that the medical examiner was called in early today to investigate." Barone thought of the ambitious young assistant medical examiner. "Hospital officials refuse to confirm or deny the reports, but several hospital employees have told us that there has been a sudden stepping up of security, and that two of the doctors have been suspended. This is Tina Gregorie reporting for *Eyewitness News.*"

The camera switched to the anchorman. "In other late breaking news tonight, a policeman was beaten to death this evening on the street, one block from Grand Central—"

Barone switched the set off.

At least they didn't have his name yet. But it would only be a day or two, at most, before his suspension would become public knowledge. Barone began to pace the length of his apartment. He had to come up with some evidence against Peter Lee, or no one would believe him.

He threw himself down on his bed and closed his eyes, squeezing them shut tightly until he could feel a teardrop begin to form at the outer corner of each lid. Sniffling in, his nostrils filled with Sylvia's scent, lingering on his sheets from the night she had spent with him. God, he needed her now. He needed her physically, and like a drug addiction, he needed her even more emotionally. But now, what he needed most was the wisdom of her counsel. She would have been able to tell him what he had to do next. It had been her quiet thoughtfulness that had first led him to search through Maurie's files.

Of course, raiding Maurie's office again was out of the question; it would be too dangerous, and besides, who would let him into the office now? Even if he could get a copy of the letter in Peter Lee's file, the psychiatrist at the University of Maryland would never step forward to discuss Peter Lee's case. And the university hospital would never even admit publicly that Peter had been a patient.

The university hospital! That was it! The hospital would still have Peter's medical records in its archives. If he could only get ahold of them, he might find some evidence, some kind of clue as to why Peter Lee had become a murderer.

He leafed through his personal telephone book, located the number of an old friend doing a surgical residency at the University of Maryland medical center. His wife answered the phone.

"Hello. This is Chuck Barone. Is Wally home?"

"Chuck Barone?" She thought out loud. "Didn't you and Wally used to play tennis back in medical school?"

Barone chuckled. "That's right. Say, you have a great memory."

"I have to," she responded flatly, "to remember what my husband looks like these days."

"I gather he's not at home?"

"Oh, he's right at home, all right. In the hospital. Our apartment is just a place that he visits every now and then."

"It's tough being a surgical resident," Barone offered.

"It's tougher being the wife of one."

She gave him the telephone number of the hospital's page operator.

The rain had eased up and the relative silence intruded upon the shattered thoughts of the young vagrant crouched in the shelter of an outcropping of rock. His eyes still burnt, as if he had not slept for weeks. He rubbed a sandy grittiness from his lashes with his filthy fingers. He had to sleep, closed his eyes again.

It was futile. The traffic sounds were a constant reminder of a world of which he would never be a part. It would never let him, fully, into the pleasures of its life, and it would never really leave him alone. He straightened one leg. The knee joint ached and the entire limb tingled. He uncurled the other leg, massaged them both. It was good to feel *something*, even if it was pain.

With considerable effort, he pulled himself to his feet. At first he was unable to feel the ground under his feet. He wobbled, caught himself by holding onto a tree. Slowly, he stumbled out of the park, into the bright lights of Fifth Avenue.

The rivulets formed by the raindrops running down the side windows of the auto made it difficult to read the addresses on the gaunt tenement buildings. Barone had been to Baltimore only once before, but he had thought he could find his way around. He rolled down the window slightly to study the partly lit address on one old apartment complex. He blinked, the spray of raindrops hitting the edge of the window forcing him to squint. At least, on a night like this, no muggers were likely to be out on the streets. On a warm, clear night in September, he knew, it would be considered at least a suicidal gesture for a white boy to cruise alone through this neighborhood.

He finally made out the address on the building. Only six more blocks to go. Barone stepped on the accelerator, too hard for the ancient Chevy, and the engine began to stall. He eased up reflexively on the gas. Don't die now, he prayed. Not here.

After an interminable hesitation, the engine caught again, and he started off down the street, a bit too fast. He would have to have his mother's car tuned up. Some of the neighborhoods she drove in were not much better than this.

Barone turned a corner. The University of Maryland Medical Center sign, still two blocks off, lit up the night. As he approached it, he could see the smaller sign, EMERGENCY ENTRANCE painted above a red arrow, pointing down a side street. The Emergency Room entrance was under a covered portico. He parked in the area marked DOCTORS ONLY and walked in the rain, past a row of ambulances parked alongside the building. An ambulance, aglow with flashing red lights sat under the portico. He waited as two paramedics rolled a stretcher bearing an elderly woman, wrapped in red blankets, into the Emergency Room. He followed them in.

A nurse greeted the paramedics as soon as they were inside the door. One of them immediately began his spiel: ''An eighty-seven-year-old woman with chest pain, EKG shows no acute changes, no arrhythmias. Blood pressure one seventy over ninety. We gave her two nitros. . . ." His voice faded as the nurse guided him around the corner into the cardiac room.

A second nurse came up to Barone. "Can we help you—" She was cut off by a young man in a green scrub shirt and blue jeans. "It's okay, Rosie. This guy is here to see me."

Barone smiled, offered his hand. "Wally, Wally Lewis." His old medical school roommate had trimmed his beard and his hair, but still looked pretty much the same. Barone allowed his face to harden in mock reproof. "You sure picked one hell of a place to have an Emergency Room."

Wally tossed back his head as he chuckled, just as Barone had remembered. "Yeah, we thought we'd put it down here where the people get knifed and shot all the time. Saves gas in the ambulances. Not like the Upper East Side of New York, where the most exciting emergency you see is some young stud who catches his dick in his zipper while trying to put on his designer jeans."

Barone smiled. "Actually, we're only two miles from Harlem. We get our share of death and devastation."

Wally nodded in mock gravity, winking. "Sure, Chuckles." Barone bristled at the nickname which, fortunately, only Wally used. "Listen, I've got to see this old lady with the chest pain. Have a seat and I'll be right back." He pointed to a cluster of plastic stack chairs in front of a Formica counter on which were spread several patient charts.

Barone sat in one of the chairs and let his head roll back on his shoulders, then to each side. His neck muscles were tense after the long drive from New York in the rain. He began to knead his trapezius muscles. He shrugged; the tension began to ease in his neck and shoulders.

"Get a twelve-lead EKG, a CBC, and an amylase." Wally emerged from the examining room, still barking orders at the nurse. He plopped himself down in a chair beside Barone. "Now, Chuckles, I know you didn't drive four hours in the middle of the night through the driving rain just to see my handsome face. And don't give me that bullshit about your needing to see an old patient record for a presentation at grand rounds."

Barone hesitated a moment too long before responding. "It's true, Wally. I have to present this patient at medical grand rounds tomorrow. He has Munchausen's syndrome, goes around passing himself off at various medical centers around the country as having different illnesses. He gets some kind of weird kick out of it if he can convince them to operate. I need to review his psychiatric records from the University of Maryland medical center."

Wally shook his head. "And you couldn't have asked me to look up the records for you?"

"The chart is probably very thick. It would take you too long."

"I read fast." Wally shrugged.

"Besides, I really need to know the entire case history. You have no idea how tough it is to present at grand rounds at New York Hospital—"

"Sure," Wally interrupted, "I know. Attendings firing questions at you from every side . . ."

Barone nodded. "And your entire future at the hospital depends on your ability to show that you really know the facts of the case you are presenting."

Wally shook his head, exhaled. "Look, Chuck, I didn't buy that bullshit over the phone. And looking at your guilt-ridden face, I really don't believe it now. But if it is so important to you that you have to lie about it to your loyal old roomie . . ." He hesitated for a moment. Barone's ears were red. "Well, I'll get you the chart."

Barone sighed. The relief in his voice was palpable. "Really, Wally, it's not that I don't trust you—"

"Sure, Chuckles. You're just testing me, right? To see how far your old buddy will stick his neck out for you."

Barone looked at the floor. "I didn't mean it to be—"

"Dr. Lewis," the nurse called down the corridor. "We have that EKG for you."

Wally stood up, resting a hand on Barone's shoulder. "You don't have to explain. Maybe someday I'll need a favor from you." He started off down the hallway, then turned, continued walking backward. "What was that patient's name?"

"Peter Lee."

The filthy young man continued walking east toward the river. The buildings, towering above him on each side, were like the legs of reproving adults as he crawled by. As he reached each building, the lights seemed to come on in every window. The people inside were staring at him. He dared not look up at them, but he knew they were looking at him. He was sure of it.

At last he reached the iron fence of the Rockefeller University. He looked back down Sixty-sixth Street. The empty street between the tall high rises was like a canyon, ready to swallow him up. The face of the nurses' residence hall, across York Avenue, glowed pink orange at him. All the lights in the building seemed to be turned on. They were watching him, too.

He reached his arms through the iron fence, into the darkness beyond. His fingers caught the bough of an evergreen. Its needles felt fresh and cool. There was relief beyond the fence. Sanctuary. He pulled on the bough, tried to squeeze himself through the grating. The metal bars tore at the skin of his face. He grasped the bars with his hands, tried to shake them. No one would let him in.

Peter loped along York Avenue, looking for some hidden entrance. Suddenly, he looked up. Directly ahead was the stark white face of the New York Hospital, lit up against the black night sky. That was where Barone had hidden Sylvia. She needed him. The path in front of him, illuminated by the harsh white light reflected off the hospital, beckoned.

"Got a patient for you."

Barone, lying on the stretcher in the darkened examining room, did not even open his eyes. "Hey, I'm just a visiting doctor, waiting for a patient chart."

"Sorry, doctor's orders."

Barone opened one eye to see a tall, dark-haired man pulling a wheelchair backward into the room. "I said"—he raised his voice with a note of irritation—"I don't work here. I came down here from New York to examine a patient chart. And I'm just trying to grab a couple of minutes sleep while I wait for it to be delivered."

The man stopped in the doorway, his voice suddenly changing to a Irish brogue, "Aye, and we've just delivered a bouncing fifteen pound set of sextuplets for ye."

Barone opened his one eye again. The delivery man, turning the wheelchair around, was Wally Lewis. On the seat of the chair were piled six volumes bound in manila covers.

Barone pulled himself to a sitting position. "Holy shit. You mean that is Peter Lee's hospital chart?"

Wally shook his head. "Nope. Only the inpatient part. The outpatient chart is locked up in Dr. Davies' office in psychiatry. Looks like your little playmate is no stranger to our corridors."

Barone shrugged. "I told you his chart might be too thick for you to wade through while we chatted on the phone.'' He sat up and began to unload the thick volumes onto the stretcher.

"Have it your way, Chuckles.'' Wally yawned. "I won't pretend that I really wanted to read through *that.*'' He pointed at the charts, stretched. "The ER is pretty quiet. I'm going back to the on-call room to rack out for a while. Enjoy yourself, and if you have any problems . . .''

"Yes?'' asked Barone expectantly.

"Don't call. G'night.'' He padded off down the corridor.

Barone pulled up a tall stool. Using the stretcher as a desk, he assembled the volumes of the chart in order. The first volume contained various insurance and administrative forms, followed by daily temperature and blood pressure charts and medication orders. The second volume consisted mostly of the nurses' notes. At the end was a series of signed permits and reports on electroshock treatments.

The doctors' notes began in the third volume. The psychiatric resident's admission note alone was ten pages long. Barone skimmed through the description of the illness for which Peter Lee had been admitted.

A twenty-year-old white male, admitted for an acute psychotic break. He had previously been in good health. His father reports that he had been a good student with many friends until his last year in high school, when he gradually become more withdrawn. He stopped going to school activities after hours and spent long periods of time alone in his room. His father had difficulty communicating with him, but he grew closer to his mother.

In college, he made good grades during his first three years. He seemed to have few friends and almost never dated. He called home frequently and had long conversations with his mother, who said he appeared to be chronically depressed.

When he came home for summer vacation two weeks ago, he had lost weight and appeared slovenly. He would not seek a summer job and spent most of his time in his room.

One week prior to admission, his mother was found dead in her bed, apparently the victim of a heart attack. Following the funeral, he was continually tearful. He would not talk to his father or eat. For the last two days he would not get out of bed. This morning his father found him in the living room having a conversation with his dead mother. The patient refused to come to the hospital, but an ambulance was called. . . .

Barone read through the rest of the admitting history and the physical examination. Peter Lee had been healthy and was physically normal. Barone continued with the resident's report of his examination of Peter's mental state.

General appearance: The patient is a disheveled young man, dressed in expensive but wrinkled and dirty clothes. He sits quietly in a chair, staring into a corner and occasionally asking a question or offering a reply as if he were conversing with someone.

Mood and affect: The patient looks sad. When asked if he is feeling low, he nods, but will not speak. Occasionally he begins to cry and once continued sobbing for several minutes.

Thought form: He does not respond to most conversation, but spontaneous outbursts show blocking of ideas and derailing of the train of thought.

Thought content: The patient's conversation with the imagined person in the corner suggests a delusional framework in which he imagines that he is being persecuted by the same people who are trying to kill his mother. He believes that they have told other people to apprehend him by broadcasting his thoughts on television and publishing them in the newspapers. He is afraid that they are placing thoughts into his mind, forcing him to kill himself or his mother.

Sensorium: He appears to be alert, but will not answer questions about where he is or what day it is. When asked if he sees someone standing in the corner, he nods but will not say who it is. However, from his comments it appears that he is talking to his mother. When asked directly, he will neither confirm nor deny this, and he will not answer any questions about his mother or her health.

Barone skipped down to the admitting impression.

This twenty-year-old man seems to have had a course of chronic personality deterioration for at least the last four years. His relationship with his mother was particularly close, perhaps the only close relationship in his life. Following her death, he has experienced an acute psychotic episode. While he is clearly depressed, I am reluctant to diagnose a primary psychotic depression. In view of the previous history of a much more chronic process, beginning in late adolescence and worsening gradually over at least four years, I would favor the diagnosis of chronic schizophrenia.

Peter Lee could not take his eyes off the majestic white tower, illuminated against the velvet black night sky. It lit up the heavens; it attracted him as if by some primordial instinct, like a moth to a candle.

It was even more attractive than a candle: While a

moth performed his arabesque without knowing why, Peter knew what the attraction was. Sylvia was there.

He walked along the sidewalk on York Avenue, head back, entranced by the alabaster monolith. He stumbled on a crack, almost ran into a drunk sitting on the ledge in front of the Rockefeller University fence. It did not matter. He was going to see Sylvia.

He approached the front of the hospital, head tilted back, as if he were admiring the stonework above the entrance to a cathedral. Or a mausoleum. He pushed through the revolving door, into the main foyer, paneled in dark stone inscribed with the names of honored donors. It reminded him of the walls of Westminster Abbey. He wondered how many of Manhattan General Hospital's honored dead might be buried in its walls or under its hallways.

"Can I help you?" Peter Lee had been staring at the stonework, ignoring the entrance guard, until he nearly walked into him. "Can I help you?" the guard repeated, in a tone suggesting that he doubted it.

Peter fumbled for a minute. He had never been stopped at the hospital entrance before. "Why, uh, I'm a doctor here."

The guard squinted at him in disbelief.

"Dr. Lee." Peter answered the implied question.

"Got an ID?" asked the guard.

Peter fished in his wallet, pulled out the hospital identification card.

The guard looked hard at the picture, then back at Peter, then at the ID again. He motioned for Peter to follow him to a desk at the side of the foyer. There he shuffled through a stack of loose papers, finally coming up with a Xeroxed half sheet. "It says here, doctor, that you have been suspended. We're not supposed to admit you onto the hospital grounds except for patient visits to Dr. van Arsdale. It's a little late for an appointment, doc."

"But I have to visit a sick patient."

"Sorry," answered the guard. "No exceptions."

"She'll die if I don't see her."

The guard's face became grim. "Look, doc, I'm just a security man. I don't know anything about medicine. If you're really that concerned about it, you can call Dr. Benson at home. There's a telephone on the desk over there." He pointed to a small reception desk across the foyer.

Peter did not move. He looked past the guard to a second security officer stationed at the far end of the main corridor. He was pretty sure he could outrun the old man he had been talking to, but the guard at the end of the hall would have time to block Peter's path.

He shrugged and walked back through the revolving door into the night.

Barone thumbed through the doctors' progress notes. It had been a long hospital stay, and the young psychiatric resident had written copious notes. He described his sessions with Peter, the psychotherapeutic maneuvering, the daily revelations, all in minute detail. Interspersed with the long daily reports were occasional shorter notes by the attending psychiatrist, Dr. Davies. Most of the latter's notes tended to temper the comments of his younger associate, adding findings which were dissonant with those of the psychiatric resident and questioning his theories of the interpersonal dynamics of Peter Lee's illness.

At one point the resident wrote:

I believe that the patient's psychotic behavior springs from some unresolved conflict regarding his relationship with his mother. The depression, in my view, is an acute process, caused by his mother's death but not necessarily related to his underlying psychotic state. This hypothesis is supported by the extent to which his delusional state revolves around his mother's continued presence, rather than grief or guilt about her loss. He is so deeply involved in his love-hate relationship with her that he cannot admit, even to himself, that the object of his all-consuming ambivalence is gone.

I have spend the last six weeks in a psychotherapeutic approach focusing on his feelings for his mother, in as nonjudgmental a way as possible. He continually skirts the central issue, acting embarrassed and pointing out that his mother's presence in the room makes any frank discussions difficult.

I have, until now, carefully avoided confronting this delusion while I have tried to forge a therapeutic alliance with the patient. I have, instead, focused our discussions on the secondary delusional concepts reported by the patient, such as his belief that people are trying to hurt him and his mother and that they are broadcasting his thoughts and movements on television. Despite intensive psychotherapy, and six weeks of both antidepressant and neuroleptic drug therapy, these delusional beliefs remain firmly entrenched.

Beginning tomorrow, I will try a new approach, implosion therapy. This form of psychotherapy, in which the patient is suddenly forced to confront his fears, has proven to be quite useful in treating phobias. I will attempt to bring the conversation around to his mother's death, and if he denies it, I will present him with the physical evidence of her demise: a newspaper obituary, a photograph of the grave site. I believe that the risk inherent in this approach is justified by the absence of progress with more conventional forms of treatment.

The note was signed by the psychiatric resident and countersigned by Dr. Davies, who offered his own terse comment.

Although I do not completely agree with the above assessment concerning the origin of the patient's problems, I reluctantly concur that some new plan of action is necessary. If the patient responds to implosion therapy, it will be strong evidence that the depression is symptomatic and not causative of the psychotic state. If he does not respond, we will have to assume that we are dealing with a psychotic depression of unusual severity, and will proceed with electroshock treatments.

The resident's note the following day was written with the same pen, but the handwriting was much scratchier and less steady.

The patient was in his usual delusional state at the beginning of our daily session, asking that we let him out because people were coming to hurt him and his mother. I asked him who these people were, and he replied that he was not sure but that he thought they were government agents or perhaps from the Mafia.

I next asked him why these people would want to harm his mother. He answered that he thought they were jealous of her. I asked why they were jealous, and he said that they wanted her because she was so beautiful.

I then asked him where his mother was. He pointed to an empty chair in the corner of the office. I shook my head and told him that I could not see her. I walked to the corner, put my hand on the chair, and said, ''She's not there.''

The patient became anxious. ''She's there! She's sitting right there!'' he replied.

I shook my head again. "She's not there, Peter. You know that she's dead."

He began to tremble. He stood up, went over to the chair in the corner, and placed his hand on the empty seat. I showed him the newspaper obituary and the photo of the grave site. "Peter," I said, "she died. That's why you are here. You had to come into the hospital. It was more than you could take, more than anyone could take. We're here to help you."

He began to sob. I offered him a tissue and told him that we could talk more about it tomorrow. His fingers gripped the back of the chair so hard that his knuckles turned white.

Suddenly he lifted the chair, then started moving toward me. I began backing toward the door. He followed me, threatening with the chair, which he now held in front of him.

I backed out into the corridor and called for help. He lifted the chair above his head, as if about to throw it at me. Two aides answered my call and we were able to pinion his arms while I took the chair away. The three of us were able to encourage the patient to enter one of the isolation rooms.

Due to his violent behavior, the patient will be kept under twenty-four-hour observation.

The signature barely looked as if it had been written by the same hand as the earlier notes.

The next page was an Emergency Room evaluation sheet, followed by a two-page neurosurgical consultation. The patient had become violent while in one of the isolation rooms on the psychiatric ward. Before the attendants could stop him, he had smashed his head several times against the wooden door to the room resulting in profuse bleeding. There was an eight-centimeter scalp laceration. Two units of blood were cross-matched and the Operating Room had been placed on call. However, skull X rays did not show any fracture and a CAT scan was normal. The neurosurgery resident sutured the scalp laceration in the Emergency Room. He estimated that there had been one unit of blood loss, but that no transfusion was necessary at that time. Two slips of paper were pasted to the chart, indicating that the two units of type AB negative blood had been released to the blood bank.

For the next two days, there were only follow-up notes by the neurosurgeons. On the third day, Peter Lee began electroshock treatments. There were no further notes by the psychiatric resident.

The thin young man sat behind the counter in a red and white striped shirt, lighting a marijuana cigarette. His sallow, pockmarked cheeks sucked in as he took a deep drag, filling his lungs with the acrid smoke. He held his breath as long as he could before expelling it.

From 3:00 until 7:00 A.M. was the dullest part of the night. His only customers were usually the night shift workers from the hospitals on the next block, who came over for a slice of pizza during their break. Most of the time, he just made dough or sliced vegetables for the next day. Which was why he was so sure that the dirty young man with the sunken dyes, leaning against the counter, was going to be trouble.

"Whaddaya want?" The counterman carefully stubbed out his joint. He tried to look the young man in the eye—he had heard that could scare away a stickup man—but the coal black eyes darted about nervously. When he finally caught them, they burned with such intensity that the counterman had to turn away.

"Some pizza." The customer was so nervous that he practically seemed to be vibrating. "Two slices."

The counterman nodded and put two cooked slices

of pizza into the oven to warm. He walked to the back counter and began kneading some dough, wondering if he should slip into the back room and call the police.

"In a box," called the customer. "I'd like it in a box."

"It ain't ready yet," the counterman replied nervously.

"I don't care. Give it to me now. In a box."

The counterman shrugged. The front of the shop was open. If the customer had a gun and meant to shoot, there was nothing he could do about it now. He placed the two slices into a delivery box, closed it up. "That will be two-fifty."

The customer hesitated.

"A buck each for the slices and fifty cents for the box," he explained, almost apologetically. He expected the young man to pull out his gun. It was time. He braced for the impact of the bullet.

Instead, he pulled out two crumpled bills and two quarters.

The counterman pocketed the money. Combat pay, he thought. I can always tell the boss I ate the pizza myself.

Peter Lee carried the box of pizza on his shoulder, partially obscuring his face, as he came in the back entrance of New York Hospital.

The guard stopped him, sniffed. "Smells pretty good."

"Pizza." Peter nodded. "For the nurses on Four East."

The guard shook his head. "No wonder so many of the night nurses are getting fat. First hallway to the left, then take the elevator to the fourth floor."

* * *

* * *

Barone paged through the progress notes made during the electroshock treatments. There were three treatments a week, extending over a five-week period. Each treatment was marked by a stereotyped note by the physician who applied the electroshock:

> Intravenous line started and patient injected with 50 mg Brevital and 5 mg succinylcholine. An airway was placed and 50 watt-seconds of current applied across the right and left temporal regions, resulting in a modified tonic-clonic seizure. Patient required mask ventilation for thirty seconds, then resumed breathing spontaneously. Returned to ward in good condition.

The progress notes from this period, written by a different resident, were considerably shorter and less speculative than the ones from the previous six weeks. The new resident mostly dwelled on the profound amnesia for recent events caused by the electroshock therapy. As a result, any serious psychotherapy was impossible, and the patient spent most of his time between treatments walking around the ward in a daze.

Around the fourth week, Peter Lee began to forget his delusions. A week later, he was barely able to remember his own name, but the psychosis was gone.

In the following week, the resident recorded her attempts to restart psychotherapy. The patient initially resisted, but by the end of the week had begun to talk more openly about his problems. In her note on the last session of the week, she reported her conversation with the patient.

> We began to discuss, for the first time, the reason for his hospitalization. He was visibly saddened and said that he knew now that his mother was dead. He

became very quiet, and I was afraid for a moment that he might be hallucinating again.

After a few minutes, he asked me if I could keep a secret. I reassured him that all of his comments to me were confidential. He then told me that, as his memory returned, he was disturbed by some dim recollections of the weeks preceding his hospitalization.

Apparently, his mother had been very beautiful, a tall, thin woman, with long chestnut brown hair and soft gray eyes. He admitted that he had always felt a certain sexual longing toward her. During the period of his depression, he came to rely on her more and more, to depend on her emotional support, as expressed by frequent close physical embraces. It was during one of those encounters that he pressed his hand against her breast when he kissed her. She gave him a cross look, and threatened to tell his father if it happened again.

The following afternoon, while she was taking a nap, he slipped into her bed beside her and kissed her cheek. She slapped him and tried to get up, but he held her down. When she started to call for his father, he placed a pillow over her face. She struggled and he pressed against the pillow until she stopped.

I tried to question the patient, gently, about this incident, but he held fast to his belief that he was responsible for his mother's death. Dr. Davies and I both believe that this is a secondary delusion caused by the patient's finally coming to grips with his mother's death, during a period of some mental confusion caused by the electroshock treatments.

During the following week, the patient did not talk of killing his mother, and on direct questioning denied it. The resident's note was short.

He has at last abandoned his delusional state and will soon be ready for discharge. He plans to return to the university to resume his senior year as a pre-medical student.

The elevator opened on 4 East. Peter Lee slipped out, laid the pizza box on a counter, and surveyed the patient room assignment board. He did not see Sylvia's name. He scanned the board a second time, but still did not see her listed. He began to panic: Maybe they had moved her.

No, he thought, they were probably just trying to hide her from him. They often had celebrities in Manhattan General Hospital, but for the sake of privacy their names were never put up on the assignment board. There was only one private room on 4 East without a patient name: 407.

He edged down the hall, sticking close to the wall. It was a quiet night, and there was a low buzzing of voices from the nurses' station but no movement in the hall. He pushed the door to room 407 open slowly.

The light over the bed was on low. He squinted at the form of the patient lying, her face partly hidden by long dark tresses, in a pool of light. It was Sylvia.

He entered the room and was halfway to the bed before he realized that there was someone propped in a chair in the corner. In the near darkness he could make out a woman, in a blue security guard's uniform. Her head was lying back, dozing.

As Peter approached, the guard stirred. He reached for the bedside table and found a metal emesis basin. The guard opened her eyes, started at the sight of the dark form in front of her. Peter brought the basin down on her head with a dull thud. She slumped back in the chair, unconscious.

He turned to the bed where Sylvia lay. At last, he thought, we are together. He brushed the strands of hair from her cheeks. The bright yellow color of her complexion shocked him at first, but he continued to stroke her cheek, which was soft and warm.

"Barone did this to you, Sylvia," he whispered. "He did this to us. He'll pay for it. No one can come between us."

He interlaced his fingers with her limp hand and held it to his cheek. Tears came to his eyes. "Sylvia, sweet, sweet Sylvia," he murmured, and laying his head next to hers, kissed her cheek.

He stretched out next to her, along the edge of the bed, and rolled her body over, pulling it against his own. He kissed her on the mouth. She was dry and slightly sweet smelling. It did not matter; he kissed her again.

His hand caressed the soft skin of her back, the plump fullness of her buttocks. He ground his hips against hers, feeling the warm pressure in his abdomen swell.

He lay back, his arm supporting her shoulders, sighed with a deep sense of fulfillment he had long dreamt of. "I'll make you mine," he whispered into her insensate ear. "Ever since I was a little boy, we have both dreamed of this."

Peter Lee sat at the edge of the bed and slid Sylvia's arms out of the hospital gown, then slowly drew it down her body. He gently caressed each small, firm breast, running his fingertips over the nipples. His breath came thicker as the sense of warmth in his loins grew. His hand ran down the soft smooth skin of her abdomen, his fingers burying themselves in the downy fur of her pubic hair.

He placed her hand over his crotch, using it to massage himself, savoring the increasing warmth and fullness that he felt. The hand slid back to the bed as he unzipped his fly and freed his swollen erection. Lying beside her, he ran her limp fingers along its shaft and cupped them over him.

"It's been such a long, long time," he whispered, mounting her. He gritted his teeth as he pressed against her, into her, rhythmically grinding his hips against her. "I love you," he growled, biting at Sylvia's ear, "I love you"—until his body convulsed in orgasm, his throat tightening—"I love you, Mother."

Wednesday Morning, September 18

Barone walked in with the usual crush of mid-morning arrivals—laboratory technicians, accountants, porters, secretaries—all of the nonmedical staff vital to running a hospital. He hunched over a bit, stared straight ahead, hoping to make himself less conspicuous, as he passed the guards at the entrance. The hospital tunnel entrance would have been safer, but there was no time. Not after what he had read last night in Peter Lee's medical records.

"Hey, you," called one of the security guards.

Barone ducked his head down and continued to walk. He had tried to call from Baltimore, but the night nursing administrator had refused to talk to him. Under Dr. Benson's orders, all she could release was Sylvia's condition: serious but stable. When he had tried to explain to her that Sylvia was in danger, she had hung up on him. He had driven back, traveling at the top speed his mother's old Chevy could muster, and parked illegally across the street. And no guard was going to stop him now.

"Hey, you there. Stop."

The guard started after him. Barone broke into a run, darting between startled workers. At the end of the foyer was an open stairwell with slate steps. He looked back over his shoulder at the pudgy guard, who was already red faced and puffing. Barone hit the stairs at full speed, taking the steps two at a time. There was no way the older man could catch him.

"Halt or I'll shoot." The voice from the bottom of the stairwell was tired but angry. The guard was a retired policeman. He was not used to having his orders disobeyed. And even if he could no longer run, he was still quite a good shot.

Barone did not look back. They would never shoot at him. Not in the hospital. Not with all these people around. He did not even break stride as he hit the first landing.

He felt the bits of plaster, blown out of the wall in front of him stinging his face before he actually heard the report of the first shot. Barone grabbed the rail at the landing and vaulted over it to reach the second flight of stairs. He heard the second shot and the high-pitched *ping* as it ricocheted off the slate steps. He was halfway up the next flight of stairs before he heard the wail of a woman on her way to her post as nurses' aide in the newborn nursery, who had been hit in the leg by the stray bullet.

Barone reached the second floor, out of sight of the guard who was still struggling up the first flight of stairs. He thought about continuing up the staircase, but knew that the guard would be radioing his location to security officers all over the hospital. In a few seconds, there would be guards in position, waiting for him to come out of that stairwell on every floor. He ducked instead into the second floor hallway, dashed down the corridor to the West Pavilion stairwell, and continued his upward climb.

Guards would probably be converging on 4 East. They would be expecting him to come up the stairwell or down the hall from 4 West. And there would be plenty of time for men with guns to stop him on either approach. He continued climbing, past the 4 West landing and stopped at the fifth floor. He peeked around the corner. A security guard was hurrying away from him, down the hall toward the East Pavilion, his keychain jangling from his belt. He disappeared into the East Pavilion stairwell.

Barone made his way cautiously down the same hall. Every few yards he stopped to listen for more running feet or jangling keys. He opened the door to the stairwell slowly; there was no sound of footsteps and no one on the fifth floor landing. Silently, he entered the stairwell and let the door close behind him. Edging over to the bannister, he leaned over to catch a glimpse of the fourth floor landing. A security guard was stationed on the inside of the door, gun drawn, pointed down the staircase. They were waiting for him to come *up* the stairwell.

Barone took a deep breath and grasped the rail with both hands. There was only one chance. Swinging his feet over the top of the railing, he pulled as hard as he could with his arms to arc his body forward, toward the foot of the staircase at the fourth floor landing. The guard barely heard the muffled sound of Barone's take-off. He did not even have time to raise his eyes, let alone his gun, before the sole of Barone's left shoe smashed into the bridge of his nose. The gun, still pointed downward, discharged, blasting a chunk of plaster from the wall of the stairwell. The two men collapsed in a pile on the floor of the landing.

Barone cursed to himself. The gunshot would draw help in a matter of seconds. He disentangled himself from the unconscious guard. There was no time to see if the man was hurt. He had to get to Sylvia.

He burst through the stairwell door onto 4 East. Two guards were already rushing toward him, one of whom had already begun to draw his weapon. Barone ran as fast as he could, smashing his left shoulder into the chest and face of the closer man. He could feel a crunching and a sharp pain ran down his arm, as he used his momentum to push the first, stunned guard into the second.

Barone rebounded from the impact, rushed down the hall toward Sylvia's room. The security guard posing as an old man, posted in the corridor in front of Sylvia's old room, was already rising from his chair, his gun drawn.

Barone ran at him at full speed.

The guard tried to take aim at him, but could not get a clean shot down the crowded hospital corridor. He hesitated, waiting for Barone to come within range. Suddenly, Barone let his legs slide out from under him on the slippery tile floor. Rolling along the hallway, he bowled over the astonished guard before he could correct his aim. The guard went flying. Barone scrambled to his feet, plunged toward Sylvia's door, ignoring the shouts from down the hall.

He hit the door with his injured left shoulder. A sharp pain ran down to his elbow and up into his neck. He stumbled to the bedside as three guards piled into the room behind him.

Barone bent over Sylvia. Strands of dark hair covered her face. He waited in agony for her to breathe.

"Hold it right there, asshole!" Two guards had their guns trained on Barone. He reached out a hand to brush the hair from her face. Still no breath sounds.

"I said hold it, you motherfucker! Touch her again and you're dead." Barone felt the cold steel of a gun barrel at the back of his head. He moved the strand of hair. If Sylvia were not alive, it did not matter. He felt the click of the revolver pressed against the back of his skull as the guard pulled back the hammer. "Just give me an excuse, asshole."

Sylvia gasped, then took a deep breath. Barone lifted his hands above his head.

"What's going on here?" asked a woman's voice

from the corner. One guard roughly shoved Barone against a wall and began to frisk him.

"I don't have any weapons," Barone complained to the wall. "I just wanted to make sure she was all right."

A guard jerked Barone's left wrist back, sending another jolt of pain up into his neck. "That's right, Dr. Schweitzer. And I'm the good fairy." He snapped on a handcuff; it pinched the skin of Barone's wrist.

"Of course she's all right." The woman guard got up from the chair in the corner. "I was with her all night."

"Sure you were," called Barone over his shoulder. "You were asleep in the chair over there when I came in."

The woman's face reddened. She rolled her eyes and began to shrug, the universal response to the ravings of a lunatic. But as she began to hunch her shoulders, an expression of pain suddenly passed over her face.

"You okay, Celia?" asked one of the other guards. "He didn't attack you, did he?"

She put on a brave face. "No, he didn't. He just ran right to the girl." She massaged the back of her skull and neck. "I must have got a stiff neck from . . . sitting in that chair all night."

"Take me to Maurie Benson," demanded Barone. "And don't leave Sylvia alone. Not for a minute."

Another jolt of pain shot up Barone's arm as the guard yanked the handcuffs upward. "Just who the hell do you think you are?"

Barone winced. "Call Benson. Tell him that I have to talk with him. Tell him that I have some new information about Peter Lee."

The guard shoved Barone through the wooden doorway. Barone winced as another flash of pain ran through this left arm and shoulder. The guard stationed himself at Barone's side and closed the door.

"You're lucky I'm even seeing you, Barone," Maurie began. "I should have just let the security guards turn you over directly to the police. But I wanted to see you one last time—in handcuffs."

Barone's face reddened. "I have some new information." He swallowed. "Peter Lee is a chronic schizophrenic."

Benson's face darkened. "Peter has a history of psychiatric problems. I have always known that. I won't debate the diagnosis with you; it doesn't make any difference. He's a competent physician, who occasionally suffers from bouts of depression. This program is committed"—Maurie leaned across the desk—"*I* am committed to giving him a fair chance. His psychiatric history does not make him a murderer."

Barone glared back. "He murdered his mother," he said slowly, "during his first psychotic break."

Maurie stared at him in disbelief. "Are you sure?"

Barone stared back. There was no need to answer.

"How did you find that out?"

Barone's face began to color. "I asked a, uh, friend of mine at the University of Maryland to read through his medical records. Peter confessed to his therapist that he had smothered his mother with a pillow. He had made some veiled sexual advances toward her, and she had brushed him aside."

Maurie's face darkened. "Are you saying that you used your medical connections to invade the privacy of another man's medical records?" The veins at his temples began to bulge. "That is confidential information, protected by the doctor-patient relationship. What you did was not only useless, it was unethical."

"Useless?" echoed Barone.

"Useless!" thundered Maurie. "Peter was in a psychotic depression. He was delusional. He felt hopeless, helpless, guilty. He would have confessed to anything, from killing his parents to killing Jesus Christ.

"I have had it with your sactimonious attempts to destroy Peter Lee's career. I'm sure that I could have you prosecuted for invading the privacy of Lee's medical records. But it will be much simpler just to have you charged with trespassing." He picked up the telephone, buzzed his secretary. "Bernice, get Sergeant Decker for me, at the Yorktown precinct office." There was a pause. "What? Why is he here?" Pause again. He glanced at Barone, sitting in the corner. "All right," he conceded. "Send him in."

A moment later there was a sharp knock, rattling the glass pane of the door. Dr. Mancia, from the medical examiner's office entered without waiting for a reply. He stared for a moment at Barone, handcuffed and under guard, then addressed Maurie.

"Doctor Benson," he began, emphasizing the title in a way that implied that he did not believe it was deserved, "we have finished the autopsy on the Grayson woman. We were unable to determine a cause of death."

Maurie had been sitting forward, tense. He began to settle back in his chair, a look of satisfaction on his face. "I told you that you wouldn't find anything." He almost smiled. "I have some—"

"I didn't say we didn't find anything. Just that we still don't know the cause of death. But we're quite certain that she was murdered."

Maurie arched forward in his seat. "What do you mean? How can you be so sure that she was murdered if no cause of death was found?"

The young medical examiner approached the edge of Maurie's desk and stared down at him. "We found semen in Miss Grayson's vagina. Very fresh."

"So what?" Maurie's face was red. "A young, attractive girl like that, she must have had plenty of boyfriends. Even when she was sick in the hospital, one of them might have visited. It happens all the time."

Mancia shook his head. "This semen was deposited after she died."

Maurie's face was ashen. "How could you know that—"

"There were several scrapes on the skin of the labia and vaginal vault as a result of intercourse, but no evidence of hemorrhage. The absence of bleeding indicates that the skin was injured *after* her death."

Maurie slumped against the back of his chair. "Are you sure?"

Dr. Mancia sneered, nodded. "Even the most valiant stud of a boyfriend would have noticed that something was wrong. No, she must have been raped by the same man who killed her."

"Where is the other medical examiner?" Maurie pleaded. "The older man. I want to talk to him."

Mancia's face remained fixed in its taunting smile. "Bernie's been taken off the case. I'm in charge now."

Maurie squeezed his fingers against his eyes, as if to hold back the tears. He brought his thumb and forefinger together against the bridge of his nose. Without opening his eyes he asked: "Did you find anything else?"

Mancia took a half step back, as if to release his pressure on his resigned prey. "Two things. Her potassium was seven point three. Abnormally high, but probably not high enough to kill a young person with a healthy heart. And we blood-typed the semen. It was AB."

"Peter Lee!" gasped Barone.

Mancia turned toward him. "What did you say?"

Barone cleared his throat. "That is Peter Lee's blood type. It was in his medical chart."

"That's a rare blood type," Maurie interjected. "Are you certain?"

Barone nodded.

"Where can we find this Peter Lee?" asked the medical examiner.

Maurie shrugged. "He was the intern who was taking care of the patients who died. I suspended him"—Maurie looked at the handcuffed resident—"at your request, when you took the Grayson girl for autopsy."

"Where can we find him now?"

Maurie shrugged. "I'm not sure. He is only supposed to return to the hospital to see"—Maurie glanced again at Barone—"to see his doctor for medical appointments."

"What kind of appointments?" asked Mancia.

"That is none of your business," replied Maurie.

"Then you had better make it my business." Mancia leaned over the desk again, glowered at Maurie. "I hope I don't have to remind you that you have already tried to obstruct a homicide investigation. If I were in your shoes, I would be *very* cooperative. . . ."

Maurie swallowed hard, stared at the blotter on his desk. "He's supposed to see a staff psychiatrist."

Mancia's jaw dropped. "You mean you knew all along that this guy was mentally disturbed?"

Maurie shook his head without looking up. "He's depressed. That doesn't make him a murderer." He sounded less convinced than he had a few minutes earlier.

Mancia bent lower, stared Maurie in the eye. "Why are you protecting this guy?"

Maurie looked down again. "I'm not protecting anyone. I made the decision to take Peter Lee as an intern, despite his psychiatric history. He had been sick years ago. But he had done very well in medical school. I thought he deserved a chance. And I still don't want to see him persecuted by some . . . some witch-hunt."

"Well, I think the police will be a little bit less understanding about it. This is a rape-murder case now. And if we can find a pubic hair on Miss Grayson that belongs to the killer, we can make a positive ID. I still don't know how she was killed, but I think that the police will want to talk to Dr. Lee about that.

"There's a police detective outside who wants to talk to you. I think you ought to be very helpful to him."

Maurie did not look up. "I assure you of my complete cooperation," he said flatly.

"Good," said Dr. Mancia. "And afterward we can go downstairs together to the press conference."

Maurie lifted his head, a look of disbelief on his face. "Press conference?"

Mancia came as close to smiling as his sullen features would allow. "I took the liberty of scheduling one for noon," he said evenly. "After we put the case on the police blotter, we got a big press response. Rather than have them come calling one at a time, picking us apart, I figured we might as well face them all together. Then you can tell them how shocked and dismayed you are"—he eyed Maurie carefully—"and how you are aiding the police investigation in every way possible.

"By the way"—he pointed to Barone—"why do you have the doctor here in handcuffs?"

Maurie dropped his gaze back to the desk top. "We caught him trespassing."

"Trespassing? I thought he worked here."

"I suspended him yesterday, along with Dr. Lee."

"Well, isn't that cute," snorted Mancia. "You have a rapist and a murderer on your staff, so you let him go and lock up the man who turned him in . . . for trespassing!"

"It's not quite like that—"

"Maybe not, but I can assure you that is how the press will view it. If I were you, I would plan on bringing Dr. Barone to that press conference. Without the handcuffs."

The glare of the lights from the television cameras was blinding. Barone blinked reflexively, directing his gaze down at the top of the table behind which he, Benson, and Dr. Mancia were seated. Then he remembered Mancia's warning not to look away from the lights: "It makes you look guilty, like you have something to hide. That's why all those people they interview on *Sixty Minutes* look so suspicious."

"Dr. Benson." The reporter from the *Post* was as short and greasy as his questions. "Just how long have these murders been occurring at Manhattan General Hospital?"

Maurie's eyes flashed at the pushy reporter before he caught hold of himself and answered evenly: "We're not even sure that there have been any murders." He refused to take the bait. "That is the purpose of this investigation. But we at Manhattan General Hospital are concerned for our patients' welfare. We are therefore cooperating fully with the authorities to make sure that this hospital remains as secure as it has always been."

"But how can you be so sure that another murder won't occur?" the *Post* reporter pressed on.

"While the *possibility* of a homicide is being investigated," Maurie corrected, "we have done everything possible to make sure that our patients are protected. We have the best and the largest security staff of any hospital in the city."

The *Times* reporter stood up and was recognized. "That's all right if the murderer is an outsider, but what if the murderer is a member of your medical staff?"

Maurie looked at Mancia. His stare was cool, noncommittal. "I'm sorry," Mancia answered, "but we cannot comment on that possibility at this time. We have, however, taken every precaution possible to prevent another incident."

"Dr. Barone," interrupted the *Post* reporter, searching for a chink in the united front. "Under these circumstances, would you want to have your mother admitted to Manhattan General Hospital?"

Barone hesitated, noticed that his eyes had drifted down toward the table again. He forced himself to look back into the searing lights. "This is a superb hospital. I would have no hesitation at all," he answered, thinking, *as long as I could get her around-the-clock bodyguards.*

Dr. Mancia stood up. "Ladies and gentlemen, this ends the question-and-answer portion of our press conference. Before we adjourn, Dr. Daniel Harris, the president of Manhattan General Hospital, would like to read a prepared statement."

The harsh lights shifted to the podium in the corner of the room. Harris, tall, silver-haired, and distinguished looking in a dark business suit, addressed the crowd. "Ladies and gentlemen of the press," he began, "I realize that your first responsibility is to present each story as fully as possible to your audience. This is almost always in the public's best interest. However, there are occasions, such as when a man shouts 'Fire!' in a crowded auditorium, that a more orderly presentation of the facts is to everyone's advantage.

"Many people in this community rely upon Manhattan General Hospital for their health care. If the story of the present investigation is not presented in a responsible fashion, many people who need our help might hesitate to come. If even one patient with cancer delayed seeking medical attention because he or she were afraid to come to the hospital, this tragedy would be greatly and needlessly extended.

"The reputation of a hospital takes decades to build. It can be damaged irreparably overnight. I therefore ask you to show the utmost restraint in reporting the present situation to the public, at least until the police have resolved whether a homicide has actually occurred. I thank you in advance for your forbearance."

He started to step down from the podium. The *Post* reporter stood up and shouted: "That's not good enough, Dr. Harris! Unless you have a suspect in custody, we don't know whether the patient with cancer is in more danger *out* of your hospital or *in* it!"

Harris stopped and turned to Mancia, who nodded back. Harris cleared his throat. "I think that press cooperation in this matter is of the greatest importance. I have been authorized to tell you that a suspect has been identified and is being sought for questioning. His name is being withheld until he is in custody." Harris looked considerably less self-assured.

"Still not good enough, Doctor." The *Times* reporter stood up now. "You are asking us to violate our most sacred trust: to report the whole truth to our readers. We can temper our reports but only if we are sure that it is in our readers' interest. As long as no suspects have been named, we must take seriously our responsibility to warn our readers away from this hospital. Now, if we could feel more confident that sufficient progress was being made in the investigation, for example, if you named a suspect, then we would be more likely to judge that our readers would not be in danger if they came to your hospital."

Harris glanced at Mancia, who arched his eyebrows and rolled his eyes to the side. The two men walked to the back of the table, facing away from the reporters. Barone could hear only bits of their conversation.

"You have to give them a name," Mancia whispered hoarsely.

"I can't do that."

"Look, Dr. Harris, they will get it eventually by bribing some police detective. Or maybe even one of your own security guards. Give them what they want, or they will drag you and your hospital through the mud."

Harris was silent for a long moment, then returned to the podium. "I have been authorized to tell you that the suspect is a Dr. Peter Lee, an intern at this hospital who was suspended one day before the current investigation began. Premature disclosure of this information could cause the suspect to go into hiding and delay his apprehension. I therefore implore you to use the utmost discretion in reporting this story.''

There was a long pause. Finally, the *Post* reporter snorted. ''I don't see how we can sit on this story for more than twenty-four hours, doctor.'' The room was filled with murmuring as the other reporters nodded assent. Then the *Post* reporter continued. ''But, Dr. Harris, if there is another murder while we are holding back, you're going to have to sell this place for a parking lot.''

Detective Sergeant George Wislocki was considerably less pleasant than the reporter from the *Post*. Dressed in an ill-fitting suit and with his silver-blond hair in a flattop crew cut, he reminded Barone of one of his high school physical education coaches. The detective barked his questions in the raspy, high-pitched voice that had resulted from being spiked in the throat during a college football game.

''I thought you said that Peter Lee was not on call the night that Herbert Brown died,'' he hammered at Barone.

''Herbie, uh, that is Mr. Brown died, uh, in the early evening, about, that is around the time that, uh, Dr. Lee signed out to the on-call intern.'' The harder Barone tried to control his stammering, the more self-conscious he became and the less coherently he could speak.

''And Anne Delbert died during the night while Dr. Lee was off call?''

''Peter Lee was seen, by a hospital security guard, entering the hospital that night.''

''I see.'' Wislocki cleared his throat. ''Very convenient. Is there any way to get into this hospital at night, through an entrance that is not guarded?''

From the tenor of his questions, it was clear that the detective had not overlooked the possibility that Barone himself could be a prime suspect. He hesitated to tell Wislocki about the tunnel system. He could not be sure who had seen him there. And he was fairly certain that Peter Lee had not used that route. Barone was not sure that Maurie would think to tell the detective about the tunnel system, and he might not find it himself. Even if he did, Barone's failure to mention it could be taken as a sign that he had not considered the tunnel entrance before.

Barone suddenly realized that his face was starting to redden, and he had taken too long to answer no. He coughed, looked down at the floor. ''Well, uh, there is also a tunnel, from the, uh, house staff apartment building. It's not really unguarded, that is, uh, you need a hospital ID to get into the apartment complex. But it is connected to the basement of the hospital. We, uh, use it to come to the hospital on calls when the weather is bad,'' he finished lamely, hoping he did not sound too suspicious.

''Hunh,'' Wislocki snorted. ''And where were you the night that Anne Delbert died?''

The color in Barone's cheeks deepened. ''I was, uh, with my girlfriend.''

''All night?'' Wislocki's eyebrows rose suggestively. Barone nodded.

''That's a pretty good alibi,'' Wislocki sneered. ''Unless she happens to be a sound sleeper. I would like to talk to her. Just who is the lucky lady?''

Barone's mouth was so dry he could not even swallow. He did not look up at the obscene little man. ''Dr. Sylvia Blackman.''

Wislocki snorted again. ''The resident who is comatose?''

Barone nodded again.

"Cute." Wislocki shook his head. "Real cute." He jotted a note in a small spiral-bound notebook. "And just what is the prognosis for her recovery, doctor?" He made the title seem more of an epithet than an honorific.

Barone shrugged; his voice cracked. "I wish I knew." He just wanted the little troll to go away.

Wislocki shook his head again. "I'll bet you do, doctor. I'll just bet you do."

Barone could feel his ears burning. He finally looked up at the smug expression on the detective's face. "Listen, sergeant," he burst out. "I've had just about as much of your insinuation and character assassination as I am going to take. You would think that I was the chief suspect, rather than a cooperative citizen."

The detective stared coolly at Barone, letting his temper fade before answering in his highest pitched, tightest voice. "For your information, doctor, you *are* a chief suspect in this case. *Everyone* who had access to the murdered patients is a suspect, until *I* am satisfied that they are cleared."

"But I, uh, I blew the whistle. I was the one who reported the problem."

"What better way to direct attention away from yourself?"

"And what about the sperm?" Barone persisted. "The murderer had blood type AB. I have type O."

Wislocki stared at Barone for a long moment. "And I suppose, doctor, that you have never heard of artificial insemination?"

Barone stared blankly.

"You know, doctor, that would be a nearly perfect frame-up. Murder the girl, then artificially inseminate her with sperm from a man with a different blood type. I understand that there is a very active sperm donation program at this hospital. I don't suppose it would be too difficult for a doctor to get ahold of some, perhaps for a 'research project'? Then you could agitate for an autopsy, to make sure that someone found the sperm. I imagine you could even cause the scratches on the vaginal wall with the medical instruments you would use to introduce the sperm. Very clever."

It took every bit of Barone's willpower not to smash the detective's arrogant face. "Are you suggesting—"

"You're damn right I am!" The detective cut him off. He brought his face so close to Barone that the latter could feel the heat of the detective's breath. "I get very suspicious when one of the chief suspects solves the case for me before I even get started. I would like to interview this Dr. Lee, but right now I consider you as likely a suspect as he is. I wish, Dr. Barone," he spat out the name, "that I had enough evidence to lock you up right now. But I would suggest that you stay in town and keep us informed of your movements. And pray that Dr. Blackman wakes up and can corroborate your story."

Wislocki put his feet up on Maurie Benson's desk. He made sure to grind the dirt of his heels into the polished wooden surface. He had a talent for identifying just what maneuvers would irritate each witness the most. In fact, he had made a science of being obnoxious. Once he got a witness to blow his cool, George Wislocki was an expert at extracting critical information and attitudes, uncolored by the witness' sense of what he thought Wislocki might want to hear.

Maurie Benson was unusually easy to get to. Wislocki guessed that he was probably always angry, perpetually on the edge of lashing out. He could see, from the patina of Maurie's old mahogany desk, the kind of compulsive care that Maurie habitually gave to everything he did. As he suspected, Maurie was already seething before he had asked the first question.

"So, how long have you known about this?" Wislocki asked.

The reply was slow, deliberate, icy. "Known about what?"

"About what, Dr. Benson?" Wislocki wore his most professionally smug expression. "How about four patients on your service, four patients for whom you are the physician of record, dying from no apparent cause?"

Maurie's voice was strained but controlled. "As attending physician, I was, of course, informed of the deaths within a few hours after they occurred. I also know that we have been unable to establish a cause of death. But that is not unusual."

Wislocki paused for a moment. This was going to be tougher than he had expected. "And you didn't think that four unexplained deaths in one week was strange?"

Maurie leaned back in his chair, pressed the fingers of his two hands together. "It was a bit against the odds but not really suspicious in itself."

"Then why did Dr. Barone decide to call in the medical examiner?"

Maurie shrugged. "I really can't account for Dr. Barone's behavior. To be fair, perhaps with his lack of experience, Barone may have felt that the unexplained deaths were unusual. He does tend to take everything personally. But I can assure you that a run of three, four, sometimes five unexplained deaths happens in our hospital several times a year."

"And no one investigates?" Wislocki raised only his right eyebrow, an ability that he had cultivated since his youth. He kept the tone of his voice incredulous.

"Never," answered Maurie. "Not if the autopsies are negative. It is a fact of life that no cause of death is found in about ten to fifteen percent of our autopsies. We expect four successive negative cases in about every two or three hundred autopsies."

"And Barone was aware of this?"

Maurie shrugged. "Perhaps. He also had an axe to grind. He was dating a female resident, Dr. Sylvia Blackman. Peter Lee had a crush on her as well. There was a lot of friction between the two of them, exacerbated by the fact that Barone was assigned to supervise Lee this month. According to the other interns, Barone was always finding fault with Lee. When several of Peter's patients died, Barone had an ulterior motive for suspecting the worst."

"When did Barone first consult you about his suspicions?"

Maurie frowned. "I believe that it was last Sunday after the death of the third patient, Anne Delbert."

"And you didn't believe him?" The tone had suddenly become accusatory.

"I told you why I did not think that the deaths were suspicious," Maurie responded irritably.

"And you took no action?" Wislocki let a note of disbelief creep into his voice.

"I told Barone to watch Peter Lee more carefully."

"So you did have some suspicion that Barone might have been correct?" Wislocki tried to force the conclusion on Benson.

Maurie began to redden. "Of course not. I mean, I thought Barone had gone off half-cocked. But I also knew that Peter Lee was becoming depressed. His performance as an intern was suffering as a result of his conflict with Barone."

"So you asked Barone to ride him a little harder?" Wislocki arched the eyebrow again.

"Look," Maurie fumed, "I always put my patients' best interests first. Sure, I was concerned about Peter Lee. But it was more important that his patients' care not suffer. I wanted Barone to oversee their care more closely than usual."

"Dr. Benson," Wislocki began with studied contempt, "if you really gave any credence to Dr. Barone's story, and if you really cared about your patients, why didn't you call in the police at that time?"

Maurie's face was red, his eyes bulging, but he restrained himself. His voice nearly cracked as he answered, "I already told you, detective. I didn't believe Barone's story. There was no evidence for it."

"What were you waiting for?" Wislocki paused to take some water; he slugged it back as if it were whiskey. "A fourth corpse?" He leaned forward in his seat, his gaze penetrating Maurie's skull. "And when the Grayson girl died, why didn't you get an autopsy?"

"The victim's family refused." Maurie's voice was hoarse; Wislocki could sense that his restraint was wearing thin.

"Then why did you refuse to call in the medical examiner to force an autopsy?"

"I couldn't call in the police!" Maurie was leaning forward over his desk, glowering at the stubby detective. "This hospital runs a census of roughly eighty-five percent occupancy, which is barely enough to keep us from insolvency. The news about a series of suspected murders would have turned this hospital into a ghost town. By the time word got out that no murders had actually occurred, the hospital would be bankrupt. I had to have some solid evidence before calling in the medical examiner or the police."

"In other words," continued Wislocki smoothly, "you tried to cover it up."

Maurie was livid. "You son of a bitch! You can't come into my office and accuse me of trying to cover up a murder." Maurie leaned belligerently across the desk, the veins at his temples bulging.

Wislocki impassively stood up and placed his coat over one arm, as if to leave. "I *can* do that, Dr. Benson," he finally said, matter-of-factly, "because I am a cop, and that is my job. Just like saving people's lives is supposed to be your job.

"Unfortunately, I have to agree with you that we have no real evidence for any murders—no cause of death, no weapon. If I did, I would have shut this place down myself. So let me put you on notice. If there is another 'untimely' death at this hospital during our investigation, I am going to have you arrested as an accomplice."

The noonday sun, reflected off the face of the hospital pavilion across the courtyard, suffused Sylvia's room with a brightness that, earlier that morning, Barone had not thought he would ever see again. He sat at the bedside, her hand enfolded in his, savoring each moment. His judgment had been vindicated. He had been right about Peter Lee. And most important, with the intervention of Mancia, he had been allowed to visit Sylvia once more.

The only one who stood in the way of his complete reinstatement was Wislocki. The detective had put a hold on his staff privileges at the hospital, pending the outcome of the investigation. He was still being considered as a suspect in the four murders.

Could it possibly be that Wislocki thought he was the murderer? No, not even the boorish detective could believe that. It had to be some kind of ploy. If he were really a suspect, Wislocki would never have agreed to let him visit Sylvia.

Or would he? Maybe it was some kind of trap. Did they have him under surveillance? Barone thought of the man he had seen by the elevators, the woman dressed in a hospital robe who had been sitting out in the hallway. Were they there to keep an eye on him?

He suddenly had a thought, began scanning the corners of the room. No video cameras. Unless they had hidden them. Was there something in the corner behind the edge of the curtain . . . ?

Barone let his head sag forward, until his chin rested on Sylvia's hand. He gazed along her outstretched arm, to her face, its sallow features frozen, like a dummy in a wax museum, constantly silent, as if she were waiting her turn to speak.

God, did he need her! He felt a longing for her all the time, but never more than now, when he was physically with her, but she, in a very real sense, was not there at all.

He held her hand to his cheek, and only when he turned it over to kiss her fingers did he realize that it was damp.

George Wislocki walked slowly up York Avenue, toward a German restaurant that he liked on Eighty-Fifth Street. As he walked, head down, watching the sidewalk, he tried to fit together the pieces of the puzzle. Never had he participated in a homicide investigation in which there was so little evidence that a murder had actually occurred. Unfortunately, the technical details necessary to prove the murder lay in the medical realm. So far even the ME's office had not come up with a cause of death; and without that, Wislocki was forced to admit, there was no case.

It was infuriating to think that a murderer could escape him because George Wislocki was not clever enough to figure out the means of the murder. That was why he had pressed the two doctors so hard. He had suspected that each of them was involved, in some way, more deeply than he would admit. But by the end of his interviewing, Wislocki knew from years of grilling suspects that each was innocent. Now he merely wanted to use them, to mobilize their technical expertise, to find the killer. Wislocki had long ago found that he got the most cooperation from a witness who felt that it was in his or her own best interest to assist with the investigation. The easiest way to achieve that goal was to accuse the innocent witness of committing the crime.

The other frustrating aspect of this case was that the suspected murderer was probably suffering from a psychiatric illness. This really presented two problems. First, it was much more difficult and dangerous to catch a psychotic criminal. The psychotic man by definition does not think rationally, and therefore cannot be expected to follow any of the usual rules of criminal behavior. There would be no reliable *modus operandi,* no set of criminal connections that could be squeezed for information, no usual haunts where the criminal could be conveniently apprehended. Totally unpredictable, thought Wislocki. And capable of incredible, remorseless brutality.

Second, and from a detective's point of view probably worse, even when a psychotic criminal was apprehended, he could rarely be convicted. By pleading insanity, the criminal would usually be acquitted, with detention only for psychiatric care during the current psychotic episode. As soon as the criminal was judged by two psychiatrists to be "not dangerous to himself or others," he was back out on the streets. Psychotic criminals were never "clean busts"; they rarely bolstered a detective's conviction record.

Wislocki started to cross Eighty-first Street but was forced to jump back as a taxi cut him off. He slapped his hand down on the trunk, to get the taxi to stop. As he began to reach for his badge, the cabbie gunned the engine. Its wheels screeching, the taxi sped off. Wislocki stared at the license plate number, then decided not to write it down. He really did not want to write up a traffic citation, and he certainly did not need to waste his time in traffic court. What he had really wanted, he realized, was to see the cabbie's face: to watch him sweat.

* * *

As the noonday sun beat down on the tangled mass of dark, matted hair, a bead of sweat began to form on the forehead, then run down the face, tracing a streak through the dirt. Peter Lee stopped, wiped his brow, continued walking down the street, still wearing his dark blue windbreaker. He did not even think of taking it off to help cool down. Removing his jacket would only leave him that much more exposed. And he already felt naked, unprotected in a harsh and cruel world.

He walked up First Avenue, talking to himself, as passersby cautiously moved to the other side of the sidewalk and sometimes across the street to avoid him. He told himself that he did not need to worry. But he did not really believe that. Not after the way he had been stopped at the hospital entrance the night before. That was Barone's doing.

Everywhere he turned, Barone was there to cut him off. First he had taken Sylvia. Now he had kept him out of the hospital. And on the street. Where it was goddamned hot!

He needed shelter. It was out of the question for him to go home. The place was haunted. It held too many memories for him to face, too many demons from his past. It was the apartment of another Peter Lee, one who had a place to work and a woman that he loved, but it was not his home any longer. Barone had taken that away from him, too.

He had to get off the street, out of the view of the people who were everywhere around him, who knew about him and despised him. People who had been poisoned against him by Barone. He had to be alone. He had to find a place. A place where he could be alone with his thoughts. Where he could be alone with Sylvia.

* * *

A good Wiener schnitzel would normally settle Wislocki's stomach, giving him a sense of weight and fulfillment in his belly. Today, however, he felt instead a churning sensation in his stomach and the taste of acid in his mouth. Wislocki wondered whether the egg had been too greasy or perhaps the Bavarian Riesling that accompanied it too tart. But the sense of rising tightness in his abdomen as he knocked again on Maurie Benson's door confirmed that it was not the fault of the food at all. If George Wislocki was committed to anything, it was the truth. He could not hide it, not even from himself. The burning in his belly came from the realization that, for the first time in many years, an investigation was getting beyond his control.

Never could he recall being so sure that a crime had been committed, with so little proof. In missing persons cases, even when no body had been found, he could usually key in on the suspects with motive and opportunity. A close investigation of these individuals would almost always reveal a critical clue as to the method, time, or place of the murder. And then all it took was dogged determination and brute police work to find the body.

In front of him now were *four* corpses. All of them had had complete autopsies, and all without establishing a cause of death. A murder without a body he could handle. But a body—four bodies—without a clear-cut murder was something Wislocki could not recall seeing in his twenty-six years on the force.

And Wislocki was certain that the four victims had indeed been murdered. His interview with Barone had convinced him of that. He had sensed that the young doctor had been hiding something, perhaps some dirty, unflattering detail, but Barone had convinced him that the four unexplained deaths were no accident. The pathology resident had confirmed that Barone had come to him with his doubts after the third death. And the

ME's finding that the fourth victim had been raped was too great a coincidence.

But Benson had also been right; Wislocki had checked out the statistics himself with the pathologist. Four consecutive inconclusive autopsies was not unusual in a large hospital; it happened several times a year. Of course, the odds against four such consecutive autopsies among the patients of one intern within a single week were astronomical. But that hardly constituted proof of a crime.

Adding to Wislocki's discomfiture was the fact that he was going to have to rely on Benson and Barone to establish that a crime had in fact been committed. And he did not like either one of them. Both doctors had too much at stake in the outcome of his investigation for Wislocki to trust them. His only comfort was that, at least, their interests were opposing.

Wislocki knocked on the door a second time, then opened it without waiting for an answer. Benson, who was talking on the telephone, looked up and scowled, motioned for Wislocki to wait in the hall. Wislocki ignored him, sat down across from the desk, listening intently to Benson's phone conversation.

"Look," said Maurie irritably into the receiver, "I'll get back to you later. I have a visitor here." He hung up. "Goddamn it, sergeant, this is a private office. You have no damn business barging in here."

Wislocki stared at Maurie as if regarding an insect he was about to dissect. "Would you rather I got a warrant?"

Maurie blanched. "What the hell do you want?"

Wislocki took out a pipe and began to fill it slowly with tobacco. It was a prop. He did not particularly like to smoke, but the pipe gave him an air of reasonableness and sophistication, and a variety of natural pauses in which to think about his words. He always used a pipe when interviewing professionals in their area of expertise. "I would like to talk to both you and Dr. Barone"— he tamped down the tobacco—"about some of the medical issues in this case."

Maurie was irate again. "Why Barone? We have hundreds of fully trained physicians at this hospital. He's just a resident."

Wislocki nodded thoughtfully. "Yes, but he's the one who first alerted us to the problem. And I want to have as many points of view as possible." Good. Benson was already on edge. He lit a match, set the matchbook down on the desk.

"Hey," barked Maurie, "there's no smoking in here."

Wislocki cocked his head. "I don't remember any city ordinance against smoking in nonpatient care areas of hospitals."

"It's hospital policy. And mine too."

Wislocki held the match over the bowl and sucked the flame down into the tobacco. He took several short puffs, exhaling the fragrant smoke slowly. "We could always do this downtown. They allow smoking in the interrogation rooms there."

Maurie was silent.

"Okay." Wislocki puffed again, making sure the smoke was drifting in Maurie's general direction. "Then let's get Barone in here, so we can get started."

By the time Barone pushed open the door to Benson's office, the room was filled with a blue haze, which contrasted starkly with the purple flush in Maurie's cheeks. There was a faint cherry odor to the air. Not until he had fully entered the room did he see Wislocki, sitting in the far corner, emptying his pipe into Maurie's wastebasket.

"That was quick." Wislocki knocked the bowl of his pipe against the rim of the wastebasket without looking up.

"I was just upstairs . . . with Sylvia," Barone offered. "Maurie's secretary paged me."

Wislocki nodded his head and motioned for Barone to be seated. He paced back and forth in front of Maurie's desk as he spoke, drawing a metal pipe cleaning tool from his jacket pocket. "I need your help," he began, eyeing Benson and Barone in turn, "if we are going to fully investigate this case." Barone nodded; Maurie sat stone faced, fuming. "We are working under the assumption that as many as four murders have been committed here." Barone nodded again; Benson's face only grew more red. "But what we are lacking is a cause of death."

Maurie finally exploded. "Then how the hell can you be so fucking sure that the patients were murdered?"

Wislocki busied himself scraping the bowl of his pipe. He tapped the charred tobacco remnants into Maurie's wastebasket unhurriedly. "I'm not." He blew a stream of air through the pipe to clear it; a bit of ash flew out and landed on Maurie's desk. "But we cannot afford to assume otherwise. If there has been no murder committed here, then the investigation merely wastes a few weeks of my time—"

"And destroys the hospital's reputation," Maurie interjected heatedly. He brushed the tobacco ash from his desk, rearranged some papers.

Wislocki pulled the stem off the pipe and withdrew a pipe cleaner from his pocket. He spoke without looking up. "If no crime has been committed, then no more deaths will occur, and the bad publicity will blow over. A year from now, this will all be just a bad memory." He pulled the pipe cleaner through the stem.

"But suppose for a moment that the dead patients were murdered." He looked up for the first time, transfixing Maurie with his gaze. "Suppose that there is a murderer out there"—he pointed out the door—"and suppose that another patient is killed in New York Hospital while we turn our heads and look the other way. Now, just how long do you think this hospital, and anyone connected with this investigation''—he stared pointedly at Maurie—''is going to last? The newspapers and television will eat us all up alive.''

Maurie turned away from the intensity of Wislocki's gaze. ''So what do you want from us?'' he asked quietly.

Wislocki sat down again, poked the pipe cleaner through the barrel, then into the bowl of his pipe. ''I just want your technical help.'' He sounded confident, sure; he felt like he was sticking his head into a lion's mouth. His only assurance was that the two doctors represented the opposing jaws, and they would never work in concert.

He looked up again at Benson, then Barone. ''I want you to tell me how these patients might have died.''

''Why don't you talk to Mancia?'' Maurie replied. ''He seems to know everything.''

Wislocki fitted the pipe together again. ''Actually, Dr. Mancia has been most helpful.'' He blew again through the pipe. ''But in the absence of an autopsy-proven cause of death, he can't make any positive statements. I was hoping that you doctors''—he gestured with the pipe—''who worked so closely with the deceased patients can tell me something, perhaps some detail of local hospital practice, that could shed some light on the deaths.''

''Our hospital policy is pretty standard,'' Maurie answered before Barone could speak. ''We have not significantly altered it in many years. And there has never been any question of unexplained deaths in the past. I don't think that our hospital practice is, or should be, at issue here.''

Wislocki did not acknowledge the response. He drew a pouch of tobacco from his pocket, unfolded it, and stuffed a pinch into the bowl of the pipe. A faint aroma of cherries wafted toward Barone.

"What about the high potassium levels then?" He tamped the tobacco down with his thumb, again staring at Maurie. "All four patients had high potassium levels."

Maurie answered quickly again. "A high serum potassium is not an unusual postmortem artifact. As muscle tissue breaks down after death, potassium is released. The longer you wait after death to take the blood sample, the higher the potassium level goes."

Wislocki pushed another pinch of tobacco into the bowl of his pipe. "But the ME's office tells me that all four patients had potassium levels that were higher than could be accounted for on the basis of postmortem changes—"

"But none were high enough to be lethal," interjected Maurie.

"Well, that's just where I need your expert opinions." Wislocki put the pipe stem between his teeth and searched his jacket pockets for a match. "Just how does excess potassium kill people?" He patted down his pants pockets, shrugged. "Have either of you got a match?"

Maurie shook his head, Barone offered a mumbled, "Sorry, I don't smoke."

Maurie knew that the medical examiner must have already answered that question for Wislocki. He was not sure whether Wislocki was merely trying to assess their reliability or whether the question was meant to anger him further. But he spoke up quickly again, to stifle any potentially embarrassing reply by Barone.

"Potassium is responsible for the spread through the heart of the electrical impulse that causes contraction, pumping blood. In the presence of high potassium levels, the electrocardiogram waveform, which usually shows the familiar spikelike pattern, becomes broader and flatter. Eventually, the electrical impulse can no longer be conducted, and the heart goes into fibrillation.'' Maurie hoped to maintain the right professional tone, just above the head of his questioner, to discourage further inquiries.

Wislocki looked slightly puzzled. ''Now what is that, 'fibrillation,' exactly?'' He began to push aside some papers on Maurie's desk.

Maurie's cheeks flushed as he tried to push the papers back. ''In fibrillation, the heart does not contract in an organized way. The individual muscle fibers each contract randomly, and the surface of the heart muscle wriggles like a bag of worms. No blood is pumped.''

Wislocki found his missing matches under a sheaf of Maurie's papers. ''So why do you give potassium to patients in the hospital at all?''

''Because''—Maurie frowned resignedly—''when potassium levels are too low, the heart becomes irritable, and it may also stop functioning.''

Wislocki pulled a match from the book. He addressed himself to Barone this time. ''And how is potassium normally administered to patients in this hospital?''

There was a moment of hesitation, as Maurie deliberately held back. ''Sometimes we give it orally,'' Barone spoke up.

''Were any of the four patients receiving oral potassium?'' Wislocki continued to address Barone, still holding the unlit match.

Barone shook his head.

''Any chance they may have got it by mistake?''

Barone shook his head again. ''Not really. Oral potassium tastes horrible. Practically everyone who receives it for the first time complains to us when we make rounds. And it would take a tremendous amount of oral potassium to raise blood levels that much.''

Wislocki wrinkled his forehead. The pipe bobbed up and down in his mouth as he spoke. "Why is that?"

"Potassium is absorbed fairly slowly from the gastrointestinal tract, and the muscles in the body act as a huge reservoir for the mineral. As soon as the potassium is absorbed, it is siphoned off into the muscles. On the other hand, if the potassium is given more quickly, for example by intravenous injection, the blood levels can get to be very high."

He paused. Wislocki still looked puzzled. "It's like filling your car with gasoline," continued Barone. "If you set the pump at a slow rate, all of the gas goes down into the tank. But if you try to fill it too fast, the gas backs up into the filler pipe."

Wislocki nodded; apparently pleased with the analogy, he set down the match. "So for the potassium levels to get that high, the potassium must have been injected into the patients. How is that done?"

"We usually try to inject potassium as slowly as possible," continued Barone, "because it is so dangerous. After starting an intravenous line, a nurse puts some potassium chloride, usually about twenty millequivalents per liter, into the intravenous bottle. That would normally be infused into the patient over eight to twelve hours."

Wislocki took the pipe from his mouth and pointed the stem at Barone. "Why so slowly?"

"The lethal dose for potassium given all at once is about forty millequivalents. We never put more than half that amount into a full bottle of intravenous fluid, and even then the nurse must use a special computerized device, attached to the intravenous line, to make sure that the patient gets no more than five millequivalents per hour."

Wislocki nodded, sucked at the stem of his pipe. "So in order to get potassium levels as high as those in the four murdered—" He stopped himself and turned to Maurie, lips curled in a near smile "That is, allegedly murdered patients"—he bowed slightly and turned back to Barone—"someone must have deliberately injected them with potassium."

"But none of the patients had lethal levels," Maurie reminded him.

Wislocki picked up his match again, struck it, but then sat looking out the window until the flame nearly singed his fingers. He suddenly shook the match out and turned to Barone. "Are there any other potentially lethal drugs that might elevate potassium levels?"

Barone shook his head thoughtfully.

Wislocki pulled a new match from the book, held it ominously over the matchbook. "So can we assume that the four patients were deliberately injected with potassium?"

Maurie broke in again. "What the hell difference does it make? Even if somebody did inject them with potassium, which I find incredible, none of them had lethal levels. There is still no evidence that they were murdered."

Wislocki struck the second match. "Deliberately injected with potassium, raped, found unexpectedly and unexplainably dead—but not murdered?" He sucked the flame into the bowl of the pipe. "That's doesn't make any sense." He puffed furiously at the pipe for a moment, then shook out the match just before it burned his fingers. "And you had better help me find out how it was done." He puffed again for a moment, blew the smoke directly at Maurie's face. "Or this investigation will drag on, and the news reports will destroy your hospital." He puffed again more deeply, exhaled a cloud of blue smoke. "And while you're thinking, I suggest that both of you provide whatever help you can in the search for Peter Lee. I think he is probably the key to this whole puzzle. If we don't find him soon, the press is going to want another whipping boy. And I think they might just choose someone in this room.''

Barone snapped on the light switch. His apartment seemed more barren, more sterile than he remembered it. He opened the refrigerator. It too was empty, except for a single stale bagel. He didn't care. He unwrapped the bagel, tore at it with his teeth. It was rubbery, tasteless. He didn't care about that either. He was just grateful finally to have something with some substance that he could attack.

Peter Lee was a wraith. Barone had spent the afternoon searching the odd corners of the hospital, places that only the residents and maybe the cleaning staff knew about. He had looked in the isolated study carrels in the basement of the library, in the chart dictation room behind the medical records department. He had asked around in the food preparation area of the kitchen, where sympathetic food service workers would often give an on-call resident an extra dinner in exchange for a curbside consultation about a backache or a missed period. Barone talked to the secretaries, the maintenance workers: Several knew Peter Lee, one or two had seen him earlier in the week but no one within the last day or two.

Peter Lee was not hiding in or about the hospital. The police had his apartment staked out and had been searching for him on the streets. One hospital guard recalled having turned him away from the hospital's main entrance the previous night, but for all anyone could tell Peter Lee might as well have been swallowed up into the earth as he walked out past the entrance gates. He had simply disappeared.

Barone was as sure as Wislocki that Peter Lee could provide the key to solving the mystery. Only the killer could tell them how he had murdered the four patients.

And Barone knew, with a conviction beyond any physical evidence, that Peter Lee was the murderer.

He crossed the room, flicked on the television set. The news was on. He sank back into the armchair, ignoring the pictures of presidential speeches and foreign battlefields. It was now, when he was unsure how to proceed, that he found himself missing Sylvia the most. He thought about his lunch hour, spent at her bedside, holding her hand, caressing her brow as she slept, the only sound in the room the incessant *beep-beep-beep* of her cardiac monitor. He yearned for her to speak. It really did not matter what she said; just the soft tones of her voice could calm him, allow him to organize his own thoughts.

The picture on the television screen caught his eye: a well-groomed reporter, in the golden evening light, standing in front of the Manhattan General Hospital main entrance. Barone remembered her from the press conference: a photogenic face who did not ask any insightful questions.

"This is Diane Cray reporting live from the Manhattan General Hospital." She had a slight lisp, the kind that would have prevented a male reporter from obtaining a newscasting job with a New York affiliate of a major network. On her, it sounded cute. ". . . Where the search goes on for a murder suspect, a young doctor from the hospital staff who is believed to have murdered as many as four patients and to have raped at least one of them. The four patients all died mysteriously, and doctors have not yet established a cause—" He switched off the set. It was already beginning. The drumbeat of negative publicity would grow louder each day, until it reached earthquake proportions, and the entire hospital would come crashing down.

He had to think this through, and he knew that Sylvia's apartment was the only place he would find the peace of mind to do it. He took the elevator down to her floor. The hallway was deserted, the blue-painted steel doors seemed colder, more forbidding than when she had accompanied him down that corridor. As he fumbled with the key, he found himself wishing she were waiting for him, just inside.

The tumblers of the lock slid open. As he pushed open the door, he was greeted at once by Sylvia's scent. He imagined her sitting across the room at the bedside. For a moment he heard the silken rustle sound of her slip against her pantyhose. He saw her dim form, moving against the slits of lights penetrating between the slats of the venetian blinds. He could sense another person in the room, breathing.

It was not his imagination. He was not alone.

He froze, reached out his hand for the light switch. It was not where he remembered it. His hand explored the wall, the only thing in the room that was moving. He held his breath. Finally he found the switch, snapped it on.

Seated across the room, in Sylvia's bedside chair, was Peter Lee. He had painted his face with Sylvia's makeup, the way a young girl does the first time she plays dress up. Barone felt a sick sensation as the scent, Sylvia's cologne, filled his nostrils. Peter Lee was sensuously running his hand, wrapped in one leg of a pair of pantyhose, across a satin slip, which he had spread across his chest.

"Peter," Barone's voice was softer, calmer than he imagined possible. "How did you get in here?"

Peter Lee ran the sheer nylon of the stocking across his cheek. "The doorman let me in. He knows Sylvia loves me."

"But we've been looking for you everywhere," said Barone.

"And all along I've been here"—Peter sighed slowly—"with Sylvia."

A shiver ran up Barone's spine. He nodded, edged

toward the telephone in the corner by the kitchen. "I know, Peter." He talked so slowly that each word seemed like an entire sentence. "This is where you belong." He picked the telephone receiver from its cradle.

"Who are you calling?" Peter leaned forward in the chair, the slip falling away from his filthy shirt.

Barone could feel his heart pounding as he dialed: 911. "Just some friends." The phone rang.

"They're not *my* friends!" Peter shouted, his voice on the edge of hysteria.

"Sure they are." Barone sounded less convinced than he wanted to.

"Emergency." A woman's voice answered.

"This is Dr. Barone. I have the man that Sergeant Wislocki has been looking for."

"They're not my friends!" Peter screamed, rising from his chair.

Barone felt behind him for the kitchen drawer.

"Where are you located, sir?"

"Manhattan General Hospital house staff residence." He felt a sharp blade against his fingertips, fumbled for the handle.

"Don't tell them!" Peter began to edge forward.

"Four-thirty-one East Seventieth Street, Apartment Ten G."

"I said don't tell them!" Peter Lee lunged. For a long moment his body seemed hung in midair. Barone's fingers closed around the knife handle. As he brought it up to defend himself, Lee impaled his left hand on the blade. The force of the impact wrenched the handle from Barone's grasp.

Peter cried out like a wounded animal. He made no effort to extract the blade from his palm. "You tried to kill me!" He looked at his hand, dripping blood on the floor, then at Barone. "You always wanted to kill me."

"No," Barone protested. "I wanted to help you, Peter."

His denial only fueled the fire. "They all wanted to kill me. And Sylvia too. You wanted to kill me so you could have Sylvia. You wanted to kill me so you could kill Sylvia!"

Barone raised his arms, open-handed, as much to protect himself from attack as to plead his innocence. "It's not like that, Peter. No one wants to hurt you."

"Liar!" Peter's leg lashed out, moving so quickly that there was no time to respond. The toe caught Barone's chin and sent him flying backward, his head hitting the wall, stunning him.

"I've got to save Sylvia!" Peter's second kick caught Barone's cheek, tearing the skin. Barone could feel the hot blood trickle down his jaw as he slid down the wall. Helplessly, he watched as Peter Lee plucked the knife from his lacerated hand. He waited for the blade to slash down, wondered if it would sink into his neck or maybe his abdomen. Instead, with his last graying vision as he slipped into unconsciousness, he watched with even greater horror as Peter Lee ran out of the apartment. To Sylvia.

Barone could not be sure how long he had been out. The world seemed to come back to him so slowly. He remembered calling the police. No one had arrived yet, so it could not be more than a few minutes. Then he remembered Peter Lee, his face made up like a Times Square hooker, running out of the room. To go to Sylvia.

He struggled to his feet, aching from the crown of his head down into his shoulders. He took a tentative step. A sharp shooting pain ran from his neck up into the back of his head. It didn't matter. It couldn't be allowed to matter. He jogged toward the hallway as quickly as he dared, the back of his skull swallowed up in searing agony.

At least the pain cleared his head. If Peter Lee tried to get into the hospital by any of the regular entrances, the security guards would try to stop him. From his own experience the other day, he had to assume they would succeed. At least they would get there in time to prevent Peter from harming Sylvia.

Would he think to use the tunnel? Peter would know about the hospital entrance guards from the previous night. But every resident and intern knew that it was possible to get into the hospital through the tunnel. Peter might very well use that approach.

Barone considered using the elevator. It would probably be faster than the stairs. But he could not imagine standing in the hallway, waiting for an elevator car, perhaps as much as two or three minutes, then taking a slow ride down, stopping at half a dozen floors for other passengers to get on or off, while Peter Lee was getting closer and closer to Sylvia. And he knew the Peter, in his frenzy, would not have, could not have had the patience to wait for an elevator either. As much as his neck and shoulders ached, he opted for the stairway. It might not be faster, but he knew that he had to keep moving. He could not stand still.

As he opened the door to the stairwell, Barone heard, several flights down, the sound of running feet. He started down the stairwell, refused to speculate. Each step sent a white-hot stab of pain up his neck.

Halfway down the first flight of stairs, Barone spotted a drop of blood on one of the steps. It looked fresh. He smeared it with the sole of his shoe. Peter Lee! He had come this way. Barone realized that he probably had just been unconscious for a few seconds. The man on the stairs in front of him had to be Peter. Barone ignored the searing jolts of pain from his neck as he bolted down the steps, taking the last three stairs at each landing with a single leap, grabbing the railing to pull himself around the corner, adding the centrifugal force to his forward momentum.

By the time Barone reached the tunnel entrance, he could hear the sound of the running footsteps receding in the distance. As he entered each twisting segment, Barone could hear the *tap-tap-tap-tap* of footsteps on the concrete floor from around the next corner, then down around the next hall. He followed the trail of blood drops, just moments behind the wounded man.

Finally, as he entered the hospital basement, he caught a glimpse of the runner ahead, turning into the next corridor. It looked like Lee. It had to be him. The man looked back over his shoulder. It was him!

Barone dug down into an inner source of strength that he had never known he possessed, ran even faster. As he reached the corner, Barone was suddenly aware that the footsteps ahead of him had stopped. He rounded the corner cautiously. The trail of blood drops continued down the corridor.

Barone walked more slowly, following the trail of blood drops, slowing to look into each doorway off the main passage. Some of the rooms were dark; muffled sounds of machinery emanated from behind the doors. The trail turned off the main corridor into a dimly lit side room. Barone looked inside. The room was filled with cardboard boxes. Boxes from intravenous bottles, from sanitary pads, from syringes, from cotton gauze bandages. In one corner of the room, the jaws of a giant trash compactor loomed open in the semi-darkness.

And there, at the foot of the trash compactor, the trail of blood drops suddenly stopped. Barone stooped down, wiped his fingers across the last drop. It was wet.

Barone had started to straighten up when he was aware, from the corner of his vision, of a shadow crashing down at him from top of the trash compactor. The sudden weight of Peter Lee landing on his back caused Barone's legs to collapse, and the two men tumbled among the empty cartons. Barone, feeling the crushing pressure of Peter's forearm wrapped around his neck, fought for breath, thrashing frantically as he tried to break free from his attacker. He felt a stinging sensation under his right shoulder blade, as Peter stabbed at his back. The knife blade bit into his shoulder muscles, but was turned aside by the bone of the shoulder blade.

Barone struggled to turn, caught Peter's right wrist. The blade, clenched in Peter's right hand, was poised like an executioner's sword over Barone's neck. Barone pushed against Lee's wrist as hard as he could manage. He could feel the torn tissues of his shoulder muscles beginning to give way. The blade came closer, the cold metal pressing into his skin.

In one last convulsive movement, Barone brought his knee up, as hard as he could, into Peter's groin. Peter arched backward as Barone rolled out of his reach and scrambled to his feet.

Barone could feel a sharp burning pain every time he moved his left shoulder. From the hallway, a hospital worker, dressed in a green scrub suit, watched the combatants circle one another. "Hey," Barone called out, "get security down here!" The man disappeared into a side corridor.

Barone realized that he was standing between Peter Lee and the doorway. He was the last obstacle preventing Lee from reaching the elevator to 4 East . . . and Sylvia. He had to hold him in until help arrived.

Peter faced him, the kitchen knife gleaming in his right hand. "You're trying to kill her, Barone!" He moved forward, circled to his right.

Barone blocked his approach. "She's all right, Peter. Just put down the knife and we can talk about it."

"We've got nothing to talk about. You were the one who took her away. You want to kill us both."

"I want to help you."

Barone backed up a step as Peter lunged, but could not get out of the way. He was spinning to his left as the blade sank into his abdomen. Both men stopped, stared at the handle of the knife protruding from Barone's belly like the key on a windup doll. A red stain began to spread out over his shirt. Barone's legs went rubbery, collapsed under his own weight. Peter Lee backed out of the room, then ran down the hall toward the elevator. Barone struggled to regain his feet, could hear the sound of the elevator door opening. His shoes slipped on his own blood as he staggered out into the hallway. Peter Lee was already standing in the elevator car, his coal-black eyes glaring at him, taunting him. Barone braced himself, yanked the handle of the knife, pulling the blade free from his abdomen. With his last ounce of strength, he threw it at Peter Lee. It bounced harmlessly off the closing elevator door and clattered to the floor.

Wislocki sat in the bedside chair, watching the fluid in the drip chamber, tracing the tortuous intravenous line to Sylvia's neck. How did he do it? wondered the old detective. Not even the doctors could tell him that. How could he inject enough potassium to raise the blood content, but not to lethal levels, and still kill four patients?

He knew that the answer was somehow here, in this room, with this girl. If he could only find the right thing to look for, he knew he could find out how the murders had been committed. And maybe by whom. And why.

Unless . . . Was it possible? Could there have been no motive behind the killings in the hospital because they had been committed in the throes of some twisted, demented, passion?

How could a man who was that psychotic have functioned as a medical intern? Or was this a case of a smart young doctor who deliberately emulated the pattern of a psychotic mind, to cover his deeper motives. . . . ?

He forced his eyes back to Sylvia, watched her irregular pattern of breathing, the only movements that she made. Somehow she had to hold the answer. Her skin, he noticed, was a pale yellow color, as if she had been tuned in on a bad color television. But her features were—

"Sergeant Wislocki?"

He jerked his head up, looked at the empty doorway. He was surprised to see that the nurse had entered the room without attracting his attention and was already standing at his side. "What is it?" he answered testily.

"There's a call for you. From the police central switchboard. Chuck Barone just called in to say that he located Peter Lee. At Sylvia's apartment, in the house staff residence—"

Wislocki was out the door before she had finished telling him the apartment number.

Lauri Sherman was sorting five and ten milligram Valiums. She checked her medication sheet once more, then plunked blue pills into paper cups marked "Garner," "Flaherty," and "Geisler," and yellow ones into the cups marked "Johnston," "Marzanno," "Beroa," and "Schnitzler." She held the last pill in her fingers, thought for a moment about giving Mrs. Schnitzler the higher dose pill—she certainly could have used it—then reluctantly dropped the yellow one into the cup.

She checked the list again. Mr. Herman needed a subcutaneous injection of heparin on this round. She unwrapped a syringe and plunged its needle into a fresh vial of heparin, withdrawing one milliliter.

The door to the supply room outside opened. "Mary?" she called. The nurse's aide was supposed to be at supper. There was no answer.

She smiled. "Dr. Korman?" Her voice was perceptibly softer. The new intern who had replaced Peter Lee was really cute. Maybe he was coming back to find something for one of the patients. Maybe he was coming back to find her. She looked over her shoulder, her eyelids fluttering a bit as she turned.

"Dr. Lee!" she gasped, stared at the makeup painted on his face. "I thought that—"

"Get out of the way." Peter began to push her aside. "But . . . you're on suspension."

"I said move!" He shoved her roughly against the wall, began to sort through the medication bins.

She was more surprised than hurt. "You had better leave here." She brandished the syringe she was holding as if it were a weapon. "Before I call security."

He turned toward her, glared at the syringe. "You want to kill her. You want to kill me too!" His leg kicked out, caught her hand; the syringe went flying. "You all want to kill me." He grabbed her shoulders and slammed her against the wall. "That's all you've ever wanted . . ." Her head cracked against the wall, she slumped. "All of you doctors . . ." He smashed her against the wall again. "And all of you nurses!" A trickle of blood rolled down the back of her skull, began to drip down the wall. "You all want to kill me!" He let her crumple to the floor.

He rummaged through the bins, tried to extract a vial of potassium chloride with his left hand. The fingers wouldn't work properly; the vial, slippery with his own blood, slid out of his grasp and back into the bin. Angrily he grabbed it with his right hand, snapped off the top. They were not going to stop him.

He meticulously filled a ten-milliliter syringe, squirted out the air bubbles in the end of the needle, handling it like some life-saving medication. "I've got to save her," he murmured to himself.

An elderly woman was wheeling a pole, from which

hung her intravenous medication, slowly down the corridor, leaning against it for support. Peter almost knocked her over as he ran down the hall toward Sylvia's room. He stopped outside the doorway, standing to one side, slowly pushed the door open.

"Who is it?" the guard inside asked. The voice was that of a woman. It came from the right side of the door. That was all he needed to know. Peter ducked his head down and burst into the room, headed straight for the guard. Before she could reach for her gun, Peter had made contact. His head smashed into her solar plexus, knocking the breath out of her and slamming her back against the wall. She struggled to breathe, began once again to reach for her gun. She never even saw Peter's shoe, as it lashed out, catching the side of her skull. Her head bounced off the wall, landed on the floor with a thud. She did not move.

He turned to Sylvia. She was lying on her back, her dark hair spread out on the pillow around her head like a halo. He bent over her, brushed his lips against her cheek. The skin was warm and soft. Alive.

He kissed her gently on the forehead. She did not stir. A hot tear ran down his cheek, splashed against her waxen face. "Barone did this to you: He ruined what we had. He destroyed us."

He sat on the side of the bed, buried his face against her shoulder. "I had to kill him, Sylvia. I had to. He tried to kill both of us." He hugged her limp body, pressed it against his own. "And now I'm here to save you. I want to make sure that no one ever harms you again."

He uncapped the syringe, stared at the needle, a fine pointed line, standing out sharply against the red orange light of dusk filtering in through the window. The lethal solution inside, backlit a cherry orange color too, was so clear he could see her form, lying on the bed, through the barrel of the syringe. He plunged the needle into the injection port in Sylvia's central venous line.

There was a shuffling sound from the doorway. Peter raised his head. Barone was leaning against the door frame, his hand pressed against his abdomen, dripping blood.

"Don't do it, Peter," he said softly.

"I have to." His eyes were fixed on Barone's abdomen. "I have to save her."

"She's going to be all right, Peter. You don't have to worry about her."

"You're a liar!" His glassy stare turned toward Barone's face. "You tried to kill me with a knife."

"I was only trying to protect myself."

"You stabbed me!"

"You tried to grab the knife blade with your hand."

"And now you want to kill Sylvia."

"I'm trying to help her, damn it. Sylvia is going to be all right."

"She's in a coma. You tried to take her away from me, and when she refused you took her away the only way you knew how. You gave her the hepatitis, you refused to take her to the hospital until the very end, and now you want to kill her to keep her away from me."

"Peter, I love Sylvia. I would never hurt her."

"You are trying to kill her."

"I am not. I'm—"

"You're trying to steal her from me."

"Peter, she loves me."

"Liar!"

"Don't!"

He pushed the plunger of the syringe.

Barone's eyes went wide with horror as he watched the trace on the cardiac monitor begin to widen out, then flatten into a sine waveform. "Help!" he screamed down the hallway, hoping to attract the attention of the ward nurse. The effort of shouting sent a white-hot searing pain through his abdomen. He braced himself to yell again. "Cardiac arrest, room 407! Call a code blue, room 407!" There was no response.

Peter Lee's face blanched as he watched the sine wave flatten. Suddenly, he bolted from the room, nearly knocking Barone over as he ran past. Barone steadied himself, looked at the monitor again. Flat line. The cardiac monitor stopped bleeping, gave out its single, continuous note, the clarion call to oblivion. Sylvia's ochre complexion was already beginning to look dusky.

Barone staggered across the room, supported himself against the edge of Sylvia's bed. He waited for the loudspeaker to give the cardiac arrest alarm. What was keeping the ward nurse? She should have called it in by now.

He lifted the receiver, dialed the operator on the bedside telephone.

The phone rang once, twice. The cardiac monitor screamed its single note. The operator was taking forever. Why couldn't she answer the phone right away? Just this once. She picked up on the third ring: "Manhattan General."

"Cardiac arrest, room four-oh-seven," he gasped.

"What's that?" the voice was routine, bored.

"I said *cardiac arrest*." The effort of shouting made his belly feel as if it were about to tear apart. "Room—"

"What room is that?" the operator interrupted.

"Four-oh-seven, damnit." The pain in his abdomen was like a hot poker. *"Room four-oh-seven."*

"Room four-oh-seven, got it," the operator repeated, as if he had just told her the weather outside. She hung up.

The monitor was still blaring its monotone. This was taking too long. It might take the cardiac arrest team two or three more minutes to get there. Sylvia could not wait that long.

Barone summoned all his remaining strength, crawled up on the bed, knelt astride Sylvia's ashen body. He placed the heel of his right hand against her chest, tried to interlace his fingers; they were slippery with his own blood and would not obey his command. From the hall he could hear the loudspeaker, finally blaring: "Code blue, room four-oh-seven. Code blue, room four-oh-seven."

He inched his palm over her warm, soft chest to the spot just below her left breast, where he had listened to her heart beat just a few nights earlier. With a herculean effort, he leaned his entire body forward, driving his palm against and compressing her chest. A hot, stabbing pain shot through his abdomen. He leaned forward, pumped again. He could not believe it: the pain was worse. He pumped a third time, gasped involuntarily after another searing white-hot jolt.

Where was the cardiac arrest team? The announcement had gone out more than a minute ago. Sylvia had not been breathing for nearly two minutes. He pumped again, pushed aside the agony from his belly. He was the only thing standing between Sylvia and Mancia, that ghoul from the ME's office. He pumped again, felt as if his guts were about to spill out of his abdomen. His vision began to gray again. He pumped harder. He had to stay conscious. Had to stay alive. For Sylvia.

Again he heard, over the loudspeakers: "Code blue, room four-oh-seven. Code blue, room four-oh-seven."

Barone tried to pump again, felt his arms buckling. His fingers slipped off her chest.

"Chuck!" Barry Grant burst into the room. "What are you doing here?

With a great effort, Barone lifted his head. His eyes were dull. "Help," he croaked, straightening up.

"Take over pumping, I'm . . ." He fell backward off the bed, was caught by the wall, sat on the edge of the windowsill. "I'm too weak."

Grant stared at the blood on the front of Barone's shirt. "What the hell happened . . . ?"

Barone shook his head weakly. "Not important . . . pump."

Grant, still staring at Barone, climbed onto the bed, began chest compression. A pair of nurses wheeled a red cart into the room. "Get the bag out," called the first nurse. "Breathe her."

"How long has it been?" Grant asked.

Barone's voice was a hoarse whisper. "Two minutes, maybe three—" His breath caught involuntarily; he held his abdomen. "It's a potassium overdose . . . give her some calcium and some bicarb." Each breath was agony.

"One amp of calcium and two of bicarb," Grant ordered one of the nurses as he continued pumping.

A surgical resident, still wearing green scrub suit, rushed into the room. "What happened?" he addressed no one and everyone.

"Potassium overdose," replied Grant. "Grab a set of electrolytes."

The surgical resident lifted Sylvia's hospital gown, palpated the groin. "Good pulse," he called out, reached out a hand. One of the nurses slapped a fresh syringe into his palm. He plunged the needle into Sylvia's groin, slowly pushing deeper and deeper, until deep purple blood suddenly gushed back, filling the barrel of the syringe. He handed the syringe to the nurse, pressed a cotton gauze over the wound.

"Does she need a central line?" he asked. The surgical resident reached one hand up to palpate her neck. "Say, who is this patient?" He looked for the first time at her face.

"Sylvia Blackman," answered one of the nurses.

The surgical resident drew back his hand, as if he had been touching a hot plate.

"She doesn't need a central line anyway," said Grant between compressions. "We put one in two days ago to monitor her fluid balance."

There was a shuffling sound from the corner as Barone suddenly tried to straighten himself. "Of course," he said. "They all had central lines!"

The surgical resident turned to him for the first time, noticed the blood stain on his shirt. "Holy shit! What happened to you?"

Barone shook his head, as if to set the question aside. "All of the patients who died," he gasped, "they all had central lines!"

The resident moved Barone's hand aside. "Jesus Christ, Barone. You're bleeding out."

"EKG is still flat line," called out Grant. "I want two more amps of bicarb, then get ready to shock her."

Wislocki suddenly burst into the room, his face crimson. "What the hell is going on here?"

A nurse ignored him, began injecting a vial of sodium bicarbonate into the intravenous line, while a second nurse prepared the defibrillator paddles. Grant dismounted and held the paddles in his hands, his thumbs resting lightly against the red discharge buttons.

"Everybody off!" he called, looking up one last time at the EKG. "Wait," he said, "she's beginning to show a sine wave pattern."

"I was just up here on the ward"—Wislocki was panting—"when I got the call that Peter Lee had been found in the house staff residence"—he gasped, swallowed—"and then, just as I'm leaving the hospital, I hear the cardac arrest called for room four-oh-seven. . . ."

"There's a QRS complex," said Grant excitedly, still ignoring the detective. "Another one. She's coming back.'' He pressed his fingers against her neck, looking for the carotid artery. ''Good pulse.''

He finally turned to Wislocki. ''Who's the old man?''

Wislocki thought he might actually have preferred to be ignored. ''Detective Sergeant George Wislocki.'' His breath was coming easier. ''I'm in charge of the murder investigation.''

Grant looked up at him. ''You almost had another one.''

Wislocki stared back dumbly, could only say: ''Is the girl all right?''

The resident nodded.

''What happened to her?''

''Potassium overdose,'' Grant replied.

''Potassium?'' repeated the detective. ''How the hell . . . ?''

''Peter Lee,'' interrupted Barone, his voice a hoarse croaking sound. Wislocki was shocked by the sight of the pale young doctor, leaning against the window, his shirtfront and pants stained with blood. ''He gave her . . . the potassium.''

''But I thought we had ruled out the potassium as causing the other deaths.'' It was more of a question than a statement.

The shaking of Barone's head was barely perceptible. ''No, he gave it''—Barone stopped, caught his breath—''by a central venous line.'' He closed his eyes. ''It goes right into the heart—'' He grimaced, held his abdomen. ''Instant death. Only takes about half as much as an intravenous dose.''

Wislocki looked to Grant for confirmation.

The resident nodded. ''It doesn't take very much potassium to kill someone if you inject it right into the heart. Like just happened to Sylvia here. But if you get the circulation restarted, the potassium washes out and the heart returns to normal.''

"And what happened to you?" Wislocki turned back to Barone.

"Peter stabbed me . . . with a kitchen knife." The air whistled against his teeth as he suddenly gasped.

The surgical resident shook his head, turned to one of the nurses. "Get me a type and cross for six units of blood on Dr. Barone. Stat. We're going to the OR."

"Not yet." Wislocki pushed him aside, placed his face right in front of Barone. "Where did Peter Lee go?"

Barone shrugged.

"Where did he go?"

Barone's head lolled back against the windowpane.

The surgical resident tried to push Wislocki aside, "I said we're going to the OR. Now!"

The old detective held his ground like the retired middle linebacker that he was. "Where did he go?" he asked again.

Barone stared out the window, down at the courtyard in front of the hospital. It might have been the film on the rarely cleaned windows or the fading light of the approaching dusk, but the world outside seemed more dim than usual. He could barely make out the form of one of the security guards, directing a limousine to the front door. And across the courtyard, the figure of a younger man with uncombed hair and disheveled clothes, who was walking almost casually toward the gates to the Rockefeller University grounds.

"Look," Barone gasped. "Down there. Peter Lee."

Wislocki pressed his face against the window. "Where?"

Barone motioned with his head. "By the Rockefeller . . . gates."

Wislocki peered through the twilight, pointed to the far end of the courtyard. "Dark fellow, by the parking area?"

Barone nodded.

Wislocki, still panting, sprinted out of the room.

* * *

Wislocki stopped at the 4 East nurses' station, grabbed the telephone. He dialed the police operator's "back door number," glanced at his watch: 7:03. The second hand turned, the phone rang once, a second time. Goddamn it, for an immediate access line, the operator was taking a hell of a long—

"Police operator number—"

"This is Sergeant Wislocki," he broke in. "I've got a six ten in progress. Put out an all units call to seal off the Rockefeller University campus, all exits from Sixty-third to Sixty-eighth Streets. Silent approach."

"Where do you want the patrol to meet you?"

"I don't. Just have them guard the perimeter. No one enters or leaves until I say so. The suspect is armed and dangerous, believed to be psychotic. I am going in after him alone."

"Alone? But, sergeant, department policy—"

"Fuck the policy!" He knew the rules as well as anyone. And he had broken every one of them over the years. It was how he had become a detective originally, and why he was still a sergeant now. "Look, this guy could blow at any time. If he sees a bunch of cops coming after him, he could start stabbing people, maybe take hostages." He caught himself. This was wasting time. He continued in a calmer voice. "I'm going in after him. Alone. Tell the others to stay on the perimeter until seven thirty. If I don't bring him out by then, they can come in." He hung up before she could call her supervisor to argue with him.

He took the stairwell down again. Lee had four minutes on him, maybe five. From the window, he had looked as if he were sauntering across the courtyard. No hurry. *No sane man walks away from a murder.* And an insane man is harder to catch, because his responses cannot be predicted.

Wislocki scuttled down the stairs, his legs pumping almost mechanically, using the railing to pull himself around each corner. At the first floor landing, he stretched out his arms, letting his weight fall against the doorway to the main corridor. He ran down the stone-paneled corridor, engraved with the ranks of past donors. If Lee continued his leisurely pace, it would still be possible to catch up with him.

The guards in the hospital lobby eyed Wislocki suspiciously as he ran through the vestibule. He flashed his shield, shouted "Police!" But he knew he need not have bothered. They would have let him through, the same way they had let Peter Lee pass only a few moments earlier.

The driveway in the courtyard was cobblestoned, an affectation that remained from the previous century. Wislocki, trying his best to keep his footing on the rough surface, caught the tip of his shoe on a stone. He tripped, caught himself, swore under his breath. He figured that they probably kept the cobblestones to impress wealthy donors, who liked the quaint humming sounds as the wheels of their limousines turned into the hospital entrance from York Avenue.

He flashed his shield at the guard standing at the gate between the Manhattan General Hospital courtyard and the entrance to the Rockefeller University campus. "Police!" he barked. The gate was closed; the guard made no move to open it.

"Sorry, sir." The guard held up his hand. "Just got a police bulletin. We're supposed to seal off the entire campus. Police are supposed to wait at the gates until seven thirty."

"That was my order, you asshole!" The guard, a short, wiry man with greasy hair, looked unconvinced. "I'm Sergeant Wislocki, NYPD." He held his shield up for the guard to read. "Did a scruffy young man, about five-foot nine, dark hair and clothes come by here a few minutes ago?''

"That could describe about half of our students.'' The guard snorted. "But yeah, a real dirty-looking kid, with his face all painted up with some kind of makeup did come in here just before the bulletin came through. He showed a Manhattan General Hospital ID, which I thought was odd, because he looked too grungy to be a doctor.''

But, of course, thought Wislocki, you let him in anyway. "That would be him.'' He shoved the gate, causing it to rattle. "Open it.'

The guard shook his head. "I've got to call in to check this out.''

"You stupid son of a bitch.'' Wislocki confronted the smaller man, bringing his intimidating bulk up so close that the guard could feel the heat of his breath. "This guy has already killed four people. If someone else dies while you're checking it out, I'll personally see to it that you won't even be able to get a job as a parking lot attendant. Now open the fucking gate.''

The guard glared at Wislocki, hesitated.

"Now!''

He unlocked the gate.

The Rockefeller grounds were cool and quiet in the fading evening light. Small patches of orange light, filtered through the overhead canopy formed by the leaves of the huge oak trees, here illuminated a small patch of grass, there highlighted the pink stones of one of the stately buildings. Despite the failing light, Wislocki navigated the shadowy walks of the campus methodically, working his way down the main footpath, carefully checking out every side path, every isolated walkway.

He was sure that he would find Peter Lee out of doors. Through long years, dealing with deranged killers, he had come to know the psychotic mind. The inside of a building, any building, would be too confining. Inner pain needed open spaces to dissipate itself.

Wislocki searched the walks, the courtyards, the tennis courts. He checked beneath the staircases, behind bushes, in back of trash cans. Peter Lee would need to be outdoors, but he would also seek a protected niche, a barrier against the storms of reality.

Wislocki was sure that he knew where to look. The main problem, he realized as the twilight began to fail, was that time was working against him. He had only asked the police operator for twenty-five minutes to search alone. It would have been difficult to convince the watch commander to hold off any longer than that. But the main reason he had not pressed for more time was that he knew the campus would be in darkness by then and the search would be hopeless. Already the lengthening shadows were yielding new hiding places that had not been there moments before. Paradoxically the more thoroughly he searched, the less likely Wislocki was to find his quarry.

He began to work more quickly, running his practiced eye over entire landscapes, searching for that vague outline, that one telltale movement. He was already leaving the small courtyard overlooking the East River when a shadow in one corner caught his eye. Had it moved? He stopped, peered into the gloom. In the deepening darkness he could barely make out . . . It moved again! A tingling sensation ran up his spine.

"Peter?" he asked tentatively.

He was sure he could detect a nod.

"I've come to help you." He stepped into the middle of the courtyard.

The dark figure reared up onto its legs, standing on a stone bench along the outer wall of the courtyard. It reached out a hand, rested it on a stone parapet. "Who are you?"

"A friend, son."

"I don't have any friends. What do you want?"

"I want to help you." He took a step closer, reached out his hand.

"Stop! Stay away."

"I only want to help." He placed his right foot forward.

"Stop!" Peter screeched, stepped up onto the top of the wall, holding onto the parapet for balance. "You're going to kill me."

Wislocki judged his distance to the wall: about twenty feet. "No one wants to hurt you son."

"Liar!" The voice was hysterical, choked with rage. "You're all liars! You wanted to kill Sylvia. You tried to take her away from me. But I wouldn't let you. And now you want to kill me too."

Wislocki opened his hands, held his arms wide apart, in the gesture of a man with nothing to hide, seeking only peace. From this position, he knew, he would also save a precious fraction of a second if it became necessary to bring his arms forward to make a grab for Peter Lee.

"I don't want to hurt you, Peter. I'm on your side."

"Barone has all of you brainwashed." The voice was righteous, indignant. Good, thought Wislocki, he is beginning to interact. "He wants me out of the way. So he can have Sylvia for himself."

"I know," Wislocki agreed. Had to keep him talking.

"But I beat him," Peter continued, his lips drawn back in an ugly grin. "I put her out of his reach." He stopped smiling, squinted at Wislocki. "And now he sent you to kill me."

He was getting out of control again. Wislocki stared at his target. In the fading light, he could barely make out the edge of Peter's pants leg, quivering. The emotional outburst seemed to be making him rubber kneed.

That was good; it meant that it would take him a split second longer to react.

"I'm a friend, Peter." Wislocki leaned forward, as if to give Peter a better view of his face. Nineteen feet away, still too far.

"Stay where you are!" Peter stepped backward on the ledge.

Nineteen and a half feet, thought Wislocki. Have to keep him talking until it gets a little bit darker, and I can gradually sneak closer. "Whatever you say, Peter. I just want to help you."

"Then go away."

Wislocki noticed a low, rumbling sound, coming from the direction of the East River. A helicopter, he thought, taking off from the heliport pad down by the river at the foot of the Queensborough Bridge.

The sound of the revving engine reverberated off the face of the apartment buildings on Roosevelt Island, bounced off the stone walls of the Rockefeller buildings. Peter nervously watched the detective, stole a quick glance down at the East River.

Wislocki used the slight lapse to lean forward, plant his right foot. Eighteen feet, maybe seventeen and a half. His thoughts ran back to his football days in college. He had been able to sack more than a few scrambling quarterbacks from distances greater than this. "I'll do whatever you say." He couldn't miss.

The rumbling quickened, became louder as a helicopter began to rise from the heliport pad.

"Then leave." The sound seemed to be coming from everywhere at once, enveloping him. He had to know where it was coming from. Peter turned to look at the river.

It was the distraction Wislocki had been waiting for. He launched himself forward, two quick steps, then a flying tackle. Peter heard the sound of the footsteps, turned back to see the awesome sight of the two-hundred-pound detective flying through the air at him.

Wislocki stretched his arms, his whole body, forward. He had the advantage of surprise. He could do it.

His arms closed around the air, still warm and rank from Peter Lee's presence. He skidded on the stone ledge, wedged his head against the parapet, snatched at . . . nothing.

He raised his head to see Peter Lee, hanging in the air, frozen in time and space. His red-painted lips were turned upward in the beginnings of a faint smile and his coal-black eyes, emphasized by mascara, reflecting the last rays of twilight, seemed to sparkle back at Wislocki like small onyx marbles. Wislocki could not immediately place the look on his face. It was certainly not fear. Perhaps it was even a bit smug. It was a look of . . . triumph.

And then, as the law of gravity inexorably began to exact its toll, Peter Lee started to sink. Terror returned once more to his features. He reached out his hand. Wislocki stretched, almost lost his own balance. His fingers grazed Peter's, grasped convulsively, as they intertwined.

There was a tremendous yank on Wislocki's arm, nearly wrenching it from its socket and pulling him forward abruptly as he broke the younger man's fall. For a desperate moment Wislocki felt himself losing his balance, being dragged over the edge, as he dug in his feet, braced himself against the wall.

When he felt himself stable, he looked over the edge. Peter Lee, dangling by one arm, had wedged one foot into the cracks in the blackened rock wall. His other hand was flailing as he tried to turn his body so that he could reach the wall.

Slowly Wislocki began to pull Peter upward. The sinews in his shoulder felt stretched to their breaking point. A white-hot pain stabbed into his upper arm as his fingers clutched Peter's hand with a grip of iron.

Wislocki used the tremendous strength in his legs to pull his upper body and his dangling quarry back from the brink. He could just see over the edge of the ledge. Peter's free hand explored the rocks of the wall as his fingers searched for purchase. Gradually he began to regain his balance, using the wall as much as Wislocki's grip for support. His other foot found a crevice, and the weight on Wislocki's shoulder lessened, allowing him to use his greater bulk to pull Peter upward.

At last Peter looked up, his face no longer a mask of terror but now showing a more complicated range of emotion, more akin to gratitude or perhaps shame. Slowly, with Wislocki's help he worked his way back up the wall. And gradually the facial expression became more set, as the onyx eyes reflected mainly anger at finding himself so dependent on his betrayer.

Wislocki gave one last hard pull backward. Peter lifted one foot to a higher perch, used his new position to push himself higher, until his free arm cleared the edge of the ledge.

And grasped Wislocki's throat. The fingers dug into his skin like the iron teeth of a hunting trap, tearing at the flesh, closing off his airway.

Wislocki gasped, tried to breathe. His lungs felt on fire, as he struggled against the suffocating grip. His face turned red, then purple, as he stared over the edge, into the fanatical mask of anger and resentment. The smoldering black eyes burnt their way through the mist that was rapidly enveloping his mind.

Wislocki desperately trying to wriggle free of Peter's grip. The fingers dug into his flesh, would not let go. In desperation, Wislocki swung his free arm forward, tried to loosen Peter's grip. He began to slip, lost his balance. Weakened by the lack of oxygen he could no longer dig in with his feet, began to feel himself being pulled back over the edge.

And then his free arm came down on the side of Peter Lee's head. He did not even seem to be willing it, as it struck viciously, came up sticky with blood, then smashed down a second and a third time, bashing his assailant's head against the blackened rocks.

The grip on his neck finally loosened. The detective, still hanging half off the ledge, watched in mixed horror and fascination as Peter's fingers slid from his hand, grasping at the air, as the space between them began to grow.

A wave of relief and then nausea swept over him as Wislocki watched Peter's body grow smaller, tumbling head over heels, toward the East River Drive. He bounced off the windshield of a white Ford station wagon. The body, its head snapped back at a ridiculous angle, cleared the railing at the edge of the jogging track and splashed into the water, finally enclosed by the stygian blackness of the East River.

Epilogue

It was the kind of day that is typically referred to as "crisp" or maybe "brisk," as the nearly October chill swept away the mugginess of the late summer. In the bright, cold sunshine it was possible to believe not only that winter was not far off, but also that perhaps it might not be so unwelcome a change after all. The tall, thin young woman, strolling along York Avenue, tilted her head back to let the sun warm her face. A sudden breeze splayed out her long, dark hair, the sunlight playing on the red highlights. She shivered, tried to pull her thin windbreaker around her. It was a futile gesture. The denim papoose strapped to her chest and abdomen extended much further in front of her than the size eight jacket could cover.

A beachball, thought the elderly man, walking in the cold shadows of the buildings on Sixty-ninth Street. She looks like she swallowed a beachball. He watched as she tilted her head back again to let the breeze catch her hair. The sunlight silhouetted her face so that, even from half a block away he thought that he recognized her. He stopped walking for a second, then started up again, quickening his pace. He did know her. He had to be sure.

"Sylvia?" he called when he thought he was within hearing range. No response. He had to be right. Maybe she just couldn't hear him. He walked even faster, called out a bit louder "Sylvia!" She had to be.

She turned. She was.

She looked at the old man. He was dressed in a shabby coat, but wore freshly polished black shoes. His face was ruddy, more than could be explained by the wind or the temperature. Like most New Yorkers, she normally did not talk to strangers on the street, but somehow this man knew her name, and she had the uncomfortable feeling that she knew him, too. She was not sure why, but she had to find out.

The old man hurried to get to the corner before she could walk away. His face did look vaguely familiar, like a distant relative out of a family album. And there was an air of authority about him, as if he were used to being obeyed. "Wait!" he called. She did.

"Do I know you?" she asked when he was within conversational distance.

He nodded. "Yes," he puffed. "At least, I know you."

Perhaps an old friend of her parents. She squinted. The wrinkles blurred, but the face looked no more familiar. "I'm sorry." She began to blush. "But I can't place your—"

"That's okay," he interrupted. "The last time I saw you, you were in no condition to remember anything. The name is Wislocki."

She sucked in the cold air in an involuntary gasp. "Sergeant Wislocki?" she asked.

"Just George Wislocki now." His face opened up into a smile. He extended a beefy hand. "I retired from the force nearly a year ago."

She took his hand. The skin was rough but warm. "A year ago?" she asked. "I hope that I didn't have anything to do with—"

"No," he lied, remembering the sense of shame and revulsion he had felt after killing a man with his own hands. And then he had had to face the suspension and demotion for abandoning departmental policy when he decided to pursue the now-famous Hospital Killer by himself. Early retirement, by comparison, had seemed the easiest way out—both for Wislocki and for the department. "It was just my time. In fact, I was overdue. You can only do police work for so long, and then you know that you have to get out." That much, at least, was true.

"What are you . . . I mean, do you live around here?"

The old detective looked up at the facade of the house staff apartment building, glistening in the sun nearly a block away. "Hardly." He chuckled without humor. "Not on a cop's pension." He cleared his throat. "No, we still live in our old place in Brooklyn. That is, the wife still lives in the old place. I got a little efficiency apartment. But it's only two blocks away."

She nodded sadly. "Sometimes that happens after people retire. A couple lives under the same roof for thirty years, then suddenly find that they can't handle being together twenty-four hours a day. Did you leave because you were bored?"

Wislocki was amazed at the ease with which he could discuss his personal life with this young woman he did not even know. But then, they were not exactly strangers. "No, she kicked me out. Said I was hitting the bottle too much."

"Were you?" She was standing close enough that she did not really have to ask.

"Yeah," he admitted as much to himself as to her. "I guess I have been." He looked for the first time into her pale gray eyes. "And what about you, Dr. Blackman?" He nodded toward the papoose. "I see that your circumstances have changed."

"That's Mrs. Barone." She laughed. "In the hospital I'm Dr. Blackman, but out here on the street, Mrs.

Barone. Or Sylvia. My mother wouldn't let me have it any other way.''

"Using an alias already?'' Wislocki grinned. "And who is your little accomplice?''

"Eva.'' She giggled. "Eva Barone.'' She patted the small, nearly bald head and held it to her breast. "Fresh from her three month checkup.''

"And where is Daddy?''

"At work''—she nodded at the hospital building across the street—"as usual.'' Sylvia seemed to glow, in a way that Wislocki had not seen since the days when his own marriage had been very young. "He bounced back from his surgery before I recovered from my hepatitis. The most difficult part for us was that while we were recovering, we were in hospital rooms on different floors.'' She glanced down at the baby's head. "At least, we were most of the time.'' She grinned sheepishly. "We decided to get married while we were still in the hospital. The hospital chaplain did the ceremony. We were in wheelchairs, still dressed in hospital gowns. Two weeks later, we found out I was pregnant.''

"How's Chuck doing?''

"He's fine now. Actually, he's lucky to be alive. The stab wound cut through his spleen and stomach. He lost a lot of blood. But the surgeon said that the knife just missed his aorta. Chuck insisted that it was his skill at gross anatomy and lightning quick reflexes that allowed him to duck his aorta out of the way in time. The surgeon says that the knife was probably just not long enough.''

They both laughed. "Anyway,'' she continued, "he went back to work last fall. We both did. Only I have been on maternity leave since July. But I'll probably go back to work next week, too.'' She stroked the baby's head as she spoke.

"I'll bet the little bugger will miss you,'' Wislocki purred. "Can I take a look at her?''

Sylvia smiled again. "Could any mother refuse the opportunity to show off her child?" She unzipped the denim covering, gently lifted the infant from the sling that supported her, cradling the child in her arms. The small hands and feet seemed to move almost randomly, the tiny fingers curling and uncurling as they clutched at the denim fabric.

The features of the infant, the mouth, the nose, the chin, were a miniature of Sylvia. The baby's skin was blushing red in the nippy breeze. She yawned, blinked in the bright sunlight, then opened her eyes, looked directly into Wislocki's face.

The child seemed almost to be glaring at him. The old detective watched for a moment, held in the fascination that the elderly have for the very young. And then his jaw dropped a fraction of a millimeter as he recognized and returned the stare from the shiny black eyes, bright as little burning coals, hiding a secret which could never be shared and a fire that could never be quenched.

IF IT'S MURDER, CAN DETECTIVE J.P. BEAUMONT BE FAR BEHIND?...

FOLLOW IN HIS FOOTSTEPS WITH FAST-PACED MYSTERIES BY J.A. JANCE

TRIAL BY FURY	75138-0/$3.95 US/$4.95 CAN
IMPROBABLE CAUSE	75412-6/$3.95 US/$4.95 CAN
INJUSTICE FOR ALL	89641-9/$3.95 US/$4.95 CAN
TAKING THE FIFTH	75139-9/$3.95 US/$4.95 CAN
UNTIL PROVEN GUILTY	89638-9/$3.95 US/$4.95 CAN

A MORE PERFECT UNION

75413-4/$3.95 US/$4.95 CAN

DISMISSED WITH PREJUDICE

75547-5/$3.50 US/$4.25 CAN

MINOR IN POSSESSION

75546-7/$3.95 US/$4.95 CAN